Praise for Brenda Minton and her novels

"This heartwarming read shows that God's plans are always greater than we can envision."
—*RT Book Reviews* on *The Cowboy's Holiday Blessing*

"Realistic struggles and tough issues are handled with strength and gentleness."
—*RT Book Reviews* on *The Rancher's First Love*

"Familiar characters and timely issues—addiction and moving beyond past mistakes—combine with touching scenes to make this a very satisfying conclusion to the Cooper Creek series."
—*RT Book Reviews* on *Single Dad Cowboy*

Praise for Kathleen Y'Barbo and her novels

"Y'Barbo's strong characters demonstrate the struggles associated with caring for a loved one with Alzheimer's in this quick, enjoyable read."
—*RT Book Reviews* on *Her Holiday Fireman*

"Y'Barbo pens a winner."
—*RT Book Reviews* on *Daddy's Little Matchmakers*

Brenda Minton lives in the Ozarks with her husband, children, cats, dogs and strays. She is a pastor's wife, Sunday-school teacher, coffee addict and sleep deprived. Not in that order. Her dream to be an author for Harlequin started somewhere in the pages of a romance novel about a young American woman stranded in a Spanish castle. Her dreams came true, and twenty-plus books later, she is an author hoping to inspire young girls to dream.

Kathleen Y'Barbo is a multipublished bestselling author of Christian fiction and nonfiction with over thirty books to her credit. She writes historical novels for Waterbrook Press and is the coauthor of two nonfiction books on divorce and empty-nest syndrome. A tenth-generation Texan, she holds a marketing degree from Texas A&M University and a certificate in paralegal studies. Kathleen is the proud mother of a daughter and three grown sons.

The Cowboy's Holiday Blessing

Brenda Minton

&

Her Holiday Fireman

Kathleen Y'Barbo

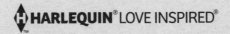

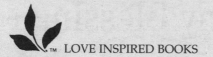 LOVE INSPIRED BOOKS

Recycling programs
for this product may
not exist in your area.

ISBN-13: 978-1-335-19994-2

The Cowboy's Holiday Blessing and Her Holiday Fireman

Copyright © 2017 by Harlequin Books S.A.

The publisher acknowledges the copyright holders of the individual works as follows:

The Cowboy's Holiday Blessing
Copyright © 2011 by Brenda Minton

Her Holiday Fireman
Copyright © 2012 by Kathleen Y'Barbo

www.Harlequin.com

Printed in U.S.A.

CONTENTS

THE COWBOY'S HOLIDAY BLESSING

Brenda Minton

Merry Christmas to all of you,
and a special thank-you to Stephanie Newton,
Nancy Ragain, Barbara Warren and Shirlee McCoy,
great friends who helped me so much
during the writing of this book.

To Bonnie, Ed and Willie,
for helping to carry the load at church.

To Mary,
for a clean house.

To my family,
for always putting up with me
during the deadline crunch.

To my editor, Melissa Endlich,
for encouragement at just the right moment.

Come to me, all you who are weary and burdened, and I will give you rest.
—*Matthew* 11:28

Chapter One

The rapid-fire knock on the door shook the glass in the living room window. Jackson Cooper covered his face with the pillow he jerked out from under his head, and then tossed the thing because it smelled like the stinking dog that was now curled at his feet, taking up too much room on the couch.

The person at the front door found the doorbell. The chimes sounded through the house and the dog growled low, resting his head on Jackson's leg. The way his luck went, it was probably one of his siblings coming to check on him. This could go two ways. Either they'd give up, knowing he was alive and ignoring them, or they'd break the door down because they assumed the worst.

He opted for remaining quiet and taking his chances. Moving seemed pretty overrated at the moment. Three nights of sleeping on the couch after a horse decided to throw him into the wall of the arena, and this morning it felt like a truck had run over him.

The way he figured it, after another attempt or two they'd give up. Unless the "they" in question weren't his siblings, but instead someone with literature and an invitation to church. Or it could be that girl he dated last month, the one that wouldn't stop calling. He covered his face with his arm and groaned. The dog at his feet sat up.

The door rattled again and the dog barked. The next time they knocked harder. Jackson shot the dog a look and Bud cowered a little.

"Thanks, you mangy mutt."

He sat up, careful to breathe deep. Bruised kidneys, cracked ribs and a pulled muscle or two. Man, he was getting too old for this. He'd given up bull riding a few years back for the easier task of raising bulls and training horses. Every now and then a horse got the best of him, though.

He got to his feet and headed for the door, moving slowly and taking it easy. He buttoned his shirt as he walked. The dog ran ahead of him and sat down in front of the door.

When he got to the door he looked in the mirror on the wall and brushed his hands through his shaggy hair. He rubbed a palm across whiskers that should have seen a razor days ago.

"I'm coming already." He jerked the door open and the two people on his front porch stared like they'd just seen a man from Mars.

He glanced down. Yeah, his jeans were the same ones he'd worn yesterday and his shirt was pretty threadbare, but he was fully clothed and decent. He ran a hand through his hair again and tried to smooth it down a little.

"What?" If they were selling cookies or raffle tickets, he wasn't going to be happy. Take that back; he already wasn't happy.

The woman frowned and he remembered her. She'd moved into the old homestead a year or so back. She wore her typical long sweater, longer skirt and her hair in a ponytail. The glasses that framed big, brown eyes were sliding down her nose. He shook his head and focused on the girl next to her. A kid with blond hair and hazel-green eyes. Man, those eyes looked familiar.

"Mr. Cooper, we… I…" The schoolteacher stumbled over her words. He was on painkillers but he remembered her name: Madeline. Yesterday he'd barely remembered his own name, so that was definitely an improvement.

He grinned because the more he smiled, the more flustered she always got. At that moment she was pulling her heavy sweater a little tighter. A week or so back he'd helped her put groceries in her car and she'd nearly tripped trying to stay away from him.

"Ms. Patton."

"Mr. Cooper," she said, pushing her glasses back in place. She was cute, in a schoolmarm kind of way. "Mr. Cooper, this young lady was dropped off at my house."

"And this young lady is my problem why?" He shifted his attention from Madeline Patton to the girl at her side.

The girl glared at him. He guessed her to be about thirteen. But for all he knew she was sixteen. Or ten. Kids grew up too fast these days. And yeah, when had he started sounding like his parents? He'd kind of thought if he didn't get married and have kids it wouldn't happen.

Wrongo.

He leaned against the door frame. The dog had joined him and was sitting close to his legs, tongue lapping up cool air.

"Mr. Cooper, it is your problem…"

"Call me Jackson." He grinned and she turned three shades of red. He could do one shade better than that. "And I'll call you Maddie."

Yep, from rose to pure scarlet cheeks.

"Madeline." Her little chin raised a notch as she reminded him. "Please let me finish."

He nodded and kept his mouth shut. Time to stop teasing the teacher. But for the craziest reason, one he couldn't grab hold of at the moment, he couldn't stop smiling at her. Maybe he'd never noticed before that her smile was sweet and her eyes were soft brown.

Maybe it was the pain meds talking to his addled brain, scrambling his thoughts the way his insides were already scrambled. Something was causing random thoughts to keep running through his mind. Worse, to jump from his mouth.

"Mr. Cooper, this young lady was dropped off at my house by her aunt. She left the girl and drove away." She paused a long moment that felt pretty uncomfortable. He got the distinct impression that she was making a point, and he didn't get it.

"Why is that my problem?"

The girl stepped forward. A kid in a stained denim coat a size too small and tennis shoes that were worn and holey. She brushed back blond hair with bare hands red from the cold. When had it gotten this cold? A week ago it had been in the sixties.

The kid gave him a disgusted look. "What she's trying to tell you is that I'm your daughter."

"Excuse me?" He looked at her and then at the teacher. Madeline Patton shrugged slim shoulders.

"I'm your daughter."

He raised his hand to stop her. "Give me a minute, okay?"

Jackson rubbed his hand through his hair and took a deep breath. Deep as he could. He turned his attention back to the girl with the hazel-green eyes. He noticed then that the blond hair was sun-bleached, sandy brown more than blond.

The kid stared back at him, probably waiting for him to say or do something. Now, what in the world was he supposed to do?

"Aren't you going to say something?" She stepped close, a determined look on her face.

"Can you give me a minute? It isn't like I got a chance to prepare for this. It's early and I wasn't sitting around thinking a kid would show up on my door today, claiming to be mine."

"Mr. Cooper—" Madeline Patton stepped forward, a little cautiously "—I know this is awkward but we should probably be calm."

"Calm?" He laughed at the idea of the word. "I didn't plan on having the postal service deliver a package to my house today. I certainly didn't expect a special delivery that walks, talks and claims to be mine."

It really wasn't possible. But he could keep some random thoughts to himself. He could take a deep breath and deal with this.

"Why do you think I'm your dad?"

The girl gave him another disgusted look and then dug around in the old red backpack she pulled off her shoulder. She shoved past some clothing and a bag of makeup. Finally she pulled out a couple of papers and handed them to him.

"Yeah, so I guess you're the clueless type," she said.

Nice. He took the papers and looked at them. One was a birth certificate from Texas. He scanned the paper and nearly choked when he got to the father part— that would be the line where his name was listed. Her mother's name was listed as Gloria Baker. The date, he counted back, was a little over thirteen years ago. Add nine months to that and he could almost pinpoint where he'd been.

Fourteen years ago he'd been nineteen, a little crazy and riding bulls. At that age he'd been wild enough to do just about anything. Those were his running-from-God years. That's what his grandmother called them. His mom had cried and called him rebellious.

He handed the birth certificate back to the kid. Her name was Jade Baker. He wanted a good deep breath but it hurt like crazy to take one. He looked at the second paper, a letter addressed to him. Sweet sentiment from a mom who said Jade was his and he should take care of her now. The handwriting had the large, swirling scrawl of a teenager who still used hearts to dot the *i*.

The name of her mother brought back a landslide of memories, though. He looked at the kid and remembered back, remembered a face, a laugh, and then losing track of her.

"Where's your aunt?"

"Gone back to California. She said to tell you I'm your problem now."

"And Gloria?" Her mother. He kind of choked on the word, the name. He hadn't really known her. Madeline Patton gave him a teacher look.

"She died. She had cancer."

Now what? The kid stood in front of him, hazel eyes filling up with tears. He should do something, call someone, or take her home. Where was home? Did she have other family? He didn't know anything about Gloria Baker.

He looked at Madeline, hoping she had something to say, even a little advice. The only thing she had for him looked to be a good case of loathing. Nice. He'd add her name to the list. It was a long list.

"I'm sorry." He handed the papers back to Jade. "But kid, I'm pretty sure I'm not your dad."

Madeline Patton had pulled the girl into her soft embrace while giving him a look that clearly told him to do something about this situation. What was he supposed to do? Did she expect him to open his door to a teenage girl, welcome her in, buy her a pony?

He had known Gloria Baker briefly years ago. He'd never laid eyes on Jade. He wasn't anyone's dad. He was about the furthest thing from a dad that anyone could get.

This wasn't what he wanted. The kid standing in front of him probably wasn't too thrilled, either.

"We'll have to do something about this." He realized he didn't have a clue. What did a guy do about something like this, about a kid standing on his front porch claiming to be his?

First he had to take control. He pointed into the living room. "Go on in while I talk to Ms. Patton."

Jade hurried past him, probably relieved to get inside where it was warm. Madeline Patton stared over his shoulder, watching the girl hurry inside, the dog following behind her. He didn't know Madeline Patton, other than in passing, but he imagined that momentarily she'd have a few choice things to say to him.

Madeline watched Jade walk into the living room and then she turned her attention back to Jackson Cooper. He remained in the doorway, faded jeans and a button-up shirt, his hair going in all directions. Her heart seemed to be following the same path, but mostly was begging for a quick exit from this situation.

Although she didn't really know Jackson Cooper, she thought she knew him. He was the type of man that believed every woman in the world loved him. Well, maybe this would teach him a lesson.

The thought no more than tumbled through her mind and her conscience took a dig at her. This situation shouldn't be about a lesson learned. A child deserved more than this.

And Jackson Cooper wasn't the worst person in the world. He'd come to her rescue last week when a bag of groceries had broken, spilling canned goods across the parking lot of the store. He'd been fishing and was suntanned and smelled of the outdoors and clean soap and was on his way home, but he'd stopped to gather up her spilled groceries, holding them in his T-shirt as he carried them to her car.

Jade had disappeared into the living room. Time for Madeline to make her exit.

"If you have this under control, I should go." She glanced at her watch. "I have to be at work in an hour."

The wind blew, going straight through her. She pulled her sweater close and stomped her booted feet. Jackson nodded, distracted. Even distracted he could make a woman take a second look.

His suntanned face was angular but strong. Fine lines crinkled at the corners of his eyes, eyes that were nearly the same color as Jade's; a little more gray than green. His mouth, the mouth that often turned in an easy, *gotcha* smile, was now held in a serious line.

"I really need to go." Madeline didn't know what else to say, or how to remove herself from this situation, this moment.

"Could you stay, just until I figure this out?" Jackson's words stopped her as she started to turn away. "Please."

Softer, a little more pleading.

Reluctant, Madeline looked at the cowboy leaning against the door as if he needed it to hold him up. She'd heard the ambulance going down the road the other day when he got hurt. They had prayed for him at her Thursday Bible study.

A smile almost sneaked up on her because his grandmother prayed for him, too. The woman who had sold her little house to Madeline never failed to mention Jackson when prayer requests were made on Sunday mornings at the Dawson Community Church. Sometimes she even included fun little details about his social life. Once or twice Madeline had heard a gasp from various members of the church.

He cleared his throat. She looked up, met his humor-filled gaze and managed a smile.

"I think it would be better if you called your family, Jackson." There, she'd been strong. She could walk away. He had people to help him.

"Right, that sounds like a great idea." He no longer smiled. "If I wanted them all over here in my business, that would be the perfect thing to do."

"They're probably going to find out about her anyway, since she stopped at the Mad Cow and asked for directions. Unfortunately she was one house off."

Madeline couldn't figure out how anyone could confuse her little house on two acres with this house on hundreds of acres. She felt tiny on the long front porch of the vast, white farmhouse that Jackson Cooper had remodeled. His grandparents had built this house after their marriage. But his grandfather had grown up in the little house Madeline bought from his grandmother.

The Coopers had a long history in Dawson, Oklahoma.

Her legacy was teaching at School District Ten, and building a home for herself in Dawson. And this time she planned on staying. She wouldn't run.

"Give us thirty minutes, Madeline." Jackson's voice didn't plead, but he sounded pretty unsure. It was that tone that took her by surprise, unsettled her.

She wondered how it felt to be him and have control stripped away by a thirteen-year-old girl. It was for that girl that she even considered staying.

She hadn't been much older than Jade when she'd found herself in a new home and a new life. She would always remember how her sister had dragged her from bed, leading her through the dark, to safety.

"I'll come in for a moment, but I don't know how that will help."

"Me neither, but I don't think you should leave her here alone."

"She isn't *my*—" Madeline lowered her voice "—problem. I don't know her. She says she's your daughter."

"Right, I get that, but let's assume she isn't and play this safe."

Okay, maybe he wasn't as reckless as she had always imagined.

"So, are you a decent cook?" he asked as he led her into his expansive living room with polished hardwood floors and massive leather furniture. The dog and Jade were sitting on the couch, huddled together.

"I don't have time to cook." Madeline tried hard not to stare, but the house invited staring. It had the sparseness of a bachelor's home but surprising warmth.

"Just asking, sorry." He smiled at Jade then at her. "So, what are we going to do?"

"Do?" Better yet, "we"? He didn't need to include her in this problem.

"Yeah, do. I mean, we should probably call someone. Family services?"

"That's a decision you'll have to make."

"Right." He pointed for her to sit down.

Madeline sank into the luxurious softness of one of the two brown leather sofas. The one opposite had a blanket and pillow indicating he'd been sleeping there.

No Christmas tree. No decorations.

Jackson stood in the center of the living room. The light that filtered through the curtains caught bits and pieces of his expression as he stared at the young girl sitting on his sofa. They stared at each other and then both glanced away.

Madeline didn't know how to help. She could deal with children in a classroom. This seemed to be more of a family situation. And she had no experience with those.

"Maybe you should sit down?" She didn't know what

else to say. It wasn't her home. Jackson stood in the center of the room, hands in his pockets. When she made the suggestion, he nodded once. Jade, sitting next to her, gave a disgusted snort.

Madeline sighed. She glanced around the big room, because the silence was uncomfortable and she wanted to head for the door. She glanced at her watch and then looked around the room again. A big stone fireplace took up the wall at the end of the room. The fire that crackled came from gas logs, not wood. A television hung over the fireplace. The walls were textured and painted a warm, natural color. If it hadn't been for the nervous energy of Jackson Cooper standing there staring at her, and then at the girl claiming to be his daughter, Madeline might have enjoyed being in this room.

Jackson moved a chair from the nearby rolltop desk and straddled it backward. He draped his arms over the back rest and sat there, staring at Jade. His legs were stretched out in front of him. His feet were bare.

Madeline picked up the throw pillow leaning against the arm of the couch and held it in her lap. Next to her, Jade fiddled with her ragged little backpack.

Madeline did not belong in this little drama. She had to come up with something to move the action along so she could escape.

"Why did your aunt leave you here?" Jackson asked, zeroing in on the girl with a question Madeline had asked and not gotten an answer for.

Madeline shifted to look at the girl, who suddenly looked younger than her thirteen years. Jade shrugged and studied the backpack in her arms.

"Well?" Jackson might not have kids, but he had a dozen siblings and some were quite a bit younger. His parents had adopted a half dozen or so children to go along with the six biological Coopers. And then there had been Jeremy.

Next to her, Jade looked up, glaring at the man in front of them. She chewed on her bottom lip, not answering Jackson's question. This wasn't going to get them anywhere.

"Jade, we need to know what is going on. We might need to call the proper authorities." Madeline smiled to herself. The word *authorities* always did the trick. The girl's eyes widened and her mouth opened.

"My aunt can't take care of me. She doesn't have the money or a house for us."

Jackson rubbed the back of his neck and when he looked at Madeline, she didn't know what to say or do. She taught English at the local school. She wasn't a counselor. She no longer had siblings. The other foster children in the home where she'd spent a few years until she turned eighteen hadn't counted.

"Maybe we should have coffee." Madeline glanced at the man sitting across from her.

Jackson smiled that smile of his, the one he probably thought conquered every female heart. With good reason. There probably wasn't a single woman under seventy living in and around Dawson who didn't sigh when Jackson crossed her path. But she wasn't one of the women chasing after him. And she certainly wasn't the type he chased.

"You know, some coffee would be good. Do you have time?"

"I can make coffee, but then I have to go. School is out but it's a teacher work day." She glanced at her watch again, and not at Jackson. "You should call your parents."

Because this had nothing to do with her.

But years ago she'd been a kid like Jade, lost and alone, looking for someone to keep her safe. As much as she wanted to run from this situation, she couldn't leave Jade alone.

Chapter Two

The schoolteacher looked at her watch again and then she sighed. He nearly sighed in unison because he didn't know what to do with the kid sitting across from him. Madeline Patton taught school. She had to know more than him.

Jackson pushed himself up from the chair, groaning a little at the spasm in his back. He held the back of the chair and hoped it didn't roll away, because if it did, he'd be face-first on the floor in front of God and everyone.

Madeline stood, too. She faced him, looking him over as he stood trying to get his balance. His lower back clenched and he managed a smile to cover up the grimace.

"Are you okay?" Madeline faced him, her brown eyes narrowing as she watched him, her gaze settling on his white-knuckled grip on the back of the office chair.

"I'm good…" He was great. "I think I'll make that pot of coffee and try to sort this out."

Some kid had knocked on his door, claiming to be his. He had broken ribs and a messed-up back. He was wonderful. Every day should start this way. He managed a smile because it wasn't Madeline Patton's fault.

"Maybe she should go with you?" he offered, a little bit hopeful that he was right about her being worried.

"No, she shouldn't." Another little glance at her watch.

"I'm in the room." The girl slumped on the couch and Bud had curled up next to her. The dog raised its head and growled at him. Yeah, well, his hackles were raised, too.

Jackson shook his head and turned his attention back to Ms. Patton. "What do I do with her?"

"I'd start with feeding her."

He sat down, hard. The chair rolled a little. "Right, feed her. I think there's more to it than that."

"I know there is." She hefted her huge purse to her shoulder.

Concern flickered through those brown eyes. He hadn't meant to play her. He was long past games. In the words of his niece, *games were so last year.*

Yeah, he was going through a mid-life crisis, but Madeline didn't need to know that. She didn't need to know that he envied Wyatt Johnson for settling down with someone he'd wake up with every morning. Man, he was even jealous of Andie and Ryder Johnson's twin girls.

Jackson had two rocking chairs on the front porch, and at night he sat alone and watched the cattle graze in the field. He was as sick of being alone as a man could get. But most of the women his age, if they were still single, were listening to their biological clocks. They were ready for rings and babies.

Which brought him back to the problem at hand: Jade Baker.

"I'll get the coffee started, then you need to make a plan," Madeline offered.

"Thanks, that would be great." He smiled at her and she didn't even flinch. He was losing his touch or she was immune. Either way, he was a little baffled.

"Where's the kitchen?"

He pointed to the wide doorway that led to the dining room and from there to the kitchen and family room. Madeline nodded and away she went, that long skirt of hers swishing around her legs.

"Why don't you just give me a hundred bucks or something and I'll head on down the road." The kid, Jade, shot the comment at him.

Jackson turned the chair to face her. She was hugging his dog. She looked younger than thirteen, maybe because she looked sad and kind of lost. Wow, that took him back to Mia when she'd landed on their doorstep twenty years ago. Travis, nearly twenty-five years ago. Jesse when he'd been about twelve. Jesse had been an angry kid. Now he was a doctor.

Jade Baker, aka his kid. She'd asked for a hundred bucks to leave. Surely the little thing wasn't working him for money? Could it be she'd been dropped off by someone who knew she resembled their family? He rubbed his thumb across his chin and studied her. She just stared at him, with eyes that looked like his and Reece's. Eyes that looked like Heather's and Dylan's.

He could smell toast in the toaster. Jade glanced toward the door that led to the dining room and the kitchen. The dog perked up, too. The girl had pulled her blond hair into a ponytail. Her jeans were threadbare and her T-shirt was stained. He didn't know a thing about her life or what she'd been through.

He hadn't really known Gloria. She'd been about his age and she'd liked hanging out at rodeos. Someone had told him she lived in the back of a van with her older sister. He hadn't believed it. He should have. The next time he'd gone through the Texas town where he'd met her, she wasn't there.

Fourteen years ago. He barely remembered her. But seeing Jade, the memories resurfaced. He hadn't loved Gloria. He let out a sigh. A kid should at least have that knowledge, that her parents loved each other.

He stood up, holding his breath to get through the pain.

"Sorry, kid, I'm not giving you money. We'll figure this out, but money isn't going to be part of the deal."

"Why not? You obviously don't want me here. With some money I can hit the road and find a place to live."

He admired her pluck. She had stood, and his stupid dog, Bud, stood next to her. "You're not even fourteen yet. You can't live by yourself or even take off on your own. And one hundred dollars? That wouldn't get you to Tulsa."

"I could get emancipated."

"Honey, at your age you can't spell that word and you can't even get a job. We'll try for plan B, okay? Let's go see what Ms. Patton is cooking up in there." He eased forward a couple of steps. Jade glared at him and started to walk away. He reached for her arm and stopped her.

"Let go of me." She turned, fire sparking in those hazel-green eyes of hers.

"I'll let go, but you're not going to blame me for not knowing about you." He'd made a lot of mistakes that he'd had to own up to. He sure wouldn't have walked out on a kid.

He would have claimed his kid if he'd known about her. If it was possible that she was his, he'd do everything he could for her. But she wasn't his. He was pretty sure of that.

"Yeah, well, you do kind of have something to do with my life and not being in it," she shot back at him, her chin hiking up a few notches and a spark in those eyes that dared him to tell her otherwise.

"I didn't know where your mother went to, and she never tried to get in touch." He had let go of her arm and they stood in the center of the living room, facing off.

"Yeah, well..." Jade stared at him, her eyes big in a little-girl face. Man, she was a tough kid. He didn't know what to do. He could hug her. Or he could just stand there and stare. He didn't think she'd want either.

"Well, what?"

"Well, you coulda tried." Her bottom lip started to tremble. "Haven't you heard of the internet?"

"If I'd known, I would have searched the whole world to find a kid of mine." He softened his tone and took a step forward.

"Yeah, right. My mom said you told her once that you never planned on having kids and so she didn't bother telling you that you had one."

"That was real nice of her to do that." He wasn't going to say anything against her mother. The kid had gone through enough, and he didn't know Gloria well enough to say much more.

She reached for his hand. "I didn't think you'd be so old."

"Well, thanks, Jade. Is Jade short for something?"

"Just Jade." She had hold of his hand. He looked at her hand in his, small and strong. Yeah, he would have been okay with having her for a kid.

The toast popped out of the toaster and coffee poured into a cup from the single-cup brewer on his counter. Jackson Cooper had the kitchen of her dreams. It didn't seem fair that he had her coffeemaker, the replica of a vintage stove and fridge she'd always dreamed of, granite countertops and light pine floors. But really, what was fair?

Life? Most often not. She'd learned that at an early age. She'd put away the baggage of her past years ago, when she realized carrying it around weighed a person down. If a person meant to let go of their burdens, they shouldn't pack them back up and heft them over their shoulder.

She pulled toast from the toaster and buttered it. From the dining room she could hear Jackson talking to the teenager who had knocked on her door just over an hour ago. A few minutes later they walked into the kitchen and their likeness floored Madeline. The two had the same strong cheekbones, the same strong mouth, and eyes that matched. Jade's hair was lighter.

Jackson walked to the sink and ran water into a glass. Madeline stood next to the counter, feeling out of place in this mess of his and even more out of place in his home. This wasn't where she'd expected to end up today, in Jackson Cooper's kitchen, in his life. When she woke up this morning, it had been like any other Friday. She'd been looking forward to the weekend and decorating her house for Christmas. Jackson hadn't figured into her plans. Ever.

She'd lived in Dawson for over a year, and even though it was a small town, she didn't run in the same circles as Jackson Cooper. Every now and then he flirted with her at the Mad Cow Café. But Jackson flirted with everyone.

"You made toast." Jackson set the glass down on the counter.

"I did, and the coffee is ready." She dried her hands and watched as he shook two pills into his hand, popped them into his mouth and washed them down with water.

"Are you eating?" He pushed a plate in her direction.

"I had a granola bar." She pushed it back. "You need something in your stomach."

"Right." He glanced at the girl that she'd delivered to his front door. "There's cinnamon and sugar in the cabinet if you want it for your toast. After we eat we'll figure this mess out."

Jade carried her plate to the table and sat down. "I don't know what you need to figure out. Fourteen years ago, you messed up." She shot him a look and flapped her arms like wings. "Your roosters have come home to roost."

"Great, she's a smart-mouth to boot," he grumbled as he picked up a slice of toast.

He took a bite and glanced out the window. He didn't sit down. Instead he stood next to Madeline, his hip against the counter. His arm brushed hers. Of course he would be comfortable in his own skin. He wouldn't feel the need for space.

She stepped away from him, picking up a pan that had been next to the sink. Not her pan. Not her mess. She grabbed a scrubber and turned on hot water. Jackson rinsed his plate and opened the dishwasher.

"You don't have to wash that." He touched her arm.

"I don't mind washing it." She rinsed the pan and stuck it in the dish drainer. She glanced out the window again. The land here rolled gently and was dotted with trees. Cattle grazed and a few horses were chasing each other in a circle, bucking and kicking as wind picked up leaves.

"Can she stay with you?"

"Excuse me?" Madeline glanced in Jade's direction and turned her attention back to Jackson.

"Look, Maddie…"

She lifted a hand to stop him. "My name is Madeline."

"Sure, okay, *Madeline.* I need to work this out and you can't leave a kid here with a single man, not when you aren't sure if that single man is her father. And I don't really want my family to know about this, not yet."

"So you want to hide her at my house?" She tapped her foot on the light pine floor and fought the urge to slug him.

"Not hide her. She needs to stay somewhere and she can't really stay here, not until we know exactly what's going on."

As much as she didn't want to, she got it. She also kind of admired him for thinking about the girl. They could call the police or family services, but then she'd end up in state custody. Jade definitely couldn't stay alone with him, a single man. What if she wasn't his? Even if she was, there were things to consider.

She glanced across the room at Jade and she remembered that first night, fourteen and alone in the Montana town she'd rarely visited as a kid. Frightened because she had fifty dollars and no one to turn to, she remembered flashing lights at a convenience store and being driven to a group home.

Fear knotted in her stomach, the way it had then, half a lifetime ago.

"Yes, she can stay with me for a little while."

Jackson watched her, his eyes narrowing. "You sure?"

"Yes, I'm sure."

"I'll pay you." His mouth shifted into a smile, revealing a dimple in his chin.

"Pay me?"

"For letting her stay with you. I can write you a check or pay you cash."

Madeline glanced at her watch. "I really have to go, and I don't want your money."

"There will be the expense of feeding her. She probably needs clothes. I need to pay you something."

Jade stood, the quick movement catching Madeline's attention, and from the jerk of his head in that direction, Jackson's also. The girl held her plate, trembling a little.

"Stop, okay? I'm a kid, not something you trade off or try to get rid of. I thought it would be different…" Jade bit down on her bottom lip and looked from Madeline to Jackson. "You were supposed to be different."

His smile dissolved. Madeline watched as he approached the girl who might possibly be his daughter. He sat down at the table and pointed for her to sit back down. He was used to girls, used to kids. He had been raised in a house with eleven other children. Now he had nieces and nephews.

"Different than what?" he asked.

"Different, that's all."

"From?"

"From my mom. I thought it would be—" she looked away "—better here."

Jackson whistled. "So far we haven't made much of an impression, huh?"

Madeline wanted to correct him, to tell him *he* hadn't made a good impression. The girl claimed to be his. Madeline was just the unsuspecting stranger who had ended up with Jade on her doorstep. And she'd gotten tangled up in this.

"No, you haven't made a great impression." Jade rubbed her eyes hard. Madeline pulled tissues out of a box on the counter and handed them to her. Jade took them with a watery smile and rubbed her nose and then her eyes.

"Okay, let's start over. Jade, I'm Jackson Cooper and I don't know squat about raising teenage girls. Today one landed on my front porch and I'm trying like crazy to figure out what to do and to keep that from being a problem for both of us." He glanced at Madeline. "And this isn't *her* problem at all."

"I don't like being called a problem," the girl cried again.

"Right, okay, you're not a problem. But you are a situation that I need to figure out. And I need a little time to do that."

"Okay."

"So for now, you'll go with Ms. Patton because that's the best thing for us to do. And I'll work at figuring something out."

"She can't go with me yet," Madeline interrupted. "I have to be at work. Now!"

"Okay, so we'll work this out. She stays with me for

now while you go to work and later we figure something out."

"Jade, I'll see you later." Madeline leaned in to hug the girl.

Jackson stood, probably to walk her to the door. She didn't need that. She didn't need any of this.

"I'll see myself out."

Jackson walked with her anyway. "You'll be back?"

"Yes, Jackson, I'll be back."

He must have read her mind.

"Thank you." He grinned as he opened the front door for her. "Sorry if I haven't been the best host. It isn't every day that I get a wake-up call like this one."

She didn't want to like Jackson Cooper. She didn't want to let her guard down. But he had a way of easing into a person's life, taking them by surprise.

"I think we've both been taken by surprise today."

Maybe she had been the most surprised. She had formed opinions about Jackson. Now she had to re-think those opinions.

Chapter Three

Jackson couldn't think of another reason to keep Madeline from leaving. He could think of several reasons why he wanted her to stay. She stood on his porch, brown hair, brown eyes, brown sweater and skirt. He couldn't quite figure her out, and he felt pretty sure that's what she planned when she camouflaged herself in brown. What she probably hadn't expected with her disguise was the fact that she intrigued him.

"I have to go." She stepped away from him, tripping over that crazy dog of his.

Jackson reached for her arm and steadied her. "Sorry about the dog. He can get in the way."

"Right, okay, I'll see you later."

"Madeline, thank you. I'm sure getting mixed up in this mess wasn't on your to-do list when you woke up this morning."

"No, it wasn't. And I'm still not sure how I feel about this. I think you should call family services."

"It's the right thing to do?" He smiled because he guessed she always went by the rules. "But then she's in the system and my hands are tied. I'd like to figure this out and then I'll make a phone call."

"She could be a runaway."

"I'm going to check into that. Don't worry, I'm not planning on harboring a juvenile."

Madeline's brows shot up. "I think you plan on letting me harbor said juvenile."

He grinned and shoved his hands into the front pockets of his jeans.

"If you go to jail, I'll bail you out."

"Thank you, that's very kind." She glanced at her watch. "I have to go. Please think about calling your parents."

The urge to lean down and kiss her cheek didn't come as a surprise. But today he had to think like Jackson the dad, not Jackson the guy who loved beautiful women. He smiled and promised her he'd think about calling his parents. But he'd already come to the conclusion that the last thing he needed was the entire Cooper clan descending on his house today.

Madeline hurried down the steps and across the lawn to her little sedan. He couldn't help but smile as she slammed the door, opened it and slammed it again before driving away. He remembered her doing that when he'd helped her pick up her groceries last week.

When he walked back inside he found Jade on the sofa, a throw blanket pulled over her body. She blinked, and offered a little smile.

"I guess you were up all night?" He eased down onto the desk chair he'd left in the middle of the room.

"Yeah, pretty much."

Jackson rolled the chair closer to her. "I'm going to

get some work done. You take a nap and later we'll figure out what to do next."

"What's next? I'm your kid and my mom is dead. What are you going to do, dump me on the side of the road somewhere?"

"No, I'm not going to dump you. I do want to check all of the facts before we make any big plans."

"Fine." She looked a little pale and her eyes were huge. "Do I have grandparents or something?"

"Yeah, you have grandparents."

She closed her eyes, a little-girl smile on her face. After a few minutes he scooted in the other direction, back to the desk and his laptop. He flipped the top up and hit the power button, all the while watching a kid who really thought he could be her dad.

He sighed and shook his head. First he checked his email because a certain bull he'd been after for a year had been put up for sale and he'd made an offer. Still nothing on that front.

So where did he begin searching for Jade Baker's story? And her mother's? Death records, obituaries and telephone directories. Every search came up empty. He had another connection, a friend who had gone into law enforcement. He typed a short email asking for information on runaways—one specific runaway, actually.

He sat back, trying to think of other avenues for finding Gloria Baker. But it wasn't her name he typed in the search engine of the internet. He found himself doing a search for Madeline Patton.

She'd been in the area for a year. She'd moved to a town where she didn't have family. She'd bought a house connected to his land. The house had once belonged to his great-grandparents. It had been their original home-stead, before oil and ranching paid off for the Coopers.

His grandmother had taken a liking to Madeline and sold that little house and two acres to the schoolteacher for almost nothing. Maybe his grandmother knew more about her than the rest of them.

Or maybe he was the only Cooper left out of the loop when it came to Madeline. That kind of bugged him.

His search of Madeline Patton turned up article after article, all from Montana newspapers. He leaned back in his chair and his finger hovered above the mouse. Her story, if she had one, should be private. But the brief sentence under the heading wouldn't let him back away. He clicked the link and started reading.

For a long time he sat there. He read newspaper articles about a child named Madeline Patton. He searched for more articles. As he read he went from pain to rage. He had never wanted to hurt someone as badly as he did at that moment, thinking about that little girl.

Man, it made him want to drive to the school and hug her tight. It made him want to keep her safe. No one should ever be used the way Madeline had been used. Exploited. Hurt.

He closed down his computer because he knew these were her stories, her secrets. She had a right to her privacy. She didn't trust him. She definitely wouldn't trust him with these secrets.

He stood, easing through the motion and then holding on to the desk as he took a deep breath. Jade remained curled in a ball on his sofa, sound asleep. He leaned over her, shaking her shoulders lightly. Eyes opened with a flutter and she pulled back.

"I have to get some work done in the barn. Are you

going to be okay here by yourself?" He figured being by herself might be something she was used to. Just guessing.

"Yeah, I'm still tired."

"Sleep on. If you get hungry there's lunch meat in the fridge and a container of chili my mom brought over yesterday."

"Thanks." Her eyes closed.

Jackson slipped on his boots and pulled on a jacket. When he stepped outside he took a deep breath of cold, December air. It felt good to get out of the house. He never would have made it in the nine-to-five corporate world. Walls were not his cup of tea. He liked open spaces, horses in the field and bulls moving around their pens.

Blake, his older and less charming brother, could have the corporate gig. If someone had to count the money, it might as well be Blake.

Jackson whistled for the dog. He came running from the field, brown splotches on his back where he'd been rolling in the grass. When the dog got close enough, Jackson groaned.

"Bud, you stink. Get out of here."

Bud wagged his tail as if being stinky sounded like a compliment.

He shrugged down into his jacket and trudged down the driveway toward the barn. Horses whinnied and trotted along the fence line. Cattle started moving from across the field.

He flipped on lights in the barn and a few whinnies greeted him. He stopped in front of the stall of the little mare he'd bought last week. She stuck her velvety black nose over the door of the stall and he rubbed her face. She'd make some pretty foals. Her daddy had sired quite a few champion cutting horses. Her brother was a champion barrel horse. If people were concerned about pedigrees, hers topped the charts.

A minute later he walked on down the aisle to the feed room. As he unhooked the door he heard a truck easing down the driveway, the diesel engine humming, tires crunching on gravel. He stepped back to the center of the aisle and shook his head. Travis, late as usual.

As much as he loved his kid brother, Jackson missed Reese. They were closer in age and understood each other a little better. But Reese was deployed to Afghanistan and wouldn't be home for a year.

It was going to be a long year. He'd be doing a lot of praying during that time. He and God would be on pretty good terms by the time Reese came home.

Travis whistled a country song as he walked through the wide doors of the stable. He was tall and lanky, his light brown hair curled like it hadn't seen a brush in days. Nothing slowed Travis down. And nothing ever seemed to get him down.

"I didn't expect to see you up and around today." Travis pulled on leather work gloves.

"Is that why you waited until noon to feed?" Jackson blew out a breath, letting go of his irritation.

"Had a cow down and had to pull a calf. I knew everyone here had plenty of hay until I could get here. And I also know you well enough to know you can't stand staying down."

"Yeah, I feel better."

"Good, but let's not go crazy, right?" Crazy, as in give himself a chance to heal.

"Right." Jackson scooped grain into a bucket and

headed for the first stall. There were only five horses in the stable; the rest were in the pasture. There were two stallions, a gelding he was training for a guy in Oklahoma City, a mare that had been brought over for an introduction to his stallion, Dandy, and the little black mare.

"You left your front door open." Travis stopped to pet the black mare. "You really think this mare is going to throw some nice foals? She's small."

"She's fast."

He didn't remember leaving the door open and wondered if Jade had woken up. Fortunately Travis let it go. He grabbed a bale of hay and tossed it in a wheelbarrow without asking more questions. He pushed the wheelbarrow down the aisle, whistling again, and Jackson knew he wasn't getting off the hook that easily. Travis didn't let go of anything. But for now he seemed to be content with a nonanswer. He shoved two flakes of hay into the feeders on the stalls. When he got to the stallion, Dandy, he pulled off three flakes.

"Don't overfeed him," Jackson warned.

Travis grinned. "He's a big guy doing a lot of work. He requires extra fuel."

"Not every feeding."

"I'm not five." Travis pushed the wheelbarrow back to the hay stacked in the open area between stalls. He piled on two bales for the horses outside.

"I know you're not." But it was hard to turn off "big brother" mode. He'd been getting Travis out of scrapes for over twenty years.

"The charity bull ride for Samaritan House is next week. Do you think you'll be able to go?" Travis was a bull fighter, the guy responsible for distracting bulls as the bull rider made a clean getaway. Or distracting bulls when the getaway wasn't clean. Sometimes the bull fighter took a direct hit to keep the rider safe. That made him a hero. Travis had taken more than his share of hits.

Jackson slapped his little brother on the back. "I'm going to take a rain check."

Travis grinned. "Really? What's going on with you?"

The Russian accent was still noticeable, even after all his years in America, and being raised as a Cooper.

"Nothing, just not sure if I'll be able to make it. If you need me, though…"

"No, we should be fine."

They walked outside. The sun was bright and the sky a clear blue, not a cloud in sight. It hadn't warmed up much and didn't seem to be heading in that direction.

The corral held a few of their best bulls. Jackson walked up to the metal pipe enclosure and raised a foot to rest it on the lowest pipe of the six-foot-tall pen. He hadn't ridden bulls professionally for several years. He trained them, sometimes hauled them and then sold them. The Cooper bull breeding program was his baby. Gage, the brother between Reese and Travis, was the bull rider these days.

Raising bucking bulls had become a big business, bigger than they'd ever thought it would be.

Travis pointed to a rangy, Holstein mix bull. "Bottle Rocket is scheduled for the championship round in Oklahoma City?"

"He is." Not one of them had guessed that little bull calf they had bottle-fed would be a champion bucking bull. But there he was, pawing at the ground and looking for all the world like a top athlete and not the sickly calf they'd saved six years earlier.

A car rumbled up the drive. Jackson didn't turn as quickly as he would have a week ago. Travis beat him to the punch. And that meant a lot of explaining for Jackson to do.

"Isn't that Madeline Patton?" Travis crossed his arms over one of the poles of the fence but turned to watch as Madeline got out of the car and then the front door of the house opened.

What in the world was she doing here so early?

"Yeah, I guess it is." Jackson turned his back to the woman and kid heading their way. He needed to think fast and distract Travis.

But of course this would be the day that Travis was focused and sharp. He pulled dark-framed glasses out of his pocket and shoved them onto his handsome face. Somehow Travis always looked studious in those glasses. And serious.

Jackson kept his own attention focused on Bottle Rocket.

"So, Madeline Patton and a kid that looks like you. Something you want to tell me?" Travis stared straight ahead, his voice low.

Jackson wanted to clobber his younger brother. Travis was like the farm dog that kept chewing up shoes, but you kept it anyway. He didn't mean to cause trouble, he just naturally found it.

"No, I don't really have much to tell you."

"Well, there are rumors spreading through town about a kid that looks like you showing up at the Mad Cow asking for directions to Jackson Cooper's house."

Travis let out a sigh and shook his head. He stepped

back from the fence and turned to face the woman and teenager heading their way.

"People in this town gossip more than they pray." Jackson walked away from his younger brother.

"Shoot, Jackson, what do you think a prayer chain is?"

Jackson didn't wait for Travis, but Travis caught up with him anyway. "Travis, I'd hope that a prayer chain is for prayer."

"Is she yours?"

Jackson glanced at Travis. "What do you think?"

"What are you going to do about it?"

Jackson shrugged. At this point he didn't have a clue. But it would help if he could find her mother. Since he'd discovered there wasn't a death certificate for Gloria Baker, he assumed she was still alive.

Chapter Four

Madeline didn't quite know what to say, not with Travis staring from Jackson to Jade and then to her. She wanted to lift her hands and back away. She wanted to explain to them all that this family drama didn't belong to her. But the girl standing next to her, what happened to her if Madeline took the quickest exit from the situation?

Common sense told her that someone else would step in. If she left, Jackson would have to turn to his family for help. She looked up, caught him watching her, probably wondering the same thing she'd caught herself wondering. Why in the world was she here? He grinned and winked.

Someday she'd regret this moment, the moment she decided not to walk away. But the past had to be conquered. She couldn't spend her life running from the fear. Standing there looking at Jackson Cooper, all of that fear, rational and irrational, rushed in, pummeling her heart.

She took a deep breath and Jade reached for her hand, holding her in that spot.

"Travis, maybe it's time for you to go." Jackson slapped his little brother on the back. "And if you can, keep your mouth shut."

Travis tipped his hat. "Will do, brother. If I can."

"Try. Real hard."

Travis laughed as he walked away. Madeline watched him go and then she couldn't ignore Jackson any longer. He stood in front of her, an imposing six feet of strength, muscle and charm.

She watched Jade's retreating back as she followed the dog into the stable. Madeline fought back the urge to run, because running was easy. Something had clicked in Sunday services a few weeks ago, about facing life with God's strength, not our own. If she couldn't be strong on her own, she could be strong, more than a conqueror, with God.

"Jackson, I know this isn't easy. I think the sooner you tell your family the better."

"I'm going to do that. It isn't as if I'm a kid who's afraid to go home and tell his dad he messed up. I've messed up plenty in my life, Madeline. I know exactly who and what I am."

That's good, because she didn't know him or what exactly he was. He could be charming and funny. He helped a woman pick up her spilled canned goods. He always showed up first when a neighbor needed help. The tornado last spring had been an example of that. He'd worked tirelessly on homes that were damaged. He'd hauled food and water to people trying to rebuild their lives.

She'd admired that about him. Admired him from a distance, of course. Distance kept a person safe.

"You're a good person, Jackson." The words slipped

out, honest but ugh, so embarrassing once they were said. She looked away, seeking Jade, making sure the girl hadn't decided to climb on a bull or a wild horse.

Jackson stared at her for a long minute and then he smiled.

"Madeline, I think that's about the nicest thing anyone has ever said to me."

"I doubt that. But honestly, about Jade…"

He glanced at his watch. "What are you doing here so early?"

"We got out at noon today. I forgot to tell you that earlier."

"Right, a holiday?"

"For the kids. A planning day for teachers." She started toward the barn, drawn by the whinny of a horse and laughter. Jackson walked next to her. She glanced up at him. "What are you going to do?"

"I'm not sure. I can't find any information on her mother's death. And I emailed a friend in law enforcement. She hasn't been reported missing."

Madeline stopped walking. "So where do you think her mother is?"

He didn't have a clue. "Maybe she's the one that's missing? I might have to drive to Enid. I'm going to keep searching because I'm starting to think she's not actually from Enid."

"You think?"

"What, you came to that conclusion first?"

She smiled because the look on his face said he clearly didn't think she could think of it first. "The thought had crossed my mind. I think there's far more to her story than she's telling."

"The guy is always the last to know." He motioned her inside the stable ahead of him.

Madeline loved barns of all kinds, but this one took the cake. Shadowy and smelling of hay and horses, it stretched from stalls to a wide aisle that led into the arena. Country music played softly and Jade stood in front of a stall petting a pretty black mare.

The girl smiled at Jackson, hazel eyes glittery and full of light. "She's a beautiful horse."

"I thought so." Jackson walked up next to the girl. "After she settles down I'll let you ride her."

"I've never ridden a horse." Jade's voice came out breathless and wistful.

"I guess that's something we'll take care of." Jackson turned to smile at Madeline and she felt a little wistful, too. "What about you, Ms. Patton?"

"I've ridden a few times with Andie Johnson."

Jade stepped back from the horse who had her head down, munching hay. "Why don't you have a Christmas tree?"

Jackson blinked at the rapid change of topics. Madeline nearly laughed because he clearly needed to adjust to how a teenage girl's brain worked. He didn't understand that a girl like Jade could have a dozen or more things going on in her mind at once.

"I guess 'cause I don't need one."

Jade's mouth opened at that revelation. "You have to have a Christmas tree. How can you have Christmas without a tree?"

Jackson shrugged. "Because I go to my parents' house and they have a tree."

Madeline didn't want to jump in but Jade turned, clearly intending to pull her in.

"Do you have a tree?" Jade asked, her attention now on Madeline.

"I have a little one." Pitiful, really. She had a pink tree with silver ornaments. It had seemed like a good idea at the time because it came pre-decorated.

Now a pink Christmas tree just seemed wrong.

"Christmas isn't about a tree." Jackson stepped in, almost defensive.

Jade blew out, obviously disgusted. "I think I know that. The tree isn't what Christmas is all about, but it kind of makes me think more about the holiday."

"We'll get a tree." Jackson herded them toward the door of the barn. "Tomorrow."

Madeline thought about tomorrow, the day she planned on baking bread, decorating her house and then working on finishing touches at the Dawson Community Center's living nativity. She also needed to run to town and buy ingredients for candy.

"We can drive my truck out to the back pasture and find a decent cedar. And if Madeline needs a tree, we can cut her one, too."

"I really don't." Madeline stiffened when his hand went to her back, lingered and then moved away. When she glanced at him his hands were in his pockets and his smile had disappeared.

"Of course you do." He looked down at her. "We'll cut down trees and then we'll come back here for hot chocolate and cookies."

Jade's face lit up. "Perfect."

Madeline wanted to disagree. Perfect would be how she'd describe her life before this morning, before being invaded by the two Coopers standing next to her. Perfect would be her little pink tree being left alone and her heart not hammering out the tune "Meet Me Under the Mistletoe."

She didn't want those thoughts, those dangerous-to-her-heart thoughts. She didn't want to be afraid. Of what, she asked herself. Afraid of rejection? Afraid he'd hurt her? Or worse.

Always worse.

God's strength. She reminded herself that she could do this, she could face her fears. She could be the strong person she sometimes knew existed inside her.

Tomorrow should be good enough to start on being strong. Today she had to deal with her emotions tumbling inside her, mocking her because she'd thought she had them locked up tight.

Jade and Jackson were still talking and laughing, discussing the plan for tomorrow. She wanted to explain that she already had plans. Instead she chose escape.

"I should go. I need to get some stuff done at my house before our big adventure tomorrow."

Jade walked away from the horse but her gaze lingered on the animal, and then turned to Jackson. Of course she wanted to stay with him. Madeline understood that. But Jade, like so many kids that Madeline knew who were used to disappointment, brushed it off. She raised her chin a notch, shrugged, and let it go.

Still, it had to hurt. Even if she knew how to pretend none of this bothered her, on the inside, where it counted, Madeline knew Jade had to be afraid.

Worse, she seemed to be counting on Madeline for strength and for guidance.

"What are you going to do for the rest of the day?" Jackson leaned against a stall door and she figured it had to be holding him up.

"Is there something you need?"

He grinned and winked. "A back rub would be good. Are you offering?"

"Do you ever stop?"

His smile faded. "Yeah, I do. I'm sorry for saying that. You might have to give me a few days to get the old Jackson under control."

"Right, of course."

"Do you think you'll be going to town today?" Jackson reached into his back pocket and pulled out his wallet.

"I had planned on picking up Christmas decorations in Grove. Why?"

"Because I thought I'd give you money for groceries since you've got another mouth to feed. And she might need some clothes and a warmer coat."

"I'm fine. You don't have to worry about me." Jade moved to stand next to Madeline, her shoulders squared and stiff. "I'm good at taking care of myself."

"I'm sure you are, Jade, but that isn't necessary. You came looking for a family and this is what family does." Jackson handed Madeline several bills and she folded the money and put it in her pocket.

"I can take her." Madeline smiled at the girl standing next to her. "We can have fun shopping."

Jade shrugged slim shoulders. "Okay, sure. So I'm leaving and I won't see you until tomorrow?"

After a long pause, Jackson eased closer, taking stiff steps that Madeline hadn't noticed earlier. She wondered if he was even supposed to be up, let alone doing chores.

"Jade, I want to spend time with you. We're going

to figure this whole mess out and I'm going to do my best to help you…"

"I don't need help. I need a dad."

His features softened. "I know, and I'm going to do my best to help you with that. But honestly, kid, I need to crash. I think my ribs are about to snap in two and my back kind of feels like a truck is sitting on it. Now that isn't the toughest 'dad' kind of thing to admit. Especially in front of two women." He smiled a tight smile. "But that's the way it is."

"Fine." Jade stood on tiptoe and kissed his cheek.

And something about him changed. Madeline watched his eyes and face shift and suddenly, Jackson Cooper became a dad. Or at least what she always imagined a dad would be if she'd had a real one.

"We should go." Madeline reached for Jade. "What time tomorrow? And are you sure you don't want me to bring something over for dinner tonight?"

"I think by nine in the morning." Jackson winked at Jade before turning to smile at Madeline. "And don't worry about me. I'm going to crash, and food is the last thing I want."

They walked back to the house together, slowly. Jackson watched them get in the car and then he eased his way up the steps of the front porch and into the house. Madeline waited until he stepped through the door before she shifted into Reverse.

"You think he's cute, don't you?"

Madeline blinked a few times at the crazy question the teenager sitting next to her had asked. Jade smiled at what Madeline had hoped would be a warning look. Maybe she needed to work on that.

"Jackson doesn't need for anyone to think he's cute. He thinks it enough about himself."

"Mmm-hmm."

Let it go, her wise inner voice said. *Let it go*. She drove on down the road, back to her house. When they reached her place she pulled up to the mailbox.

"Could you reach in and get my mail?" She pulled close and rolled the window down for Jade.

"Sure." Jade reached into the box and pulled out a few pieces of mail. Rather than handing it over she sifted through it. "Hey, a Christmas card from Marjorie Patton. Is that your sister or your mom?"

Madeline grabbed the mail and shoved it in her purse. "It's no one."

Jackson woke up in a dark living room, the dog at his feet growling. He groaned and tossed the pillow across the room. Twice in one day. In one long, long day. The doorbell chimed again and he pushed himself off the couch, groaning as he straightened, stretching the muscles in his back.

Things to do tonight: sleep in own bed.

"I'm coming, already."

He threw the door open and immediately backed down. "Sir."

His dad stood in the doorway, the look on his face a familiar one. At almost thirty-four, Jackson should be long past that look from anyone. But there it was, the "buddy, you're in big trouble" look.

"Come in, I'll put on a pot of coffee."

Tim Cooper stomped the mud off his boots and stepped inside the house. "Smells like dog in here."

"Yeah, the stupid dog refuses to sleep outside. Either

he's worried about me, or he just doesn't like the cold. I'm going with the cold."

"Probably. You're walking like you're eighty years old."

"Yeah, well, I feel older than that."

"What spooked that horse? Did you ever figure it out?"

They reached the kitchen and Jackson motioned for his dad to sit down while he filled the water reservoir on the coffeemaker and pushed the power button.

"I think it was a loose door banging in the wind. We both know that isn't why you're here."

"I can be here for more than one reason. Your mom is worried because she tried to call and you didn't answer."

"I was dog-tired."

"I told her you were probably asleep."

Jackson reached for the bottle of painkillers on the counter and then he put them back. It wasn't so bad he couldn't walk it off. "And the other reason you're here?"

"Travis has a big mouth."

"Right, I figured as much. Something about the words 'Travis, keep your mouth shut' tends to loosen his mouth like an oiled hinge."

His dad kind of laughed. He took his hat off and sat it on the table. "She isn't yours?"

"Probably not." Jackson sat down next to his dad. He fiddled with the stack of mail he'd left on the table earlier that day. "But my name is on her birth certificate."

"Where's her mom?"

"Your guess is as good as mine." Jackson got up to make the coffee. He put a cup under the nozzle. "Black?"

"Yeah. Oh, your mom sent dinner. It's in the truck and I'll bring it in before I leave."

"Thanks. You know, I'll never learn to cook if she keeps feeding me."

"She isn't going to stop. I've tried. And she's itching to fix this situation for you, too."

Jackson set the two cups of coffee on the table. "I'll fix this myself. The fewer people involved the better."

"I don't think your mom thinks that she's one of the people who shouldn't be involved. She said to tell you she'll expect to see you tomorrow."

"Give me a few days. I'm trying to figure this out without hurting Jade."

"Is that her name?"

He nodded and took a sip of coffee. "Yeah, Jade Baker. I knew her mom. But you know…"

"Yeah. Might need to head to the doctor just to make sure."

"I will. I'm not turning her out in the cold. I'm not going to call the state yet. I'm not going to have her in the system at Christmas."

"Where is she?"

This is where it got tricky. He sipped his coffee and gave himself a minute. His dad answered his own question.

"Travis said Madeline Patton was up here today."

"She was."

"Madeline, huh?" Tim grinned kind of big, the way a man did when he'd raised a bunch of sons. "Not your normal cup of tea."

"I've never been a tea person."

"No, you haven't." Tim lifted his cup and finished off his coffee. "Don't hurt her. If you don't want big trouble with your mother, remember that people think of lot of Madeline."

"I'm not chasing the schoolteacher, if that's what you think." He shook his head. "And I'm not eighteen years old. So thanks for the advice."

Tim stood. He put a hand on Jackson's shoulder. "She's the kind of woman a guy marries."

Yeah, that said it all. Put him in his place. Jackson, who had done his running around and then settled down on this farm with a dog and some livestock, had yet to outrun his reputation. It sure felt like he couldn't do enough good deeds to undo what the people around here thought of him.

He stood to follow his dad out of the kitchen, and he couldn't stop one last attempt at denial. "I'm not planning to marry Madeline Patton."

His dad laughed. "When do things ever go the way we plan?"

"This is different. She's helping with Jade."

"Right, of course." He slapped Jackson on the back. "Careful, son, the word *never* usually leads right where you never thought you'd go."

Jackson stood on the front porch, thinking of all the times he'd said never. It wasn't until his dad's taillights disappeared that he remembered his dinner in that truck.

Fortunately he'd lost his appetite.

Chapter Five

A light snow had fallen overnight, just enough to dust the grass and the trees. Madeline drove her car up the long driveway to Jackson Cooper's ranch. The old farmhouse with the wraparound porch looked pretty with the powdery white snow sprinkling down. In the field the cows stood tail to the wind, snow sticking to their thick winter coats.

"This sure ain't Oklahoma City," Jade whispered.

"What? And don't say 'ain't.'" Madeline pulled her car in at the side of the house.

"Nothing. And I'm sorry." Jade already had her door open. "I bet he's still sleeping."

"No, he isn't. I saw him walk out of the barn."

"Oh, okay." Jade slammed the door of the Buick and ran toward the big barn.

Madeline waited. And she worried. What happened to a girl when she thought she'd found a fairy-tale parent who would make everything right, and then found herself let down? Heartache? Madeline remembered a father, but he hadn't been her real father. She blocked the memory because too many other memories chased after it. Yesterday she'd gotten a card from her mother. Her mother always managed to find her. Madeline couldn't run far enough or fast enough to outrun Marjorie. She would never escape the past.

She never answered the cards or letters. Usually she moved and hoped it would be the last time. No matter how much Marjorie apologized or said she wouldn't hurt her, that she just wanted a chance to talk, Madeline couldn't believe.

The one person she wanted to see had disappeared off the face of the earth. She'd searched for her sister the way Jade had searched for Jackson. She hadn't found Sara. Maybe she had married. Or changed her name. Madeline had been given that option years ago, to change her name.

But she was Madeline Patton. She didn't know how to be anyone else. She'd always felt as if she had to face this life, not change her name and become someone else. Not that it hadn't occurred to her. Not that she didn't think a change of name would be a great way to start over.

"Come on!" Jade had raced ahead but she turned back, hugging her new coat to herself.

Madeline nodded and smiled. She followed at a slower pace, not quite as excited about spending the day with Jackson. Dealing with him. It exhausted her just thinking about it. He had too much energy and twice as much charm.

"You coming?" Jade headed her way. The dog ran out of the barn and caught up with her, nipping at her pant legs.

"I'm not going to run."

"You're walking too slow. We're going to get a Christmas tree." Jade reached for her hand.

"I know and it's twenty degrees out here."

"Right, that makes it more like Christmas."

Jackson walked out of the barn, smiling and waving when he saw them. "I have everything we need in the truck. I'll get it."

"Coffee?" Madeline shivered inside her coat. When she looked up, met his gaze, he smiled. And then he let his gaze drop.

"Where's the schoolteacher?" He winked at Jade.

"What does that mean?" Madeline looked down at herself and then up at him.

He moved his hands in circles. "You're in jeans. And you're not wearing your glasses."

Jade laughed, loud and silly. "I did it. I talked her into wearing jeans and putting in the contacts she never wears. You can't chop down a Christmas tree in a skirt."

"I see." Jackson took a step closer. "Not a bad change, Maddie. Not bad at all."

"It's jeans and contact lenses." She shot him a look and he raised both hands in surrender, his smile fading. She pulled her heavy coat a little closer. "And my name's Madeline."

"You're right, it's just jeans and a new coat. People change clothes every day."

Jade raced into the barn. A second later she ran back out, her face beaming. "It's a wagon, Madeline, a real wagon."

The pumpkin will be your coach, Cinderella. Make sure you're home by midnight.

She grimaced and pushed fairy tales from her mind as she walked into the barn to see what had Jade jumping up and down this time. The girl went from defiant and strong-willed to giddy in the blink of an eye.

Maybe changing with the ease of a chameleon was a Cooper trait and the girl had gotten it from Jackson. Hazel eyes, blond hair and the ability to shake off pain and become someone else.

As they walked through the open double doors of the barn, Jackson touched her arm, his hand cupping her elbow. "It's a Cooper tradition. I know we aren't going with the family, but I thought we should do this the right way."

A buckboard wagon pulled by two honey-colored horses stood in the wide center aisle of the barn. The harness jangled as the two large animals nodded their heads up and down, chewing on the metal bits in their mouths.

"I told you." Jade ran to the back and started to climb in. The dog jumped around her feet, happy, it seemed, to have someone in his life who could be easily excited.

"Climb in." Jackson led her to the front of the wagon, indicating with a nod the little step and a handle on the side of the wagon.

"We're really going off into the field in a wagon."

"We really are." He put a hand on her waist.

Her hand froze in midair, inches short of the handle as his touch lingered. She closed her eyes and exhaled. Pleasure and fear mixed like some crazy concoction that made her brain fuzzy and her heart ache.

The woman in her wanted to know that someone could find her attractive, someone could see how special she was. Someone could want to love her. She wanted to believe someone could melt her heart and make her feel whole.

She wasn't sweet sixteen and never been kissed. She was twenty-eight, and in the arms of a man she'd never felt more than distance and the wild urge to escape.

The child in her, that little girl that had hidden in closets and tried to run, wanted to escape because this man shook her heart, and because another man had made her feel dirty to the depth of her soul.

And it had taken years of counseling to get past that pain.

It had taken a faith that renewed and taught forgiveness to get her past the hatred. She still needed to work on the part of the plan that said she could love herself.

She had never let a man inside her heart because she'd never wanted to feel that pain again. She never wanted to be betrayed again.

Jackson stood behind her, his hand still light on her waist. Jade laughed and played with the dog, unaware. Jackson stepped closer.

"I'm just helping you in the wagon, Maddie."

She nodded and his hand moved to her back as she stepped up and into the wagon. As she settled into the seat he led the horses from the barn. She ducked as they went through the door, but there wasn't really a need. In the back, Jade had settled under a blanket with Bud the dog.

Jackson, stern in a way she'd never seen him, tipped his hat to her and then walked around and climbed up next to her. They didn't speak as the wagon started on a worn trail toward an already open gate.

He had nothing to say and her heart seemed to be tripping all over itself, trying to catch up with twenty-eight years of emotions and new revelations about herself.

She folded her hands in her lap as the wagon bumped

and jostled along the trail. No cattle or horses grazed in the field they were traveling through. The winter morning was cold and quiet. Even Jade seemed to be too excited to talk. For once.

Madeline found herself wanting to talk nonstop. For once. Talking would be easier than the silence, easier than delving into that moment back in the barn. A moment when she'd wondered what it would be like to turn into his arms, to be held by him.

She nearly laughed at that thought. What would Jackson Cooper do if a church mouse like her threw herself at him? A smile crept across her face. He'd die of shock. He'd run for his life.

He surely wouldn't know what to do.

Not that women didn't pursue him. But Madeline Patton in pursuit would probably scare ten years off his life. It scared ten years off hers just thinking about it.

"Here we go." Jackson pulled the team up and set the handbrake on the wagon. Jade hurried to stand, wobbling and grabbing the back of the bench seat he and Madeline were sitting on.

"What are you two waiting for?" She hopped over the side, the dog, Bud, jumping after her.

"We're coming." Jackson glanced at the woman next to him. She'd been quiet the whole trip out. Not that fifteen minutes of silence was impossible for a woman, but he thought her silence said everything she wasn't willing to say.

He wasn't about to push his way into her life, to tell her she didn't have to be afraid, that he wouldn't hurt her.

He had hurt women, not intentionally, but because

he hadn't ever been the guy that wanted to take a few dates and turn them into something more. Yeah, she was smart to keep her distance from someone like him.

But if he was going to have a cup of tea…

Crazy thought. He wasn't a tea-drinking man.

"We should get down." He said it smooth and easy, as if he hadn't just been having thoughts that shook him from his comfort zone.

Last summer he'd teased Wyatt Johnson about Rachel Waters, telling Wyatt that the woman would get under his skin. And he'd been right. They were married now and as happy as any two people could be.

He knew better than to let a woman get under his skin. Even one as sweet as Madeline Patton, with her quiet ways and soft smiles.

She looked up at him; her mouth opened as if she meant to say something. Probably something he didn't want to hear. He didn't think she would be the type to call a man names, but he'd been called a few in his life.

"Thank you."

That was it. And he didn't even know why she was thanking him. Before he could question her she hopped down out of the wagon and walked away. Her new coat was brick red. It was a crazy combination with her brown hair hanging loose and the wind blowing it around her face. Her boots left tiny prints in the light dusting of snow. She turned to look back at him, catching her hair back from her face with her hand.

"You going to join us?"

Yeah, he was joining them. He stepped down out of the wagon, landing with a jolt that shot through his pancreas or something. He took a deep breath and whistled as he exhaled.

"You okay?" Madeline called back.

"Yeah, I'm good." Great. Wonderful. Happy.

He grabbed the chain saw out of the back of the wagon and followed the two ladies on a merry chase for the "perfect" tree.

"You know there isn't a perfect tree, right?" He trudged along behind them, smiling a little as they circled a tree close to twelve feet high.

"What do you call this?" Jade turned and then she started singing, "Oh Christmas tree, oh Christmas tree."

"I call this too big for my house." He walked on and they followed after him.

"Scrooge," Madeline whispered as she moved past him.

"You'd better believe it." He snorted and she laughed. And he wondered if she realized how much fun she was having. "So how'd it go last night?"

She stopped and her gaze remained on Jade who had skipped away with the dog to survey a tree she'd seen and it had to be the one.

"She's a mess." Madeline smiled and started walking again. "And now my house is a mess. I think you need a turn at the trail of clothes, water on the bathroom floor and dishes on the counter."

"And deny you the pleasure?"

She sighed and didn't laugh. "Seriously, Jackson, her mom has to be out there somewhere. We can't keep her here forever."

"I know that. I've got someone working on it. I'll find her."

"And then what?" Madeline looked up at him, her brown eyes locking with his. "Send her back? What if it isn't a safe situation? What if…"

Jackson got it. "What if you get attached and can't stand to let her go?"

Madeline shrugged. "She's heading back."

"Right, of course. And you're very good at skipping out on answering questions."

"What, are you going to tell me you won't get attached? Or that you won't worry? I know relationships are easy for you. Are they that easy to walk away from?"

Jackson stopped, stunned, and more than a little mad. "That's a great assessment from someone who doesn't really know me."

"I'm sorry." She reached for his arm. "That was unfair."

"A little." Not too much. The old saying that the truth hurt might have worked for this situation. Not that he planned on telling her that bit of information.

"This is it!" Jade pointed to the biggest cedar on the place. It had to be twenty feet. "It's perfect."

"Really? Perfect for what, the White House? Let's see if we can't find something a little smaller."

She did the teenage eye roll and walked on. He didn't have a single parenting bone in his body. He was a fraud. The only thing he knew to do was mimic things he'd heard his dad say over the years.

"What about this one?" Madeline pointed to a medium-size tree.

"Hmm, yes, it's good. It isn't very full. It doesn't have huge open gaps." Jade walked around the tree. "Yes, this is good. And we need one for Madeline's."

"No, we don't have to do that." Madeline shot him a look.

He remembered his sister Mia, when someone would

offer her something that she thought was too much and she didn't want to be a bother. He smiled at the memory.

"Of course you need a tree." A kid in his life for twenty-four hours and he'd suddenly turned into his dad.

Maybe he'd wake up and this would be a dream. Or a strange version of *It's a Wonderful Life*. This was his world invaded by domesticity. He could almost hear the angel, Clarence, telling him that his life would be better with a family. Without them his home was empty, quiet.

Now how was peace and quiet such a bad thing?

"I really don't need one." Madeline had already spotted one. He knew it the minute she smiled.

"That one, right there. The small one?"

She nodded and smiled at him. "Please."

"You got it, Maddie."

She didn't correct him this time.

He left the chain saw on the ground and picked up the handsaw he'd brought. It would take about five minutes to cut through the trunk of a little bitty cedar. The part he'd forgotten about was the kneeling down part. That meant him on the ground, cracked ribs and all, pushing a saw back and forth. Through one of the toughest little cedars he'd ever seen.

By the time he finished the second tree, standing up just about wasn't an option.

He backed up, on his hands and knees, inhaling through the sharp pain. Jade had hold of her tree and started dragging it toward the wagon. Madeline stood in front of him.

"Need help?" She didn't smile.

"I'm afraid to admit that I do." He sat back up, moving into a squatting position that proved to be pretty overrated.

She stood there a long moment and then she reached for his hands. He made it to his feet, holding on to her as he stretched and the muscles in his back relaxed. Briefly.

"Phew, that was fun."

She was still holding his hands. She looked up, her eyes wide and deep-down hurt, the kind that took years to heal. Inside those dark eyes of hers he saw the little girl she'd been. He wanted to wrap her in his arms and protect her. He wanted to promise no one would ever hurt her again.

He let go of her hands because he wouldn't be the guy that broke her heart. She needed someone safe and dependable. How was that for being the grown-up, responsible guy? He'd have to share this moment with his dad.

The day Jackson Cooper used self-control.

What in the world had happened to him? Had he grown a conscience? Changed? Maybe all of those prayers uttered at Dawson Community Church on his behalf were suddenly being answered.

He chuckled.

"What?" Madeline had backed away, as if she'd suddenly come to her senses.

"Nothing, just thinking about prayers said on my behalf."

"What does that mean?"

"Are you going to say you haven't heard my mother or grandmother stand up in church and spill their guts about my life and how I need to come back to God?"

"That isn't really something to joke about." Madeline's eyes narrowed and he felt very chastised, for a second.

"I'm not joking. I know what they say. I grew up in church."

"They don't gossip about you, if that's what you think. They love you and worry about you."

He smiled at her ruffled feathers. "I know. But I'm not so far from God as they all think. I pray. I read my Bible. I'm not dating a different woman every night of the week. I've hardly dated at all in the last six months." As if she really needed all this information.

They walked side by side back to the wagon. Jackson had pulled on his gloves and he dragged the bigger tree behind him. Madeline stopped him a short distance from the wagon. She put a hand on his arm.

"Why don't you go to church?"

He shrugged. "Got out of the habit, I guess. Years of running around, rodeoing, sowing those wild oats. God and I are working it out."

"I see. So when they ask for prayers for you on Sunday, should I tell them you're good?"

He grinned. "One of these days I'll show up and prove it myself."

"That would be nice. You know it breaks your mother's heart that you're not in church."

"I'm not the only one."

"I know. She wants all of her children in church with her."

"Have you always gone to church?" He lifted the cedar tree and tossed it into the back of the wagon. Jade had a stick and she tossed it for Bud to fetch. He watched her for a minute, wondering how much of her story was true. She didn't seem to be a heartbroken kid. Instead she acted as if she might be on the adventure of a lifetime.

"She's a cute kid."

"Yeah, she is." What in the world should he do with her? He couldn't just move a kid into his house and be her dad. He hadn't been sitting around his house thinking he wanted a kid cluttering up his bathroom, leaving dirty clothes on the floor and asking for money to go to the movies.

He watched her hug his dog when the heeler jumped up, front paws on her stomach. Truth time. He'd been thinking a lot lately about how empty his life had become.

"She's just looking for a family." Madeline's voice sounded wistful to him.

"I know."

"She admitted she researched your family when she found the birth certificate. A real family, that's what she wanted."

"So where is her mom?"

Madeline looked from the girl to him. "Try Oklahoma City."

"Gotcha." He whistled, and Bud came running back. Jade loped after him, her cheeks red from running and playing in the cold.

"Time to go?" She looked in the back of the wagon. "Where do I ride?"

"Up here with us."

She grinned big and climbed into the seat. He stood behind Madeline and waited for her to get situated and then he climbed up, sitting next to her. They were pushed together by Jade on the end of the bench seat.

Madeline swallowed, he saw her throat bob, saw a

flicker of a pulse in her neck. If ever a woman needed a man who would make her feel safe, it was this one.

She needed a Prince Charming, someone like his brother Blake. Yeah, Blake wouldn't hurt a woman. He'd set her up in a nice house at the edge of Dawson. He'd buy her a pretty diamond ring and bring her flowers. Blake was a cold fish, though. For good reasons, Jackson figured, but still, his big brother needed to learn how to let go.

He'd have to do one better than that for Madeline. She needed someone. He smiled down at her. But not him.

Chapter Six

The horses picked up the pace on the way back to the barn. Their easy trot jangled the harness. Madeline sat sandwiched between Jade and Jackson. She shivered, not because of the cold, but because of him. She closed her eyes and breathed in the cold air.

Jackson drove the team past the barn and to the front door of the house. "I'll unload the tree and take the horses back to the barn."

"Where are your decorations?" Jade nearly bounced from the seat as they pulled up to the house and the team came to a jarring halt.

Madeline grabbed the girl and held her in the seat.

Next to her, Jackson pushed his hat back a notch. "Well now, that's a good question. I guess I hadn't thought about decorations."

"You have to have decorations," Jade insisted, hopping down from the wagon and joining the dog who had already done the same.

"No, not really. I haven't put a tree up in years. Let's take it inside and when I go to the barn I'll look in the storage shed."

Jackson eased himself down from the wagon, not as quickly as before. Madeline filed away that information about him, because it changed who he was in her mind. Jackson Cooper, selfless? Willing to put himself through all kinds of agony in order to ensure a child had a Christmas tree?

He was the man holding his hand out, offering help getting down from the wagon. She could refuse and do it herself, looking stubborn and a little silly. Or rude. She could take his hand and risk everything.

Risk what? She bit down on her bottom lip and his hand still reached for hers. She nodded and stepped over the side of the wagon. His hand touched her waist, her arm. She landed gently on the ground. When she looked up it was into hazel eyes that danced with laughter.

Smile, she told herself, make it easy. Jackson Cooper dated tall, leggy blondes and polished brunettes. He didn't date mousy schoolteachers. She knew the drill. She would always fit the role of person most likely to help. She had always been the one a guy called if he thought she could help him hook up with someone else. And she had always liked filling that spot, because it didn't hurt so much if expectations were low. It didn't hurt if you didn't get too close.

As she stood there gathering herself, he opened his mouth as if he meant to say something. But he didn't.

"We'll make hot chocolate." She stepped away, turning to go inside.

"I'll be right back." He walked to the front of the wagon and took hold of the first horse in the team. "If you want hot chocolate there's a mix in the cabinet. Mom makes it every winter."

"Thank you." *Say something smart and witty*, she

pushed herself. But she'd never been the smart, witty type. She'd never been the flirty one, batting her eyelids or saying cute things. She'd been the bookworm, hiding behind glasses and her studies.

She'd been the one hiding from life, protecting herself.

How in the world had this become her life? Laughter and a barking dog reminded her. A mix-up had dropped a child in her life and somehow tied her to Jackson Cooper. She could have dropped Jade off yesterday and driven away, not looking back, not thinking she had an obligation of any kind. Somewhere out there Jade, more than likely, had a mother who wanted her back.

"Let's go inside." She motioned for Jade as she walked up the steps.

As she walked through the front door of the house she did what she knew to do. She put all of her crazy emotions in a box and shoved them to the back of her mind.

"Do you think he has any cookies?" Jade followed behind her with the dog, who left muddy paw prints on the wood floor.

"I think the dog should stay outside." Madeline pointed to the paw prints.

Jade had already moved on. "Where should we put the tree?"

"It isn't my tree or my house so I'm not going to make that decision."

Jade glanced at her but didn't seem to be too bothered. "He wouldn't have a tree if it wasn't for us."

"I'm not even sure why I'm here," Madeline said out loud.

That got Jade's attention. The girl turned quickly, her

eyes widening and her smile dissolving. "I'm sorry. I mean, I guess you probably have other things to do?"

"No, not really." She would have been at home knitting another scarf. She might have been cleaning her kitchen or reorganizing her cabinets. "Jade, where's your mom?"

Deflecting. Always safe. Not always fair.

Jade's eyes got huge and the color drained from her face. She walked away, the dog right on her heels.

"Jade?"

"It's none of your business. Remember, you're the person who got stuck with me. I came here looking for my dad and instead I'm staying with a lady who sleeps with every light in the house on."

The front door closed. "Problem here?"

Jackson walked into the living room, carrying a rubber tub with a lid. He'd shed his jacket and was dressed in jeans and a button-up shirt. If he felt the tension, he didn't show it. He took off his hat and hung it on a hook.

"No, there's no problem." She offered Jade an apologetic smile but the girl walked away.

"Let her go." Jackson said it in an easy, relaxed voice. "She'll get over it. She's too excited about the tree to stay mad for long."

"I asked where her mother is," Madeline admitted. "I thought she might talk to me."

"Talking isn't always easy."

"No, it isn't."

He pulled the lid off the box. "We could get you a dog."

"Excuse me?"

"It can't be cheap to have all of your lights on all the time."

She pulled out a string of lights that looked as if they were from the last century. "What do you know about my lights?"

"I've driven by a few times and wondered."

"I'm fine."

He looked up, his hazel eyes asking questions she didn't want to answer.

"Are you really?"

The question made her wonder. Then she answered, and it didn't hurt, it wasn't a lie. "I really am."

Of course she had doubts. She did sleep with the lights on. But she'd come so far and she'd grown so much. But why did he ask? What did he know about her fear?

She didn't want his sympathy.

"We should go check on Jade." She backed away from him, but not fast enough. His hand shot out, stopping her escape.

"Jade's fine. She's rummaging through my cabinets and snooping through the kitchen. I'm getting you a dog."

She shook her head. "I don't need a dog."

"I'm either going to teach you to shoot a gun, or I'm getting you a dog."

"I don't really want either."

His hand still held her arm but he hadn't moved closer. "I know, but trust me on this. There's something kind of nice about coming home to a dog. It makes a house less lonely."

"I can get my own dog." It was her last attempt to hold on to independence and to take a stand against a man who had stormed her life as easily as Jade stormed his.

"I owe you for helping me out with Jade."

"I didn't have to help."

"No, you didn't." His hand slid down her arm to her hand. "But I'm glad you did."

"Jade," she whispered and glanced back over her shoulder.

"Right, Jade."

Jackson watched Madeline's retreat. He walked a little slower, giving her space, giving himself time to get his head together. What in the world was he thinking?

So she slept with the lights on. When had that become his problem? She'd been his neighbor for over a year. He said hello to her when they passed on the street or bumped into one another walking into the Mad Cow. He'd seen her lights on late at night, and he'd wondered about it. So now he knew and he thought he needed to buy her a dog to make her feel safe?

He needed his head examined.

Bachelor pad. That's what his house had been designed as. He walked into the kitchen and nearly groaned. The two females who had invaded his life were standing shoulder to shoulder mixing milk with his mother's cocoa mix. A plate of cookies had been set out on the counter. It smelled and looked like Sally Homemaker had moved in.

It smelled kind of nice, the combination of hot chocolate, cookies, popcorn and… Madeline's perfume. He leaned against the counter and watched the two of them have what looked like a mother-daughter moment.

"Did you find decorations?" Jade turned, a spoon in her hand. Her eyes sparkled and she smiled. Happy. And she wore it like new clothes, something she'd wanted and never had.

"Not much. I did find a couple of old tree stands. One for mine, one for the tree you're taking to Madeline's."

Madeline looked at her watch. "I have to go soon."

"We have to decorate his tree." Jade stirred the cocoa and then lifted the spoon to take a sip. Madeline took the spoon from her hand and tossed it in the sink. Jade's mouth opened. "Why'd you do that?"

"I don't want to share germs."

"Fine." Jade grabbed another spoon and turned to Jackson again. "We can string the popcorn if you have a sewing kit around here. And maybe make some snowflakes."

"Sure, why not," he grumbled as he pulled cups from the cabinet. "Would you like to crochet doilies for my tables?"

Jade laughed and pointed to Madeline. "She can do that."

Madeline looked away, her cheeks turning crimson. The hot chocolate steamed and she ladled the liquid into the cups he'd set next to the stove.

"I bet she can." He grinned at Madeline's back because she had turned away from him and was pretending to be busy with the cocoa.

"We need to hurry," she finally said. "I have practice tonight."

"Cool. Can I go?" Jade leaned close to Madeline.

"I tell you what, we'll go do something this evening. Madeline has to practice for her part in the nativity. We'll let her do that and you and I will go somewhere."

"Together?" Jade's eyes lit up and her smile radiated.

"Yeah, together."

Madeline turned with a cup in her hand. She held it out to him and said nothing. She didn't need to. She needed a break from Jade. She needed a break from him. He got that. Sometimes he needed a break from himself.

They migrated to the living room with a tray of hot chocolate and cookies. Jade carried the popcorn and the miniature sewing kit he'd found in the cabinet. As they settled down to the task of making decorations, Jackson pushed the tree into the stand and picked up the string of lights.

He unfolded the ladder and headed to the top with lights and a pulled muscle in his back. Madeline looked up from cutting into folded paper to make a snowflake for his tree.

"You okay?" she asked, her eyes narrowing as she watched him.

He looked at the scene below him. A woman and a child making Christmas decorations. His floor strewn with craft paper and ornaments. It looked like a picture from a Christmas card, not a picture from his life. Maybe the life he could have had?

"Yeah, I'm good."

Thirty minutes later, with the creative talents of Jade and Madeline, the tree changed from the sad Charlie Brown tree they'd dragged in from the field into a real Christmas tree. Jade had even found a prize: a tiny bird's nest leftover from last year. She'd moved it from the inner branches and placed it front and center, filling it with tiny eggs made of colored paper.

"It looks good." He hadn't contributed much, just a star for the top and the string of lights. But it was a decent-looking tree, even with the big empty space on the side they'd pushed close to the wall.

"Now we have to decorate Madeline's tree," Jade

proclaimed as she hung the last foil star. "She has real decorations."

"Hey, don't diss my tree." Jackson plugged in the lights. The strand of multicolored lights flickered and came on.

"I'm just saying." Jade smiled a cute kid smile. "Anyway, this is a good tree."

A knock on the door and they all froze. Madeline looked at him, then at Jade. Jackson shrugged and pointed at the dog who had decided to bark his fool head off. Bud sat down, tail wagging, but a menacing snarl still curled his lips.

"I'll be right back." Jackson touched Jade's head on the way to the door. "Stay in here."

When he opened the door a police officer stood on his front porch. Jackson stepped out the door and closed it behind him.

"Jackson, Douglas Clark called about the kid you have staying with you."

"She's not staying here. She's staying with Madeline Patton."

"I see. Can you tell me who she is and how she came to be here?"

"Well—" he paused because the only thing he had was Jade's birth certificate and her side of the story "—she's my daughter."

"Jackson, we need to clear this up. You have a minor who could be a runaway. That's not something we can turn our back on."

"I get that, Lance, but if she's my kid…"

"If she's not?"

"My name is on her birth certificate."

The officer started to get a grim look on his face. "Jackson, we need to try to contact her mother."

"Gotcha. What if I promise I'm trying to do that? Look, I don't want the kid in state custody. Not this close to the holidays."

"Find her mom."

"I will." Jackson stood his ground in the door but Lance didn't turn to leave.

"Jackson, I have to talk to her."

"We're decorating the Christmas tree."

Lance laughed at that. Why did everyone find it so amusing when he did anything slightly different? "That's pretty domestic."

Jackson motioned Lance inside. They'd met on occasion, usually at a fire or an accident that volunteer first responders were called to. That was the thing about a small town, a rural county; people knew each other. They knew stories. They knew where to find someone without getting a map or directions.

Sometimes that could be a good thing. Sometimes it got under a guy's skin.

They walked into the now-empty living room. Empty except the twinkling, pitiful tree and leftover decorations scattered across the floor.

"She must be in the kitchen."

Lance nodded and walked next to him through the living room and dining room. When they entered the kitchen Jade turned, her eyes going all glittery with tears. Madeline moved closer and shot Jackson an accusing look.

"You called the police?" Jade trembled, her face draining of color.

"No," Jackson said. "Not this one."

"Young lady, I need your full name and address." Lance stood in a relaxed pose but his eyes shifted, taking in the room, the setting. Cop training. Jackson could have told him to relax, no one would jump out from behind a door. But that training kept a guy safe on the job.

Jade hiccupped a little.

"Jade, honey, tell him." Madeline, soft-voiced and sweet but still shooting daggers at Jackson.

Jackson should do something. He should step forward, put an arm around her. He'd been raised in a close family with parents that were always there for them, holding it together during the worst times.

Jackson tried to grab hold of those experiences. He might not be Jade's dad, but he could step up and be who she needed him to be. Tim Cooper had been the best dad in the world. He still was a man whose example could be followed.

"Give her a minute, Lance. She's a kid." Jackson stepped closer to Jade. "Go ahead. Tell him what he needs to know."

She nodded and wiped at her eyes. He put an arm around her shoulder and pulled her close for just a second and then released her. She smiled up at him and sniffled.

"I'm Jade Baker. My mom is Gloria Baker. We live in Oklahoma City."

"Your mom is alive?" Jackson had known, but he'd been willing to believe her until he found out the whole story.

Jade didn't answer. She cried. Tears slid down her cheeks and she shrugged.

"We need to contact your mother." Lance pulled a pen from his pocket. "Do you have her number?"

"Yeah, but good luck finding her."

"What does that mean?" Jackson leaned back against the counter, watching Jade shift from foot to foot. She looked up at him, tears pooling in her hazel eyes.

Man, he hated tears. He glanced at Madeline and her eyes were overflowing. Though he'd grown up with emotional females, he'd never gotten good at handling tears.

"Jade?" Madeline had the soft touch, the gentle voice that the kid needed. He shot her a grateful smile.

"She's never at home. She leaves for days at a time. The reason I came here is because I found my birth certificate and decided I'd find you and see if you were any better than her."

"Did you leave her a note?" Lance wrote on the pad and barely glanced up.

"Yeah, I left her a note. But she doesn't care where I go as long as I'm out of her hair. She's high most of the time and that's what she cares about, her next score and how to pay for it."

"Let's try to call her." Lance waited and Jade recited a number. He pulled out his cell phone and held it to his ear. After a few tries he gave up. "No answer."

"I told you." Jade looked down at the floor, at the dog sleeping at her feet. "I wanted a real Christmas with a real family."

"You're truant from school. You're a runaway." Lance ticked the crimes off on his fingers.

"I'm with my dad," Jade insisted and Jackson couldn't

get a word in to dispel that fact from her mind. "And I can go to school here."

Lance sighed and shook his head. "I have to call this in. I'm going to leave it up to you, Jackson, if you want to be responsible for taking her home."

"I'll take her home." He didn't look at the woman gasping in disbelief or the kid shedding tears that dripped down her cheeks. "Next weekend. I have to make a trip to Oklahoma City with a bull calf I've sold. I can take her then."

"Keep trying to make contact with her mom. And you might want to contact a lawyer to see what your legal rights are."

"I'll do that."

Lance put the pen back in this pocket. "Jackson, don't get me in trouble with the sheriff. I'm just doing my job and I can't afford to lose my career over this."

Jackson leaned forward and shook the other man's hand. "I'll walk you to the door."

Lance pointed a finger in Jade's direction. "Running away is serious. I could call a juvenile officer. If my boss tells me to, I'll have no choice. And let me warn you, if you're thinking of running again, don't. It's December. It's cold. There are people out there who would hurt you. You're just lucky that you ended up here, with one of the best families in the state. Think about that."

"I will." Jade's eyes overflowed again.

"Take it easy on her, Lance." Jackson growled the words as they walked out of the kitchen.

"I'd love to, Jackson. But I want her to know how dangerous this is. Some kids get in the habit of running and they never stop. They end up in serious trouble, sometimes in permanent custody of the state. I don't want that to happen to her."

"You're right, but she's scared enough."

"So, you have a kid."

Jackson shrugged. If he gave up too much information, Lance would probably haul Jade in. A simple shrug and let it go, that had to be his answer for now.

He couldn't let Jade go, not now, knowing her story. That Cooper DNA was catching up with him. Take in strays and fix people. His parents had a dozen kids and more foster children because of that trait.

After watching Lance's patrol car drive away, Jackson walked back in the house. Jade and Madeline were waiting in the living room. He glanced at his watch. "We should probably eat lunch."

Madeline looked at her watch. "I need to go. I have practice."

"Okay, gotcha. What about your tree?" Jackson smiled at Jade. Her eyes and nose were red.

"I can put it up later. Jade…"

"Can stay with me. We'll cook dinner and have a nice meal waiting for you when you get home." Jackson stuttered over the words. "I mean, when you get back."

He felt itchy all over. His life didn't include a woman coming home and a kid hanging stockings on the fireplace mantel. It wasn't even a real, wood-burning fireplace.

"You don't have to do that." Madeline slipped into her coat. When she struggled to find the left sleeve, he pulled it out for her and held it as she slid her arm through.

She looked up, soft eyes and a soft smile. She smelled

like hot cocoa and vanilla. He inhaled and stepped close, but then he backed off, remembering. But he couldn't let it go, not completely. He brushed a hand through her hair, pulling it loose from the collar of her coat, letting his fingers linger in the silken strands.

He took a deep breath and stepped away from her. "We'll see you later."

She nodded and hurried out the door.

Behind him Jade laughed. "I thought you were like some Casanova guy that knew all about women."

"I am and…" He grimaced. "I'm not. You know what, go clean up the kitchen."

He needed to get his act together, as his dad used to say. He needed to get his head on straight and think smart. His dad had said that too many times in his life. It had started when he dated Julia Hart. Two years older than him, and someone his mother didn't want him seen with. Julia hadn't lasted two weeks. His dad had made sure of that.

Jackson shook his head, remembering. And realizing his dad had been right most of the time.

Sometimes, though, a guy had to take a chance. He walked into the kitchen where Jade was busy putting away the dishes.

"I have an idea."

"I love ideas." She wiped at the few stray tears that rolled down her cheeks. "What is it?"

He didn't shake his head at the realization that she was just a kid, and she didn't really have anyone. But the thought hit him, broadsided him. A kid should always have someone.

Madeline had been a kid who needed someone. Probably still needed someone.

"It's a surprise for Madeline and you can help me." Jade's eyes lit up and he only hoped that Madeline would be nearly as excited by his plan.

Chapter Seven

What Madeline loved most about Dawson was that everyone knew everyone else. What she loved least was that everyone knew everyone else's business. As she walked through the Dawson Community Center, formerly Back Street Church, she got the feeling that everyone knew. Or maybe they only thought they knew something.

She slipped past a group of teenagers who were preparing to be citizens of Bethlehem. She had a role as shepherdess, one of the few who were overwhelmed by the presence of angels in the sky on that first Christmas morning. She didn't see it as a lowly role, but as one of the most important.

It symbolized something to her, that the angels appeared to mere shepherds. Not to kings, to the wealthy or religious, but to poor shepherds watching their flocks by night. Thinking about it made her heart rush with love for the God who had loved her that much.

She hurried down the steps to the basement of the community center. Beth Hightree looked up when Madeline walked into the dressing room. Newly married,

Beth smiled with a certain glow. She held out a robe. "There's my last shepherd."

"Sorry, I meant to be here earlier." Madeline took the robe.

"I'm sure you did. Tell Jackson you have to be here early tomorrow."

"I don't know…" Madeline stopped mid-denial and shook her head. "Beth, I…"

She didn't have a clue what to say. How in the world did these people spread information so quickly?

"You don't have to explain. He's cute. He's single. You're cute and single."

"It isn't like that."

What was it like? It was a shared secret. It was about helping a neighbor who, until yesterday, hadn't even been a friend. She looked up, making uneasy eye contact with Beth.

She wouldn't lie to her. She wouldn't lie to anyone, but Beth was more than a friend. Beth, Jenna McKenzie and Madeline had formed a support group in the last year. Each had gone through a difficult situation and survived. As survivors they knew being strong meant holding on to each other and lifting each other up. Staying strong.

Beth had survived an abusive marriage.

Jenna had survived injuries suffered in Iraq.

Madeline had survived her abusive nightmare of a childhood.

They had done more than survived. They had escaped. They had overcome. They were still overcoming.

"Madeline?"

She looked up, smiling at Beth. "It isn't what you

think. I can't share what Jackson is going through. But I can tell you that I'm fine."

"Really?"

The two sat down on a little bench. Madeline held on to the rough cotton robe she still needed to change into.

"It's crazy, really. I've spent my life living in my little shell, protecting myself."

"And Jackson Cooper is cracking the shell?" Beth smiled big, her brown eyes sparkling with humor.

"No, I mean, I can't even call him a friend. I guess he's just a surprise. He's also a nice person."

Beth laughed at that. "Yes, he's a nice person. He's a flirt. He's dated more women than most of the Cooper men put together. But he's nice. He's actually sweet. And he's the last person you need to open yourself up to."

"Right. You're right." She stood and slipped the robe over her head. It hung to the floor and then some. "I think it's too long."

"I have a feeling you got the wrong robe. I saw Johnny Scott leave here in a robe about two feet too short."

"We can trade next time."

Beth handed her a long piece of rope. "Here's a belt. We can blouse it out over this and maybe you won't trip on your way up the stairs."

"That works for me." She wrapped the rope around her waist twice and then pulled to blouse the top of the robe. "Beth, I'm not going to get hurt. I'm just helping Jackson with something."

Beth nodded and reached for a box of safety pins. "I know, Madeline. The whole town knows."

Great. "There aren't any secrets in this town, are there?"

"Nope. Well, a few, but usually they get found out eventually."

Beth's words were innocent, teasing, but Madeline's mind went elsewhere, thinking about how things might change if everyone knew her secret.

"Madeline, are you okay?"

She nodded because words wouldn't come. Her throat tightened with emotion and she turned away. A hand touched her shoulder.

"Madeline, you have friends here who love you."

"I know." She hurried out of the room and up the stairs.

She knew she had friends who loved her. But suddenly she wanted more. Suddenly she wanted what she'd never wanted before. She wanted to be loved forever by a man who would walk next to her and never let her down. She wanted a man who could hear her story and not run or make her feel as if she'd done something wrong.

She didn't know if such a person existed. She remembered being little and looking up at a man she'd called Father, only to find he couldn't be trusted at all. He'd bought her ice cream and pretty dresses, and he'd taken her to the movies.

He'd taken everything from her and left her with nothing but nightmares, guilt and a heart that had closed itself off to the idea of ever being loved.

She walked outside, into bright sunlight, through the crowds of people who considered her a friend and neighbor. God had changed her life in the last few years.

He'd brought her here. He'd taught her lessons about love and forgiveness.

Now it seemed as if she might be on the brink of learning another lesson, about God and about herself.

Someone touched her arm. She turned and smiled at Dixie Gordon. "Shepherds are over here. And it looks like you might have the wrong robe!"

"I think I might." As she followed Dixie her thoughts turned to Jade and Jackson, making it hard to concentrate on being a shepherd.

Out of the blue it hit her, she wanted to go home. She wanted time alone to think. She shook her head as she tripped over the robe. She wanted to be with Jade and Jackson, doing whatever it was they were doing.

She looked up, wondering how God could ask her to put her heart on the line this way. Of course she wanted to trust. But this felt like jumping into quicksand, knowing full well what it was before she jumped.

Who would do that?

The puppies barked and chased each other in the fenced-in yard. Jackson watched Jade run with them, then sit to let them crawl on her lap and lick her face. They were sable and black balls of fluff, wagging tails and sharp eyes.

Adam McKenzie shook his head and didn't say anything.

"I want a male." Jackson leaned on the fence. "They're nice-looking pups."

"Best German shepherd puppies in the state." Adam glanced his way before settling his attention back on Jade and the mother dog who had crawled up next to her for attention. "Not a mean bone in that mama dog's body. I found a male that was a good match."

"So a great pet as well as a great guard dog?"

Adam nodded. "Sure, they'll protect you. Why do you need a guard dog?"

"It isn't for me. It's for Madeline Patton."

"Oh, okay."

The tone said it all. Jackson waited for Adam to say more but Adam had turned his attention back to the girl inside the fence and the puppies. Jade picked up a puppy and it wriggled close to her, giving her face a crazy bath. She laughed and then rolled on the cold ground with the dog. "This one."

He nodded in agreement. Definitely that one. He still wanted to know what Adam McKenzie wasn't saying about him buying a dog for Madeline. What did he want Adam to do, talk him out of it? Tell him to back off before he got hooked into something he couldn't get out of.

Or better yet, tell him not to hurt her. That thought had run through his mind more times in two days than he could count.

Two days, and here he was buying a dog and remodeling her house. Yeah, big words telling Wyatt Johnson that Rachel would get under his skin. Big words, buddy.

"Talking to yourself?" Adam turned, a big grin on his face. Adam, ex-pro-football player, could squish him like a gnat.

"Not at all. We'll take that one."

Adam opened the gate for Jade to exit with the puppy.

"Fine by me, but he's a she."

Jade looked up, eyes big, pleading. But she didn't say anything. He'd learned something about her. She was pretty used to disappointment. When he'd announced that he'd have to take her home at the end of the week, she'd accepted with a quiet dignity unusual for a thirteen-year-old kid. She'd accepted it the way kids accepted when they were not ever getting what they wanted.

A home and a family shouldn't be one of the things a kid had to wish for. A kid shouldn't have to accept going back to abuse. And every time he thought about a hurting child, he shouldn't also connect dots to Madeline Patton.

He let out a long sigh and shook his head. His life was no longer his own. Not one but two females were getting under his skin.

"A girl puppy is fine." He touched the spiky, wet nose of the shepherd pup. "What do we call her?"

Jade held the puppy up, looking her in the face. "Angel."

"Angel?" He grimaced and shook his head. He should have known better than to let her name the dog. "Sure, why not. She's a guardian angel."

"Exactly." Jade pulled the puppy close again.

"How much?" Jackson pulled out his checkbook and Adam shook his head. "Adam, I'm buying the dog."

"Consider it a Christmas gift."

"I can't do that. I tell you what, I'll write you a check for Camp Hope."

"That's a deal." Adam took the check and slid it into his shirt pocket. "Have fun with that dog, Jade."

She smiled. "I will. But I have to go home next week. This is just a vacation."

A vacation from reality. Jackson put a hand on her shoulder and guided her back to the truck. *Thanks for putting a knife in my heart, kid.*

"Jade, you and I have to do something on Monday."
He opened the truck door for her and she looked up.

"What's that?"

"We're going to the doctor for a test. We need to make sure we know what's going on so we know how to fight."

"How to fight?"

"Yeah, for you to be able to stay here, we have to have proof that you're my daughter." Heat climbed up his cheeks.

Jade climbed into the truck. "Sure, okay. But I am your daughter."

Yeah, he kind of wished she was. When the test came back with the results he knew they'd get, what then? What happened to Jade when she learned the truth?

When he pulled into Madeline's drive, Jade and the puppy were sleeping in the passenger side of the truck. Wake them up or leave them? He decided to let them sleep. He could get his ladder set up, find the electric box and get his work done before Madeline got back.

In a perfect world.

As he set the ladder up, the truck door opened and the twin tornadoes scrambled out. The dog ran to the corner of the yard. Jade chased after her. Jackson climbed the ladder, smiling as he listened to Jade talk to Angel. The puppy yapped and ran in circles.

He'd bought motion lights for the front porch and the back. When Madeline came home, she'd have security lights that came on with any motion. Maybe this way she could sleep at night without being afraid.

It didn't feel great, climbing the ladder. But it felt better than a few days ago. He reached for the old light, slipping it off the bracket and unscrewing the wire nuts that held the light to the light box. He wasn't an electrician, but he knew enough to hang a light.

In the yard Jade laughed and the puppy barked, yipping as the two of them raced around a tree. Every kid should have a dog. He let out a sigh, then froze as the ladder wobbled.

He looked down, the puppy stood on her hind legs, front legs on the first wrung of the ladder.

"Jade, could you get the dog?" He held the new light up to the wiring and twisted the correct wires together. He needed to connect them with the wire nut and then do the other set of wires.

Jade raced across the lawn to grab the puppy. "Sorry."

He let out a long breath and worked the other two wires together. "No problem."

The light fit into the box and he used the old screws to attach it. In a minute he'd flip the switch and make sure it worked.

The ladder wobbled again. He glanced down. That dog meant to kill him. He held tight and whistled to get Jade's attention. She'd gotten distracted, pulling Christmas lights out of the box he'd bought. She wanted Christmas lights on the front of Madeline's house.

The dog ran to the other side of the ladder. A ten-pound puppy shouldn't be able to push a ladder over. Jackson reassured himself with that bit of reality.

He grabbed the old light off the rafter of the front porch roof and slid the tools into his tool belt. He didn't want to make a scene, but he wasn't crazy about heights. A car came down the road and he knew Madeline would be home soon. It might be her now, catching him in the process of surprising her.

It wasn't.

"Here are the Christmas lights." Jade held them up, a strand of new lights.

"Sure, okay. Find the middle and I'll hook them here first."

She stretched them, pushing away the puppy who thought she'd found the best chew toy in the world. Finally she handed them up, bent where she'd found the center. He hooked them over a planter hook already in place.

Finished, he climbed down, more than a little relieved to be back on the ground. Good, solid earth. He stretched to relieve the tension in the middle of his back.

"You look a little weird," Jade announced as he moved the ladder to the end of the porch. "You okay?"

"Of course I am." He climbed the ladder and pulled the hammer from the tool belt around his waist. He pulled a nail out and made a makeshift hook for the end of the lights.

"Perfect. But hurry, she might be here in a few minutes."

"I'm hurrying. Is there even a place to plug these in?"

"Yeah, over by the door. You'll need an extension cord."

"Gotcha." He moved the ladder to the other end of the porch. The ground didn't look too level and the ladder wobbled as he climbed.

"Uh, be careful."

"You think? I'm recovering from cracked ribs and a bruised kidney. If I go down, kid, I'm taking you with me."

She laughed and he shook his head. "No respect for old people," he grumbled.

"You're not that old."

"Thanks, I think." He hammered a nail into the wood trim of the porch roof. "There we go. She has a security light and Christmas lights."

"Isn't she too old to be afraid of the dark?" Jade moved close to the ladder.

"People are afraid of a lot of things, Jade."

"Yeah, I guess." She shook the ladder and he screamed. "Chicken."

"I'm going to get you, good."

She ran, laughing. The yapping puppy went with her. He saw another car. He turned and waved as Madeline came up the drive. Before he could make adjustments, the ladder swayed. He leaned, trying to push it back the right way. Slowly it fell backward, taking him with it.

Jade screamed. Madeline's car door slammed and she yelled.

As if he could answer as he jumped. He landed on his feet a short distance back from the ladder that crashed to the ground.

Madeline got to him before the dog. "Are you okay?"

He nodded because he couldn't really get the words out yet. These two women were determined to make him look like a weak little girl. He brushed a hand through his hair and inhaled sharply.

"Phew, that was close."

"You think?" Jade snickered and he reached for her. She moved quickly and got away.

Madeline looked up at her porch and then at him. "You put up Christmas lights."

"One better. You now have motion lights. Well, one motion light. I still have to put up the one for your back stoop."

"Jackson, you don't have to. I'm fine."

"You'll be able to sleep with the lights off." He didn't stay to discuss it with her. He picked up the ladder and headed around the side of the house, moving a little slower.

She appeared as he set up the ladder and pulled the second light out of the box. "You didn't have to do this."

"I know I didn't. I'm being a good neighbor. I should have thought of it sooner."

She stared at him, big eyes searching his face, questioning him. Probably questioning his motives, he guessed.

"Why? Why would you think of it sooner? For all you know I'm a night owl, an insomniac, addicted to computer games and coffee."

"You drink tea. Probably herbal. And you live out here by yourself."

It didn't sit right, knowing her story and her not knowing that he knew. He'd have to tell her. But how did he tell her, basically a stranger, that he knew her secrets?

"Jackson, whose puppy is that?"

He climbed the ladder and pretended to busy himself removing the old light, but he looked down at the woman standing close, holding the ladder. She didn't smile when she looked up. She didn't look away, either. He thought she had the sweetest face he'd ever seen. Pretty. She was definitely pretty. And he hadn't noticed till now because she hid behind those sweaters and big glasses.

"The puppy is yours, too. It's easier to be in the dark if you're not alone."

"I can't take a gift like that."

He hooked up the new light and twisted the wire

nuts. "Yeah, you can. I've dragged you into my life and you've not asked for a thing in return. I wanted to do this for you."

"It wasn't necessary. I was helping a neighbor."

"That's what I'm doing." He climbed down. "And if you want to flip your breaker, we'll see if this works."

She nodded once and walked away. He watched her go, and he couldn't believe how much he wanted to go after her. But he stood his ground because he'd already warned himself that he wouldn't hurt her. She wasn't a woman he could casually date and then walk away from.

She had too much at stake. Too much to lose.

Madeline flipped the switch and stepped back outside to see if the light worked. Jackson stood nearby, looking up at the unlit light. He walked past and it flickered and came on. He stood beneath it in the gray light of early evening. She couldn't look away.

Jackson Cooper probably topped the list of eligible bachelors in Oklahoma. And he had just installed lights for her to sleep more securely at night. He stood in her yard, a cowboy in faded jeans and a dark blue flannel shirt. His blond hair spiked a little when he took off his hat. His slow, easy smile revealed a dimple in his chin.

Years ago she'd realized she could look at a man like Jackson and feel nothing. Which was better than the fight-or-flight instinct of her childhood. But feeling nothing had felt hollow.

Hollow but safe.

Jackson made her feel safe. But he wasn't. He could break her heart.

Because he made her feel.

"It works." He walked toward her, slow and easy, casual but she saw his grimace of pain.

"It does. Thank you."

Jade rounded the corner of the house, the puppy at her heels. "Hey, the lights on the porch work. Come and see."

Jackson reached for her hand. Madeline drew in a breath as his fingers clasped with hers and she allowed him to lead her around to the front of her house.

"Well, look at that, you have Christmas." He tugged her close, sliding her hand with his into the pocket of her heavy coat. His fingers curled around hers, around her emotions, her heart.

She needed space. She needed to breathe deep and clear her head. She moved a step away, focusing on the glittery lights that ran along her porch roof. It took a moment for her world to settle, for her thoughts to settle. The man standing next to her had done this. For her.

A sneaky thought poked at her, asking her why he'd done this. What did he want? She brushed the suspicions aside. Jackson Cooper had done something nice for her. *Let it go.*

"Thank you." She stepped closer to the house. The floodlight he'd installed came on, taking her by surprise, making her laugh. "That might be extreme."

"You'll have to get used to it, but it'll light up the yard like it's daylight out here. And remember that every possum that crosses its path will probably set it off."

"I'll remember."

She would remember this Christmas, the year that

a runaway girl pulled her into Jackson's life. The year her emotions had sprung free, totally out of control.

This moment equaled sneaking a peek at wrapped presents under the tree and then trying to shove them back into the paper, to make it the way it had been before.

An impossible task.

Jackson reached down to pet the puppy, groaning with the movement. "Jade, you need to take this dog in and feed it."

The girl turned from the lights and called the dog. The puppy ran to her new best friend and she scooped her up and headed into the house. The last thing Madeline needed in her life was a puppy. Close to the last thing she needed.

Jackson smiled down at her, his face shadowed by the brim of the cowboy hat he'd placed back on his head. "I should go."

"I could cook dinner. To pay you for all the work you've done and all the muscles you pulled jumping off the ladder." Madeline should have kept her mouth closed, let him leave.

"I'm good and we stopped at the Mad Cow. Vera cooked up fried chicken and the fixings. It's in the fridge."

"Thank you again." It sounded like a broken record now. His little kindnesses were taking her life in so many new directions she didn't know what else to say. "You can stay."

Common-sense Madeline had clearly left the building, to be replaced by out-of-control Madeline, her evil twin who obviously didn't think about broken hearts and the pain of the past.

"Thanks, but I'm going to clean up my mess and go home to crash." He picked up a few tools he'd left on the porch. "I'll get the ladder if you'll put this in the back of the truck for me."

"I can do that." She took the box, carefully avoiding eye contact with probably the most gorgeous man she'd ever met.

She walked to the back of his truck and set the box in the metal toolbox behind the cab. He returned carrying the ladder, walking a little slower. He grinned as he lifted the ladder and set it in the back of the truck.

Madeline brushed back her hair and shivered in her coat as a cold wind picked up, scattering dried leaves left over from autumn across her lawn. She looked up and he had moved closer, his hazel eyes settled on her face, watching her, touching her with a look.

When his hand touched her arm she closed her eyes, waiting, telling herself not to run from this, not to run from feeling too much. His fingers touched her chin, turning her to face him.

Grounded, she was grounded. Reality, not fear. She was in her yard. The earth was beneath her. The truck was close enough to touch. A car drove by. A neighbor honked. She opened her eyes, no longer afraid. Much.

His hand moved to her cheek, sweet and easy. His fingers tangled in her hair and she looked up, wanting to know what it meant to be the woman in his arms.

When he pulled her close she froze for just an instant, then she exhaled and let go. He leaned in, soft breath and mint. The tangy scent of his cologne mixed with the winter air, a sharp breeze and wood smoke from the neighbor's fireplace. His hand slid to her waist and he held her for just a moment.

And as quick as that, he backed away, leaving her standing there in her driveway, unsure. Shaken.

He smiled and shook his head.

"Madeline, you're tempting, and self-control is not one of my strongest character traits. Some would say I have no control when it comes to beautiful women." His fingers touched her cheek, feather-soft. "But I always keep my word and I'm going to do that right now and walk away."

She backed away from him, not sure how to take this moment, this goodbye. Her heart raced and she breathed, trying to catch up. Jackson Cooper tipped his hat and got into his truck.

As she stood there trying to make sense of what had happened, he backed out of her drive and was gone. She had put her heart on the line, taken steps she'd never taken before. She'd been rejected.

Jackson Cooper, known for his many relationships, for having a constant string of women, had held her and walked away.

So what did that make her? Chopped liver?

For a long time she stood in her driveway, shivering in the cold wind and trying hard not to be hurt by his rejection. But it did hurt. Because she'd held her emotions in check for so many years and when she'd taken a step toward someone, the man had walked away.

It hurt because his daughter was in her house and she'd have to see him again tomorrow.

As she walked back into the house she told herself

it didn't have to be him. He didn't have to be the man she took a chance with. She could find someone safe. Someone who wouldn't break her heart.

But she had a hard time convincing herself.

Chapter Eight

Jackson had to admit to a moment of real doubt as he walked up the steps of Dawson Community Church. Church, for the first time in... Well, he'd gone to funerals and weddings, but hadn't gone to church in ten years or more.

Except Christmas and Easter. He'd done the holidays for his mom.

Today he walked up the steps and through the door for... Himself? Jade? Or maybe for Madeline? Because last night he'd walked away from her, seconds short of a moment that he figured would have changed his life and hers in ways he couldn't take back.

His dad had warned him Madeline wasn't someone to play around with. Madeline had stories that he couldn't begin to fathom and pain that he wished he could take away. He wanted to hold on to her and promise no one would ever hurt her again. He was the last person to make that promise.

Church had already started. He walked through the double doors and into the vestibule. He stood there rethinking the impulse that had put him in church on a

Sunday morning, dress boots and new jeans, a button-up shirt he'd actually ironed. He took off the black cowboy hat he'd shoved on his head as he got out of the truck and held it in his hand.

Someone stepped forward, reaching for his hand. Ryder Johnson. Not much more than a year ago Ryder had been single and he'd planned on staying that way. Now he had a wife and twin baby girls.

"Jackson, good to see you," Ryder whispered as he pulled him into a comfortable man hug and slapped him on the back. And then Ryder ruined things by whispering, "And look, the roof is still in one piece."

"Yeah, thanks." Jackson spotted a seat on the back pew. The piano played and the choir sang "I'll Fly Away."

"It really is good to have you here."

"Good to be here." Jackson sat down and Ryder went back to his seat next to his wife, Andie.

Jackson settled into the seat by himself in an empty pew. A few people looked back, wondering. His Gram sat near the front next to his dad. Her smile split her face and she nodded and looked up, thinking God had, at long last, answered prayers for the grandson gone astray.

He closed his eyes as the choir took their seats and Jenna McKenzie sang a solo. He felt someone move close, sit next to him. A body brushed past him. He opened his eyes and smiled at Jade, who'd taken her place to his left. And Madeline to his right.

Oh yeah, this wouldn't be a rumor starter. And a match on dry wood wouldn't start a fire. Right! By the end of the day everyone in town would be talking and they'd have a hard time deciding what to discuss first. Jackson Cooper had gone to church and the roof hadn't caved. Madeline and a girl that looked a lot like him had sat next to him in church. So much for slipping in unnoticed.

"You're here." Jade grabbed his hand. She peeked past him to Madeline. "I told you."

"Shhh," Madeline warned. "We're in church."

Jade nodded but she held on to his hand.

Somehow he managed to focus on the sermon about killing giants with faith. A decent twist on a story he'd heard all his life. Giants. He'd had a few that he'd faced in his life. He couldn't really say what had pushed him out of church. Maybe a lifetime of being told to get up, to clean up, to stop acting up? Maybe being busy, being gone on Sundays? Maybe shame for the things he'd done that he knew would make his mother blush and probably make God none too happy?

Today didn't really push him to the top of any spiritual mountains. Everyone in town knew him for what he was. Today they would think he was a dad. The kid sitting next to him, holding on to his hand like he was some kind of hero, thought he was her dad.

Maybe they'd think he was involved with everyone's favorite teacher. He had to admit, he didn't dislike the notion of people thinking he'd managed to snag someone who smelled like a spring morning.

Her arm touched his.

"Lunch at the Cooper Ranch after church," he whispered close to her ear.

She shivered and he moved his arm, settling it on the back of the pew behind her. Lunch with the family, a Sunday tradition. Even when he didn't go to church he still had lunch with the family. Most of the time.

But he never took a woman with him. The word *date* slipped into his mind. He'd never taken a date to Sunday lunch. That hadn't seemed right. Not attending church hurt his mother enough without him adding a woman to the mix.

He settled his attention on the front of the church and something shifted in his heart. It happened when he saw his mother sitting next to his dad. Travis sat next to her. And Mia. And Lucky and his wife and kids.

Reese would have been there, but he'd joined the army and recently shipped out to Afghanistan.

Blake, probably busy with bank business, didn't attend church.

Heather went to church in Grove. She liked anonymity.

Jesse was probably on duty at the hospital.

Dylan had a load of bulls in Texas, and Gage was busy riding bulls.

Sophie did her own thing these days, and usually it had nothing to do with the family.

Everyone had lives, stories and places to be.

He should have been here sooner. If not for himself, for his mom. The look on her face when she turned at the end of the service drove that thought home. Yeah, he should be there for God, for himself, but his mom was the one looking right at him, with tears in her eyes.

After the closing prayer everyone stood, people moved and he had enough sense to know that most of them were heading his way. Jackson in church on a Sunday that wasn't a holiday? They'd all be wondering why.

"Hey, brother." Travis clasped his hand and shot a look from Madeline to Jade. "You coming out to the house for lunch?"

"I plan on it."

Travis leaned in close. "You bringing your little family?"

Jackson squeezed the hand that still held his. "Travis, don't make me have to take you out back."

Travis laughed and pulled away, a good-natured pup who needed a serious thump on the head. "Nothing wrong with settling down, brother. The three of you look kind of nice together."

Jackson reached but Travis moved a little quicker these days.

And then his parents stepped close. This had gone from a decent idea to one huge complication. Jade was in his mother's arms and his mom stared at him, eyes wide, lots of questions and answers.

Sooner or later he would have to talk to Jade, explain things to her. But looking at her in the middle of his big family, watching her smile and laugh, he knew it wouldn't be easy and it would break her heart. He could give the kid Christmas with his family. That's what she wanted, a family.

"Are you coming out to the house for lunch?" His mom still held on to Jade and with her free hand she reached for Madeline, pulling her close. And they were all looking at him.

Yeah, he'd planned on lunch with his family. Now that plan seemed to include the two females who were doing a lot to complicate his, up to now, uncomplicated life. Yesterday it had felt good to do something nice for Madeline. It had felt pretty decent to spend an afternoon with Jade.

But taking them home to his family felt a little…

He pulled at the collar of his shirt and wished it was not quite so hot.

"Jackson?" His dad shot him a look.

"Of course we're coming out for lunch." He avoided looking at Madeline but he couldn't miss the very pleased smile on his mother's face.

Sandwiched on the truck seat between Jade and Jackson, Madeline tried to make herself smaller. She sat up straight and kept her shoulders in. The truck turned and she slid a little toward Jackson in his new jeans, his dark cowboy hat covering blond hair that managed to look a little messy and made him a whole lot cute.

For the first time in her life, she felt young. She felt like a sixteen-year-old in a pickup on a Saturday night. It felt good. And frightening.

"Nervous?" Jackson smiled, eyes crinkling at the corners, and then shifted his attention back to the road. He reached to turn up the radio and an old Randy Travis song filled the cab of the truck. *Forever and ever, Amen.*

She'd never thought about loving someone forever. She'd always thought that being single meant being safe from being hurt. Safe now seemed to be a thing of the past.

"Of course not. Why would I be nervous?"

He laughed loud. "You and I both know that this isn't a simple lunch. The minute you sat down next to me, everyone in Dawson had us paired up and started wondering when we'd be announcing the big day."

She choked a little because she hadn't expected him to put it so bluntly. "Thanks."

His left hand firmly on the wheel, he moved his right arm and slipped it around her shoulder. His fingers tweaked her sleeve, and her arm buzzed beneath his touch.

"It's okay, Maddie, we'll get through this and in a week or two, people will realize you were the person rescuing me and Jade."

Why didn't that make her feel any better? Because he'd just let her know, in a sweet way, that she wasn't anything more than the person helping him out? Why did it suddenly, painfully, matter?

They pulled up the driveway that led to the main house of the Cooper ranch, the Circle C. Cooper Creek flowed through the field and circled back through the stand of trees farther on. The house, a big, brick, Georgian place, sat back from the main road. Trees lined the driveway.

The Coopers were everything a family should be. The Coopers were everything she'd ever wanted. Probably everything Jade had ever wanted. Not that they didn't have problems, but when they did, they drew together and held on to each other.

She'd never really had a family. Hers had been a group of people and it had never been safe or nurturing. Foster care had been a respite for a few years but she'd been too closed off at that time to get attached to her foster parents. She'd kept in touch for a few years but she'd finally stopped writing.

"They don't bite." Jackson leaned close as he pulled to a stop behind another car. Lucky's family piled out of an SUV. Jackson's hand rubbed her arm and he pulled her close for a brief instant.

"I know they don't." But her heart pounded hard, achingly hard. Not because of the prospect of lunch with the Coopers, but because Jackson's arm around her held her tight.

He held her tight and she wasn't afraid, not of him.

"You okay?"

"I'm good." Not good.

Her heart crumbled a little with the knowledge that it was this man who made her feel safe. It shouldn't be him. It didn't make sense that safety and fear should tangle together in her heart, pushing against each other.

Jade had already jumped out of the truck. Jackson reached for his door and settled one last look on her before pushing it open. "Time to face the music, Maddie."

"So sweetly put." She ignored the hand he held out. "I should have gone home. You could have spent this day with Jade and your family."

"My mother would have taken a switch to me if you hadn't come along."

"I doubt that."

He laughed and pulled her close. "Darlin', you have no idea. My mom is probably thinking you're one of the answers to her prayers. All our lives she's prayed for God to send the perfect person into our lives at the perfect moment. And she has no doubt that God will honor that prayer."

"But I'm not..."

"You won't be able to convince her of that." He leaned close, and she wondered if he meant to kiss her. He didn't. He flicked her chin with his finger and stepped away.

She obviously brought this new self-control out in him. *Way to go, Madeline.* For the first time she wanted to be held and for the first time in his life, Jackson Cooper had self-control.

Madeline took a deep breath and stood a little straighter. Time to face the music. She managed a smile and to not melt when Jackson held her hand and walked her up the steps of the big house, straight into the circle of trust that was the Coopers.

Jade didn't seem to have a problem. She stood in the middle of Jackson's very overwhelming family and allowed them to pull her in.

"What's for lunch, Mom?" Jackson's thumb brushed the top of Madeline's hand and he didn't let go.

Angie Cooper turned, smiling big, reaching for Madeline and forcing Jackson to let go. Madeline loved Angie Cooper. She was gracious, dignified and always kind.

"Madeline, thank you so much for helping Jackson with this...situation."

"It hasn't been a problem."

Angie's smile softened as did her expression. "Of course it hasn't. But it means so much to us."

Coopers were everywhere. They were laughing and talking, teasing each other. Angie Cooper continued to talk, not bothered at all by the constant commotion around her. Her family. Jackson's family.

Madeline nodded in answer to Angie's questions. In the blink of an eye Jackson stood next to her. She smiled up at him, pretending to be strong, because she'd pretended for a long time. But in the middle of this family she felt so much like a fraud, because she'd never had a family, not a real one.

She was strong. She'd spent the last fifteen years telling herself she was a survivor, not a victim. But survivors still had to deal with the past, with fear, with leftover anger and resentment.

With baggage that didn't unpack itself.

She'd done a lot of baggage unpacking. There were a few little things she still carried around with her, she knew that. But eventually she knew she'd let it all go. She'd trust enough to let it go.

She brushed a hand across her cheeks to wipe away stray tears that had trickled out before she could get control of her emotions.

"Let's walk." Jackson took her by the hand. "Mom, we'll be right in to help set the table."

Angie Cooper shot her son a narrow-eyed look. "Jackson."

"Five minutes." He winked at his mom.

Madeline thought about telling him no. But for Jackson, his charm seemed to come naturally. He could wink at his mom, smile and they all went along with his plans. At that moment she had no choice but to go with him. She either went or she fell apart in front of his family.

Somehow he knew that she needed a minute to gather herself. Later she would thank him for that little bit of intuition. Later she might even wonder how he knew her so well.

Hand in hand they walked out the front door, down the steps and across the lawn. Neither of them spoke, which was good. What would she say when they did speak? Sorry for being so ridiculous?

At a small gazebo at the edge of the lawn they finally stopped. Jackson smiled down at her, a gentle smile. No wink. No flirty grin. "I wanted to make sure you're okay. I thought a little fresh air might help."

She nodded, unsure. "I'm fine, really I am."

He stood in front of her, and she felt as if he saw everything about her. Including the things she didn't want him to see. He touched her cheek. "You're sure? Because I recognize that 'need to escape this family' look."

"I'm sure." She laughed a little because she had been thinking exactly that.

Was that part of Jackson's charm? He could read people and it made a woman think that he really cared, really understood? Of course that was it, and for that reason alone she should back away.

He shouldn't be the man she wanted to kiss. She moved closer and his brows arched. His hand moved from hers. He slid it around her back and held her close. But he didn't kiss her.

Okay, fine, she would make the first move. She could do this, even if she fainted in the process. She didn't plan on living her life in a box, afraid to feel. Braver than she'd ever been in her life, she stood on her tiptoes and rested a hand on his shoulder. Jackson whispered her name as he bent and drew her close. Telling herself she wouldn't regret it, she touched her lips to his, closing her eyes to the landslide of feelings that slammed her heart.

"Madeline." He pulled back first.

"I'm sorry." She didn't know what else to say. "I can't believe I did that."

"You don't have to apologize." He winked—a little of the old Jackson obviously still existed.

She had kissed Jackson Cooper and he had pulled away. Now she had to go back in the house with him, sit at the table with him, and pretend it didn't hurt to be rejected, to be the woman that Jackson Cooper could resist.

She blamed herself. She'd taken a single moment

and turned it into something it hadn't been, ever. He had done a few sweet things for her and she'd obviously taken it wrong. Last night she'd thought he would kiss her and he hadn't. She should have learned then that he wasn't interested.

As she hurried up the steps he called her name. She didn't turn back. She wouldn't. She'd been humiliated enough. For years she'd been praying that God would help her move past her fear. This probably hadn't been His plan.

The front door of the house opened. Heather Cooper, blonde, petite, pretty, smiled. "Madeline, Mom told me you were here today. She said to find you and Jackson."

Heather peeked around her. "There he is." And then her attention refocused on Madeline, and Madeline wanted to melt into the concrete of the front porch. "Are you okay? What did he do?"

Nervousness turned to hysteria. Madeline giggled and then laughed. She turned to watch Jackson walk up the steps, still the gentleman, shrugging and saying nothing.

"Nothing happened." Madeline wouldn't let him take the fall for her mistake. "Nothing at all."

She hurried inside the house and left Jackson with his sister. Nothing at all had happened. Nothing would ever happen. Jackson had given her the space she needed to come to her senses.

He had rejected her. That knowledge settled in her heart where it felt heavy and cold. And she had to go in to lunch with him, sit across the table from him and avoid looking his way.

Which she could do because she'd always avoided him. She needed to do that for a little longer, and then she would put distance between them. Jade could stay with his family. Madeline could go back to her life. Thanks to Jackson, she could walk away without regret.

At the moment, thanking him was the last thing she wanted to do.

Chapter Nine

After a pretty miserable lunch, Jackson loaded Madeline and Jade back into his truck and drove them to the church where they'd left Madeline's car a few hours earlier. A five-minute ride felt like five hours with neither of the women in his truck speaking. The younger one seemed to be talked out—finally.

The older one looked hurt and wounded. Exactly what he hadn't wanted to happen. He'd been doing his best to protect her and she'd messed that up royally.

Jackson pulled his truck into the church parking lot, stopping next to Madeline's sedan. Jade dozed in the seat next to him. Madeline had managed to sit near the door this time. He had thought long and hard about that kiss, about the hurt look on her face when she ran away.

He couldn't let her go home thinking this was about her. The woman who hid behind big sweaters and glasses needed to understand that he hadn't rejected her because of her.

But when would he tell her, and what would he say? Nothing for now, not in front of Jade. Not in the church parking lot when he would be driving home and she'd go back to her house.

"Jade, climb on in Madeline's car. I'll follow you back to your house." He nudged the sleeping teenager.

"We'll be fine." Madeline opened the truck door. "I'll bring Jade to your house in the morning before I go to work."

"I know I don't have to follow you, but I'm going to. We need to talk."

Madeline moved for Jade to get out of the truck. "We don't need to talk. Really, I don't want to talk. I think we've said it all."

"We actually haven't said a word and I want to explain."

"No, thank you." She got out and closed the door.

Jackson watched as she rummaged through her purse for her keys. She had reverted to glasses today and a big brown sweater with a denim skirt. He shook his head as she fumbled, dropped her purse and then opened the car door and tossed it in the back seat. Angry gestures. Mad at him or mad at herself?

After she drove away Jackson sat there in the parking lot, thinking about a lot of stuff, most of which didn't make sense. He didn't need this. His life was fine. He had his ranch. He had his family and friends.

This church that had always been in his life, he even had that, when he wanted.

When he wanted? On his schedule, his time?

Okay, he got that God might not like that idea. So this was all some "jerk you up by the seat of your pants" faith plan? He remembered the chorus of an old hymn his grandmother loved.

No turning back, no turning back.

He could argue all day that he kind of liked the old Jackson, the old life, but God was sending a pretty clear message. No turning back. It set him back on his heels a little, and he took a long time getting back on the road.

Tomorrow he'd move forward. He'd go to his doctor in Grove.

He'd try, again, to get hold of Gloria Baker.

And he'd fix things with Madeline.

Tonight, though, he'd find a way to get his mind off the crazy twists and turns his life had taken. First he drove past Madeline's, making sure she and Jade got in the house safely. The porch light burned bright. She'd parked her car under the carport.

He turned his truck around in her driveway and headed back to town, in the direction of Back Street. He had work to do on the living nativity. Since the horse had thrown him and then Jade showed up, he'd kind of neglected his job of building Bethlehem.

The front porch light of Dawson Community Center cast a wide arc of light across the front lawn of what had once been his family church. There were a lot of memories tied to this little building. Most were pleasant, some weren't.

One that he had mixed feelings about had to do with Jeremy Hightree, his half brother. They'd grown up together, not knowing that they shared the same father. Today they were probably closer than ever. But the relationship was still strained. It took a lot for a guy like Jeremy to let go of pride and resentment. Jackson figured Jeremy had done better than he would have.

After parking he grabbed tools out of the back of his truck and walked across the lawn to the makeshift buildings. An inn, shops, and on the other side of the lawn, the manger scene. He needed to work on the inn. He strapped a tool belt around his waist and hooked the hammer into the loop.

"What are you doing here tonight?"

Jackson turned, smiled at Jeremy and pulled nails out of his mouth so he could talk. "Thought I'd get some work done. I've kind of fallen behind on the job."

"From what I heard, you fell off a horse. I didn't expect you for a few more days."

"We don't really have a few days, now do we?"

Jeremy shrugged and walked a little closer. "No, I guess we don't. Saw you at church today. A little advice?"

"I'd rather you not give me advice, if you don't mind. It wasn't that long ago that you were running hard and fast from anything that had to do with Dawson." Jackson grinned and avoided looking at Jeremy. "As a matter of fact, I remember a dozer aimed at this building."

"Right, I guess you've got a point."

"I guess I do." He placed a nail and lifted the board that needed to be attached. "What would you do without me, anyway?"

"Oh, we'd manage." Jeremy stepped closer and Jackson saw that his brother wasn't smiling. "I'm just going to go ahead and say this."

"Really?"

Jeremy nodded and for a second Jackson wondered if he was about to get punched. Jeremy smiled but his eyes were steel-hard in the evening light.

"Jackson, if that kid is yours, you'd better not leave her out in the cold."

When an old dog got riled, he bristled. Jackson felt a lot like an old dog but Jeremy looked a little ahead of him, more prepared for a fight. He put the hammer down and took a step away from Jeremy. He got it. He knew why Jeremy would say something like that to him. Jeremy had spent most of his life feeling like baggage that got left on the side of the road.

"I think you know me better than that." Jackson picked the hammer up again. He tapped the nail into place, and reached for another. "And you don't really know a thing about this situation."

"I know that everyone in town is talking about a kid showing up on your doorstep claiming to be yours and looking a lot like you."

"People assume a lot, don't they?"

"Maybe they do, but sometimes the facts point to the obvious answer."

Jackson pushed a tarp out of the way and pulled a piece of plywood across the opening. "I'm really not going to have this discussion with you."

Jeremy didn't budge. He didn't back down. "I guess it isn't any of my business. And I guess I'm making it my business because she's a kid and I know what it feels like to be that kid, wanting to be a part of a family."

Jackson exhaled a whole lot of frustration. He finally looked at Jeremy, shaking his head and wishing he'd gone on home. Instead he'd come here thinking he could work alone, get his thoughts together and figure out what to do.

That's what he got for thinking.

"She isn't mine."

Jeremy stared for a long minute and then looked up at the sky. When he zeroed in on Jackson, it felt pretty uncomfortable. Jackson's attention focused on a closed fist and then on the hard stare.

"Really?"

Jackson picked up another board and nailed it to the frame of what would soon be the inn that turned Mary and Joseph away. For all eternity it would be the inn that turned away a baby, the son of God, the savior.

But the story would have changed if Jesus hadn't been born in that manger, the humblest of circumstances. He might not go to church every Sunday but Jackson got that God always had a plan. Things came together for a reason.

A young girl had landed on his doorstep. For a reason?

"Jeremy, she isn't mine. I know that she looks a lot like a Cooper and my name is on the birth certificate. But I'm about one hundred percent certain she isn't mine."

"'About'?"

"I'm done with this conversation. I'm either going to finish the inn or knock you into the middle of next week. Which do you prefer, brother?"

Jeremy raised his hands and backed away. "You go right ahead and finish the inn."

"Thank you, I will." Jackson pounded another nail with Jeremy watching.

Of course he wouldn't be quiet for long. Finally he cleared his throat and stepped forward again.

"She's a cute kid and she seems pretty high on you." Jeremy cleared his throat again. "As a matter of fact, she isn't the only one who seems to really like you these days. Two women, is that a record?"

"It isn't a record and you're a piece of..."

Jeremy slapped him on the back, laughing loud.

"Jackson, I'm the best thing that ever happened to you. I'm your brother."

"I don't know how you think that's a good thing."

Jeremy backed toward the door. "Well, I haven't knocked you on your can yet. And I put up with you coming over here in the evening, making noise and bellowing like an angry bull."

"I put up with you on Sundays and holidays." More than that, but he wasn't in the mood to be congenial.

"I'm going to give you a sweet little niece or nephew in about eight months."

Jackson froze, holding the board, pretty amazed. "Seriously, you and Beth?"

"We're having a baby."

"Congratulations." Jackson meant it, but today it didn't come out as easily as it once would have. Today he could only think about the little girl who wasn't his and the woman who had kissed him this afternoon, unsettling him, and changing his mind about a lot of things.

"Thanks. It's going to be a big change for us." Jeremy grinned and snorted a laugh. "At least we get to work up to it. No *'surprise, it's a teenager'* for us."

"You're a laugh a minute."

"I try. Hey, it's getting late and Beth will wonder where I am. Why don't you head on home? We'll get some more work done here on Wednesday."

"Yeah, I think that's a good idea." He slipped the hammer into the tool belt and stretched, groaning when the muscles between his shoulders protested. "I think it's time to go home and put my feet up."

"Let me know if I can do anything to help." Jeremy walked out the door ahead of him.

"Yeah, I'll do that."

A few minutes later Jackson drove down the road, slowing as he got close to Madeline's driveway. Every light in the house was on. A week ago he would have gone on by, wondering about her, maybe smiling.

Tonight he pulled in, parking behind her car.

It took her a few minutes to answer the door. He knocked a little louder, rethinking the decision to stop by. The puppy barked and Jade shouted, which meant he couldn't leave now. He had to stand there, not quite sure of himself. He pushed his hat back and waited.

Who was he kidding? His mom said he'd been sure of himself since he turned three and managed to kiss Annie Butler on the cheek in the church nursery. He grinned, not that he remembered, but he liked that story. Even if Annie hadn't ever dated him.

Commotion erupted inside the house. He peeked between the curtains and saw Jade race through the hall, the dog following her. Madeline yelled that she would get it and for Jade to get in the shower.

Wow, domestic. Family. Not at all what he had been thinking about. A book on the table and a coffee cup. Pictures on the walls. The smell of wood smoke filled the air. A cat hopped up on the porch and sat looking at him, licking its paw and blinking the way cats did.

The door opened a crack. Madeline peeked, sighed and opened the door the rest of the way.

"Why are you here?"

He shrugged. "Guess I felt like we have unfinished business."

"Really? I think it's all been said. Jackson, can't you let a woman crawl off and hide without you chasing her down and making her remember that she made a fool of herself?"

He moved a little into the door. "You didn't make a fool of yourself, so that isn't why I'm here. And I'm afraid I do like to be the one who chases the woman."

"So this is because…" Her cheeks turned pink. "Because *I* kissed *you.*"

"And hurt my male ego?" He smiled and then laughed. "It isn't that at all. Why don't you invite me in for a cup of tea? It's cold out here."

And he wasn't a tea person. But he thought she probably was. He could hear water running and knew Jade would be out of the shower soon.

"Okay, tea." Madeline led the way through a house he'd been in hundreds of times in his life. His great-grandparents had lived here. His grandmother had grown up here.

Jackson took a seat at her tiny dining room table. A poinsettia graced the center. She'd put her Christmas tree in the corner of her little dining room. Jackson watched as she moved around the kitchen heating water, finding tea bags and placing cups on the counter.

After a minute he stood, because he couldn't sit and watch her. He had to stand near her, watch her expressions, her serious brown eyes. He knew her story, but he wanted to know everything about her. He wanted her to share her dreams with him. He wanted to hear her laugh.

He'd dated a lot of women who talked nonstop, whose constant stories about themselves grated on his nerves. This woman didn't talk enough.

"The other day when I was looking for information on Gloria Baker," he said, leaning against the counter.

Madeline kept her back to him. She poured steaming water in the two cups. "I searched your name."

She nodded but still didn't turn to look at him. "Okay."

"I know what happened when you were a little girl."

She poured hot water in the cups and didn't look up. It took everything for him to stay in that spot, watching her, not moving toward her, not reaching for her hands that trembled, not putting an arm around her when she shivered.

He knew all the right moves. He'd spent his life studying women, figuring out how they ticked. He knew how to make them feel special. This time he didn't know. Or maybe he did. Maybe standing there, letting her pull herself together, not reaching for her was the best move.

It was just a new page in his life. A new game plan.

"Why are you telling me this?" Her voice trembled but there were no tears.

"I'm telling you to explain that I didn't pull away because of you. I pulled away because of who I am. I don't want to be another person that hurts you. And let me tell you, I'm the guy who could. I've had plenty of angry messages on my answering machine. I've dated a lot of women and most of them are no longer in my life. A few still send me Christmas cards. Thirteen years ago one of those women put my name on a birth certificate as the father of her child. I'm keeping my distance because I don't want to hurt you."

"What did you learn about me?" She turned, handing him a cup of tea before walking away. He watched her take a seat at the oak dinette.

When he'd searched her name he hadn't really expected to learn anything. He hadn't expected to learn information that would change his life. Maybe hers.

"I guess I learned everything. Or at least the facts available on the internet. But there's more to you than that story."

"It isn't something I share with many people, Jackson. It isn't a great opening line. Hi, I was born and raised in a cult. My mom worshipped a man who convinced her that all of the women owed him their little girls."

"You were a victim."

She shrugged. "It's my past. It changes how people think of you when they learn something like that. Doesn't it?"

He moved to the seat across from her, carrying the cup of steaming tea in a tiny little cup that represented the woman staring up at him with liquid brown eyes and a soft smile that trembled and faded.

"I'm sorry." What could he say? That he wanted to find that man and hurt him for what he'd done to her and countless other children. He didn't need for her to share the story of a man who used little girls as objects, dividing them amongst his disciples, marrying them off at young ages after their innocence was already stolen from them. He didn't want for her to have to tell him the story in her words. The story was on her face, in her eyes and hidden in her heart.

But she'd survived.

Her hands trembled as she sipped the tea. The cup clattered in the saucer when she set it on the table. He kept his hands on the porcelain cup of amber liquid, thinking it should make him calm, but it didn't.

"You don't have to be sorry." She smiled up at him,

brave, amazing. Too good for him. "Unless you mean you're sorry for snooping."

He laughed a little, surprised by her smile, her soft laughter. "I am sorry about that. I'm sorry if anyone ever treats you differently because of what you've been through. You are more than what happened to you in that place."

"I know." She sniffled a little and reached for a napkin in the basket on the table. "I get caught feeling blessed because I escaped with fewer scars than so many of the children. And then I feel guilty because I escaped. I owe Sara everything."

"Your sister?"

Madeline nodded again. She held her cup of tea in both hands, not drinking it. He sipped his, waiting, not wanting to push.

"She took me to town. And then she disappeared. I haven't seen or heard from her since."

"Your parents?"

"I don't know who my real father is. My mother finds me and sends a Christmas or birthday card every year or so." She glanced toward the hall, toward the bathroom where water still poured from the shower.

"Your mother is out of prison?"

She nodded. "Jackson, I'm glad I can help you with Jade, but you have to understand. I've spent years trying to convince myself that it wasn't my fault."

He held the cup of tea because he wanted to hit something. Or somebody.

"I've been numb. I've been afraid. And over the years, I've been happy with my life." Her brown eyes twinkled. "Even when I sleep with the lights on."

Jackson reached for her hands. He moved them from

the cup and he held them in his. "I haven't had a lot of experience with this, but I think I make a pretty good friend."

She laughed at that. And laughed some more. When Jackson started to let go of her hands, she held tight until her laughter dissolved and she had to wipe her eyes.

"What's so funny?"

She laughed again. "You, being a girl's friend. The idea of it makes you turn a little red." She touched her neck. "From here up."

Footsteps in the hall meant they were about to have company. Laughter and the dog barking. Madeline smiled. "You have definitely unsettled my life. My neat little house is suddenly chaos, clutter and a Christmas movie come to life."

"I hope that's a good thing. I think we've both been a little unsettled this week."

"More than a little." Her eyes darted toward the door. Still no sign of Jade. "I think she's not as happy as she pretends to be."

"I think you're right about that. I think she's trying to pretend this is some great adventure."

"We can't run from life."

"No, we can't." He stood, leaving the nearly empty tea cup on the table. Maybe he was a tea person after all. "I'll see you tomorrow."

She followed him to the door. He could still hear Jade and the dog. They were probably in the spare bedroom at the back of the house. It was probably better that she didn't crash in on this conversation.

He knew Madeline's story. She still didn't know his. He thought that one was better saved for after the doctor's appointment he'd made for the next day. A DNA test and a check-up.

"Jackson, thank you." She stood on the front porch, hugging her sweater around her thin frame. The full moon captured her features, her big eyes and sweet smile.

"You're welcome." He leaned in, kissing her good-bye. An easy kiss on the cheek. "I'm getting very good at this."

Her eyes narrowed. "At what?"

"Nothing."

He tipped his hat to her and walked down off the porch, whistling a song and thinking that maybe self-control wasn't such a bad thing. But she didn't need to know that.

They were friends. He could give her a simple kiss on the cheek to tell her good-night, or an easy hug. He could be there for her, make her feel safe. Friendship.

Yeah, simple, easy, friendship.

He'd keep telling himself that.

Chapter Ten

Mondays were always hard for Madeline. The kids were fresh from the weekend, lots of energy, homework not done and attitudes definitely not in check. This Monday proved to be even more difficult. She couldn't relax and the kids were bouncing off the walls. When she left at the end of the day she wanted nothing more than a long soak in the tub and a nice, easy dinner. Maybe takeout from the Mad Cow.

But halfway home she remembered Jade. She remembered Jackson. She remembered all the ways her life had changed in the last few days. And none of it had been her doing. A few weeks ago in their Sunday school class Clint Cameron had taught how God changed our lives to make more room for Him and His plan. She hadn't really thought about it before. She'd made her own changes, such as buying a home, forcing herself to stay and not run.

God had brought other changes. She hadn't thought about Jade or Jackson in that light. She'd thought about Jade on her doorstep as a mistaken address and bad directions.

What did any of this have to do with her? Maybe God wanted to use this situation to show her that she could open up to people. More specifically, that she could trust a man. Of all the men she should be expected to trust, God picked Jackson Cooper? Why not someone like James Wilkins, the nice teacher who had asked her to lunch on occasion?

Why not the very handsome coach from the Tulsa school where she'd taught?

She pulled up to her mailbox and pulled the mail out, shuffling through the letters, junk mail and an electric bill. Another card from her mother. She tossed the mail, all of it, on the seat next to her.

Why another card? Wasn't one unopened card at Christmas enough? Didn't the lack of a response tell her mother what she needed to know, that Madeline had no interest in a relationship with her?

Madeline pulled up her driveway and parked. She sat for a long time, not wanting to move. She wanted to run again. But she wouldn't. She looked at her little house, now adorned with Christmas lights and two new motion lights.

People in Dawson cared. They wanted her in their lives. Jackson Cooper had installed security lights to make her feel safe. She had a church family and neighbors. She picked up her mother's card but she wouldn't open it, not yet.

Instead she forced herself out of the car into the cold December day that gusted and blew. The cold went right through her and she shivered down into her coat.

When she walked into her house she was slammed by more changes. Kid stuff. Jade had left dirty dishes on the counter. Madeline quickly washed them and put them away. A towel had been left on the bedroom floor. She tossed it in the hamper, wiped the sink and tub and then made the bed in the spare bedroom.

Neat and tidy, everything in its place. She turned to the sound of whimpering. They'd left the puppy on the screened-in back porch. Madeline groaned, knowing this wouldn't be pleasant.

The rug had been chewed to pieces, as had her slippers that she'd left on the floor. The stink of it made her gag and she backed away. The puppy whimpered and plopped down, resting her little head on big paws. Madeline glared at the little renegade.

"No messes in my house, puppy." She pushed the dog aside and reached in the cabinet for paper towels. "My house, my life, is neat and tidy, not messy."

The puppy did a little dance around her feet, barking and nipping at her boots.

"You really don't care, do you?" She leaned to pet the fluff ball. "Neither does he. He doesn't care that I don't want my world turned upside down. No, he brought you, and a child."

He'd pushed his way into her life, her thoughts, her dreams. No one belonged in those places. Dawson had been her safe place. Until last week.

She stomped into the kitchen for a spray bottle of the strongest cleaner she had. The puppy whined at the door.

"Oh, *now* you want to go outside?" She pushed the door open and watched the little dog race outside.

It chased blowing leaves, sniffed grass and then found a stick to chew on. Madeline pulled on rubber gloves, held her breath and started to clean the mess that should have been Jackson Cooper's to clean. Yeah, she should call him and tell him to come down and clean up after his rotten puppy.

If it hadn't meant having him in her home, all male and smelling good, she would have. But she didn't want his faded jeans and cute grin cluttering up the place that way.

Tires squealed and she heard a horrible yelp. The puppy. She tossed the cleaner and paper towels and ran out the front door. A truck sat in the middle of the road and an older man had picked up the puppy.

Jade's puppy. Her puppy. The stupid, sweet, messy puppy.

"I think she's okay." The farmer, a neighbor named Clark, held the ball of fur. "I tried to stop but she was chasing something."

The puppy whimpered and stared with dark eyes. Her little body trembled. "I should take her to a vet."

"I think you probably should. I'm real sorry. She came out of nowhere."

Madeline closed her eyes to the surge of tears. "I let her out. I didn't think about her running across the road."

She didn't know a vet. She didn't know anything about dogs. Or cats. Or cows.

"Let me put her in your car." The farmer, in bib overalls and a straw cowboy hat, trudged through the ditch and up the hill. "Do you know where to take her?"

"I'll figure it out."

"Doc Marler is good. If you can catch him."

She nodded and her mind spun in crazy circles trying to think about dogs and vets and what to tell Jade. A new batch of tears streamed down her cheeks. She'd have to tell Jade.

"I think she'll be okay. And if you send me the vet bill, I'd be happy to pay it."

Madeline rubbed the useless, silly tears from her eyes. "No, I'm the one who let her out and didn't watch her."

"Well, you let me know how she is. She's a cute little pup."

"She is, isn't she?" Madeline sighed and shook her head. "I didn't know I wanted a dog."

The farmer left the dog in her car and headed back down the driveway. Her cell phone rang. She pulled it from her pocket and groaned when she saw the caller ID. She didn't need this, not right now. And then, she did. Because he would know what to do.

She answered her phone with a quick hello and then said, "The puppy got hit by a car. I don't know what to do."

Her body trembled the way the puppy trembled. The poor little thing hunkered in her front seat, holding her front leg out.

"I'll be right there." Jackson's voice over the cell phone undid a little of the fear. He wouldn't leave her alone to handle this. Of course he wouldn't. He helped everyone. He rebuilt tornado-damaged homes and searched for missing children.

When he pulled up a few minutes later, she breathed a little easier. Jackson jumped out of his truck and headed her way. His smile shot clean through her, tender and unexpected. And she started to cry.

"Hey now, what's this all about?" His voice had a huskiness that undid every last shred of calm. "The puppy is going to be fine. Look at her, she's getting all worried about you."

Madeline nodded but she couldn't stop the tears. Everything inside her broke loose and she couldn't shove it all back inside. The puppy whimpered and belly-crawled to the edge of her car seat.

"Shh, you're okay." Jackson pulled her to him and held her in strong arms. "Shh."

She sobbed against his shoulder and knew that the strange calm seeping into her body, into her heart, was from him. Safe. And suddenly, not so safe.

"I thought she was dead." Make it about the dog, much easier to make it about something other than the Grand Canyon splitting open inside her heart.

"A puppy against a truck. She beat the odds today." He still held her. His lips brushed her hair and he didn't let go.

"Jade will be so upset."

"She's fine. I called and she's going to stay the night with Heather. Doc is waiting for us."

"Thank you." Madeline moved from his arms, brushing her hand across her face. "I'm a mess. And I need to run inside and get my purse."

"You aren't a mess." He brushed hair from her face. "Get what you need and I'll put her in my truck."

She nodded and rushed back into the house for her purse. She turned off lights on her way out and locked the front door. When she got to the truck Jackson had the door open for her.

The puppy crawled close, head resting on Madeline's leg. She looked quickly at the man sitting next to her. A friend. He had said it himself. They were friends.

The local veterinarian had been in town most of Jackson's life. He had even delivered a baby once, years ago. It had been a stormy night and the woman, a dairy farmer's wife, had gone into labor while Doc had been there taking care of a sick cow. When things had moved a little too quickly, Doc delivered Jasmine Porter.

Jackson parked and got out. Madeline, still pale and shaken, held Angel in her lap. He'd heard her murmur a few prayers, even promise the dog that she did like her and was glad she had her. He smiled as he helped the two of them out of the truck.

"You know, you didn't do this to the dog."

"I was really angry that she chewed up my rug and made a mess in the utility room."

"So every time a dog's owner gets mad, God sends a truck to teach them a lesson?" He kind of chuckled, and she shot him a look that took the humor right out of the moment.

"It isn't funny."

"It kind of is, if you think about it. I don't think life works that way. I don't think God works that way. He doesn't get us back every time we have a thought He doesn't approve of."

"I know." She smiled a little. "I know it's a crazy thought. I'm a woman, we get at least three crazy thoughts a week."

"I'll try to remember that." He opened the door and she went through, still holding the puppy she hadn't really wanted. He smiled as he followed her inside. He couldn't stop smiling.

Something must have happened to him when he got tossed off that horse. Maybe he'd hit his head and they hadn't realized.

A door to the left of the desk opened. Doc walked

out, slipping into a pale green jacket as he did. He nodded at Madeline and the dog before turning to Jackson.

"How old?"

"Eight weeks, Doc. Looks like her front leg."

Doc's bushy gray brows shot up. "You're a vet now?"

Jackson laughed. "Doc, you're more than a vet."

"Yeah, I'm the guy that…"

Ran Jackson off when he took Doc's daughter out a few times. But since Doc had the only veterinary clinic in Dawson, they'd worked past the resentment.

Doc took the puppy from Madeline.

"I'll take it back for X-rays. You two stay here."

Madeline stood in the center of the room, looking a lot like a woman letting go of a kid for the first time. Jackson looped his arm through hers. "I'll buy you a cupcake if you'll stop looking so guilty."

He led her to the vending machines at the end of the room.

"What kind?" He pulled a few ones out of his wallet.

"I love cinnamon rolls."

He fed the dollar into the machine and pushed the button. The package of cinnamon rolls dropped down and she reached in and grabbed them. "Thank you."

"Something to drink?"

Madeline shrugged. "Water. I'm so sorry that I dragged you over here. I know you're tired and still trying to heal up. And you have other things to do. You have a life."

Pink flooded her cheeks and he grinned at the rush of random words that spilled from her lips.

"I do have a life." He fed a dollar into the machine and pushed the button for a bottle of water.

"I mean, you know…"

He laughed. "You mean…women?"

"You know what I mean. Don't make me say it."

"Dating women is something I do enjoy. I'm a single man. That makes it okay."

"Right, I know that." She took her cinnamon rolls and the bottle of water back to one of the hard plastic chairs that lined the wall near the door. "I'm apologizing because I know this is keeping you from your life. I can't even, I don't know…"

He sat down next to her. "You can't, you don't what?"

"I could have called Jenna or Beth. I have friends. I do have a life." She glanced at her watch. "I have play practice in two hours."

"I know you have a life."

"I just panicked and when you called, I blurted it out."

"And I offered." He couldn't tell her the truth, that he liked being the person who came to her rescue. "Don't worry, she'll be fine and as soon as she's taken care of, we'll head over to Back Street."

"We?"

"I have some work to do over there."

"Oh, okay." She reached for her purse and pulled out a stack of mail. Her face paled a little and she looked away, shoving the letters back into the side pocket of her bag.

"Bad news?"

She shook her head and her shoulders slumped. "My mother sent me another card."

"What does it say?"

"I didn't open it. I don't open them."

"Why?"

She looked up at him, staring as if she thought he'd

dropped off another planet. Okay, maybe he should get this, but he didn't. Women weren't the most understandable creatures in the world. Beautiful, nice to hold, but definitely not easy to understand.

"Why would I open it?" She held it in her hands and he wanted to take it from her, open it himself.

"Because you need to."

"That sounds easy." She smiled up at him. "So, just open this card and, 'tah-dah,' everything is better?"

"No, but I think it would be a beginning. Look, Maddie, I know that my family looks pretty great from the outside, but we've had our problems and we've learned that it's best to take care of situations from the get-go. Don't let it drag on. Don't let it take root."

"It's already rooted, Jackson. This is more like having to weed a garden that's been let go."

"I understand."

She put her hand on the edge of the card and tore just a little. "This isn't easy."

"No, I bet it isn't. But remember, the only thing in there are words, and if you don't like them, toss them in the trash, burn them, never open another card from her."

"Right." She slid her finger under the flap and pulled out a Christmas card.

Emotions flickered across her face as she read. Jackson watched, waiting, not pushing. She bit down on her bottom lip and then her eyes closed briefly. Finally she shrugged and handed him the card.

"She was pregnant, sixteen and living on the streets. She thought Rainbow Valley sounded peaceful, like a place to raise a baby."

"Are you glad you read the card?"

"It changes things." She took the card back, looked

it over again and then slid it into the envelope. "But it doesn't change what happened. It doesn't answer the other questions. Now I have more questions. Why didn't she leave?"

"I guess those are questions only she can answer. But maybe not questions to answer in a card."

"Sara wasn't really my sister."

Jackson moved his arm, encircling her slim shoulders and pulling her close. Two weeks ago she'd been a neighbor, not even a friend.

"Maddie, did you ever think that the two of us would be sitting here together sharing huge events in each other's lives?"

"Never."

He laughed at her strong response. "You make it sound like the worst thing that could have happened to you."

She looked up and took him by surprise. Her hand touched his cheek, rested there and then moved to his shoulder. "It hasn't been the worst thing at all."

The door opened and Doc walked out, carrying the injured puppy. His weathered gaze shot from Madeline to Jackson and he shook his head. "Some things never change. Here's the dog. And here's the bill."

"Is she going to be okay?" Madeline touched the dog's back.

Doc handed Jackson the slip of paper. "A broken leg, but she'll heal quickly enough. You paying?"

"I can…" Madeline reached for the bill.

Jackson shook his head. "No, I'll pay for this."

Madeline took the puppy and held her close. The same puppy she hadn't been too fond of yesterday. Jackson wrote out a check for the vet bill and walked her out the door.

"What's the deal between you and Doc?" she asked as Jackson opened the truck door for her.

"He caught me parking with his daughter about sixteen years ago and he has a long memory." Jackson waited for her to get in the truck and then he leaned in close. "And back then he had a pretty good aim with his shotgun."

"He shot you?"

"Nope, he shot the tires off my truck. I had a hard time explaining that one to my dad."

He closed the door and walked around to the driver's side. The story had grown over time and with numerous tellings, but his version was still the truth. And maybe knowing it would show Madeline why he was the last person she needed her name connected with.

But maybe it was a little too late to be thinking about that.

Chapter Eleven

Dawson Community Church cancelled Wednesday-night services. With just three weeks until Christmas and less than two weeks before the living nativity was scheduled to begin, it was decided they needed more practice, so everyone involved would meet at Dawson Community Center. Madeline had planned on picking Jade up after school but Jackson told her he'd bring her with him.

Madeline pulled into the community center parking lot shortly before six. People were already there. Lights had been plugged in outside, huge shop lights with bright halogen bulbs. She walked up to the building, searching the crowds for that familiar face.

Searching for Jackson. She shook her head and told herself to stop. Before long Jade would be going back to her mother. Jackson would go back to his life and she'd go back to living in her empty house, uncluttered, unencumbered, empty. And she would be happy for that day to come.

Really she would.

"Madeline."

She turned quickly, spotted Jade and smiled. "You have ketchup on your chin."

Jade scrubbed at her face with her hand. "Better?"

"Yeah, sure." Madeline rubbed away the last smudge of ketchup. "What did you have for dinner?"

"Jackson made corn dogs."

"Nice." She turned, saw Jackson walk through the door and averted her gaze, returning her attention to the girl in front of her. "Did you have a good day?"

"Yeah, but he's a grouch."

Madeline nodded and decided to let it go. "Come downstairs with me. I have to get dressed and you can hang with me. If you want?"

"Yeah, I want. How's the puppy?"

"Same as this morning, pitiful. I think she isn't as bad as she wants us to think."

Jade laughed at that. "I think she loves the attention." And then the girl's smile faded. "I'm going to miss her."

Because this weekend they were going to Oklahoma City to try and find her mother. "I know, but you'll get to see her again."

"When?" Jade walked next to her, small and slim, a kid who worked hard at being strong.

"Soon. I promise."

"Right."

Madeline turned to the girl. "Jade, I keep my promises."

"Yeah, probably."

"Hey, where are you two going?" Jackson appeared next to Madeline.

"Downstairs to get dressed. Don't you have something to build?" Madeline had realized something lately. She didn't know how to have an easygoing conversation with a man. She tried but it came out more like an order, less like banter.

"I do have work to do. I'll catch up with you later."

Madeline nodded and then he left. She ignored Jade's knowing glances and headed downstairs. Next to her Jade giggled.

"What's so funny?"

"The two of you, acting like you don't like each other or like you haven't been spending a lot of time together."

"We haven't been spending time…" Okay, they had, but not because they wanted to. He had made her a cup of tea Monday after they got home from the vet. He'd listened as she told him little details about her childhood. He'd given advice about finding Sara.

"Yeah, you like him," Jade teased.

"No, I don't. I mean, I do, but not…" She groaned at the direction the conversation had taken. "Jade, I'm not discussing this with you."

"Fine, that's okay. But can you do me a favor?"

They were in the kitchen of the community center, surrounded by people, and Madeline didn't know if she wanted to continue the conversation around so many pairs of ears. But Jade's hazel eyes locked with hers, begging.

"What is it?"

"Tell him to keep me. I'm his daughter and I can't go back."

"Jade, I can't make this decision for him."

"Then you keep me. Call family services and tell them that my mom isn't fit. You're a teacher, they'll believe you."

"I can't do that."

"Of course not. If I hadn't messed up and gotten the

address wrong, you'd still be doing your own thing and you wouldn't be bothered with us."

Madeline hugged the girl. "Yes, I would still have my uncomplicated, uncluttered life. I would be sitting alone in the evening in a quiet house with no one to talk to."

Although a little silence would be nice. With Jade in her home, in her life, silence seemed to be a thing of the past. When Jade left, would Jackson also be a thing of the past?

"I need to get in costume." She brushed off the thoughts that didn't make sense.

"What do I do?" Jade followed her into the dressing room.

"You can come with me and watch."

Jade sat down on a stool and watched as Madeline got ready.

"A woman called my da…" Jade looked down and shrugged. "Called Jackson today."

"Jade, that's personal." Madeline tied the fabric belt around the waist of the costume.

"Yeah, I guess. I heard him tell her he couldn't see her right now. And I think she must have asked when he could see her and he said he didn't think he'd be seeing her anytime soon."

Madeline pretended she wasn't listening because hadn't she just said that this information was personal? She didn't need to know what Jackson told women that called his home. Honestly, she didn't care.

Much.

Jackson slid the paper with the DNA results back into his pocket along with the other medical information. He had work to do. There were people everywhere.

He sighed and walked through the crowd to the back of the manger. He'd been helping with the star, getting it in place so that it would shine over Bethlehem and the baby Jesus.

Beautiful Star of Bethlehem. He could almost hear his great grandmother singing the song. The memory brought a smile and he hadn't had much to smile about today. He had a lot to think about.

When he turned from the tower holding the star he saw Madeline and Jade walking together, heads bent toward one another, whispering and smiling. He smiled, seeing the two of them together. Yeah, he had a lot to think about.

Later he'd talk to Madeline. He stopped working for a minute to think about that decision. He'd been thinking about her all day, thinking about talking to her, about telling her his news, how his day had gone.

And then he'd anticipated her reaction to the medical tests and the secret he didn't want to share. He watched her walk into place, surrounded by sheep. Jade watched from a short distance away.

Someone walked up behind him. He turned, nodded and tipped his hat to Wyatt Johnson. Wyatt grinned big and turned his attention from Jackson to Madeline, back to Jackson.

"Watch out, that one will get under your skin." Wyatt Johnson smirked a little. Payback for what Jackson had told him last year.

"I don't think so, Wyatt."

Wyatt laughed, loud. People turned to stare and Wyatt thumped him on the back, jolting him and making him flinch a little.

"Watch the ribs, if you don't mind." Jackson rolled his shoulders to unkink the muscles.

"That's right, you got tossed last week. You aren't the first guy around here with some broken ribs."

"I'm not as young as I used to be." He grimaced, knowing he sounded way too much like a country song.

"Right, you're not. So what's wrong with taking time to get to know one of the nicest single females in this town?" Wyatt watched his own wife head their way. Something stabbed at Jackson's heart. Jealousy? Nah, couldn't be.

"Nothing wrong with it, Wyatt. But I think she's a little out of my league."

"She probably is." Wyatt raised his hand to thump Jackson on the back a second time and Jackson moved to the side.

"Could you not?"

"Oh, sorry, didn't know you were so weak."

"Right, weak."

"You're not your normal humorous self." Wyatt turned to watch the beginning of the living nativity as it got underway. His voice lowered. "Seriously, is there anything I can do to help?"

"No, not right now." Jackson shoved his hands in his pocket, feeling the paper that he'd gotten that day. "I'm good."

"Well, it was good to see you in church on Sunday. You plan on coming back this Sunday?"

"No." He had to explain, not leave Wyatt hanging. Although that would have been fun. He watched the progression of Mary on the donkey, Joseph at her side.

He finally turned and smiled at Wyatt who had the

good sense not to push, but he looked pretty tense with all of those unasked questions rolling around inside him.

"Wyatt, I'll be back. I'm taking Jade to Oklahoma City this weekend." He watched Mary and Joseph exit the inn, looking young and perplexed. "But I'm coming back. I guess I got tired of going and having to face questions, a few accusing looks, my own guilt."

"So what's changed?"

Jackson didn't mean to but he looked in the direction of Jade. And Madeline. He tried to brush it off, to pretend it had nothing to do with either of them. It really did have more to do with him.

"I guess a guy has to face his life. Time to make some changes."

"She's a cute kid."

Jackson nodded but didn't say more. Yeah, Jade was cute. She looked like him. She had his eyes. Sometimes it looked as if she had his smile.

"She's great," Jackson agreed. She had somehow survived a childhood that hadn't been much of a childhood and a mother who hadn't been a mother.

He refocused on Madeline as a shepherdess. As he watched the angels appeared. Madeline went down on her knees, covering her head with her arm. Jackson walked away from Wyatt. He walked closer to the scene of the shepherds leaving the field and walking toward the manger. He stood close as Mary revealed her newborn son and angels began to sing. The shepherds bowed at her feet.

Jackson stood there waiting for normal to return. But it wouldn't and he knew that. He'd changed. Maybe this was the new normal? Maybe this was his new life? Something had to be wrong with him. He'd turned down a date today with a woman he'd gone out with off and on for the last two years. She was a lawyer's daughter and owned a clothing boutique in Tulsa. She was uncomplicated.

He'd turned her down because of the shepherdess kneeling not ten feet from him. The same shepherdess who looked up at that moment and caught him staring. Yeah, he was definitely losing control of his life.

Jade saw him standing there, watching. She smiled big and bounced away from the group she'd been crowded in with. A kid who thought she was his. He thought about her future and it left a pretty big space in his heart because she deserved a home, a life with people who cared about her.

Tomorrow he would try again to contact her mother. And if he couldn't, then what? He had a load of bulls to take to Oklahoma City. He could try to find her. But he couldn't keep Jade indefinitely. He couldn't expect Madeline to raise her. He'd considered talking to his parents.

But this one was in his court.

The program ended. Jade stood at his side, a skinny kid in a big, puffy coat. Her cheeks were pink from the cold and her nose was red. She smiled up at him.

"This is great." Her tone was all happiness and sunshine.

"Yeah, it is." He pulled her close to his side for an instant and thought about moments in the future and how it would change everything for her.

"Is it time to go now?"

He nodded and watched as Madeline spoke to a few people and then slipped away from the crowd. He watched her. He couldn't stop watching her. He smiled as she walked toward him, toward Jade.

"That was great." He thought about the three of them, arm in arm, leaving together.

"Thank you. It feels as if it is all coming together."

"Yeah, it does." He felt Jade move away from him, but he couldn't stop staring at the woman in a shepherd's costume. He couldn't stop thinking about holding her close, making her feel safe.

"I'm going inside." Jade punched his arm. "They're serving hot chocolate and cookies."

"Go for it. We'll leave soon," he called out after her. She raised a hand to let him know she'd heard. It made him feel like a dad. Strange, really strange that it could happen so easily, this change in his life.

"Are you okay?" Madeline stood in front of him still. She had zeroed in on his mood. She knew how to do that and it unnerved him a little.

"I'm good." He didn't reach into his pocket for the piece of paper. "I'm going to try again to contact her mother. If I can't, I have to drive down there and look for her."

Madeline's gaze drifted to the church, to the door Jade had just skipped through. "I know. It's a shame though. I mean, I know I can't keep her, but I wish she could stay."

He reached for Madeline's hand. "Let's walk."

"Oh, okay." She hesitated, glancing toward the church. Small crowds gathered in front of the building, talking. A few people looked their way.

Yeah, rumors, gossip. He knew the drill.

"We can talk later," he said, because he didn't want to give people a reason to talk.

"Is this about Jade?"

He nodded once and released her hand. When he did she touched his arm. It would have been easy to hold on to her, to make this about him, not about Jade. But it was about Jade. In the short span of a week his life had become all about a kid.

And a woman.

"I should go." What he meant was he should escape.

"No, you should come inside."

Madeline hooked her arm through his. He knew that took a lot for her. He knew that easy gestures weren't always easy, sometimes they took real courage. He pulled her close to his side and leaned to drop a kiss on the top of her head.

"Inside, huh? Right into the midst of gossip and speculation?"

She laughed a little. "Are you afraid?"

"Shaking in my boots."

"I'll be with you." She said it in a breathless way and he looked down to see if her expression matched. She looked up at him, surprise flickering in her eyes.

He had to dig up a little of the old Jackson to get hold of this situation. "Promises, promises, Maddie."

She didn't pull away. Instead she turned, still holding his arm and they headed toward the church. She didn't let go. He didn't want her to.

Chapter Twelve

The phone rang and rang as Madeline unlocked her front door. She tried to hurry but her fingers were numb from cold. Jade stood next to her, hopping up and down a little. The wind whipped against them, a cold, north wind.

Finally she pushed the door open and they rushed into the warmth of the living room, greeted by wood smoke and Angel barking from the laundry room. Jade ran past her, heading for the dog, of course. She could hear the girl calling to the animal as she hurried through the house.

"Don't throw clothes everywhere," Madeline warned and then in a quieter voice because it didn't matter added, "I have a hall tree."

She hung her coat and kicked out of her boots before picking up the phone and checking the caller ID. The number didn't look familiar. It didn't have a local area code. She pushed the number for voicemail and listened. Her heart raced as the message played and then she slammed the phone down.

Not at Christmas. She didn't want to do this at

Christmas. Forgiveness needed to happen, she got that. She even thought she had forgiven. But she didn't want her mother forcing her way into this life, a safe life with safe people.

Her world had already been upended by a young girl and a confirmed bachelor who wanted safe help. She was safe. Her life was safe. She plopped down in the big easy chair she'd bought when she first moved in.

The perfect chair for quiet evenings alone, reading a book, drinking tea. Safe.

Loud laughter reminded her she didn't have a quiet evening ahead of her. Then footsteps. Jade ran into the room carrying the puppy that licked and licked her face.

"She's glad to see you." Madeline smiled in spite of herself. Being alone was overrated. Jade made noise and clutter worth it.

This weekend the girl would be gone. Madeline's heart broke a little for her, because she knew how it hurt to be jerked around at that age. Maybe she'd keep Jade. Maybe she'd file for custody if Jackson didn't plan on doing something.

Why wouldn't he? He was her dad. He had to do something.

"Can I go to work with you tomorrow?" Jade plopped down on the sofa with the dog.

"I can't take you to work with me." She would have loved to. Jade needed to be in school. "Jackson is going to spend the day with you. He has a lot of work to do, he said, and you can help."

"Oh, that's cool." Jade leaned in for the puppy to lick her face again. "I love this dog. I've never had one."

Madeline smiled as she watched dog and child. "Me, neither. I think you love her more than I do."

"Do you love my da…" Madeline's heart broke a little more for Jade, even if this did sound like a tricky question coming at her. "Jackson?"

"We should go to bed." Cop-out.

Jade hugged the puppy and giggled. "She needs to go outside. And you do love him."

"I don't. Jade, love is more complicated and takes more than two people being thrown together. It is more than just simple emotions. It's about two people being connected, really caring about each other. It's about wanting to share lives and everything, good or bad, that goes with life. It takes time to find and build a love likc that."

"I think you could love each other, get married and we'd be a family." Jade's tone was wistful and sad. "Don't you think?"

Madeline sighed because she didn't know what to say. She let her heart trip over the idea of being in love with Jackson Cooper. Complicated. He made her life way too complicated, and she avoided complicated as often as possible.

"I think it really is bedtime. You're so tired you're delirious." Madeline pushed herself out of her favorite chair and reached for Jade's hand. "It's cold but the puppy has to go outside."

Jade giggled. "Too late. You should see your laundry room."

"I'm seriously going to make Jackson Cooper come over here and clean up the mess. By the time this is over he's going to owe me a new floor."

"Yep, you love him."

She swatted Jade, a playful swat. "Give me the dog and you go brush your teeth."

All of the right mom words were coming out. It took her by surprise that she knew those things to say, because she'd never had a mother who said them. And now her mother wanted to be in her life.

No. Madeline couldn't go there. She could forgive, but letting the woman in her life, that she couldn't do. Jade headed into the hall but she stopped and glanced back.

"Are you okay?" The girl bit down on her bottom lip and her eyes, so much like Jackson's, studied Madeline's face with intensity that unnerved.

"I'm good, just tired."

"Okay, I'll brush my teeth." Jade smiled a sweet smile. "I think he could love you back."

"Jade, go." Madeline cringed on the inside. That definitely sounded like a mom voice.

The phone rang again. Madeline held the puppy in her arms and stared at the caller ID. The same number. She closed her eyes and waited for it to stop ringing. Slowly her hand descended, picking it up. Because she wouldn't run anymore. She couldn't. She had to face the past to move on with her life.

"Hello?"

"Madeline? It's me. It's your mother."

Madeline's world went dark for a moment. It spun. It faded and then righted itself. The puppy licked her face. She set her down on the floor and held the phone against her ear.

"Madeline?"

"I'm here." *Breathe. Breathe.* She leaned against the wall, trying to block images of her mother's face, smiling, telling her it would be okay. But it wasn't okay. Her mother led her to the man who abused her. Tore her life apart. Her mother waited for her. Held her. Told her she was sorry.

Sorry?

"I know you don't want to talk to me."

"Really, so why are you calling?" Madeline sank to the floor. The puppy crawled into her lap. Jackson had been right about having a dog.

"I'm calling because I have to. I need to." Her mother sobbed from hundreds of miles away. "I'm in Tulsa."

"No." Not hundreds of miles. Tulsa. A little more than an hour's drive. "No."

She waited but the world kept spinning. Faster and faster.

"I want to see you."

"No." She couldn't get another word out. She couldn't form another response. She couldn't even tell the woman on the other end to go away.

Because a part of her still wanted a mother? Because she knew she needed to forgive?

But not this woman. Not now.

"Madeline, I was young. I made mistakes."

"Mistakes?" Madeline shuddered as she released a breath. "Mistakes are something a person makes in their checkbook. Mistakes are when you say the wrong thing or buy the wrong car. Those are mistakes. You didn't make a mistake. You allowed your only daughter to be abused."

"I know." A long silence, sobbing on the other end that Madeline couldn't be sorry for. But she was. "I hurt you. I wanted you to know that I was afraid, too."

"Oh, okay, well, thank you for sharing that. I'm sorry you were afraid."

"This isn't going well."

Madeline closed her eyes and tears slid down her cheeks.

"No, it isn't. I can't talk to you right now."

"Maybe soon? I have a job and an apartment in Tulsa. I wanted to be close to you so I moved here."

"I have to go." Madeline hung up.

A few minutes later Jade kneeled in front of her. She didn't take the dog. Instead she curled close and hugged Madeline. "Are you okay?"

Madeline nodded. She tried to smile and reassure Jade, but she couldn't. Her heart ached. Her throat tightened with the tears, the emotion. She wanted to crawl inside herself, the way she'd done as a teenager. She wanted to hide from the pain and close herself off from feeling.

But she couldn't go back. God had done too much in her life. She couldn't go back to being the person who hid from life.

Jade hugged her hard and let go. "I'll be back."

Madeline nodded. She knew Jade walked away. The puppy, limping and hopping, followed. Madeline hugged her knees close to her chest and took a deep breath. She had to get it together.

She needed to take care of Jade, not let the girl take care of her. She leaned her head on her knees and prayed for strength to get through whatever her mother would throw at her in the coming weeks. She prayed for strength to truly forgive.

And then the front door opened. Madeline looked up. Jade stood nearby. She pointed at Madeline and Jackson nodded. In the blink of an eye Jade disappeared and Jackson was at her side. He leaned and lifted her into his arms.

"Why are you here?" Madeline leaned into his shoulder, finding it hard to believe that he had showed up when he did. Jade had called him, of course she had. And he was here. Her heart wanted to open up like a flower in early spring reaching for the sun.

He carried her to the couch and sat down with her held against him, his arms strong and holding her close to his side. She closed her eyes. This is what safe feels like, she told herself. To be held.

She thought of all the times God had held her. Through the toughest times of her life. Held and kept her anchored in faith.

"Jade called. She was worried."

"I'm fine." And then she cried. She flooded his shirt with her tears and he stroked her hair and told her everything would be okay.

She believed him.

"What happened?" He reached for the tissue box on her table and handed it to her, but he didn't stop holding her, making her feel safe.

"Do I have to talk about this?"

"Not if you don't want to." He wrapped her in protective arms and held her tight. She leaned into his strength and she couldn't force herself to move.

"My mother has not only found me, she called and she's living in Tulsa. She'll be there when I decide I want her in my life."

Jackson sighed. She felt the rise and fall of his chest. His hand slid down her back. "I know this isn't easy, but I know that you're strong. And you know I'll be here."

"I know." Did she? Why would he be here for her? She couldn't ask those questions. For the moment she had someone in her life who promised to be there for her.

Jade had asked her if she loved him. No, of course not. She was a grown woman. She knew better than to think she'd fallen in love with him. They'd been thrown together for a short time because of a teenager and a dog. They'd somehow forged a friendship.

"Maddie, I mean it." His voice, soft and husky, warm near her ear. She wasn't in love with Jackson. Attracted to him, definitely. But love?

She looked up, intending to tell him something brave and witty, if only she could think of something. When her lips parted he leaned and met her with a kiss that made her forget doubts, fears, pain. He brushed her lips with his, feather-soft, once, twice. She clung to him, exploring this moment, no fear, no desire to run, only a need to stay in his arms. His lips touched hers again, lingering this time.

The dog barked; Jackson pulled away. His eyes widened a little and he smiled. "Maddie, Maddie, you do push a man to forget his convictions."

"Right, Jackson, that's me, the temptress."

They both laughed and he pulled her close. "More than you know."

The dog hopped into the room. A moment later Jade followed, a knowing little grin on her face. "I'm going to bed."

Jackson stood and pulled the girl into an easy hug. He kissed the top of her head and ruffled her hair. "Thanks for calling me."

"Anytime." Jade's gaze dropped to Madeline. "I took the dog out."

The evidence was in her face. The pink cheeks. The red nose. Her eyes glistened a little.

"Jade, are you okay?"

Jade nodded. "I'm good."

Madeline patted the couch next to her and Jade plopped down. Madeline hugged her tight. "It really is going to be okay."

"I know it is. Right?" Jade looked up at Jackson.

Madeline followed the look and what she saw frightened her. Jackson put on a good front. He smiled and Jade probably believed him, that everything would be okay. The look in his eyes, a look he sent Madeline, told her otherwise.

Jade seemed convinced. "Good night."

The girl hurried down the hall, the dog trying to follow.

"What's going on?" Madeline asked as Jackson paced her floor.

Jackson pulled a piece of paper from his pocket and tossed it her way. He put a finger to his lips and she got it. Everything wasn't okay. He sat down next to her again.

What she read slammed her heart. She knew he must have felt this way or worse when he read the results. The DNA test showed that Jade Baker could not be Jackson Cooper's biological daughter.

She didn't know what to say.

Madeline handed him back the paper and she couldn't look at him, couldn't see the sadness in his eyes. Or would it be relief?

When she did look at him, she saw concern and worry, not relief. It made her heart soar a little.

"Now what?"

"I'm not sure what to do." He rubbed the back of his neck and then leaned back on the sofa, closing his eyes.

Madeline didn't know what to say. She reached for

his hand and waited, because he needed time and she knew he needed a friend. A friend. He had those. He had family. And he was sitting next to her, on her couch, lost.

"Jackson, we have to find her mother." She held his hand tight, wishing she could do more.

His thumb brushed her fingers. "Yeah, I know. Thank you for being a part of this. 'We' sounds much better than me, alone."

She wondered about that. He seemed good at being alone.

"Of course I'll do what I can. I love her, too."

"I know." He let out a long sigh. "I have to tell her she isn't mine. And I have to take her back to Oklahoma City to her mother."

"I'll go with you." The words rushed out. Jackson's hand tightened on hers. He lifted it and held her palm to his lips.

He moved to the edge of the couch, leaning for a moment over clasped hands. Madeline's hand rested on his back and he turned, smiling.

"And I have to go now. Because you're amazing and I…should really go."

She followed him to the door, trying to figure out the sudden change.

"Maddie…" He leaned and kissed her goodbye, soft and slow, ending with a sigh as he walked away.

Madeline wanted to run after him. She wanted to call him a coward for running. She was the one who ran but she hadn't. This time she hadn't run. She hadn't hidden inside herself.

She watched him drive away, headlights in the dark night. Somewhere a coyote howled. She could hear trucks on the distant highway. Lost, she stood there in the cold of the open door because Jade might have a point. A teenager understood Madeline's feelings better than she understood them herself.

Jackson fired up the tractor the next morning and hooked a round bale to take out to the cattle in the back pasture. Madeline hadn't gotten there yet with Jade but Travis had shown up and he'd be in the barn when they arrived.

He drove along the fenceline, stopping to open a gate when he got to the field where they were grazing the beef cattle. He hopped back in the tractor and eased it through, then got out to close the gate again. He latched it tight because he had no intention of chasing down a hundred plus head of cattle today. Sleet had started to fall an hour earlier. Nothing major but enough to make the cold pretty miserable.

As he climbed back in the tractor he heard a pitiful sound. He stood on the step and looked around but didn't see anything out of the ordinary. The cattle were a good hundred yards out. They were grouped together, fighting the wind and sleet. As he headed their way they started to move. He'd brought a bale out yesterday but he planned on moving several bales today. He also needed to corral the young bulls he would be selling this weekend to a breeder just outside of Oklahoma City.

The City, as it was more popularly referred to. When someone was going to the City, everyone knew what they meant—Oklahoma City.

A dark form in the grass caught his attention. He lowered the bale of hay and backed off from it. The cattle were already moving in, even though they still had hay. He'd need to check the automatic waterer, to make sure it wasn't frozen.

He hated the cold. Even in the enclosed tractor, complete with heat, he felt it down to his bones. The wind whistled. Maybe the sound of the wind made it seem even colder. Whatever, he was ready for spring already and winter hadn't really hit yet.

The dark shape moved and he saw that it was a calf. The form next to it didn't move. He headed the tractor in that direction. Not a good morning for a downed cow. As he got closer the cow still didn't move. She didn't even raise her head.

Even worse. He jumped down from the idling tractor and eased toward the bawling calf. Cold air gusted, blowing against him. The calf appeared to be a few hours old, and half frozen. The sleet coated its dark fur, still wet, but icy.

"Not a good way to start your life, little guy." He scooped up the bawling calf, took a last look at the momma cow to make sure his assumption was correct.

She was gone. He walked away, holding the calf. Part of farm life. Yeah, he knew that. He'd learned the lesson early in life. Sometimes animals died. People died. He guessed for some people it got easier.

He reached to open the tractor door and pushed the calf inside the cab, following it. "Now what in the world are we going to do with you?"

A few minutes later the tractor rolled toward the barn and he knew what he'd do with this calf. Madeline's car parked in front of the barn gave him the answer he needed. He drove past the barn to the equipment barn. Tractors, an old farm truck and a couple of stock trailers were parked under the roof of the three-sided, open-front building.

Jade ran toward him as he got out of the tractor and headed for the barn. She didn't seem to notice the cold and he remembered how his grandfather had always said that cold got colder as a man got older. He grinned, remembering.

"A calf!" Jade's eyes lit up. "Where's its mom?"

"Gone." He didn't want to say more. He didn't want to see her eyes full of tears. But he knew it had to happen. Just like eventually he'd have to tell her that she wasn't his.

"What happened?" Madeline had walked up behind Jade. She looked so good this morning, he wanted to grab her up in his arms and thank her for being in his life.

He didn't know who would be more shocked if he did that. Probably better if he let it go. The tender vulnerability in her eyes last night warned him to go easy, move slowly.

Jade was petting the sticky, wet calf.

"I found him with his mother. It happens." He hated that it did. "We need to get him a bottle and get him warmed up."

"He won't die, will he?" Jade's eyes widened as she looked from him to the calf.

"Of course he won't." Jackson led them all into the barn. Travis had left. "Where'd Trav go?"

"He had to get home and start packing for Tulsa." Madeline's voice trailed off when she said the name of the nearest city. "School got cancelled due to the weather."

"Yeah, I can imagine that. Let's get this little guy

settled and a few chores done and I'll take you girls to the Mad Cow."

For lunch. And he didn't care what people said or how they talked.

"What can we do?" Madeline followed him into the feed room.

"I'll hold him if you can grab that bottle and mix the calf starter. In that rubber tub, a scoop of the starter and then fill the bottle with water from the sink in the bathroom through that door." He pointed to the door across from them. "Jade, grab a towel out of that cabinet and let's get him dried off."

"Got it." Madeline already had the lid off the tub. Jade pulled a towel from the cabinet and rubbed it over the calf.

"A little harder than that, kiddo. We need to get him dry and warmed up."

"Poor calf," she crooned as she rubbed the calf he'd set on the floor of the feed room. "Everyone should have a mom."

And that sent an arrow to his heart. Every kid should have a family, too. His mom had tried to give a home to as many as possible. He'd learned at an early age that family didn't necessarily have to be about blood connections and DNA.

"Here it is." Madeline returned, a city girl in jeans and a heavy coat, lace-up suede boots to keep her feet warm. She knew how to blend.

She handed him the bottle, her hands covered in crocheted gloves that were probably pretty worthless in the cold, especially if they got wet.

"You need better gloves." He shoved the bottle into

the fighting calf's mouth. The calf turned his head one way and then the other. "Hold his head."

"Okay. Why doesn't he want it?"

"It isn't his momma. Give him a minute to realize it's food and he'll take to it."

Madeline held the calf's head and Jackson opened his mouth. The calf let out a little moo and then clamped down on the giant-size baby bottle.

"There he goes."

Jade moved close. "Aww, just like a baby."

Jackson laughed. "Yeah, a baby who will someday weigh close to a ton, have horns and be able to run you into the ground. Don't let him fool you. He isn't a pet."

"But he's cute," Madeline insisted. He'd put the calf on the wood floor and it wagged its tail and pushed against the bottle he had handed over to Jade. Slobber flew, dripped down the calf's chin. Jade laughed and held tight to the bottle.

"He's strong."

"He is strong," Jackson agreed. "And cute. But still, he's going to grow up to be…"

"A big, mean bull." Madeline repeated his warning with a little laugh.

He shot her a smile and watched her cheeks turn pink. Yeah, he hadn't lost it completely.

"Right."

Madeline kneeled next to the calf. "You aren't planning on sending this thing home with me, are you?"

Jackson widened his eyes and pointed to his chest. "Me, do that to you?"

"Yeah, you're going to do that to me." She pulled off her city-girl gloves and stroked the calf's back. "Where would I put a calf?"

"You have an empty barn and a corral."

The sucking air sound meant an empty bottle. Jade pulled the bottle from the calf's mouth and it chased after her, butting against her, wanting more. She laughed and stuck out her fingers. The calf brought his long tongue around her hand.

"What do we do now?" Jade kneeled in front of the little bull calf.

"For now we'll put him in a stall with plenty of straw to sleep on and feed him again later."

"He'll be all alone." Madeline stroked the calf and looked at him with kind of pleading, kind of accusing eyes. Great, an orphaned calf and two big-hearted females.

"Yes, he will. But that's about the only option. He wouldn't survive on his own in the pasture." He picked up the calf and headed toward an empty stall, trying to figure out a way to undo the sad look in Madeline's eyes. It hadn't been but a couple of weeks ago that he'd just do what he had to do and that would have been the end of it.

A female around the place changed everything. They brought emotion into farming. He sighed and shook his head because now he couldn't walk away without it bugging him, too.

He put the calf in the stall and turned, smiling because he was going to be the hero. "I'll get a goat to keep him company."

"A goat?"

"Yeah, Ryder Johnson has a few goats that he sometimes pairs up with foals. We'll stop by there on our way back from the Mad Cow."

Jade leaned in, looking at the bawling, unhappy calf. "Can't we get him a friend now?"

He shook his head and pulled out his phone. "Let me call Ryder."

He made the call and fifteen minutes later Ryder pulled up to the barn and led a big, fat goat into Jackson's barn. Ryder grinned, tipped his hat and handed the lead rope of the goat to Jade.

"Told you to buy a goat." He shot the comment at Jackson.

"Right, I should have listened to you." Jackson opened the stall door and the goat walked right in, eyed her new companion in unblinking silence and grabbed a mouthful of straw.

The calf stopped crying as the goat moved closer.

"Perfect." Madeline smiled and watched as the calf followed the goat around the stall. Jackson shook his head. It was that easy to make her smile.

And he'd never cared more about making a woman happy. That thought made him want to jump in his truck and drive far and fast from this situation and this moment. Realizations like that one didn't come around very often.

It had never happened to him before.

"Now, can we go to lunch?" He slipped a convincing arm around her waist and moved her toward the door. Ryder walked on out but turned as they followed.

"Let me know if you need anything else." Ryder grinned. "Like advice."

"I doubt I need advice from you." Jackson glared and Ryder didn't seem to notice.

"Of course not. I mean, why would you need advice? You've been ranching all your life."

"Exactly. I'm very good at ranching."

And they both knew they weren't talking about ranching. Madeline walked away, fortunately not getting it. She followed Jade to the fence and one of the horses walked up to let them rub her neck.

"Nothing changes a man like a good woman and a kid."

Ryder pushed his hat down on his head a little tighter.

"I haven't changed." Jackson didn't have a woman or a kid, not really. He watched them walk down the fence line and he knew it bugged him, that Jade wasn't his. That Madeline wasn't his.

"Gotta go. Andie and the twins are ransacking the house. She's decorating. They're chewing and dragging stuff everywhere."

"It'll be a great Christmas for you all."

"Yeah, it will. See you later, Jackson. I think your Christmas is going to be different than you expected, too."

Jackson would have agreed, but he knew that the DNA test undid any ideas he'd had about Jade having a Cooper Creek Christmas. He wondered if she'd have any Christmas at all with her mother.

For a brief second he tried to tell himself it wasn't his problem, but it was and it cut deep, thinking about her alone at Christmas.

He whistled, loud and shrill. Madeline and Jade turned and headed his direction. "Let's get some lunch."

They all climbed into the truck together. Madeline in the middle next to him. Jade did that on purpose every time.

Chapter Thirteen

The Mad Cow Diner looked like Christmas come early. Madeline walked in next to Jackson and Jade. She tried to pretend she went to lunch with someone like Jackson every day. But the stares from the locals reminded her that she couldn't fool them or herself. She'd been here a year and she'd never dated. When well-meaning friends tried to match her up with a nice guy, she always said a polite "No, thank you."

She stared at the Christmas tree and decorations, trying to ignore the heat creeping up her neck. Jade grabbed her hand and pulled her toward a nativity, hand-carved by a local artist. The tree sparkled with clear lights and Christmas music played softly on hidden speakers.

Last year she'd been in town just a few months and she'd joined Vera for Christmas at the Mad Cow. Vera always had a big meal for folks in town without family. Madcline had received the same invitation for this year.

Vera walked out of the kitchen, wiping her hands on her apron. She grinned big when she saw them. "Well, Merry Christmas."

Madeline smiled back. Vera had switched from her normal blue dress to a red dress, white apron and a Santa hat.

"Merry Christmas, Vera." Madeline accepted the other woman's warm hug and skittered a look sideways to find Jackson heading their way.

"Isn't that nativity beautiful?" Vera put an arm around Jade. "A man in our church carved that for me. I love the look of love on Mary's face. She'd just had the most perfect baby in the world, and she had to wonder why God had brought this moment to her. I always wonder how she felt, being so young and being put in that situation. I think she must have felt as awed as the shepherds."

"I think the cows were awed, too." Jade grinned as she looked at the scene. "We have a calf."

"Do we?" Vera's brows arched and she turned to look at Jackson.

He shrugged and let it go. But Vera didn't. Her gaze shot up and she smiled. "Why, Jackson Cooper, look at that, Madeline is under the mistletoe."

"Vera." Madeline tried to step away.

Jackson caught her hand, a wicked grin on his face. He smiled at Vera and then at her again. His hand on hers was rough and warm. "We can't ignore mistletoe. Vera would be crushed."

"I would indeed." Vera smiled big. "I move it every morning because I want to keep things interesting."

"But—" Madeline looked around the restaurant, half-full and everyone staring at them. A table of women giggled and pointed.

Jackson grinned and her heart stopped protesting. She stopped wanting to escape. How did he do that?

When he stepped close she wobbled a little and he slid a hand to her back, steadying her. "One little kiss won't hurt."

She nodded but wanted to disagree. It could hurt, very much. He leaned and dropped the sweetest of kisses on her mouth. When he pulled back, his smile had faded.

"Maddie, I'm all out of self-control. Good Jackson has left the building."

Vera laughed. "From the look on her face, I think Good Maddie has left the building, too."

Madeline shook her head. "I'm very much still here."

Vera clucked a little and moved them in the direction of a corner booth, out of view. She said, "I think what the two of you need is a nice bowl of chicken and dumplings. Weather like we're having calls for comfort food. The weatherman said today that we've had two weeks of below normal temperatures."

"Chicken and dumplings do sound good, Vera." Jackson's hand remained on Madeline's back and he reached for Jade who had stopped to look at Christmas cards taped to the wall. "This way, kiddo."

As they walked people were talking behind their hands and nodding in their direction. Madeline pulled her jacket a little tighter around herself and blinked fast to clear her vision. Why did moments like this make her want to hide again?

Being stared at, whispered about. It had all been too much a part of her life all those years ago. Being interviewed by police, going before judges and lawyers, facing her mother that last time. Her heart squeezed tight.

A hand touched her arm, guiding her to the booth and into a seat. She scooted across the bench and took the spot closest to the window, sighing with relief when Jade sat next to her.

"What are we going to do for the rest of the afternoon?"

Madeline looked up from her menu when Jackson asked the question. Jade, seated next to her, grinned. "I'd like to ride a horse."

"We could do that, in the arena. This weather isn't great for riding." Jackson's gaze settled on Madeline and she didn't have an answer. He didn't look away for a long minute and she focused on the menu, unable to meet the questions in his eyes.

"What about Christmas shopping?" He smiled up at the waitress approaching with an order pad.

They stopped to order and then Jackson returned to the previous conversation, pulling them back to the subject with him.

"So, Christmas shopping?" He picked up the wrapper from his straw and turned it into a paper wad that he flicked, hitting Jade in the nose. "I'm kind of an expert on shopping with women. It comes from having a half dozen sisters."

"Christmas shopping sounds fun." Madeline stirred sugar into the super-strong coffee that Vera was famous for.

"We can drive into Grove." Jackson reached for the sugar bowl that Jade had nearly emptied into her iced tea. "I think that's enough."

Jade didn't smile. She didn't laugh. "I have to go home tomorrow. I won't be here for Christmas."

Madeline ducked her head and waited for Jackson's answer. But her heart broke for Jade who just wanted a family for Christmas.

"Jade, I'm not going to leave you on your own. I promise."

Jade shrugged her slim shoulders like it didn't matter. But it did matter. It mattered more than any of them could say. To a girl who had nothing, not even family, it mattered.

"You don't even think you're my dad."

Jackson leaned forward, resting his arms on the table. "What do you mean by that?"

"Why else would you need a DNA test?" Jade fiddled with her napkin, tearing it into little pieces. "You're looking for a way to skip out on me."

"I'm not." He tossed his hat on the bench and brushed a hand through his hair. "Jade, I'm a bachelor. I've been single and on my own for a long time. I'm not going to know how to make 'dad' decisions right off the bat."

"Right, yeah, whatever." Jade hunkered, her shoulders curved forward and her head down. "I'll be okay."

"Jade, you'll be more than okay. I promise."

The waitress appeared with their chicken and dumplings, as well as a big basket of rolls and salads for the three of them.

"Let's eat and have a good day. Tomorrow we'll figure something out."

Jade nodded but she wouldn't look up, wouldn't make eye contact with either of them. She blew on a steaming bite of chicken and dumplings but didn't take the bite. Instead she looked down at the bowl, tears dripping down her cheeks. Madeline touched her hand and smiled when Jade looked up at her.

"It'll be okay. I know people have told you that before, but Jackson isn't going to let anything happen to you. He's going to be there for you."

And then Madeline looked at Jackson, pleading without words for him to keep the promise she'd just made for him. He had to be the person this little girl needed. Someone had to be there for Jade.

Two hours later Jackson still couldn't shake the way Madeline's words back at the Mad Cow had shaken him. Jackson in Charge wasn't the name of this little family drama. The only person Jackson really knew how to take care of was Jackson.

Somehow, though, a kid and a woman had become a big part of his life. He walked behind them as they browsed the second flea market of the day. They were looking at fancy little tea cups that wouldn't hold more than a thimble of liquid. While they looked at tea cups he tried to remember who he had been a week ago.

"This one is pretty." Jade picked up a cup and handed it to Madeline who held it up to the light and examined it.

The guy gene didn't allow him to see a thing different about that cup. It looked like every other cup they'd looked at.

"It's beautiful." Madeline turned to him, big smile, eyes dark and pulling him in. He was about to tell her he agreed.

He couldn't stop himself.

"It is pretty." He blinked because he didn't drink tea. He didn't shop in flea markets for old tea cups that other people had been drinking out of for years.

She laughed and he knew he'd blown it. "You're not good at this."

"Sorry, I'm not a tea person. Or a cup person."

"Or a flea market person." Madeline put the cup back

on the shelf. "We should go to a store with guy stuff. Fishing poles and guns."

"Madeline, do you want that cup?"

She shook her head. "Even I wouldn't spend that much for a cup. Let's go, before you break out in hives."

How far gone was a guy when he picked up the flowery tea cup and carried it to the counter? As he paid he told himself this was going to pass. But watching the delight on Madeline's face when he handed her that bag holding the perfect tea cup, he wasn't quite sure. He wondered if he needed to go back and buy another dozen of those cups, because if each one put a smile on her face, it was worth it.

She led him out of the store by the hand, Jade skipping ahead of them.

"What am I going to do?" He watched the girl walk ahead of them, window shopping.

"Tell her the truth." Matter of fact Madeline.

"Yeah, sounds easy, doesn't it?"

"It won't be. She wants to be a Cooper. And who could blame her. She wants you for a dad. Any little girl would."

That did more than surprise him. He stopped walking, but kept his eye on the teenager a short distance ahead of them. Okay, he couldn't let it go. He turned to look at Madeline.

"Why in the world would a kid want me for a dad?"

"Really?" Madeline watched Jade, too. "You don't get that? You have everything to offer. You're a good man with a wonderful home and a family. You can take care of her, make her feel safe."

"Keep talking, you're starting to convince me." He grinned down at Madeline and she turned away, cheeks a little pink. "I never thought you'd think so highly of me, Maddie Patton."

"I'm not talking for me. I'm talking for a young girl who has grown up in a pretty unstable home."

"But I'm not that man, Maddie. I'm not dad material. I'm a bachelor who does a barely decent job at taking care of himself. And the most important fact is the one we both know. I'm not her dad."

"No, but you're the closest thing she has to one."

"What am I supposed to do about that?" He was the closest thing Jade Baker had to a dad. That didn't say much, but he knew it was true. He wasn't anyone's dad. But this girl needed someone to be there for her.

This relationship couldn't be walked away from. This wasn't a Friday night in Tulsa with a waitress who only expected one night, a decent dinner and empty words. This was a kid who expected someone to be there for her forever.

It was Madeline, standing next to him, believing he'd do the right thing. He whistled softly and shook his head. She was looking for the same thing, someone to be there for her, forever.

"Hey, what's going on back there?" Jade turned from a window and hurried back to them, sliding a little on a slick spot in the sidewalk.

When would he tell her? The thought came to him, that he didn't have to tell her. He could let her believe the DNA test came back positive.

But he wouldn't lie to her.

"We're coming." He smiled and headed up the sidewalk with Madeline at his side. "See anything you couldn't live without?"

She shrugged slim shoulders. "I thought we could go in that jewelry store. They have homemade jewelry."

"Let's go." He opened the door for the two women to walk in ahead of him.

It looked like trouble to Jackson. A jewelry store plus two females equaled serious trouble any way he looked at it. Not that he hadn't given women jewelry before. For Christmas. To say goodbye. Once, a long time ago he'd bought a promise ring for a girl in school. After another month of dating he realized forever felt like, well, forever. He'd taken the ring back and her brother had knocked him almost into eternity.

His phone rang, saving him from the ohhing and ah-hing as Jade and Madeline went from display cabinet to display cabinet. Saved by the bell, he walked outside to take the call.

"Jackson Cooper, bring my daughter back." The voice on the other end didn't sound at all familiar. The words slurred and mumbled, forcing him to plug his opposite ear.

"I can't hear you."

"This is Gloria. Bring my daughter back. She's not your kid."

"So you did get the messages I left." He walked a short distance away from the front of the jewelry store. "Listen, Gloria, I can't really talk right now. I'm bringing her back tomorrow. But we're going to discuss this situation."

"We aren't going to discuss anything. She's my kid and I could have you arrested."

Anger shot through him, white hot and making his heart beat hard in his neck. He swallowed a lot of things he knew he shouldn't say in favor of carefully chosen words.

"Don't worry, the police know that I have her. My question to you is, why didn't you call sooner? Why didn't you file a missing persons report?"

"That's none of your business. Jade knows how to take care of herself."

The anger took a pivotal turn for the worse and he had to stand there for a long minute, finding a way to respond without making the situation worse. "Gloria, she's thirteen."

Gloria laughed, loud and harsh. "Right, and you care?"

"Yeah, I care."

"Just bring her home."

The phone went dead. Jackson stood with the cell phone in his hand watching the steady stream of traffic down the street. A hand touched his arm. He turned and Madeline gave him a cautious look.

"Problem?"

He shook his head and pocketed his phone. "Nothing I can't handle. Let's go back inside and see if Jade found something wonderful she can't live without."

"She found several items that fit that description."

"What about you?"

"No, I'm not a jewelry person. And as interesting as their jewelry is, I'm more of an antiques girl. There's something about owning something that someone treasured for years, or generations."

"Gotcha." He touched her back with one hand and reached to push the door open with the other. Antiques. He filed that away for future reference.

The whirlwind of a teenager grabbed him and for the

next fifteen minutes pointed out every awesome thing she could find. And then she told him she didn't want anything. She was happy just to look. Jackson hugged her tight. If he'd had a kid, he'd want her to be just like this one. He'd want her to be wild about living life, meeting people and experiencing new things.

He bought her a matching set of jewelry and she threw her arms around his neck and whispered, "I love you, Dad."

Over her shoulder he caught Madeline's soft-hearted expression, eyes filling with unshed tears. "You're welcome, kiddo."

She deserved a dad. Tomorrow he would have to tell her the truth. He knew, from talking to Gloria, that if he didn't, Gloria would. It would hurt less coming from him. Nothing in the world would keep it from hurting, though.

"We should probably head home." He paid for the jewelry and handed the bag, all decorated in bows and swirls, to Jade.

Madeline stood next to the door waiting for them. "Good idea. I have to be at practice in two hours and I bet that puppy is going crazy wanting outside. And that's your fault, Jackson Cooper."

"My fault?" He opened the door for them. "What, exactly, is my fault?"

"The puppy at my house making who knows what kind of mess."

"Oh yeah, the puppy. Okay, that probably is a little bit my fault."

"So you'll come over and clean up her puppy messes?"

"Nope, but I'll buy you dinner tomorrow evening."

Jackson gave her his best smile because he couldn't take a chance that she'd say no.

"Tomorrow? But you'll be in Oklahoma City." Her eyes widened and her chin came up a slight notch as she got what he meant.

"You said you would go with us."

Madeline remained quiet as Jade moved ahead of them, drifting to the front of a store that held a display of tie-dyed shirts.

"She has to go home, doesn't she?" Madeline slowed her steps, and Jackson matched his to hers.

"I wish she didn't, but Gloria is pretty determined. She wants her daughter home and she pointed out that Jade isn't mine."

"She put your name on the birth certificate."

"I know. But the DNA proves otherwise."

"So this is the end."

Jackson nodded and he couldn't look Madeline in the eyes. Yeah, this was the end. Jade had to go home. Madeline would be out of his life. Everything would go back to normal. He'd go back to his life. They'd each go back to their respective lives. Whatever lesson he'd been expected to learn would be over.

It sounded easy but it hurt like crazy to think about it. Tomorrow his life would be his own again. No, he wouldn't be throwing a party anytime soon.

Chapter Fourteen

A quiet house. Madeline walked through her front door after work on Friday and thought about how this quiet used to be normal. No Jade. No Angel the puppy. Heather Cooper was babysitting the dog for her until they got back from taking Jade to Oklahoma City. No noise and no clutter.

After today her life was her own again. No more Jackson Cooper messing around in her business, or her emotions. She should sigh a sigh of relief over that one. Good riddance!

She dropped her bag by the hall tree and kicked off her boots. But she didn't have a lot of time. Jackson wanted to leave for Oklahoma City in an hour. That meant packing an overnight bag, changing clothes and tidying up a little before he got there to pick her up.

The plan included them staying one night in Oklahoma City. She would stay in a separate hotel room with Jade, to keep the girl safe and watch her. Tomorrow morning they would take Jade to her mother. And then they'd head home. Alone.

End of story. End of this little chapter in her life.

This very complicated, cluttered chapter. As she walked through the hall the phone rang. She ignored it. It quit ringing but immediately started again. Madeline reached for it as she headed to her room to grab extra clothes.

"Hello."

"Madeline, it's me. It's your mother."

Madeline cringed and then she groaned. "Stop calling me."

"It's almost Christmas. I just wondered if maybe you would reconsider seeing me. Please. If you would just see me, just once?"

"Do you know what happened to Sara?" Madeline grabbed jeans out of her closet and two sweaters. She shoved pajamas into her bag and extra warm socks.

A long pause and then her mother spoke again. "Honey, I'm sorry."

"Sorry? I think we've established that. You're sorry and you want to be forgiven." Madeline leaned against the wall and closed her eyes. And as much as she fought the urge to stay angry, to stay bitter, she wanted to forgive. The little girl in her cried out for her mother.

Over the years, every now and then, she'd thought about what it would be like if her mother came back. If her mother could be the person she wanted her to be, needed her to be. That dream had seemed far better than the thought of always being alone with no family to turn to.

"Madeline, Sara…" Across the line Madeline heard a sniffle and then a sob. "Honey, she killed herself the night that she took you to town. She wanted you safe, I think. She did what I should have done."

Madeline walked to the window and looked out at

the barren December landscape painted in shades of brown and gray. Bleak. Winter was always so bleak.

This moment felt like winter. It ached deep down inside, frozen and cold.

"I have to get off the phone now." Madeline held the phone to her ear as she slipped into jeans.

"Maybe before Christmas we can talk again?"

Madeline nodded even though the woman on the other end couldn't see. "I'll pray about it."

"Thank you. Oh, Madeline, thank you."

The call ended. Madeline sat on the edge of the bed and thought about the girl who hadn't really been her sister. Sara hadn't saved herself. She had given up. And no one had ever told Madeline. They'd allowed her to search, to ask questions, and they'd hidden the truth from her.

Maybe she could have found the truth if she'd tried a little harder? The one thing she couldn't have done was save Sara.

A car honked. She shoved her makeup bag and extra clothes into an overnight bag, slid her feet into boots and jerked her coat off the hall tree on her way out the door.

Jade jumped out of the truck and motioned for Madeline to climb in. Always pushing her into the middle. Madeline shook her head and climbed in. Jackson smiled big as she slid across the leather seat. He tipped his hat a little and winked. As she slid close she realized how good he smelled. And how good it felt to sit next to him.

The door slammed and Jade reached for her seatbelt. She didn't smile, though. Instead she watched out the window, shoulders slumped. Madeline touched her arm and Jade turned, smiling just a little.

"It'll be okay."

Jade shrugged. "Yeah, sure it will."

"We're not walking out of your life, Jade." Jackson shifted gears, his hand brushing Madeline's knee. She scooted a little closer to Jade.

"Right, I know." Jade looked out the window again, ignoring them.

Were they so different, she and Jade? Madeline thought not. Both had mothers they wanted to escape from. Madeline had escaped once and then she'd had to escape again. And again. She wasn't going to run anymore. This time she would face her mother. She'd been learning that facing fears sometimes meant overcoming them, seeing them for the tiny ant hills they were rather than the mountains they appeared to be.

Maybe her mother would be another mountain conquered.

Maybe someday Jade would conquer her mountains, her giants. It took faith, learning to rely on faith.

A hand touched Madeline's. She turned her attention from Jade to the man sitting next to her. Jackson Cooper. Her fears had changed from how he could hurt her, to how he could break her heart.

She hadn't expected that.

"How was your day?" He slid a quick look her way before turning his attention back to the road.

"Good day at school. My mother called again." She meant to be strong but her voice broke a little. Jackson shot her another quick look.

"You okay?"

"Good. I'm good." An easy smile to prove the point.

"Are we going to stop and eat?" Jade turned from the

window to ask the question. "Are you taking me home as soon as we get to Oklahoma City?"

"We will eat. I do need to check in with your mom as soon as we get to town, but I thought you could stay with us tonight. I reserved two rooms, one for the two of you and one for me."

"Cool, a hotel. The only hotel I've ever stayed in was the shelter when Mom…" Jade's words faded off and she turned her attention back to the window. "How come you had to bring bulls?"

Madeline glanced back at the trailer hooked to the truck.

"I'm selling them." Jackson looked in the rearview mirror. "We'll stop at a ranch outside of the city, unload the cattle and drop the trailer. I'll pick the trailer up on our way back home."

"*Your* way back home," Jade corrected with a big frown.

"Jade, this isn't goodbye."

"Yeah, I know." She reached to turn up the radio. "Silent Night" filled the cab of the truck.

Madeline started singing. Jackson glanced at her, a quick look at her profile. Jade kept staring out the window for a minute but then she couldn't help herself. He figured that's what Madeline intended. Pretty soon Jade and Madeline were both singing. An elbow jabbed his gut.

"Broken ribs, remember?" He grunted and grimaced a little.

"Sing." Madeline smiled up at him, innocent and sweet.

He hadn't sung "Silent Night" in years but he joined

them for the chorus. The chorus went high. They laughed at him.

"Hey, you said to sing."

"We changed our minds." Jade looked pained and stuck her fingers in her ears. "Please don't sing again."

"Give me another chance." He cranked the volume to George Strait singing a Christmas song. "This is more like it."

Madeline openly laughed. "You're not even going to tell us that you compare to George Strait."

He winked and grinned at her. "I'm a cowboy. I have jeans and a…cute grin."

"You're full of yourself." She shook her head and started singing.

For the next two hours they sang to the radio. Jade finally fell asleep. He didn't know if Madeline had intended for it to be such a great distraction, but it had worked. He owed her.

Jackson slowed the truck for the turn that would take them to the small town where he had a buyer for the bull calves in the trailer.

"Are we almost there?" Jade blinked a few times and then rubbed the sleep from her eyes.

"Almost." Jackson took the next right. The trailer lurched and the truck pulled a little. "We'll eat after we drop these calves."

"I'm starving." Jade again. She stretched and then leaned her head on Madeline.

He pulled up the driveway, dialed his phone and listened to the man on the other end give directions on which gate to back up to with the trailer.

"Give me fifteen minutes. The two of you can stay in here where it's warm."

Madeline nodded and watched him get out of the truck. He looked back in at her. Lately he'd wondered a lot what she thought about him. If he had any sense at all he wouldn't want an answer to that question.

Thirty minutes later Jackson was back in the truck and they were on the road. He cranked the heat and tossed his gloves on the floor of the truck. "Man, it's freezing out there."

"Is that sleet?" Madeline nodded, indicating moisture hitting the windshield.

"Yeah, I think it is. And maybe freezing rain. We need to get to Oklahoma City." He glanced at his watch. "I wonder if it's doing this in Tulsa."

His parents and brother were in Tulsa heading up a charity bull riding event for Travis's favorite charity, a group home for children taken from their parents. Kids like Jade. Hopefully the weather didn't mean the event got cancelled.

The frozen stuff hit the windshield. He flipped on his wipers and turned the heat to defrost. They were driving through Oklahoma City and already cars were sliding off into the ditch. Good thing he'd left that stock trailer behind. He'd pick it up on his way home.

"Can we eat now?"

Jackson shook his head. "No, we're going to see your mom first. And then we'll head for our hotel and order from room service."

Out of the corner of his eye he saw Jade wringing her hands and biting her lip.

"Jade…" He stopped because he wouldn't tell her again that it would be okay. She'd heard it enough. He didn't know what would happen, so how could he make promises?

The GPS gave directions to the address Jade's mom had given him. It was dark and the houses were dark. People stood on porches, walked out to cars. Houses were boarded up and looked empty. The house they stopped in front of didn't look much better than the abandoned houses.

"Home sweet home." Jade opened her door and got out.

The freezing rain had stopped but it was still cold. Jackson slid a little as he got out. He reached back in for Madeline. Jade had already headed up the sidewalk.

Gloria, not the Gloria he remembered from years ago, but a thinner version with stringy hair and a gaunt face, stepped outside. She shivered in her thin T-shirt and skin-tight jeans.

"Did you tell her you're not her dad?"

Jackson shot Jade a look, saw her face pale, her eyes widen.

"Not like this, Gloria."

"Well, she's got to stop living in a fantasy world, thinking she's some princess who got lost. This is it, sweetheart, home sweet home."

"Gloria, stop." Jackson rushed up the steps, reaching for Jade as the girl bolted.

"You should have told me." Jade slipped from his grasp and ran down the steps, down the sidewalk. At the street she turned. "I thought I could trust you."

"Jade, you can." But how could she trust anyone? "Come back and talk."

When he realized she didn't plan on talking, he went after her. But she was gone. She disappeared into the dark night. Madeline ran to his side, yelling for Jade to come back. They walked down the street together, past houses with loud music cranked. People shouted and cars honked.

"Where'd she go?" Madeline shivered next to him.

"It's hard to tell. Maybe she has a friend around here somewhere. Maybe Gloria knows."

They walked back to the house. Gloria had gone inside.

"How does this happen?" Madeline asked as they walked to the front door. "How does a life get this out of control?"

"Wrong choices build up." Jackson shrugged and slid an arm around the shivering woman who didn't have to be here with him. "So, your mom called again?"

"She wants to see me. I'm thinking I might. I don't know. She told me that Sara killed herself."

Jackson pulled her close to his side. "I'm sorry."

She nodded and reached to knock on the door. "The important thing now is finding Jade."

Gloria opened the door. In the light from the living room her skin looked yellow and dry. She scowled at them as if she couldn't remember who they were or why they were there.

"What?"

"We didn't find Jade." Jackson pushed the door open. "Mind if we come in?"

"I'd rather you not."

"Right, but we are." He led Madeline into the smoke-filled living room. It stank of old food, cigarettes and unchanged cat litter. "Where do you think she went?"

"What do you care? You're not her dad." Gloria plopped down on the sofa and lit another cigarette.

"My name is on her birth certificate. You did that."

She shrugged. "Yeah, well, I couldn't think of anyone else to put on there. I wanted her to have a dad. You seemed decent."

"Did you think I was her dad, Gloria?"

"No, not really. I just thought if something ever happened to me, you'd be contacted and the kind of family you came from, you wouldn't leave a kid on her own."

He tensed and shoved his hands into his pockets. He'd never wanted to hurt a woman, not once in his life. This one pushed him pretty close to that point. "Where is she?"

"Probably at that preacher's house. Maybe at a friend's house. She'll be home tomorrow. Once she calms down and realizes her little vacation is over."

"Don't you care about her at all?" Madeline's voice shook and Jackson reached for her hand. "She's a child. She needs you."

Gloria stood, got in Madeline's face, the whites of her eyes as yellow as her skin. "Don't come in here and tell me how to raise my daughter, Princess. Yeah, you're one of those do-gooders who ain't never had to suffer."

"You have no idea what you're talking about." Madeline stood tall. "But I do know that Jade deserves for you to be her mother."

"You take her then." Gloria dropped back to her seat on the couch and waved them away. "You take her."

"Take her?" Jackson stepped closer. He kneeled to put himself at eye level. "Gloria, are you okay?"

She turned away but not before he saw tears streaking down her cheeks. "Hepatitis. But it doesn't matter. I'm done with that kid running away every time something happens that she doesn't like. You're not her dad, but your name is on the birth certificate. Take her with you. Give her to your family or something."

She coughed into her hand and then lit another cigarette.

"You all need to go. I have somewhere I need to be." She slid her feet into shoes and grabbed a jacket off the chair next to her. "I don't know where she is. Come back tomorrow and maybe she'll be here."

As she got up and started to walk away Jackson grabbed her thin arm, ignoring the marks on her arms. He tried to remember the person he'd met fourteen years ago. A young woman and her sister traveling and having adventures.

"What about Jade?"

Gloria laughed, a croaking sound that ended in a cough. "Take her, Jackson. I don't want her. Give her to your girlfriend. Take her to your family. Or call the police and have them pick her up. I've had a good time not worrying about her."

"Really?" Madeline stepped between Gloria and the door. "Is that really how you feel about your daughter?"

Gloria stopped to grab a beat-up, dirty purse. "Get out of my house."

"No, I want to know if that's how you really feel about your child." Madeline shook so hard Jackson didn't know if she'd stay on her feet or fall over. But she didn't appear to be about to back down. She had the look of a mother tiger about to do battle for her cub and he wanted to hug her.

"Look around you." Gloria swung a thin arm around the dirty living room. "This is it. This is all I have. One more mouth to feed. That's what Jade is. She needs stuff. She's always wanting new clothes. She wants to go places."

"You'll sign over custody?" Jackson stepped close to

Madeline. "I'll get a lawyer tomorrow and have something temporary drawn up."

"Yeah, sure." Gloria's eyes glistened. "I'll sign."

Jackson pulled out his wallet. "Take this."

"You buying my kid, Jackson?"

"No, Gloria, I'm helping out someone who used to be a friend."

Gloria motioned them out of her house without saying anything and then she walked down the sidewalk. Jackson stood on the front porch, unsure of how this whole situation had happened.

"What do I do now?" He glanced down at Madeline.

"Find your daughter?"

Yeah, and he had no idea where to start. Somewhere on this street of mostly dark houses, a few with a sprinkling of Christmas lights or a tree showing through a window, Jade had taken refuge. She was hiding from them, thinking he had let her down.

Madeline reached for his hand. "We'll find her."

We.

Chapter Fifteen

They didn't find her. Madeline woke up the next morning with the sun peeking through the heavy curtains of the hotel and an empty feeling in the region of her heart. They'd driven for hours. They'd stopped and asked people on the street if they'd seen a young girl. They'd called the local police for help.

Jade had disappeared. Madeline looked at the other bed, still made. Jade should have been in that bed. She should have been safe, knowing that Jackson loved her the way a father loved a daughter.

That thought did fill Madeline's heart. It filled up empty spaces, that Jackson could love Jade that way, in a way that would make a girl like Jade feel safe, secure, not afraid. If only Jade knew.

Madeline forced herself to get up and get ready for another day. She prayed, the way they'd stopped and prayed last night, she and Jackson, that they'd find Jade safe. She closed her eyes thinking of that moment that Jackson had reached for her hand and said they'd forgotten something.

How could they have forgotten to pray?

She opened her eyes and looked in the mirror. She prayed again, but this time for herself, not for Jade. Her heart had moved into foreign and very dangerous territory. Her heart, crazy, inexperienced organ that it was, wanted to run away with emotions that were new.

Someone pounded on her door. She peeked through the peephole and saw Jackson standing in the hall. He had his hat in his hands and he was looking up, waiting. She pulled the door open.

"Any news?"

He shook his head. "None. Let's grab some breakfast and we'll see if we can find her."

Madeline looked back into her room. "Should I pack my stuff?"

"No, I already reserved the rooms for a second night. If we find Jade, we can go home, but if we don't, we have a place to come back to."

"We'll find her." She grabbed her purse and coat and pulled the door closed behind her. "She's hurt and she's running but she'll be back."

Hurt and running were two things Madeline knew from experience.

Outside the hotel it was difficult to tell that there were any problems in the world. They'd stayed in a quaint section of Oklahoma City called Bricktown. Arriving late last night Madeline had seen the twinkling of Christmas lights and heard music, but neither of them had been in the mood to enjoy the city.

They'd gotten a cup of coffee and headed to their individual rooms. Now, Bricktown surrounded them. Bricktown, once a warehouse district, a place where industry thrived, had been reinvented, and turned into an entertainment district with restaurants and other attractions.

They walked along the canal, watching steam rise from the water. Neither talked for a long time.

"We should eat something." Jackson led her toward a restaurant that appeared to be open. "I could use coffee."

"That sounds good." Madeline walked through the door he opened for her.

Weeks ago she would have looked down, avoided touching him as she walked through the door of the Mad Cow. Today she looked up, smiled and hoped he'd return the gesture. She wanted to comfort him, to reassure him.

The door eased closed. Jackson leaned, touching his forehead to hers. "Thank you."

She nodded, still close to him, unable to move away. "You're welcome."

"What am I going to do with a kid?" He laughed a little and then pulled back from her. "What was I thinking?"

"You were thinking that Jade needs a family and you can give her a wonderful family."

The hostess led them to a table. When they were seated Jackson reached for her hands. "I'm not a family. I'm me. I'm a single, almost thirty-four-year-old man who has never had a relationship that lasted longer than two months. To be honest, Madeline, you're about the best relationship I've ever had."

"That's not promising, is it?" She pulled her hands from his and reached for the menu, a laminated card stuck between the sugar bowl and the napkin holder.

"I think it is." He nodded at the waitress when she brought a pot of coffee to their table.

Madeline smiled up at the waitress. "I'll take biscuits and gravy."

Jackson ordered the same. "I called a lawyer this morning. He's a friend of my brother Blake's and he lives here in Oklahoma City. He's writing something up for us and he's going to meet us at Gloria's."

"That's good. I only wish we could find Jade and tell her."

"We're going to find her. I'm not leaving here without her."

After they'd finished eating, they walked the block to the parking garage. Jackson spent part of the time talking on the phone, first to his parents, then the police and then the lawyer. Finally he slid the phone into his pocket and Madeline asked the question that had been on her mind since the previous day.

"Jackson, from the very beginning, you seemed to know that Jade wasn't yours."

He pulled out his truck key and kept walking. Madeline had to pick up her pace to keep up. He had her door open and she stopped, waiting for him to answer. He helped her in the truck and then he stood in the open door.

"I knew she wasn't mine because I can't have kids." He closed the door and walked away.

Madeline leaned back in the seat, closing her eyes against the pain she'd seen in his eyes. When he got in next to her she opened her eyes and looked at him. He started the truck and shifted into Reverse without speaking.

"I'm sorry. It's none of my business."

"No, it isn't. But now you know. She isn't mine. It was never possible. I had a bad case of the mumps as a kid…" His voice trailed off and he focused on driving.

"But you didn't tell her. You allowed her to stay."

Jackson sighed and yanked off his hat. He tossed it on the seat between them and he didn't look at her. Madeline reached, touching her fingers to his. He moved his hand so that their fingers laced together.

"Madeline, I let her stay because I thought 'what if?' And I let her stay because she was a kid who wanted a family bad enough she was willing to hitch a ride and forge a note to find one. I also didn't want her taken into custody, not at Christmas."

"So am I the only one who knows your secret?"

"That I can't have kids? My family knows."

She shook her head. "No, I mean the other secret. The part about you being one of the most decent men in Dawson."

"You've forgotten that I'm the Jackson that dates a different woman every week. I'm the guy who keeps my mother and grandmother on their knees praying I'll come back to church."

"Right, you're that Jackson." But he wasn't that Jackson at all. Not anymore.

He glanced at her and laughed. "Don't get that look in your eyes like you've discovered something wonderful and noble about me, or some secret that explains my wicked ways. I am who I am, Madeline."

They finished the drive to Gloria's in silence. Madeline didn't need to ask for further explanations. Jackson was who he was. Note to self: don't get attached to a cowboy who breaks hearts for a hobby. Even when that cowboy is noble to the core.

* * *

Jade was sitting on the front porch of her mother's house. Jackson pulled up and a big, dark blue sedan pulled up right behind him. That would be the lawyer and his wife, the notary. As Jackson got out of the truck, Jade walked into the house, ignoring him.

Madeline was ignoring him, too. That was for the best. She was tea. He was coffee. She would someday want to get married and have babies. He could picture her in a little house, a baby in her arms, some nice guy coming home from his office job.

He wanted to hurt that nice guy with the office job. But right now wasn't the time to be plotting against fictional people in Madeline's life. Now he had to deal with Jade. That had to be his focus.

"George, do you have the paper?" Jackson held his hand out, shook the hand of the lawyer and then took the paper he handed over.

"Right here. Are you sure about this?"

"Yeah, I'm sure. I've never been more sure about anything." Almost anything. Madeline stood a short distance away. When he smiled at her she looked away.

Gloria opened the front door of her house and dragged her daughter out. Jade jerked away from her mother. She stood on the porch, still wearing the clothes she'd worn the day before. Today, though, her look of defiance had multiplied. She seemed to be daring all of them to speak to her.

Madeline didn't seem to care what Jade's look said. She walked right up the steps and gathered the girl into her arms. She whispered and Jade shot him a look. Her eyes got big, watered, and her nose turned pink.

What in the world was he thinking?

"Jade, do you want to go home with me?" He handed the paper to Gloria. "Sign this."

She jerked it from his hand and looked it over. "Fine, give me a pen and get her out of here."

Her words were cold, callous. Jackson didn't know if Jade noticed, but her mother's eyes didn't reflect that tone. Her eyes watered and she had to look away, to brush the tears from her cheeks.

Gloria signed the paper. Jackson signed it. The lawyer signed it. Jackson turned to Jade. "Hug your mother."

"She isn't my mother."

Madeline gasped and Jackson shot her a look. He didn't need another emotional female in this mix. He turned to Jade, now officially in his custody. "Hug your mother."

Jade had walked off the porch but she stomped back up the steps and she hugged Gloria. Gloria held her tight for a minute and then let her go quick. She stepped back and looked away. "You go with Jackson and try to behave. I want you to visit."

"She'll visit." Jackson didn't know what to do now. This time he let Madeline handle it. She hugged Gloria and gave her a phone number. In case she needed anything.

They were walking down the sidewalk when Gloria ran down and grabbed Jade again. She held her daughter tight and then whispered, "I did my best. I'm sorry."

Jade stared at her mother, unsure. "I know. Thank you for letting me go with Jackson."

"Yeah, okay." And then Gloria ran back up the steps and into the house.

"Let's go home." Jackson opened the door. Madeline

climbed in last this time. She put Jade between them and he figured that said it all.

On the drive home he had plenty of time to think about the situation he'd put himself in. Jade slept next to him, her head resting on Madeline's shoulder. Madeline had fallen asleep as well.

He turned the radio on low but he didn't hear the music. He had too much to think about. Like what in the world would he do with a teenager? He didn't want to dump Jade on his parents. He'd take her to his sister Heather and then figure out a plan. He guessed he'd need a live-in housekeeper. He'd also have to put her in school as soon as possible.

When he stopped to pick up the trailer, Madeline woke up.

"I guess we're not home?"

He shook his head. "Just an hour out of the city."

By the time he got back in the truck she had fallen back to sleep. He looked at her, sleeping like that, and he wondered what it would be like, to have a life with a woman like Madeline. A man would be blessed to have her as a wife.

He wanted to be that man.

In thirty-three years he'd never had that thought. Not this way, in a way that settled in his gut, twisted him up inside. Yeah, there had been women, most of them not exactly the kind he'd take home to his mother, that he'd dreamed about marrying.

This woman, though, she'd gotten under his skin. He could see her raising a bunch of kids, growing old with a guy, having grandchildren.

Children and grandchildren. He knew someday she'd

have those things. She'd have everything she deserved. But not with him.

She'd get married. He'd stay in his old farmhouse, raising Jade, sometimes dating. Maybe he wouldn't date. That game was getting old, as old as he was.

He drove through Dawson, one main street, convenience store, feed store, Vera's. He waved as a neighboring farmer walked out of the feed store. At the edge of town he turned on the paved county road that led to Cooper property, and Madeline's little house in the middle of the vast acreage that belonged to his family.

"Madeline, we're almost there."

She woke up, blinked a few times and rubbed sleep from her eyes. "Wow, I slept the entire way?"

"We had a rough day yesterday. You needed the sleep."

When he pulled in her driveway, she gathered up her purse and overnight bag. "I would walk you to the door, but I'd better get her home."

"That's okay, I'm a big girl." She smiled at him, a sweet as honey smile. "Goodbye, Jackson."

He tipped his hat and smiled. "Goodbye, Madeline."

She had already jumped out of the truck and was going up the sidewalk to her front door. She stopped on the porch and waved.

Goodbye, Madeline. As she drove to the community center for practice, Madeline tried to forget that empty goodbye a few days ago. She'd known when she stepped into Jackson's life that he was a player. She'd known that the only reason he'd dragged her into his life was to help him with Jade.

She parked her car and walked up to the church. Beth Hightree met her at the steps.

"You look down tonight."

"I'm not down. I mean, not really. I'm just tired."

Beth nodded and Madeline thought she'd let it go. It would be good if she let it go. "I heard that Jackson brought Jade back home with him."

"He did."

"And she isn't his?" Beth walked with her through the old church sanctuary.

"Nope. But his name is on her birth certificate."

"Amazing. He's always had a big heart."

A big heart. Madeline nodded but she didn't want to talk about this anymore. She wanted to forget that Jackson had a big heart, that he cared about people. She wanted to remember him the way she used to think of him, as the man who knew how to charm, to smile and flirt but not remember a woman's name.

Beth continued to stare at her, obviously wanting an answer.

"He has a big heart." There, she'd agreed. Now let it go. Move on.

Beth laughed a little and reached to hug Madeline. "Oh, honey, you've fallen in love with that awful rogue."

"No, I haven't." Madeline reached for her shepherd's robe. "I helped him out when he needed help. End of story. Which is why I haven't talked to him since Saturday." She hadn't meant to add that.

"And you're going to let it go, just like that? Maybe he's been busy with Jade and hasn't had a spare minute to get in touch with you." Beth helped her pull down the rough, cotton gown. She handed Madeline the belt.

"Or maybe he's moved on. He's Jackson Cooper. Isn't that what he does?"

Beth took the belt from her hands and looped it twice around her waist, tying it at the side.

"In the past that's what he did. But I think he probably misses you as much as you miss him."

"This isn't me missing him. This is me being tired and ready for Christmas to be over."

"Right, you want Christmas to be over. You love Christmas."

"I do love Christmas." She loved the music, the decorations and most of all what the story meant to her life and to her faith. "I love it without the drama. And I don't mean the living nativity. I mean Jackson drama, Jade, and now my mother."

"She's contacted you again?"

Madeline pulled the shawl over her head to cover her hair.

"She wants to see me."

"You can't."

Madeline met her friend's concerned gaze. "I think I have to. I've thought about not seeing her. But I think I need closure. I need to face her. I have to do this or it will always control me."

"If you want, I'll go with you."

They hugged and Madeline nodded. "I'd love for you to go with me. I'm not running anymore, Beth. I'm not going to flee in fear that she'll find me. If I face her, I won't have to run again. I can stay here and let this be my home."

"I'm glad because I wouldn't want you to leave." Beth smiled a teasing smile. "And I think Jackson would miss you, too."

"I think what we need to do is get up there for this last practice."

Because she could only deal with one thing at a time. She would deal with her mother, with forgiving. Jackson was something she didn't want to think about. She didn't want to think about how he made her feel, or how much it hurt to think of that very quiet goodbye.

Jackson had needed a friend. Madeline smiled as they walked out of the dressing room. "You know, I'm just the person a guy calls when he needs a really big favor."

"I think the Jackson I know, that I grew up with, doesn't call a woman to rescue him."

No, he didn't call at all. He said goodbye without even adding the cliché, "I'll call you." Goodbye means goodbye.

Chapter Sixteen

A few days before Christmas, Jackson walked through his house and it hit him that everything felt empty. Jade was staying with his grandmother for a few days. Madeline hadn't spoken to him since the day he dropped her off at her house.

The Christmas tree lights were unplugged. There were no gifts under his tree. It felt as much like Christmas as a hot day in July. Jackson Cooper, this is your life. This was reality.

He'd always liked it this way, empty, clean, quiet. Until it got filled up with Jade and Madeline, this life had been fine with him. They'd given him a brief glimpse into another world.

The doorbell chimed and the dog ran through the living room barking. Jackson yelled that he'd be there in a minute. When he opened the door his grandmother marched in, looking like a woman on a mission. With his grandmother, it was all about appearances. She had on her favorite hat, gloves and a dress coat over a pantsuit. And everyone knew that Myrna Cooper loved her blue jeans. Suits were only for business and church. He grinned as she swooped in and he knew that he was her business.

"Where's Jade?" He looked behind her, looked at her car parked sideways in the drive.

"She's with Heather. They went Christmas shopping. Dear goodness, turn on some lights, this place looks and feels like a morgue. It's Christmas. Are you Scrooge?"

She walked ahead of him, flipping on lights, opening curtains. She plugged in the tree. "Nice tree. Buy some decorations next year."

"I like the homemade ones." Made by Madeline and Jade.

"Well, I never thought of you as the pitiful grandson."

"What does that mean?" He followed her into the kitchen where she turned on the coffeemaker. "I hear Travis brought a woman home with him. Harden's daughter?"

"Yeah, she's a looker."

Jackson laughed. "Gram, you're one of a kind."

She shrugged bony shoulders and turned to point a finger at him. Rings sparkled and bracelets clinked on her arms. "You're a mess."

"Could you explain what this visit is all about?"

"I'm here to save you."

"I think I've been saved. I'm even back in church. What more could you want?"

"I'm here to save you from your pitiful self. It was sweet of you to bring Jade back and give her a home, but you can't expect the rest of the family to raise her."

"I'm going to raise her."

"I know you are. You're going to find yourself a wife and you're going to raise that child the way she deserves, with you as a dad and with a decent woman as a mom."

"Gram, I'm not getting married."

"Oh, posh, stop that nonsense." She pulled a ring off her finger and handed it to him. "This ring was my grandmother's. I guess it's older than dirt, but it means something to me. It's about family, about history. You take this ring and you ask Madeline Patton to marry you."

He choked a little and put the ring back in her hand. "I don't know what you're up to, Gram, but I'm not asking Madeline to marry me."

"You hard-headed fool. That girl loves you and I'm pretty sure you love her, too."

He poured two cups of coffee. "I'm not in love. She helped me out. We're friends."

She frowned at him. "You're going to make me lose my witness if you don't stop acting so noble. Fine, you aren't sure. Date her for a while and then ask her to marry you."

"I'm not going to marry Madeline Patton."

Gram patted his cheek with a cool hand. He braced himself for it. Three little pats and then a good whack. He blinked and shook his head.

"Jackson, stop feeling sorry for yourself. Marry the girl."

She pushed the ring back into his hand. "And I don't want your coffee. It's always too strong and it gives me heartburn. I want you to invite Madeline to Christmas with the Coopers. She shouldn't be alone and you shouldn't want her to be alone."

"I'll think about it."

That pointy finger poked him in the gut. "You'd better do more than think about it. Now, I'm going home and I want you to get out of this house and go Christmas shopping. This place is a disgrace."

"Thanks, Gram, glad you approve."

She laughed as she walked through the house, grabbing her coat on her way out the door. "I love you, Jackson. You're my favorite."

"Gram, you say that to all of us."

She turned, smiling big. "I mean it, too."

That evening Jackson took Jade to see the living nativity. They took the tour of Bethlehem, met the innkeeper who turned Mary and Joseph away and then were led to the manger where the baby Jesus had been born. Through the crowds of people Jackson watched for the shepherdess who had touched his heart in a way he'd never expected.

Six months ago his brother Lucky had told him that someday he'd pay. He guessed this was what Lucky had meant. A woman had finally changed everything for him. She made him think about someone sitting next to him in those rocking chairs on his front porch.

He watched as she kneeled before Mary, Joseph and the baby Jesus. From Heather he'd learned that two days ago she had gone to Tulsa to see her mother. Beth had gone with her. He should have been the one to go with her.

Angels sang. The people in the crowd sang. The story of the birth of Jesus. The lighted star cast a bright light over the area, illuminating everything. Including the tears streaking down Madeline's cheeks.

"Are we going to talk to Madeline?" Jade had hold of his hand. Today he'd gone shopping and when Heather brought Jade to his house, the girl had screamed and raced around the house because of the gifts under the tree. His grandmother had been right. He'd played the part of Scrooge a little too well.

"Yes, we'll talk to her."

Jade led him through the crowd. Madeline had walked away from the other shepherds. She saw them heading her way and she froze.

"Madeline." Jackson didn't know what to say. He tried to remember a time in his life when a woman had left him speechless.

This had to be a first.

"Jackson." She smiled at Jade. "Hey, Jade, how are you?"

"I'm great. I have a ton of presents under the tree. And there are some for you, too."

"What?" Her gaze shot to Jackson's, asking questions.

The ball was in his court.

"We were wondering if you'd come to Christmas with us."

She looked at Jade and then at him. "Christmas?"

"With us," he repeated.

"Please." Jade grabbed her hand. "It won't be Christmas if you aren't with us."

Jackson reached for Jade. "She might have other plans. Do you have other plans?"

"No, I don't have other plans."

"Then you'll come." Jade didn't let her answer, but grabbed her in an exuberant hug. "Yeah!"

"Jade, she didn't say she would." Jackson shook his head. "I'm sorry."

"I'll go with you. What time?"

"We'll pick you up Christmas morning. Early. Maybe seven."

"I'll be ready."

Jackson took a step back because it would have been easy to reach out, to hold her. When it came to Madeline he was still fighting for self-control.

Christmas with the Coopers. Madeline spent the next two days worrying, telling herself not to worry, being excited and then telling herself to stop. She had to get control of her emotions, shove them back in a box where they were safe.

Jackson had invited her for Jade's sake. Or maybe because the Coopers knew she'd be alone and they were just being polite. She didn't have to be alone on Christmas. Just over an hour away she had a mother living in Tulsa. Not that she was ready for serious family bonding with Marjorie. Not yet. They had talked. Marjorie had explained about growing up being shipped from relative to relative, getting pregnant and being on the streets until she'd formed a friendship with a group of people she thought would take care of her.

Madeline felt sorry for her mother. But the scars of the past were deep and healing would take time.

Beth Hightree had offered to let Madeline spend Christmas with her family, the Bradshaws. She didn't want to intrude on their family gathering, either. Yet she'd said yes to Jackson and Jade.

She'd even bought them gifts. Books for Jade because she loved to read. For Jackson, a coffee mug and gourmet coffee. She'd made candy to take for the rest of the Coopers. And there were a lot of them. Although a few would be missing. Reese had recently been sent to

Afghanistan. Dylan had taken a load of bulls to California and on his way home he'd hit bad weather. He wouldn't be home for a day or two. That meant he'd miss Christmas with his family.

On Christmas morning she paced the living room, waiting for Jackson to show up. Hadn't he said he'd pick her up? What if he'd meant for her to drive herself? She paced back to the kitchen because she didn't want to look overly eager should he show up. If he hadn't changed his mind.

Her heart kept telling her to trust him, to give him a chance. If she didn't want to be judged for her past, Jackson shouldn't be judged for his. Not that he'd been the victim. She groaned at the wild storm of thoughts sweeping through her mind.

Deep breath, calm down. He hadn't invited her for any reason other than that Jade probably wanted her there. Another deep breath. That made perfect sense. Jade had missed her.

The doorbell rang and the puppy, cast-free now, ran in circles, barking and jumping. Madeline slowed her pace and walked calmly to the door. She opened it and a bouquet of flowers and balloons attacked.

"Oops, sorry." Jackson moved the bouquet and smiled.

Her heart did a triple back flip. He grinned and pushed his hat back a little.

"What's this?"

He handed her the vase. "Merry Christmas."

"Thank you." She tried to smell the white roses and red carnations but balloon strings were everywhere. "These probably don't mess on the floor or chew up slippers."

"Not that I've heard of, but if they do, let me know." He followed her inside and she carried the vase of flowers to the kitchen table.

When Madeline turned, he was standing right behind her. She stepped back and looked up, afraid, excited, a million different things at once. Afraid of him, afraid of what he'd say or wouldn't say.

"We should go." She reached for her purse.

"Where's your coat?"

"Hanging on the hall tree."

Jackson nodded and instead of walking away, he reached for her hand to stop her. "You forgot to read the note on the flowers."

"I didn't see it."

Jackson reached for the note and opened it. He cleared his throat. "Allow me."

"Okay." Her voice trembled. Her hands trembled. Her heart did something that felt like trembling. Or longing?

"Dear Madeline, will you go steady with a cowboy who might be, very possibly is, in love with you?"

"Are you in love with me?"

"Honey, I'm so in love with you I can't see straight."

He touched her cheek. Then he leaned, still holding her close, and kissed her sweetly, stealing her heart, taking her places she'd never imagined. In his arms she was cherished. She was loved.

When he backed away, she rested her head on his shoulder. "I love you, too. I was just so afraid."

"Afraid?"

She nodded and then looked up. "Afraid that you wouldn't love me. Everything in my past, I just thought…"

He kissed her again. "You're strong, brave and beautiful. Yeah, sometimes that is too much. It floors me that you're even standing here with a renegade like me."

"I don't know what to say." She didn't know what she could say, not without losing it right there, standing in front of him.

"Madeline, you have to go into this knowing that I can't have children. I'll adopt as many as you want to fill that old farmhouse with. But that's something I've been running from for a long time."

"We have Jade."

"We." He hugged her tight. "I love it when we're a 'we.'"

Jackson reached into his pocket, laughing a little at the surprised look on Madeline's face. "I know we just started going steady—" he glanced at his watch "—two minutes ago, so this probably seems like the shortest courtship in the world, but I have another question I'd like to ask, and if I don't do this right, my grandmother is going to flog me good."

"Okay."

"Now bear with me, I'm not as young as I used to be and you might have to help me get up."

She laughed. He shot her a look, trying to appear offended that she'd laugh at him.

"Jackson, please don't."

"Are you really going to laugh at a man who is trying to propose the way his Gram expects him to propose, the way a gentleman proposes?"

She laughed until tears sprang from her eyes. Jackson reached for a napkin on the kitchen table and handed it to her.

"Now let's start over. And please, no laughing. I got

a two-hour lesson on courting and proposals last night."
He winked and Madeline turned pink. "I think Gram
might have mentioned that the courting part of the process should last at least six months and then the proposal. But I've always been a renegade when it comes
to love. I'm afraid if I don't get this ring on your finger,
you'll chicken out or realize I'm not much of a catch."

"Jackson, I love you. But really, I do think we should,
um, date? For a few months at least."

"Stop talking, you're throwing me off my groove.
You know, I used to have a groove until you came along
and completely threw me for a loop." He took off his
hat and tossed it on the table. With her hand in his
he dropped to one knee and fished the ring out of his
pocket again.

"Please, stop." Tears poured down her cheeks. Jackson stopped.

"Are you going to say no?" He didn't know how long
he could stay on one knee. He wasn't many weeks this
side of being tossed into a wall.

She shook her head. "I'm not going to say no, but it's
so much and it's Christmas and…"

He grinned big and she smiled. "And you love me because I'm crazy and nothing like any other man you've
ever met. Madeline, you need a man like me, someone
strong and stubborn. I'm not going to let you go. I'm
not going to hurt you."

The ring in his hand, more than a hundred years old,
sparkled and the metal heated in his hand. He slid it on
her finger. "My great-grandfather gave this ring to his
wife. When my grandmother got married, they gave it
to her to wear. She wanted you to have it because she
wanted you to know that when you marry me, you're a

Cooper. We marry for life and we hold on to each other through life's storms."

"Did your grandmother tell you to say all of that?"

He grinned and shook his head, but then he nodded. "Some of it."

Madeline fell to her knees in front of him. He forgot about his aching knees when she cupped his cheeks in her sweet hands and moved close, touching her lips to his.

He forgot about everything but Madeline and how it felt to hold her in his arms. He'd spent a lifetime thinking he'd never get caught, only to find out that it wasn't about getting caught, it was about falling. And falling.

With Madeline, he thought he'd be falling in love with her for the rest of their lives. He told her that and she wrapped her arms around his neck and buried her face in his shoulder.

"Madeline, will you marry me?"

She nodded. "I will."

"Then you'd better help me up and we'd better get to the house before they send out a search party."

She stood, reaching for his hands and pulling him to his feet.

"Where's Jade?" Madeline's eyes watered and her nose was pink.

"I'm right here."

They turned and Jade was standing in the door of the kitchen with Angel the puppy. "I think that was about the sappiest proposal ever."

Madeline reached for his hand and held it tight. "I think it was the sweetest proposal ever."

Jade ran forward and hugged them both. "The best

part is that I'm going to have a family. Merry Christmas!"

"Merry Christmas, Jade." Jackson hugged the girl who was his. It didn't matter what the DNA test said—in his heart, she was his daughter. They were a family, and he'd never had a better Christmas or been more blessed in his life.

Epilogue

June

Jade looked out the window of the Sunday school classroom they were using to dress for the wedding and she whistled softly. "Maddie, you have to see this."

Beth ran to the window and shook her head. "No, Jade, she doesn't. It's a surprise."

Madeline tried to slide past Beth but several pairs of hands caught her and kept her from getting a look outside.

"No, ma'am, don't even think about it." Angie Cooper held her veil. "Jackson went to a lot of trouble and you're not going to ruin it for him."

Madeline closed her eyes but she giggled. "You remember his proposal, right?"

Angie laughed. "He couldn't walk right for a week. And he was supposed to keep the ring until after you'd dated a few months."

"Exactly. So I really need to see what's out there. Someone, please?" Madeline looked around the room, hoping for someone willing to spill the secret. Her bridesmaids, Jenna, Beth, Heather and Jade, all shook their heads.

The only other person in the room shook her head, too. Madeline's mother, Marjorie, was a thin, tiny woman. She no longer looked beaten down by life. Her eyes had a spark that hadn't been there months ago when they'd met in Tulsa. They were getting to know each other again.

Madeline had a family. She smiled at Jade, remembering a teenager who had defied everyone to get that exact same thing for herself.

Jade twirled in her pale yellow dress. "I love this dress."

"Don't get it dirty," Madeline warned. "Or trip over the hem."

"I won't." Jade weaved, dizzy from turning in circles. "I wish I could go to Hawaii with you."

"Sorry, this is a honeymoon for two. When we get home we'll take you to Florida, remember?"

"I remember." Jade's smile brightened. "And I get to stay with Grandma Angie while you're gone."

"Yes, you do." Madeline looked in the mirror at her simple, white dress. Straight lines, no beading or lace. She'd never thought about weddings or what she would wear. She'd never dreamed of honeymoons or even the man who would change her life.

And yet he had existed anyway. All of those years of closing herself off, afraid to feel, afraid of being hurt again, and God already had the perfect man for her.

Jackson Cooper. She smiled at her reflection in the mirror. In a million years she wouldn't have thought e would be the one. It wasn't that long ago that she'd avoided looking him in the eye when he helped pick up her spilled groceries.

Today he would stand before God, in the presence of these people, and he would become her husband.

She would become Madeline Cooper. Maddie Cooper. She closed her eyes as love and contentment overflowed. When she opened them, Beth stood behind her, smiling.

"Look what God did, Madeline. He took all of your fears, your past, your insecurity upon Himself and gave you this new life, this new hope."

The door opened. Jackson's sister Sophia, self-appointed wedding coordinator, smiled and motioned them all out the door.

"Time to get this show on the road."

"Very romantic, Sophie." Heather patted her sister on the cheek as they filed out of the room.

"I don't have time for romance."

"Of course you do." Angie Cooper shook her head and then kissed her older daughter's cheek. "Romance will find you."

Tim Cooper, Jackson's dad, stood at the entrance to the church sanctuary, ready to walk Madeline down the aisle. He looked so handsome in his Western-cut tuxedo. But Madeline's gaze slid past him to the front of the church. Tim placed her hand on his arm and they started down the aisle, the bridesmaids walking in front of them.

Madeline had eyes only for the man at the front of the church. Jackson Cooper, the man she would spend her life with. Fifteen minutes later he slipped a wedding band on her finger, sliding it against the ring his grandmother had provided. They said "I do" and he pulled her to him, kissing her as if he would never let her go. And then he led her down the aisle and out the doors of the church.

To her surprise a white open carriage was parked in front of the church. Adorned with white roses, it was pulled by four white horses. A man in white livery stood next to the door of the carriage, holding it open for them.

"Surprise." Jackson leaned and kissed her cheek.

"It's a wonderful surprise."

"Throw the bouquet," someone shouted.

Madeline turned her back to the crowd and tossed the yellow daisies and white roses. The bouquet landed right in Sophia Cooper's hands.

* * * * *

Dear Reader,

Welcome to Cooper Creek! I've gotten very attached to Dawson, Oklahoma, and to the Cooper family. With twelve siblings I think there will be plenty to keep us busy. Most importantly there will be plenty of cowboys. And of course wonderful heroines who make it easy for those cowboys to fall in love.

Jackson Cooper has been around Dawson for a while and it seemed only fitting that he be the first hero in this series. Jackson has watched his friends and neighbors falling in love and getting married. He warned Wyatt Johnson that Rachel Waters would get under his skin. For some reason, Jackson Cooper, resident ladies' man, thought he was immune to love.

Like so many of us, Jackson had his ideas about his life. God had a different set of plans. So make a cup of coffee, or tea, put on some Christmas music and step into the world of Dawson, Oklahoma, at Christmas time.

Blessings,

Brenda Minton

Questions for Discussion

1. Madeline Patton finds herself in a situation she wants to walk away from. Instead she puts herself and her heart on the line by agreeing to allow Jade Baker to stay in her home. Why would she make that decision?

2. Jackson Cooper asks Madeline to let Jade stay with her. He has several reasons. What are they? Do you agree with the choices he made?

3. Jackson is torn when he looks up Madeline on the internet. Like so many of us, he was curious. But learning her story put him in a situation where he had more knowledge than perhaps he had wanted. How does this information change his relationship with her?

4. Jackson has a certain reputation, but as we get to know him we see that being a "ladies' man" is just one facet of his personality and life. Who is the real Jackson Cooper?

5. Madeline receives a card from her mother that she doesn't immediately open. Why doesn't she want to face her mother's words? What would you have done?

6. Why has Madeline been in the habit of moving? Why is it important for her to stay in Dawson?

7. Jackson goes back to church. Did he have a real reason for walking away from his faith?

8. Why do you think Madeline sleeps with the lights on? She has faith but still struggles with fear. How does Jackson help her through these fears? How does she help herself?

9. Madeline is hurt by what she sees as Jackson's rejection. How does this draw her out of her shell?

10. Why is Jackson being so careful in his relationship with Madeline?

11. Jackson remembers the chorus of his grandmother's favorite hymn. The lines in the chorus are "No turning back, no turning back." What do the words mean to Jackson in his personal growth? In his relationship?

12. Jackson knew from the beginning that Jade couldn't be his child and yet he allowed her to stay. Why do you think he allowed her to stay?

13. Madeline has forgiven her mother but there is still pain. Is it realistic to think she should give in and develop a relationship with her mother or is caution the best way to handle this relationship?

14. Jackson and Madeline fall in love rather quickly and both realize that they need more time to get to know one another. Love is based on more than immediate attraction. What is the basis for their relationship, beyond those first feelings of chemistry?

HER HOLIDAY FIREMAN

Kathleen Y'Barbo

In memory of Ryan Euan,
for a life well lived in a time far too short, and
for those in whose hearts he will continue to live.

As charcoal to embers and as wood to fire,
so is a quarrelsome man for kindling strife.
—*Proverbs* 26:21

"It's just dinner."
—Robert Turner

Chapter One

"Leah, somebody needs to tell the guy at table seven that we closed twenty minutes ago. He just ordered another plate of fried shrimp then had the nerve to ask me to bring him a dessert menu."

Leah Berry looked up from the list she was making to see the young waitress scowling at the offending customer. Dark hair, muscles and a leave-me-alone expression marked him as a guy who wasn't expecting company or, apparently, planning to leave, even though the sign on the door was clearly marked with the news that Pop's Seafood Shack was only open for lunch on Wednesdays until 3:00 p.m. from the first of November through the end of the year. It was now 3:20 p.m.

Much as Leah needed to get over to the stables and see to the horses, it wasn't worth losing a customer over. If she'd learned anything since she left her curator's job at The Galveston Preservation Society last spring to run the family restaurant, it was that the customer came first.

"Be nice and go fill his tea glass," she said firmly. "And smile when you hand him that menu."

The waitress, barely out of her teens and more set on a modeling career than one in food service, opened her mouth to complain then obviously thought better of it. Kate Murdoch hadn't quite taken to being a waitress but she was willing to work for what the restaurant could afford to pay her during the winter season. Plus, her father was the mayor of Vine Beach and an old friend of Pop's. Much as Leah hoped Kate made a success of her modeling dreams, she didn't wish for it to happen soon.

Grabbing a menu with one hand and the tea pitcher with the other, Kate wound her way through the maze of tables to where the stranger sat mesmerized by the view of the Gulf beyond the wide expanse of windows. He offered the waitress a nod then went back to gazing at the water again. Leah watched to make sure the future super model offered no evidence of her irritation.

"I told you we needed a rule about ordering all-you-can-eat in the last hour before closing," Kate said when she breezed past to deposit the empty plates. "He's picking at the shrimp and staring out the window. Seriously. I'm so over this."

"He probably just doesn't realize we're only open for lunch on Wednesdays," she offered to Kate's retreating back.

Orlando, her father's best pal and the only cook Pop's Seafood Shack had ever had, stepped into her line of sight. Arms crossed over his barrel chest, Orlando seemed to study the U.S. Navy tattoo on his forearm before lifting his gaze to Leah's.

"What?" she asked softly as she once again set her work aside. "We hold the kitchen open until the last diner's done. House rules, even on Wednesday. You know that."

"Don't get all riled up, Lee-Lee." The cook went back to studying the inked insignia as he managed a shrug. "Just thinking of the bottom line. Overtime for the two of us plus all that food the guy's putting away means you're losing a whole bunch of money. I'd put up the closed sign and flash the lights, if it were up to me."

Leah sighed.

He reached to touch her shoulder. "Look, kiddo, I know it ain't the way your pop would've done things but this is a new day." Orlando sent the diner at table seven an irritated look. "And new days call for new ways. That home you're keeping your father in ain't cheap, and I know you're not making enough here to cover what the insurance doesn't."

When Orlando got in a mood, humor was always the best remedy. "So you're saying I should stay open on Wednesday evenings, too? What would the choir down at Grace Bible do with their star baritone stuck behind a stove frying shrimp?"

Tossing his apron aside, the cook headed across the room, hit the switch on the open sign and slid the dead bolt on the door. When the guy ignored the gesture in favor of reaching for his tea glass and draining it, Orlando made a great show of returning to the kitchen. The diner, however, returned to his menu as if nothing had happened.

"Least now we guarantee no one else shows up," Orlando grumbled as he snatched his apron and stalked back to the grill.

The man in question looked up. Their gazes collided, and Leah nodded. Apparently it was time for dessert at table seven. She turned to call for Kate only to find her dressed in her street clothes. "Where do you think you're going?"

"I've got a date." She gestured to the clock on the kitchen wall. "Seriously, you remember what it's like to be in love, right?"

Not really. Leah bit back a response and nodded. "Go. This time."

Kate was gone before Leah could say anything further. Again the sole remaining diner met her gaze. Pasting on a smile, she grabbed for the order pad.

"Ready for dessert?" she said as sweetly as possible. "Pie's good today. Chocolate, coconut and—"

"Banana cream," he said along with her but his Texas drawl drowned out hers. "Yeah, I know." He set down the menu and she noticed his dark blue T-shirt emblazoned with the logo of the Houston Fire Department. "But what I'd really like is another round of redfish. Then we can talk about pie."

"Redfish," she echoed.

"Yeah. Is that a problem?" His gaze swept the room before once again focusing on her. "I'm surprised this place is so empty. The food's not bad."

Not bad? Leah opened her mouth to offer a candid response then thought better of it. "Well," she said carefully, "it *is* Wednesday."

"Yes," he said slowly but obviously without a clue, "it is."

Out of the corner of her eye, she spied Orlando walking toward the control box for the lights. Leah shot him a look before returning her attention to the diner.

"So…" Leah paused. "Redfish?"

"Redfish." He dismissed her by picking up his phone.

"Redfish," she echoed as she returned to the kitchen. "And not a word from you, please."

"Wasn't planning on it," Orlando said, though his expression stated the opposite.

She returned to the table with the tea pitcher in hand. "Sweet, right?"

This time, the fireman offered a dazzling smile. "Yes," he said as he pushed away his phone to offer up his tea glass. "Thank you."

His smile caught her by surprise. She glanced down at the brochures spread across the tabletop. "Looking to rent a place?"

He hurried to shove aside the pages. For a moment he seemed to be trying to decide how to answer.

Leah finished pouring the tea then set down his glass. "I didn't mean to pry. It's just that it's rare we get renters down here this time of year and…" His expression remained unreadable. "I'll just go check on your food."

When she pressed through the kitchen doors, Orlando gave her a look over his shoulder before nodding to the half-filled plate. Leah frowned and silently filled up the remainder of the platter with shrimp and headed toward the dining room. The old cook meant well, but she'd not let Pop's high standards slip for the sake of the balance sheet. If they lost money on the handsome fireman, so be it.

A covert glance told her the fireman had folded away his real estate papers. "Here you are," she said with a smile. "Is there anything else I can get you?"

"No, thanks."

"All right then. Enjoy." She tucked the tray under her arm and took a step away from the table.

"Wait."

Leah turned to scan the plate and then the table. "Did I forget something?"

His gaze was steady but his expression softer. "No. I did."

She waited a second before shaking her head. "I don't understand."

"My manners." He studied his hands then looked up at her. "It's not exactly my best…" The fireman shook his head. "No excuses. I've been rude. Please accept my apology."

Any lingering irritation at having to stay open well past closing time evaporated. "Hey, don't worry about it. We all have our bad days."

"Yeah," he said under his breath as he looked away.

An awkward silence fell. "Okay, well," Leah said, "I'll just let you enjoy your shrimp."

"Wait. If you're not in a hurry, can you answer some questions about Vine Beach?"

Ryan clamped his mouth shut. Had he actually asked a total stranger for help?

Yup, he had. But her eyes were kind. And he was tired of being alone. Especially today.

He dared a look at the redhead and saw that she seemed to be considering the question. "You don't have to," he hurried to add. "I mean I'm… I was just thinking maybe you could fill me in. I'm new here." He gestured to the stack of real estate listings, meager as they were. "Guess you already figured that out, though."

She glanced over her shoulder at the older fellow watching them from the kitchen door and then she nodded and sat. "Sure, why not?"

Ryan reached across the table to offer his hand. "I'm Ryan," he said as his gaze collided with wide green eyes, noted a sprinkling of freckles. "Ryan Owen."

"Pleased to meet you, Ryan Owen. I'm Leah." Her grasp was firm as she took his hand.

"Just Leah?" he said.

"Leah Berry." She paused only a second as if gauging whether the name held meaning to him. "So, what brings you to Vine Beach?"

There were a dozen possible answers. He decided on the easiest. "Work. Apparently the city's been without a fire chief since…"

"Since my father's illness," she supplied.

Now what? With those green eyes pointed in his direction, his mind went blank. "I'm sorry," he finally managed to say.

"No, it's fine. He's…well, it was time for him to retire. Welcome to Vine Beach," she said with the beginnings of a smile. "I'm glad the position's been filled. Pop would be glad, too."

He let out a long breath. "Maybe he could give me some pointers, then."

Her smile disappeared. "I don't know. He's not… well."

"Right. Sure." It didn't take a genius to figure out he'd just stomped all over a touchy subject. "So, anyway, I've kind of put everything off until the last minute and now I'm scrambling for a place to stay. I thought I'd just get a hotel room but apparently the hotel's closed until February."

"Yes, the owners spend the winter with their children in Florida. I always thought it was funny to leave one beach to vacation at another one." She chuckled.

"But then I'm easily amused. Anyway, I might be able to help you find a short-term rental until you can figure out where in Vine Beach you'd like to live permanently."

Permanently. That word and Vine Beach refused to fit in the same sentence as far as Ryan was concerned.

"Don't need much. It's just me and my dog." He reached for the real estate papers. "I can't make much sense of these. Looks like my choices are pretty slim. Either take a room over the beauty shop courtesy of my new boss or spend a whole bunch to rent a big place on the highway."

"Hmm...." She picked up the first paper and began to scan it. "Ima's Beauty Shop or the highway? Slim pickings indeed. Let me see if I recognize any other local addresses in here."

While she read, he watched, something that felt oddly natural given the reason for today's lunch. Mourning his late wife, Jenna, wouldn't bring her back, and neither would keeping the promises she'd extracted from him before she died.

And yet here he sat keeping at least one of them, the one about moving to the beach, while working hard to remember the others. Something about the redhead's smile made him feel better about giving up everything he'd worked for to come and live at the beach where he'd be starting over with not much hope for advancement. When a guy was chief of a department where he was the only paid employee, the only ladder to climb was the one on the ancient and apparently little-used fire truck.

"Here's one." Her gaze lifted to meet his. "It's two blocks from the high school and walking distance to downtown." She turned the paper around to point to an ad he'd somehow missed.

"Three bedrooms, one bath and a fenced yard," he read. "Sounds perfect. What's the number?"

He punched them into the phone as Leah read them off. A moment later, he had the landlord on the phone. "So it's already leased," he said after he'd given the man the reason for his call. "Thanks anyway."

Leah made a face and Ryan chuckled despite his dashed hopes. "Apparently the new science teacher at the high school got to the place before me. Oh well."

"Oh well indeed." She set the paper aside. "I'd offer our barn but I don't think it'd be too comfortable what with the holes in the roof and the lack of heat or plumbing."

He followed her gaze out the window toward a broad expanse of rolling grassland populated with a dozen or more golden palomino horses. Off in the distance was a building of substantial size, its wooden exterior silvered with age. Just beyond the barn was a smudge of black on the horizon, possibly the burned ruins of a home. His interest immediately piqued.

Ryan's attention returned to the barn. "Is that yours?"

"It is," she said, her voice soft, almost dreamlike. "It's been in the Berry family for generations. The house, too. Or, rather, it was until recently."

He shifted to look at the ruins again. "It burned?"

"Yes, back in March." She shook her head. "Hey, you know what? There are a whole bunch of weekly rentals here that I bet are sitting empty. I'd rent you ours but I'm living in it right now." She shook her head. "Don't ask."

He laughed. "All right. Any suggestions where to start?"

"I'll make a call. How can I reach you?"

Ryan tore off a corner of one of the real estate papers and reached for a pen. Jotting down his cell phone number, he handed it to Leah. "Don't need much. Just a place to sleep and maybe a yard for the dog. Beach view would be ideal, but I doubt that'll happen."

He could hope though. Nothing like waking up to the sound of waves just outside his door.

Leah's brows gathered. "You have not because you ask not. At least that's what the Bible says. So, you start asking and I'll make a call or two and see what I can find out. When do you need the place and how long are you planning to stay?"

"Now," he said. "Last week, really. It's already Wednesday and I start work Monday morning."

"Oh, goodness. Okay, so how long?"

"Six months?" By then he'd have fulfilled his promise to Jenna and could be on his way back to the Houston Fire Department. At least that had been the plan when he had applied for his leave of absence.

The redhead folded the paper in half and slipped it into the pocket of her jeans then rose. "I'll get right on this. In the meantime, can I bring you some pie? It's—"

"Banana cream," he said along with her. "Yes, please, but maybe I ought to get it to go."

Again her brows furrowed. "Why's that?"

He nodded toward the old cook who'd been eyeing them suspiciously for the past five minutes. "I'm guessing I've overstayed my welcome."

"Ignore Orlando. He tends to be a bit overprotective."

Ryan snatched up the check and opened his wallet. "Nothing wrong with that. So how about I settle up this bill while you box up a slice of pie?"

Only when he climbed behind the steering wheel of his Jeep with the pie on the seat beside him did the reality of what he'd just done hit him. Not only had he invited a strange woman to sit with him on what would have been his first wedding anniversary, but he'd ended up giving her his phone number.

Closing his eyes, Ryan rested his head on the back of the seat and let out a long breath. When would this get easier? As he backed out of the parking lot of Pop's Seafood Shack he had a feeling things were about to get a whole lot worse before they got better.

Chapter Two

Orlando now stood at the entrance, his stance unmistakably paternal. "What happened over there?"

"Just helping a stranger to find a place to live in Vine Beach. Apparently he's taking Pop's old job as fire chief." At Orlando's surprised expression, Leah continued, "It's fine. He seems nice. I told him I'd make a couple of calls."

"How about you let Riley Burkett help that stranger?"

She thought of the Realtor whose recent marriage to the town veterinarian's mother had caused him to scale back on his real estate business. "I thought he wasn't going to work during the off-season."

Orlando shrugged. "Won't know unless you ask him." His eyes narrowed. "Besides, you don't know this man from Adam and I'd rather you not get too involved in his personal life."

She shook her head. "Are you serious? I don't know a thing about Ryan other than the fact he's looking for a place here."

"Ryan is it?" Orlando shook his head.

Leah linked arms with Pop's best friend. "He's the new fire chief, remember? I was just being nice."

Orlando gave her a skeptical look before placing his weathered hand over hers. "Any fellow who wants to spend time with you will have to spend some time with me first."

She almost opened her mouth to remind Orlando that she was, in fact, well past the age where she needed that sort of supervision.

"I'll be sure to let you know soon as a fellow wants to spend time with me. Now, go on home. I don't mind finishing up here."

"I'll go, but lock the door behind you." Orlando paused to glance across the highway. "Guessing you'll make a stop at the stables before you go home."

She shrugged. "Until I can afford to hire someone to do it, I'm in charge there, too."

Orlando's expression softened. "Maybe it's time to let those horses…"

"Go?" Leah shook her head as she thought of the half-dozen palominos that were left of the once-expansive Berry herd. "I can't do that, Orlando. Not yet."

She released her grip on the man who'd taken over where Pop left off then felt the unexpected sting of tears. With a quick hug and a word of thanks, she sent Orlando on his way. Then, turning the lock behind her, Leah set to work. By the time she stopped, the place had been thoroughly mopped, shined and polished, though it didn't really need a bit of it. But she felt better, or at least she'd worked out the majority of her frustration.

Pop had been decidedly worse when she'd visited this morning. Though she knew she'd eventually lose him to Alzheimer's disease, Leah mourned every step on the way down the slippery slope.

A few minutes later she'd locked up and driven the short distance across the highway to her favorite part of the family property, Berry Hill Stables. Carefully avoiding looking over in the direction of the burned-out shell that remained of her family's pre–Civil War home—the latest casualty of her father's inability to function safely on his own—Leah turned toward the pasture. There the last remaining horses from the once-plentiful herd were waiting.

"No ride today, Maisie," she said as climbed up on the bottom rung of the fence and petted the palomino mare's sand-colored mane. While Leah was busy with Maisie, the mare's partner in crime, a glorious filly named Boo, ambled up and nudged at the pocket that both horses knew would contain their favorite snack.

Leah pulled out two apples, offering one first to the impatient Boo then to the more tolerant Maisie. The sound of tires on gravel caught her attention, and her heart sank.

"Oh, please. Not today," she said under her breath.

Jack Murdoch—land developer, current mayor of Vine Beach and an old friend of Pop's—honked his horn, sending the skittish Maisie and the rest of the herd galloping for open pasture. Boo, however, munched on her apple from a safe distance as the pickup approached. By the time the old man pulled his truck to a stop a few feet away and turned off the engine, Leah found she could force a smile. No matter how she felt about Mayor Murdoch and his real estate investors, she'd not allow him to see it on her face.

The old man's gaze swept the horizon, no doubt taking in the ruined home, the still-sturdy barn and various outbuildings that dotted the vast golden prairie. Bordered by the horizon to the north and the beach to the south, Berry land also included Pop's Seafood Shack and the little oceanfront cabin where she now lived.

"Good afternoon, Mayor. What brings you out this way?" she said, anxious to be rid of her guest.

"Had a nice visit with your daddy just now." He smiled. "Told me to tell you he misses seeing you."

"I was there this morning," she said before she could stop herself.

Pop's memory issues often caused him to forget who'd come to see him. It took all she had not to remind the mayor of this. Instead she kept her mouth shut even as she began to aim her prayers skyward. If the Lord answered quickly enough, Leah just might find a way to remember her manners.

"He also told me to tell you he'd be just fine with you letting all this go." The mayor swung his attention to meet her stare. "You know that restaurant ain't up to fire code, and the house over there ought to have been torn down the night it burned. It's plain foolishness that keeps both of them standing."

Leah's fists clenched. Still she said nothing. Though it was quite possible Pop said just that, it was also true that he'd neither remember nor agree with the idea should she ask him next time she saw him.

Not that it mattered, for she had the final say in all legal matters now, not Pop.

Finally the mayor let out a long sigh. "Look, honey, we're on the same side here." Murdoch rested his elbow on the open window of the truck. "All the boys and I are trying to do is help."

"Then, please, let *the boys* know I appreciate their concern. However, Berry land is not for sale. Not now, and not ever." She mustered up one last sweet smile. "So, thank you for the visit, but now that you've delivered your message, I hope you'll understand that I've got things to do."

To punctuate her statement, Leah turned her back on the mayor and headed for the barn. She'd almost reached the weathered barn doors when she heard the truck engine roar to life.

"I'm just trying to make things easier for you, Leah. I don't understand why you insist on being so stubborn," he called over the sound of the engine.

She picked up her pace, stuffing her fists into the pockets of her jeans. Between Pop and Mayor Murdoch and Vine Beach's annoyingly handsome new fire chief she'd just about had it with people for today. And while she could do nothing about the lingering worry over her visit with her father, there was something she could do about Jack Murdoch.

Intent on calling the care facility to have the mayor removed from the list of approved guests for Pop, she realized she'd left her phone in the car. Just as well, she decided, for that was a task better undertaken after she'd calmed down a bit.

The mayor whipped around his vehicle to drive between her and the barn. "Look, I came out here as a favor to your daddy. One day you're going to wish you'd listened to us."

"Thanks for stopping by, Mayor Murdoch. I'll be sure and tell Pop you were here."

Leah slipped inside the cool shade of the barn and waited until the mayor was gone. Only then did she give vent to her anger. Thankfully, the pitchfork was nearby. As she stabbed the implement into the fresh hay, all Leah could think was that while the Lord knew what He was doing, she had absolutely no clue.

Ryan returned to his house in Houston's Heights neighborhood just as the sun was setting. Climbing out of the Jeep, he could hear his bullmastiff's bark of greeting from the backyard. "Hey, Chief," he called. The For Rent sign was gone—likely picked up by the Realtor this afternoon—as was the lockbox that had hung on the front door.

He stepped into the front parlor of the house he and Jenna were supposed to have shared together, then shut the door behind him. Ignoring the memories and regrets that danced around the blanket-wrapped furniture and across the oak floors, Ryan made his way through the maze of boxes stacked in the dining room to slip out the kitchen door. The deck was broad and shaded, the swing gently swaying in the crisp November breeze.

The old swing was his thinking place, the spot where he went to sort out whatever was bothering him. More than one of his buddies had suggested he go see a grief counselor to deal with the lingering guilt of Jenna's death. Maybe someday he would, but not until the Lord made it obvious that it was time.

Chief came loping toward him, a ball in his massive jaws. He scratched the dog behind the ear then tossed the ball far into the yard. As the bullmastiff gave chase, Ryan's phone rang.

The number was unfamiliar, but the area code was not. Vine Beach, Texas.

"Owen here," he said by habit.

"Hi, Ryan, this is Leah. Leah Berry?"

The dog crossed the deck to deposit the ball at Ryan's feet. Once again he threw it. "Leah, yes, hi."

"Hi."

Her pause let him hear the ocean in the background, a sound that made him smile. For all the reluctance he felt leaving Houston and the fire department, he certainly had no problem living at the beach. If only the circumstances were different. Then maybe...

"So, I gave your name to a friend of mine from church. His name is Riley Burkett. He's a part-time Realtor and he may have a few rentals for you to check out."

"Thanks. I appreciate that."

"I'm glad I could help." Again the waves crashed in the background, a stark contrast to the sound of traffic on Heights Boulevard and the persistent noise of a car alarm going off in the distance.

"Are you at the beach right now?"

"I am," she said.

"Then I'm jealous."

"You'll be here soon enough." She paused. "So, anyway, Riley knows you're in a hurry to find a place. He said he would try to catch you tonight so maybe the two of you could go out looking tomorrow. I told him I'd let you know he would be calling."

"Hey, that's great. I owe you, Leah."

"Don't worry about it. I'm glad I could help." Another pause, this time punctuated by the screech of a gull and what sounded like the meowing of a cat.

"Thanks. And I mean it. I owe you." He took a deep breath and let it out swiftly.

"No need to owe me, Ryan. Really. I'm glad to help a friend."

He hung up not knowing whether the friend she referred to was him or this fellow Burkett.

Chief now dropped the ball at Ryan's feet. This time he ignored it to step inside, allowing the dog to follow. He'd kept out just enough in the way of kitchen utensils to scrape together a grilled-cheese-and-tomato-soup meal. And while it wasn't bad, it certainly didn't compare to the seafood feast he'd had for lunch.

Ryan looked down at Chief who waited discreetly for any scraps that might come his way. The company had been better at lunch, too.

He let his mind rest on Leah for just a moment. Although she'd been a little wary, or angry, or both, he couldn't deny that she was…pretty.

Chief gave him a look as if he could read Ryan's mind, then lay down at his feet. Ryan leaned over to scratch the dog behind his ear then tossed him the remains of the grilled cheese.

"She's just a nice lady who offered to find a…" Ryan rose, shaking his head. It was the one-year anniversary of his wedding to a woman he'd barely been able to build a life with before he'd lost her. He was in no position to think of anyone as "pretty."

He opened the back door and let Chief out, then stood in the twilight. The car alarm had ceased, and the road noise had quieted to allow the sounds of the night to rise. Snagging his Bible off the counter, he made his way to the swing and settled down under the porch light.

His reading this morning had come from Exodus, a passage detailing the tribe of Israel's flight from Egypt by way of the less-traveled road. Ryan estimated he'd read that passage dozens of times, and never had he noticed that when the Lord finally allowed the tribe to make their escape, He did not take them through the most direct and obvious route.

Ryan opened his Bible to read the passage again. This time he had to wonder: Was God doing the same thing with him? Was Ryan following Him down the less-obvious route—one that led through Vine Beach, Texas—or was he merely allowing a deathbed promise to send him in the wrong direction?

Ryan went to bed that night turning the question over to the Lord and awakened without an answer. But at least he had a plan. And that was better than what he'd had for the past year.

The next afternoon, Ryan arrived at the address Riley Burkett had given him. Situated across from the City Hall building where Ryan would have an office starting Monday morning, Burkett Realty was on the ground floor of a century-old building that also housed a beauty salon and a clothing store. Both were decorated for fall despite the warm salt-tinged breeze and the complete lack of fall foliage on the trees surrounding the courthouse and adjoining *Vine Beach Gazette* building.

When Ryan stepped inside Burkett Realty, he was kept waiting only a minute before a woman who introduced herself as Riley's wife, Susan, ushered him into a back office. Burkett was an older man with a head full of gray hair, a fact that surprised him given the enthusiasm he'd heard on the phone. With a pace much quicker than Ryan expected, they made short work of visiting the handful of rental properties available for long-term lease.

He settled on a one-room furnished cabin situated a

few steps from the sand with an upstairs deck that ran the length of the house. The yard was small, something Chief wouldn't much like, but it was fenced and that would have to do.

After returning to Riley's office to sign the lease, all that remained was to head back to Houston for the few things he'd be bringing with him. The movers would deliver the rest of it to storage. Then there would be nothing left to remind the new tenants of the man who never managed to bring his new wife home to the house in the Heights.

"You're all set," Burkett said. "Is there anything else I can do for you?"

"Actually there is," Ryan said. "I'll be looking for a church down here. Any recommendations?"

Burkett grinned. "Glad you asked, son. I can help you with that." He wrote down the name and address of a church on the back of his business card then handed it to Ryan. "I head up a widowers group called Starting Over, and Susan and I mentor the newlyweds."

Widowers group. Ryan glanced down at the card.

Riley Burkett, PhD, LPC
Certified Grief Counselor

"Wait. I thought you were a Realtor."

"I am." The older man looked down at the card he'd given Ryan. "Don't know how that card got into the wrong place." He gestured to a second cardholder. "I meant to give you one of those. Want to trade me?"

"No," Ryan said slowly. "I think this is the one I'm supposed to have."

"Really?" He gave Ryan an appraising look. "And why is that?"

"Long story." He paused to weigh the lease in his hand. For a second he considered telling Riley about Jenna, but the words wouldn't come out. "Thanks for your help."

Riley looked at Ryan carefully. "Anytime, son. Anytime."

As he shook Riley's hand, Ryan wondered if he could talk to Riley, if he could find some relief from the guilt that seemed to follow him around and weigh him down like a boulder on his soul. After all, he couldn't keep it to himself forever.

As he left the office, Leah stepped out of the beauty salon and right into his path. "Hey, stranger," she said, her impossibly green eyes stopping him in his tracks.

Chapter Three

"So you found a place?" Leah asked Ryan, noticing the lease he held in his hands.

"I did, thanks to you," he said. He smiled at her for a moment, and then looked down at the painfully eye-catching, oversize zebra-and-pink disposable sandals she wore postpedicure. Meant only to get her from salon to car, Leah had certainly not expected to be greeting Ryan in them. Nor did she intend to show off the pink flowers Ima had painted on both of her big toes to just anyone. She felt herself blush as Ryan's smile became a grin.

"So," Leah said as she affected a casual pose and tried to act as if the ridiculous footwear and silly flowers were as normal as the sneakers Ryan wore, "tell me about your new place."

"According to the rental ad, it's steps from the water with an efficient layout and recently remodeled kitchen and bath," he said. "Pretty much describes every place Burkett showed me except the one up above the beauty salon. The difference with this one is that the owner was willing to lease it for six months instead of by the week. That's a testament to Mr. Burkett's persuasive powers."

"Yes, I can imagine he'd be persuasive." Across the way Jack Murdoch's truck pulled into the parking space reserved for the mayor. Leah purposefully returned her attention to Ryan without acknowledging the older man's wave. "The place sounds wonderful," she said.

"It's nothing fancy, but it's much better than living over Ima's Beauty Salon, that's for sure."

"Living on the beach takes some getting used to, but it does beat inhaling chemicals and listing to blow dryers and Frank Sinatra all day."

"Just Frank Sinatra?"

"Ima's a big fan of Ol' Blue Eyes." She shook her head. "Don't worry. There's a barber shop up on the main highway, so it's likely you'll never have to experience it unless you're called on to do a fire inspection or something."

He gave the front window of Ima's a quick glance then grinned. "I'll take your word for it. Now, other than Pop's—where I'm sure you've dined a time or two—is there a good place for lunch in this town?"

"Lunch?" She thought a minute. "There's the Pizza Palace, but I don't know if it's open for lunch. Frankly I avoid it unless I'm babysitting for the Wilson girls because the noise is deafening and the pizza isn't exactly gourmet fare."

He glanced up at the sky then down the street. "I have an idea. Where's the nearest deli?"

"Inside the Beach Mart on Vine at Main," she said. "Just around the corner. Why?"

"How about we have a quick lunch, so I can thank

you for all your help? Maybe a few sandwiches on the beach?"

Leah's first thought was that she should turn him down. After all, he *was* a stranger. And also the new fire chief.

She looked at Ryan's hopeful expression, and changed her mind.

It was just lunch. Not a date. Just a thank-you. And apparently it would be deli food from the Beach Mart.

Just then, the mayor stepped out of his truck. "Great," she said under her breath.

"Leah?" the mayor called.

Ignoring him, Leah regarded Ryan with a smile. "Sure. Why not?"

"Great," Ryan said. "Let's take my Jeep."

"Wait right there," Leah said as she held up her hand to silence him. "I need to…" She pointed to her toes then headed for the front door of Ima's, escaping the mayor easily. "Just hang on, okay?"

Once inside, the sound of Frank singing "I've Got You Under My Skin" chased her across the room and into the corner devoted to Ima's boutique items. There amid the rhinestones and sequins that covered all of the clothing and most of the accessories, Leah found the adorable sandals she'd been eyeing for the past month.

Snatching up a pair in her size, she found Ima and retrieved her debit card. A sly glance out the front window told Leah that Ryan was leaning against the Jeep, arms crossed and his attention focused down the street. Mayor Murdoch was heading for the courthouse door.

The music paused then switched to the unmistakable introduction to "Strangers in the Night." "I thought you were waiting until these went on sale." Ima rang up the purchase then handed back the card to Leah, her heavily mascaraed eyes sweeping the length of her. "Guess you can't go on a date in a pair of throwaways, can you?"

Leah slipped out of the disposables and then pulled the sandals from the box. "It's not a date," she said as she balanced on one foot to carefully slide into the shoe. "It's just…" She paused to repeat the process then tuck the temporary sandals into the empty box. "Ryan's new to Vine Beach and…never mind. It's just lunch. Not a date."

"I don't know, hon," she said as she turned her attention out the window. "That handsome fella? I doubt he's thinking it's just lunch."

She slid another covert glance outside. Ryan had shifted positions and now watched her through the window. When their gazes met, he grinned. Oh, my, but he was handsome.

Leah looked away, collecting her idiotic thoughts. "Don't be silly," she said as evenly as she could manage. "He's taking Pop's job as fire chief. Why would I want to invite that kind of trouble? Can you imagine what my father would say if he found out?"

"Carl didn't take it well when he had to step down, I'll give you that," Ima said. "And then there were the questions about…" She shook her head. "Never mind. Strictly speaking, as someone who knew your pa since we were knee high to a grasshopper, I guarantee he'd like anyone you like."

"Miss Ima, really it's—"

"Not a date. Yes, I know. Still your father would be pleased. Or at least he would have if that Alzheimer's hadn't…" Ima waved a hand that sparkled with a hefty sample of the rings and bracelets she offered for sale.

"Forget I said anything. Just go and enjoy your date. And, girl, those sandals look adorable with your outfit."

"It is *not* a date." She looked down at the denim capris and plain black T-shirt she'd thrown on this morning when her entire plan was to have a pedicure then read on the beach until it was time to head over to Pop's for the evening crowd. "But thanks."

Ima nodded, her expression indicating the moment the door closed she'd be on the phone telling someone what she'd just seen. And heard. Though likely she'd forget to mention that Leah had indicated several times over that this was not a date.

She emerged into the November sunshine and offered Ryan a penitent look. "Sorry you had to wait."

He opened her door, then closed it behind her. When he'd settled behind the wheel, he offered a sideways look. "Nice shoes."

Leah couldn't help blushing for the second time in ten minutes.

Ryan tried not to cringe. *Nice shoes?*

He mustered a smile as he buckled his seat belt and started the car. "So, that grocery store? Where was it again?"

Leah nodded toward the south. "It's on the corner of Vine and Main."

He backed out of the parking space and headed in that direction. "So you're okay with a picnic?"

"Definitely pro-picnics," she said with a chuckle.

"Great." If she'd said she preferred some kind of indoor dining, he'd be back at Pop's again. Not where he wanted to take her on their not-a-date.

Besides, Burkett had mentioned that the spot offered a good view of the burned-out ruins of the Berry home.

The Beach Mart was easy to find, situated as it was on a corner just beyond the church and nursing home. He parked the Jeep but lagged a step behind Leah as she headed inside.

He wanted to thank Leah, absolutely. But he also had become more than a little curious about the fire at Leah's family home. After all, he was the new fire chief.

Of course, there was another reason for this picnic—a tiny spark of hope that threatened to flare into something really nice. Maybe even a friendship. Nothing more, of course. Just friends.

Because this was just lunch.

A get-to-know-each-other lunch.

A thank-you lunch.

Get a grip, he told himself.

"So," Leah said, "where are we going for this picnic?"

"Mr. Burkett told me about a place he takes his grandkids fishing. It's over by the lighthouse. I thought it might be nice to go take a look," he said as they headed back to the Jeep with their food.

"I know just the place you're talking about. Pop used to take me there. It's perfect."

A few minutes later, Ryan stopped the Jeep in front of the old lighthouse. According to Mr. Burkett, the place had been standing longer than any building in Vine Beach, an honor that belonged to the Berry place until a few months ago.

Ryan had tried quizzing Burkett about the fire, to no avail. Only the information about the dock's view had been forthcoming. Apparently the subject was a sore one in Vine Beach, one a newcomer best not bring up.

But as fire chief it was his duty to investigate suspicious fires. And though he'd not seen the ruins close up, the fact that questions on the topic caused such discomfort was reason enough to suspect something was not right.

Of course, could he ask Leah about the fire without stirring things up between them again?

Snatching the bag of sandwiches and drinks, Ryan turned his back on the lighthouse to follow Leah down the sandy trail that wound between the grassy dunes. A bend in the path and suddenly there was the Gulf of Mexico lapping against a dock that jutted far out into the blue-gray water. To his left was the city of Vine Beach, almost close enough to hear the gulls begging at the marina, and straight ahead beyond the dock was what appeared to be an island.

"That's Sand Island," Leah said as if reading his mind. "It's a great place to picnic, too."

"Duly noted."

Ryan shifted the bag and glanced to his right. Burkett was correct. From this vantage point he could easily make out the broken and charred columns—three at his count, though there could easily have been four or five.

The house sat on a ridge overlooking the Gulf on one side and, from what he could imagine, rolling fields where palominos grazed on the other. It must have been a beautiful place.

Leah came up beside him and shaded her eyes with her hand. For a moment, she said nothing. Then, silently she turned to walk toward the dock.

Ryan followed her, watched her spread the Beach Mart plastic tablecloth over the ancient boards, and then settled down beside her to place the bag of food and drinks between them.

Below the dock, waves lapped against the pilings then rushed past to break on the sandy shore. Unlike the beach, however, these waves were gentler. More motion than foam.

"There's a sand bar about forty yards out," Leah said as she handed him his pastrami on rye. "It keeps the surf from breaking so hard." She found her sandwich then tucked the bag under the tablecloth. "Makes for great fishing and, if you're a little kid, some seriously good swimming."

"Sounds like you're speaking from experience," he said as he unwrapped his lunch. "Must have been quite a view from up at the house."

"It was." She said the words softly, as if she might be remembering. And then, just as quickly as it appeared, her look of nostalgia disappeared.

Ryan knew he had to tread softly.

He searched for something to fill the silence that lengthened uncomfortably between them. "Have you always worked at Pop's?"

She chuckled. "No. Pop wouldn't hear of it. He insisted I get my education and see the world."

"And you did?"

"I did."

When she didn't seem inclined to elaborate, Ryan continued. "But now you're back in Vine Beach."

"I am." A trio of gulls screeched overhead, temporarily distracting her. "So, Ryan, what makes a Houston fireman decide to leave the big city behind and take a job in Vine Beach?"

Interesting. Either Leah didn't want to talk about

herself or she didn't want to talk about the fire. He took a bite to stall the answer that he didn't want to give.

"Miss Leah!" a child squealed.

Ryan followed the sound to spy a fair-haired girl of no more than seven or eight racing down the path. A few steps behind came Riley Burkett carrying a pair of cane poles and a small cooler.

Giving thanks for the welcome redirection in conversation, Ryan left his sandwich and climbed to his feet. "Hey there," he said.

"We meet again." Burkett grinned at Leah as she rose to hug the girl. "Hope we're not crashing the party."

"No," Leah said. "Not at all. Ryan and I were just having a sandwich to celebrate his new lease."

Ryan gave her a sideways look. Is that what they were doing? Celebrating? He hadn't thought of it that way, but the idea bore considering.

"'Preciate you giving Ryan my number, Leah," the older man said as he set down the cooler at the edge of the dock. "I think he managed to find a nice enough place, don't you?" He winked at Leah.

Leah shook her head, puzzled. "I don't know. I haven't seen it. But it sounds nice."

Riley looked confused. "I thought—"

The girl raced past to tug at Burkett's sleeve. "Grandpa Riley, can we fish now?"

"Sure we can, Brooke." He nodded toward Ryan. "But first I'd like to introduce you to a new friend of mine."

She looked up at him all eyes and freckles and her smile revealed two missing front teeth.

"I'm Ryan," he said as he stuck out his hand to shake. "What's your name?"

"Brooke Wilson. Just Brooke, not Brookie. My daddy calls me Brookie but he forgets I'm not a baby sometimes." She gave Ryan an appraising look. "Are you Miss Leah's boyfriend?"

"No," he said in unison with Leah. Chuckling, he added, "Pleased to meet you, Brooke Wilson."

Leah nodded toward the cooler. "How about I help you bait your hook and we see what you can catch?"

She brushed past Ryan to take the cane pole from Riley. Brooke reached into the cooler and handed Leah something that looked strangely like a piece of hot dog.

"What're you using for bait there?" Ryan asked as he moved toward them.

"My lunch," Brooke said. "Grandpa Riley promised if I ate one of my hot dogs I could take the other two fishing."

"Hey," Riley said. "At least it got her to eat her lunch. You have no idea how hard it is to get that child to eat. She'd rather do just about anything instead of sit down for a proper lunch. Everything's yucky. Except hot dogs, that is, but only occasionally."

Leah finished fitting the bait onto the hook then tugged at the girl's ponytail. "Shouldn't you be at school?"

"Teacher workday, apparently," Riley said. "Her sisters are busy working on their Girl Scout cooking badges with Amy, so Susan and I were treated to an afternoon with Brooke."

"Lucky you," Leah said, and her tone and expression showed she meant it. "Come on, Brooke. Let's go see what you can catch for dinner."

She screwed up her face into a grimace. "Fish are yucky."

Riley chuckled. "See what I mean?"

"Cute kid," Ryan said.

"Yes, she is." He looked past Ryan, presumably to watch Leah and Brooke for a moment. "My grandbabies are the blessing I never expected I would have."

"Oh?"

The Realtor returned his attention to Ryan. "I married young but my first wife and I were never able to have children. When she passed away I didn't think I'd marry again, much less inherit grandchildren in the bargain. Then I met Susan at church and got to know her. Before long she and the Lord changed my mind about marriage." He shook his head. "Her son Eric's the town veterinarian. He's married to Amy, who gave birth to my grandson six weeks ago."

"That's great, Riley," Ryan said.

Brooke squealed, and Ryan turned to see that the girl had indeed caught something. Leah had kicked off her sandals and now stood with the waves lapping at her ankles as she held the fishing line a few inches away from the hook. At the end of the line was a wriggling fish. From this distance it looked like a small flounder. November in Texas. Ryan smiled. Where else could a trip to the beach less than two months before Christmas include getting wet without shivering?

"Be right there, honey," Riley called before he once again regarded Ryan. "All I know is that God sure turned my world upside down, but everything worked out okay."

He watched Burkett trot away. God had turned his world upside down, too. Would he ever feel that way? By the time he'd said goodbye to Burkett and his granddaughter and deposited Leah back in front of the beauty salon, he still had no answer to the question.

"You've been awfully quiet," she said as she reached for the door handle.

"Just thinking," he said. "Sorry about that."

Her smile was genuine. "No, it's fine, actually," she added after a moment's silence.

"Leah," he said slowly as he once again attempted to ask about the fire. "Tell me about what happened to your home. The fire, I mean. If you want to."

"Not any more than you want to tell me why you're in Vine Beach, apparently."

She looked away. "I had a nice time."

So he'd hit a nerve. Ryan paused only a second before deciding to allow her abrupt change of topic. "Me, too." He slid her a grin he hoped matched hers. "Guess I'll be seeing you around Vine Beach."

"Count on it," she said, as she returned her attention to Ryan. "Especially if you like the food at Pop's."

"Which I do."

She climbed out to lean against the door. "Banana cream pie's our specialty, you know, but my favorite's the buttermilk."

"Buttermilk pie? No, thanks."

She straightened to close the door then regarded him through the open window. "Have you tried it?" When he shook his head she continued. "Then don't knock it until you have. Now take care, fireman. I've played hooky from the restaurant for too long. Orlando's going to be wondering where I've been."

"Yes, ma'am," he said to her retreating back.

A thought occurred and he leaned out the window

to call her name. When she turned to face him, he said, "You didn't tell me what days you offer buttermilk pie."

Again she smiled. "Every day," she said. "Lunch and dinner."

His laughter echoed in the suddenly empty Jeep as he watched her toss her red hair in the breeze then climb into an SUV parked a few spaces down. He was still watching as the vehicle pulled away and disappeared down Main Street.

Again the question of what God might be doing tugged at his mind. And again, no answer came. But he did have a new job to prepare for and a dog waiting back in Houston for a ride to his new home. And that was enough to think about for now.

That and the twinkle in Leah Berry's eyes when she invited him to Pop's for buttermilk pie.

What would happen to that twinkle when Leah found out he was about to start digging for information on the mysterious fire that destroyed her family's home?

Chapter Four

Ryan shifted into Reverse and was about to pull out onto Main Street when he spied Mayor Jack Murdoch standing beside his truck. As their gazes met, the mayor motioned for him to stop.

"What's up, Mayor?" Ryan called.

The old man crossed the road to lean against the fender of the Jeep. "Got a minute? I thought maybe we'd take a ride. Save me the time of showing you around come Monday morning."

He thought about it. With nothing back in Houston to hurry home to, there seemed no harm in taking a spin around town with his new boss.

"Sure. Why not?"

Nodding, the mayor gestured toward his vehicle. "We'll take mine."

By the time Ryan reached the truck, the mayor had the windows down and the engine humming. They made their way along Main then turned left at Vine Beach Road as silence reigned, which was fine by Ryan. He never did well with small talk anyway.

"Where'd you end up settling?" the mayor finally asked.

"Here, actually," Ryan said as the collection of beach houses came into view around a bend in the road. "The yellow one with the green shutters is mine." *For six months, anyway* went unsaid, but barely.

Murdoch answered him with an agreeable nod then adjusted his hat and drummed his fingers on the steering wheel. "You were something over in Houston. A regular HFD superstar."

Ryan stole a sideways glance at the mayor and wondered what else the man knew about his days at HFD. "I just watched and learned, and I guess did all right."

"You did more than all right, boy." He paused and worked his jaw a bit, looking as if he were chewing on the words he would say next. "I'm sorry about the loss of your wife."

So he knew. Ryan mustered up a nod of thanks but otherwise kept silent. The polite conversation that went with being a widower had yet to get any easier.

"Must have been tough," Murdoch said. "What with you being a first responder and nothing you could do to save your bride."

The image that statement brought forth was one Ryan knew would never permanently leave his mind. The image of his wife floating unconscious, his inability to revive her. It was all there just as if it had only occurred.

"Yeah," he managed to say, but only because he figured no response would cause Murdoch to keep talking. "So what's out here that you wanted to show me?" he asked to change the subject.

Up ahead, Pop's Seafood Shack loomed, its tin roof and pale weathered boards shining almost golden in the afternoon sun. Mayor Murdoch pulled the vehicle to a stop at the edge of the lot and shut off the engine. Instantly the dull roar of the waves filled the air.

While Ryan watched, the mayor reached into his pocket and pulled out a tin. Offering a mint to Ryan, who declined, he then popped one into his mouth. Murdoch chewed on the spearmint for a moment. Finally, he shook his head.

"I'm just going to be plain honest, Ryan. That all right with you?" When Ryan nodded, the mayor continued. "You're young."

"Yes, sir," he said, though it had been a long time since he'd felt it. With thirty on the horizon, *old* seemed as if it was heading toward him like a freight train.

"When your uncle Mike called me, I didn't see how I could manage a full-time fireman's position here in Vine Beach, what with the winter here and the tourists pretty much gone. But Mike and me, we go way back, so I decided I'd do what I could. 'Sides, we were gonna have to replace Carl Berry before tourist season anyway. Thing is, he never took a salary for it, though nobody expected the new guy to do the same."

He looked to Ryan for a response. "Yes, sir" was the best he could do. Ryan knew Uncle Mike had gone way out on a limb to call in a favor from his old army buddy, but he had no idea the last chief had done it free.

But then Uncle Mike knew how important it had been to Ryan to do as Jenna had asked and make a new life at the beach where the two of them had one day hoped to live. Not in Galveston. It was too soon to move there, given the amount of time they had spent planning their future lives in that city.

Instead, he'd gone to Uncle Mike to ask him to look

out for any jobs in beach towns that weren't too far from Houston and home. To his surprise, the Vine Beach job had come just in time for their anniversary. Even now Ryan didn't know whether that was an omen or just one more way for him to torture himself about a marriage that was over before it ever got started.

"Then I thought, well, I do need to carefully consider my responsibility to the good people of Vine Beach. And part of that responsibility means keeping them safe, sometimes from themselves. Don't you agree?"

Now, that was a strange statement. "I suppose so," he said slowly.

Murdoch's attention shifted to the restaurant and rested there. "Some folks, they just don't see the need to follow the rules." He jerked a thumb toward Pop's. "A firetrap if ever I've seen one. Not that I'm the expert. That'd be you."

A man didn't have to look hard to see the potential for danger in the ancient wood structure. And danger was what he specialized in preventing. Strangely uncomfortable, Ryan looked away. Thus far he'd only made one friend in this town, and even that friendship seemed rife with potential problems. Not a good sign.

"Leah—she's Berry's daughter—runs the place now that he's..." Murdoch's voice trailed off. "Anyhow, she's just about as hardheaded as it gets, but you probably know that having just spent some time with her." When Ryan ignored the statement, the older man continued. "Can't figure why she stays when she had that good job with the historical folks in Galveston." Murdoch looked at him as if he might have the answer.

Ryan thought back on her reluctance to elaborate on her reasons yesterday. "People do things for all sorts of reasons," he said. "But not everybody likes to talk about them."

Murdoch's *harrumph* told Ryan how the mayor felt on the topic. After a minute, he leaned back against his seat and toyed with the brim of his cap. He seemed lost in thought. Then, quick as that, he reached to turn the key in the ignition.

As he did, he fixed his attention on Ryan. "I'm no expert but this place probably ought to get a look-over when you start your inspections."

Ryan shifted position. Whatever ax Jack Murdoch had to grind against the owners of this restaurant, he wanted no part in it. And not because he'd come to know Leah Berry, even slightly. But once again, he found himself thinking of the job he'd been hired to do.

Thus, he answered carefully but firmly. "I figured to start with the schools then the hospital and nursing home since they're of greater public importance."

The mayor gave him a curt nod. "Makes sense. But when you do get around to Pop's, don't let that pretty redhead distract you from your job. If there are fire code violations, it's your duty to report them and see they're corrected."

"Sir, with all due respect, you hired me to do a job and I intend to do that job," Ryan said.

Sure, Leah was pretty—especially when her eyes shone as she helped the Wilson girl bait her hook. But Ryan wasn't about to let anyone compromise his reputation. Not that a woman like Leah would ever ask him to.

He could tell that about her already. She had integrity.

The mayor nodded. "Glad to hear it, son," he said.

He made a quick left onto a road so narrow the

truck's side mirrors nearly brushed the fence posts on both sides. "See that place over there?"

Murdoch gestured across the highway to the burned-out shell of the once-magnificent Berry home. To the right of the main building were several other structures that he could see much better on close range. The nearest to the road was definitely a weathered barn while the remainder were most likely a collection of storage buildings of some sort.

When he once again spied the horses, Ryan's interest piqued. He judged them to be outstanding horseflesh, and his fingers itched to grab a bridle and chase one down. Not since his rodeo days had he felt such a tug to be astride a horse galloping across a pasture. And from the look of the land in front of him, there was plenty of space to ride.

A vast golden prairie swept from the lighthouse near the beach to the horizon, the grass swaying with the breeze coming off the Gulf of Mexico. He could almost feel the saddle under him.

Once a cowboy, always a fireman. Ryan's dad was fond of teasing him with that saying. And yet, there was more to his love for horses than his former glory days as a bronc rider.

"That there's Berry property, too," Murdoch said, tearing Ryan from his thoughts. The old man gestured to the land unfolding in front of them. "House was a beauty until the big fire back in March. Too bad about that." He shook his head. "Well, anyhow, there's probably a violation or two out there. I'd have to check on the statutes, but I don't think it'd be safe to leave a building in that kind of condition."

Ryan sat up a little straighter, interested to hear what

the mayor had to say about the Berry fire. "While you're looking for those statutes," he said. "I'd appreciate if you'd get me a copy, too."

"Be glad to."

"So," Ryan said as his gaze swept the ruins, "tell me about the fire."

Murdoch shook his head. "Went up fast, but then the place was close to one hundred and fifty years old. Carl was chief then, but in name only, really."

"What do you mean?"

Gray brows furrowed. "Well, things stay pretty quiet around Vine Beach. Not a whole lot to do for the fire chief, but then I told you that when you interviewed for the job."

He had, though Ryan didn't much mind. Six months here and he'd be gone. All the better if he had an easy run of it.

"Carl hid his trouble pretty well, so while there had been talk of replacing him, nobody on the City Council wanted to be the one to bring it up formally."

"What was wrong with him?"

"Alzheimer's disease," Murdoch said as he shifted into gear and headed the truck back toward the main road. "Once the house nearly burned up around him, well, we all knew something had to be done. That's when Leah quit her job and came back here to run things."

"So you're saying the fire was accidentally set by Chief Berry?"

"I'm saying nothing of the sort. We had a hard rain that night. Could've been lightning. Or with the age of this house, a gas leak might've been the reason. I just know that whatever happened, Carl's lucky to be alive. That place went up way too fast."

"I see." He watched the landscape roll by, the sea breeze tossing the breakers against the beach in the distance. Something in Jack Murdoch's tone told him there was more to the story. "So where is he now?"

"Carl? He's got a little place at the assisted-living facility just down from the harbor."

He remembered his conversation with Leah regarding her father. Just to see what the mayor would say, he added, "I wonder if I ought to pay him a visit. Maybe get some pointers from him."

"Wouldn't advise it." Murdoch shot him a sideways look. "He's suffered enough. I'd rather him not know he's lost his job, too."

"Wait, you mean he doesn't know he's not the fire chief?"

"Didn't see the need to tell him, and my guess is Leah hasn't, either." Murdoch signaled to turn onto Main Street. "Anything you need ought to be in the files, though. Nobody's messed with them since Carl left. Didn't need to." A shrug. "Like I said. Not much happens here in Vine Beach."

When he arrived at work Monday morning, Ryan discovered that the mayor hadn't been exaggerating—not much happened in Vine Beach including fire inspections. While the schools and nursing homes had been checked over most recently, there was nothing in the file that showed the last time Pop's Seafood Shack had been inspected. Only when he came across a bundle of papers in the back of the filing cabinet did he find a certificate of inspection.

It was dated 1973.

For a second, Ryan considered asking the mayor if he knew where Chief Berry would have kept current inspection certificates for Pop's. But he quickly thought better of it.

The last thing Chief Berry—or Leah—needed was someone questioning the chief's work.

On his desk was the list of locations needing inspections. Starting tomorrow he'd be making those visits. He'd get to Pop's in due time.

And yet, what if the place really hadn't been inspected in forty years? Could he live with the fact that he'd ignored the information he now had if something happened to Pop's before he could make his inspection?

Leah. It was possible Leah had the certificates. He picked up the phone and dialed her number.

"Ryan," she said when she answered. "Good to hear from you."

In the background he could hear people talking. "Have I caught you at a bad time?"

"Actually we're getting ready for the lunch rush, but I have a minute."

"I just have a quick question. You may already know the answer."

"Sure," she said as someone called her name in the background. "I'll try. What do you need to know?"

"I'm looking through the files here and can't find a fire inspection for your restaurant after 1973. Do you happen to know if your father kept certificates for Pop's separate from the City Hall files?"

"I can tell you they're not here. I've been doing the paperwork for the restaurant since March and I've found nothing like that. Just a bunch of tax stuff. Receipts and the like. Some of it goes way back to before I was born. Apparently Pop didn't like to throw anything away." She paused. "At least he kept neat files. He was a stickler for that."

That matched up with what he'd found here at the office. Still he had to ask once more. "You're sure? Nothing at all that might look like an inspection?"

"Positive. Why?"

He leaned back in his chair and closed his eyes as the sinking feeling took hold. "Just wanted to be sure. Thanks."

"Is something wrong?"

"Just making sure the files here are complete, that's all."

"All right." A loud noise split the silence. "Okay, I've got to run, but the offer to try our buttermilk pie's still good."

"Thanks, Leah," he said as he leaned forward to rest his elbows on the desk.

Unfortunately the next time he showed up at Pop's Seafood Shack, it wouldn't be for the pie.

Leah slid the phone into her pocket then leaned against the counter. What had that been about?

"I've got to check something upstairs. I'll be right back," she called to Orlando. He waved in acknowledgment then returned to stirring the sauce for the bread pudding.

The warm scent of pudding baking chased Leah up the narrow rear stairway and into the tiny cubicle Pop called his office. Really nothing more than a glorified broom closet with a view, the lone window offered the best place to watch the sun rise and set over the Gulf.

Settling onto Pop's chair, Leah let out a long breath as she ran her fingers over the handle to the cabinet. Inside were thick files filled with documents related to the restaurant, everything from the building plans to old menus and bank statements. Though she knew the contents by heart, Leah once again searched the files for anything that looked like a fire inspection.

"Leah?" Orlando called. "Everything okay up there?"

She stood and closed the door behind her. "It's fine." Leah met Orlando at the bottom of the stairs. His expression told her that he was still curious. "Just looking for some papers," she told him. "A fire inspection. Do you remember the last time the restaurant had one?"

The cook shrugged. "That was Carl's department. I just fry the shrimp."

"And look after me," she said.

"Just doing what I promised your pop I'd do." But her lighthearted tone didn't stop Orlando. "Why're you asking about a fire inspection?"

Leah didn't immediately reply. There was no need to upset Orlando.

"You can't fool me," he said as he placed his work-roughened hand over hers. "Now just spill it. What's got you worried?"

All the starch went out of her. "All right. Let me ask you something. Do you think Pop would purposefully skip the fire inspections on this place?"

"Your father's a good man. I can't imagine he would do that."

"Regardless of the reason, I'm afraid that's exactly what has happened. I've got no records on file of inspection results, and I can't imagine that Ryan would call and ask me to check for them if he had any results on file up at the courthouse." Tears brimmed, but Leah blinked them back. "We won't pass, will we?"

To his credit, Orlando appeared to give the question due consideration. Finally he sighed. "I'd like to say we will, but I just don't know. What I do know is that you're worrying way too much. Now, why don't we finish the lunch rush and you can take the rest of the day off?"

"I can't do that," she said.

"And why not? Monday evening's always the slowest night of the week." He held her at arm's length. "I promise I'll call if the crowd gets too big for Kate and me to handle. Okay?"

"You sure?"

"Just as sure as I am that the Lord's going to handle what we can't."

Leah chuckled. "Now you sound like Pop."

"Good." He made a serious face. "Now get back to work or I'll have to tell the manager."

Chapter Five

With the Monday lunch rush behind her and the evening preparations being handled by Orlando, Leah's thoughts and her SUV turned toward home. There she could forget for just a little while, maybe immerse herself in a good book and pretend she didn't have yet another Pop-related issue to deal with.

No fire inspection indeed. She sighed as she climbed out of her vehicle and closed the door behind her. "No," Leah said under her breath. "I will not worry about that today. Tomorrow has enough troubles of its own. No need to borrow any more."

Reaching the steps leading to her upstairs porch, a plaintive yowl alerted Leah to the fact she was not alone. She looked up to spy Baby, her oversize orange tabby, sitting midway up the steps and eyeing her lazily through half-open slits.

As she began her trek up the stairs, an awful barking started from somewhere beyond the hedge of oleanders. The tabby's ears went back, and her substantial tail puffed even larger as she moved carefully across the porch to wait beside the door. The barking continued, and from the sound of it, the irritated canine inside the rental next door was no lapdog.

Leah turned the key in the lock, and the door swung open on hinges that could use oiling. Perhaps later, she decided as she paused in the doorway to let out a long breath. In the nearly eight months since coming to live here, she'd painted every surface in the studio-style cabin—except the planked pine floor—her favorite shade of eggshell white and draped the windows and frame surrounding her corner bed in gauzy curtains to match.

The only reminder of the grand antebellum mansion that now lay in ruins was the ornate desk under the window. Once holding pride of place in her grandfather's office, the cherrywood beauty was now the resting place for her laptop. Thankfully the piece had been on loan to the Vine Beach Public Library when the fire struck or it, too, would have been lost.

She took a step inside, the temptation to leave the door open to the unseasonably warm salt-tinged breeze tempered by the fact she'd be listening to the mutt's noise along with the waves. Closing the door firmly behind her, Leah pulled a sandwich out of her bag and put it away, then took the mail and went to her desk.

With the remainder of a rare free afternoon ahead of her, she tucked a book under her arm and opened the door to see if the barking had stopped. When silence greeted her, Leah went back to the fridge for a bottle of water then downstairs to settle into her favorite deck chair beneath the faded red umbrella on the beach. Baby ambled over and joined her at a respectable distance, her pampered paws untouched by the grit of the Vine Beach sand. A moment later, she turned up her nose at the ocean and slipped between the hedge of oleanders that marked the line between the Berry property and the yellow rental next door.

"You're really prissy for a beach cat," Leah said with a chuckle before opening the book and diving into the story.

Three chapters later, a loud meow followed by a hissing noise that could only come from the orange tabby interrupted Leah's reading. She looked over her shoulder to spy Baby racing toward her with what appeared to be a rope-style dog toy. Following close behind was a massive and unfamiliar dog. When the cat ducked beneath Leah's lounge chair, the canine attempted to follow.

Her book and chair went one way while she and her water bottle went the other. Only when she stood to dust off the sand did she realize the enormous brindle-colored dog was now chasing the cat up the stairs.

And the door was open.

By the time she reached the threshold, the destruction was complete. Baby was perched atop the refrigerator in the corner of the kitchen hissing like mad while the oversize mutt barked as if calling her down to come and play.

The warring pair had not gone straight to their current posts, however. Sandy paw prints the size of her fist raced across the wood floor and decorated the sofa. One of the gauze panels surrounding her bed hung askew as if the beast had gotten caught in it before tearing free.

Leah reached for her copy of *Texas Monthly* and rolled it up then approached the dog carefully. A glance at the animal told her that he easily outweighed her.

When he placed his mitt-sized paws on the counter and cast a look her way, their eyes were at the same height.

Brandishing the magazine, she moved a step closer. "Get. Out. Of. Here," she said through clenched jaw.

The dog paused only long enough to blink twice then returned his attention to Baby, whose hissing and howling did nothing to help the situation. Again, Leah waved the magazine at the dog. This time, the animal ignored her completely though his tail thumped loudly against the cabinet door.

Leah was poised to make another attempt when a shrill whistle split the air. The dog froze and looked back toward the open door. Another whistle and he loped past her, making a hasty exit.

Tossing aside the magazine, she stormed out onto the deck and down the stairs in pursuit of whatever idiot owned the disaster with paws. At the bottom of the steps, she made a sharp left turn and slammed into a wall of gray fabric.

The collision knocked her backward, and Leah went reeling into the stair rail. Her head slammed against the wood, and instantly she saw stars. A pair of strong arms caught her and pulled her upright to steady her on her feet.

"Look out, there. Did you hit your head?"

"I'm fine," she said, though her field of vision was limited to a gray *Firemen's Training School* T-shirt and, oddly, something that looked like a belt draped over one shoulder. When her brain caught up with her eyes, she realized the belt was actually a leash. Leah moved her gaze higher and noticed her rescuer looked very familiar.

Ryan Owen.

Before Leah could respond, the massive dog returned and began dancing circles around the two of them. Baby, now safely out of reach in the rafters over the carport, peered down with disdain, offering only the occasional hiss or switch of her tail.

"Sit, Chief," Ryan said sharply, and the dog obeyed at once. And though his tail continued to thump against the concrete, his attention was now completely on the man with the leash. The man who still held her in his grip.

Their eyes met. One dark brow rose.

"You're my neighbor?" she said as she made the connection.

"If you live here, then yes, I am." He seemed even more surprised than Leah.

"I guess that must be the reason Riley Burkett thought I'd seen your new place," she said.

"You feel a little unsteady on your feet," he said as he leaned back to give her an appraising look.

"I'm fine," she said despite the fact the fireman's presence was more than a little disconcerting. Especially when he held her this close. And she could smell the masculine combination of soap and salt air on his clothes. See the curve of his smile from a whole new angle.

"Leah?"

Her senses cleared. "Yes, I'm fine. Really."

When he released her, however, Leah took a step back and the horizon tilted. He caught her before her head could slam into the rail again.

She said a quick prayer that the ground might swallow her up before she said, did or thought anything else that might cause further humiliation.

"You need to sit down." Ryan led her by the elbow to a chair. "Okay, now I'm going to go put Chief inside, but I'll be right back."

He quickly attached the leash to the dog's collar and led him away through a gap in the hedge. Leah let out a sigh as she closed her eyes and rested her hands in her lap. Above her, Baby yowled. She opened her eyes to look up. The cat appeared to be more upset with her than with the dog.

"Look you," she said to the fuzzy feline. "You're the one who went over there and asked for trouble. Don't blame me if it followed you home."

The sound of footsteps coming around the corner alerted Leah to Ryan's return. She mustered a neutral expression.

The fireman stepped into view. "Don't think he'll be paying you another visit anytime soon. At least I hope not. No clue what got into him."

"Oh, I know exactly what caused the excitement. Wait right here," Leah said as she recalled the dog toy that Baby had hauled home. "I've got something that I think might belong to you."

She turned and grabbed for the nearest solid object to steady herself then made her way as best she could through the sun-dappled shade to the stairs. Reaching the second-floor deck, she heard the unmistakable tread of sneakers on wood behind her.

Turning, she saw he'd followed, though at a respectable distance. "Looks like you listen about as well as your dog." Regretting her harsh tone, Leah added a quick but somewhat nicer, "Please wait."

"No offense, but you're looking a little unsteady. Just wanted to be sure you didn't fall." Ryan crossed his arms over his chest and leaned against the rail. "If it looks appetizing, you're welcome to keep it to cook for dinner."

Only when the corner of his mouth turned up in the beginnings of a grin did Leah realize he was making a joke. She shook her head then went toward the door, intent on hurrying the process of returning the soggy length of rope and ball.

Unfortunately, her bare foot found one of the shells from the bowl formerly on the coffee table and she let out an awful yell.

Her neighbor came running, bursting through the open door and crunching precious seashells beneath his sneakers until he reached her side. "What happened?"

She looked down at the trail of broken shells then up into eyes that seemed truly concerned. And began to cry.

"I'm really sorry about Chief. I just brought him back from Houston yesterday and he's not used to his new surroundings yet," he said as he picked pieces of what once was a beautiful and perfectly formed sand dollar from the sole of his shoe.

"It's not this," she said as she used her sleeve to swipe at the traitorous tears streaming down her cheeks. "It's just…" A sob caused her to pause. "It's just that I've had a lot on my mind, what with trying to keep the restaurant going and the stables and now there's the issue with Pop that will probably cause it all to…" This time she closed her mouth of her own accord. "I'm sorry," she said when she knew she could manage it. "I didn't mean to unload on you."

"Hey, it's okay," he said. "I've had a bad day or two myself lately. I don't mind listening."

She dabbed at her eyes again. "I think you've already listened to me enough for one day."

"Leah, anything I can do to help..."

Leah squared her shoulders and blinked back further tears. "I'm fine. Honestly. Weak moment, okay?"

He nodded, looking at her closely. "Okay. So, where's the dead animal?"

"Dead animal?"

Ryan nodded. "That's what he usually tries to drag into the house."

Leah rose to pick her way gently across the floor to her desk. "There's no dead animal. Just that toy over there. Well, and this mess."

He opened his mouth as if to say something then must have thought better of it. Instead, he moved toward the kitchen where he found the dustpan and broom.

"Please," Leah said as she dug in the desk drawer for tissues. "Leave that alone. I'll take care of it."

"Not a chance." He leveled her an even look that told her not to argue, then set to work. "Go back to reading your book."

"How did you know I was reading?"

Ryan gave her a sheepish look. "We share a beach, Leah," he said before turning again to his task.

"Right." Leah blew her nose then tossed the tissue into the trash before grabbing another. By now what was left of her mascara was surely cascading down her cheeks. The extent of the damage became clear when she excused herself to go wash her face in the bathroom sink.

Scrubbing the tracks of Maybelline off her face only left red splotches behind. And not even Visine could remove the red from eyes that still threatened to spill over with tears.

Leah turned her back on the mirror and stepped out into the living area only to spy Ryan emptying the dust-pan. He turned to gesture toward a Hefty box, and to his credit his expression gave no indication of the hor-ror he must be witnessing on her face.

"Hope you don't mind but I found these in the pantry. Now why don't you go sit down and rest a little? You hit your head pretty hard." He went back to his tasks without waiting for her response.

Though she complied without comment, Leah paused frequently to give in to the urge to watch Ryan's prog-ress. Before long, he'd made short work of reducing the mess in the kitchen to the contents of a black garbage bag. Setting the trash aside, he moved into the center of the room where he made an attempt to right the arrange-ment of pillows. Leah stifled a smile as she watched the thoroughly masculine man fumbling around with the placement of the frilly decorations.

Whether he gave up or deemed the decor appealing, Leah couldn't say. If nothing else, he'd achieved a rigid symmetry that she'd never be able to replicate. Unlike her random-toss technique, Ryan had made sure each pillow was equidistant from the next and not a one dared lean even a millimeter out of line.

Kneeling beside the coffee table, he gingerly placed the whole shells back into the bowl then swept the bro-ken shells onto the dustpan. "Guess I owe you more of these," he said as he emptied the contents of the dust-pan into the garbage bag.

"Won't take long to replace the broken ones," she said.

With a nod, he turned to assess the bed curtains.

"Did you hang those yourself?" When she nodded, Ryan glanced up at the ceiling and the fabric dangling from the end of the rod. "If you've got a stepladder, I think I can fix this."

"Downstairs." She moved toward the door.

"No, you sit right there. I'll go get it. Just tell me where to find it."

Leah paused. "It's hanging on a peg in the storage room," she said to his back.

His footsteps retreated down the stairs. When she was finally alone, Leah closed her eyes. Her head throbbed in the spot where she'd thudded it against the wall. *What a day.*

First she'd learned that Pop hadn't inspected the restaurant since 1973. Then she'd poured out her heart to Ryan about how hard things had been since she'd come back. And now her apartment was in shambles and she'd probably given herself a concussion.

Not to mention the fact that her father's replacement was a charming, handsome man...who had moved in next door and was now in her house.

Clearly a concussion wasn't the only reason her head hurt.

Chapter Six

"Found it," Ryan called as his feet hit the wooden steps. A moment later, he came through the door carrying the folding step stool. "This ought to be an easy fix," he said when he had the stool in place.

"Actually, I used the ladder when I hung them." Leah rose. "Didn't you see it down there?"

"I did but this one was easier to get to." He gave the situation a look. "This will be fine."

Leah shrugged. Ryan was at least a head taller, so perhaps he could get by with just the step stool. Still, the ceiling in this cabin was awfully high.

"Trust me," he said as he waved away her look of protest with a sweep of his hand. "I'm certified on ladders."

"Funny," Leah said.

Ryan climbed the step stool and made a grab for the curtain rod. The fabric encasing it refused to budge. He gave a pull but only made things worse.

"Oh, no," Leah called as she hurried to help him unravel from the tangle of fabric. The job was made all the more difficult by the fact that Ryan refused to be still and allow her to assist him.

"I'm making a mess of this," Ryan said.

"Welcome to my world." She sank down on the floor beside him and reached for the curtain's rod. "Here, let me help. I'll thread the curtain back on while you hold the rod steady."

Perhaps it was the mummylike curtain wrappings he was attempting to unravel, or maybe it was the look of pure exasperation on his face. Whatever the reason, a giggle rose in her throat.

It wasn't funny. Really, she had no business laughing when her whole world could be falling down around her should the restaurant fail inspection. Just as the curtains had fallen on Ryan Owen.

The thought propelled her giggles into actual laughter.

"Well, I'm glad I could at least lighten your mood," Ryan said as he cast the last of the fabric aside.

Leah stifled her laughter to nod. "Yes, you've done a great job of that. Thank you."

"Long as you don't tense up, you can usually come out fine."

He grinned and dimples appeared at the corners of his mouth.

"Too bad you're not certified on curtains." And with the comment, her giggles returned.

This time Ryan joined her. "No, I guarantee the instructors at the Houston Fire Department haven't even considered that one."

Leah released the wad of curtains in her hand. "Odd that you would choose to leave the big city to come here."

"Not really. It's what I needed to do."

"I see," she said, though she really didn't.

"Yeah, life's funny. Just when you think the Lord has your path clearly marked, He goes and moves the road. At least that's what my wife used to say."

"Wife?" Only after the word came out did Leah realize she'd said it aloud.

"Guess I didn't mention her." Ryan ducked his head. "Um," he said as he lifted his gaze to meet hers. "She's gone. She died, is what I mean. On our honeymoon."

Leah's smile froze.

"It was a diving accident. I should have been able to revive her, but…"

With no good response handy, she bundled the curtain fabric into a pile then rose to begin folding it. Ryan climbed to his feet and grabbed the opposite corners. As their fingers met, Leah looked up into his eyes and found Ryan studying her.

Say something. But no words came. So Leah offered her next-door neighbor a smile and turned her attention to the fabric in her hands.

They continued folding until the curtains were stacked neatly on the kitchen counter. Ryan righted the stool and climbed up to look at the ceiling. "Looks like the hook came out. I've probably got one in my truck."

As soon as he disappeared down the steps, Leah groaned. "Nothing like sticking your foot in your mouth, Leah." She thought about everything Ryan had just said, about losing his wife on their honeymoon a year ago. What a horrible thing to go through. Her heart nearly broke for Ryan, though she knew he didn't want anyone's pity.

She walked outside and moved to the rail to rest her

elbows on the weathered wood. The temperature was relatively comfortable for November but the clouds boiling on the horizon threatened rain before dark. Leah sighed. A stormy night certainly suited her mood.

Baby rubbed against Leah's ankles, purring loudly. When Ryan turned the corner and headed up the stairs, the cat skittered away.

He set his toolbox on the deck then disappeared downstairs to return with the ladder. "Figured I'd give your idea a try," he said with a lift of his brow. "Give me just a second and I'll be out of your way." After he brought the toolbox in, he returned for the ladder. "I might need your help getting those curtains on the rod," he joked, obviously trying to lighten the mood.

She watched the fireman disappear through the door with the ladder balanced on his shoulder. "Sure," she called to his retreating back.

Rather than follow Ryan inside, Leah watched from the door as he set up the ladder. This time his repair was swift and successful. When he reached for the folded fabric, she stepped in to help thread the curtains onto the rod then handed them to Ryan to hang.

"All done," he said as came down from the ladder to put away the tools.

She watched his dark head bent over his task and wondered whether to bring up the topic of his wife again. Before curiosity got the better of her, Leah busied herself adjusting the curtains then securing them with tiebacks. Still she wondered about the late Mrs. Owen. How young had the poor woman been when she died?

Was her death the reason he left an apparently good job with the Houston Fire Department to move to Vine Beach? Too many memories in Houston?

Leah shook her head. What was wrong with her? She'd always been a private person—more now that Pop's illness had progressed—yet why was her mind so focused on invading the privacy of someone else?

She couldn't help herself. Ryan was clearly a man in pain, and she wanted to ease his burden somehow.

Even though the smart thing to do was stay away from the man who had the potential to shut down her restaurant—and change her life forever.

Ryan fitted the ladder back in place then gave it a tug to make sure the hooks held. Given the issue he'd just fixed upstairs, he wouldn't take anything for granted as far as hardware in this place. Satisfied that the ladder was safely stowed, he sprinted up the stairs with the intention of getting his toolbox and making a quick escape.

He hadn't intended to tell Leah everything he'd told her, but she was just so easy to talk to. It had been a long time since he'd told anyone even a little bit about what had happened. It felt good.

He'd planned on throwing a steak on the grill and enjoying it while he watched the sunset. Maybe he'd offer to grill one for Leah, as well. A couple baked potatoes and a glass of sweet tea and they'd have a fine meal.

The thought stopped him cold.

This was the woman who ran the restaurant that he was about to shut down. The woman whose house mysteriously burned down. He needed to keep his distance.

He paused at the door. Leah was standing stock-still, her back against the kitchen cabinet and her thoughts seemingly miles away. The afternoon sun streamed in through the window behind her and caught her profile in its fiery glow. For a moment, her beauty took his breath away.

"I'll grab my toolbox and the step stool and get out of your way," he said before he could make another mistake.

Leah jumped as he interrupted her thoughts. Pretending he didn't notice, Ryan moved past her to fold the step stool flat then reach for his toolbox.

He'd almost escaped when Leah called his name. "Yeah?" he said as he turned around to face her.

"Thank you," she replied.

Ryan hesitated only a moment before offering up a nod in response then made his exit. Only when he reached his house did he slow down. That woman was dangerous for him, and it had nothing to do with the fact he'd walked out of there with broken shells in his shoes and a fresh set of bruises from battling a set of curtains.

He climbed the stairs and slipped inside his temporary home. Navigating the boxes with Chief at his heels was dicey, but he managed it. He opened the fridge to grab a bottle of water then tackled the job of unpacking that he'd put off last night when he had arrived back in Vine Beach.

The first two boxes emptied quickly as he filled up the kitchen cabinets with the few items he'd deemed necessary for his new life. All the fancy things—the crystal, china and other things that Jenna had insisted on registering for—were stowed away along with the furniture he'd sent to storage. Memories of that life didn't belong in this one. That had been his reason at the time.

If only it were that simple.

Ryan lifted another box onto the counter and opened

it. This one was filled with books, the topmost being the Bible that had seen him through the past year. He set it aside and made quick work of filling the bookshelf in the corner.

Another half hour of work and he was almost done. Chief had given up on gaining Ryan's attention and moved to the sliding glass door where he had a bird's eye view of all that went on down at the beach. The dog seemed enthralled, though to his credit he didn't dare bark every time a beachgoer strolled past. He did lift his head when Ryan crossed the room to stand beside him.

Lumbering to his feet, Chief pawed at the door. "Not just yet," Ryan said. "One more box then maybe we'll take a jog before dark. How's that, boy? Can you wait?"

The dog settled back down, leaving Ryan to return to his work. Letting out a long breath, he took a swig of water then yanked at the tape holding together the last carton. Ten minutes later the box was empty and his unpacking complete. He added the flattened box to the stack by the door then carried them down to put away in the storage closet.

Though the hedge between his place and Leah's was thick, he could see through the swaying leaves that her vehicle was still in the driveway. Ignoring another urge to invite her to dinner, he grabbed Chief's leash and headed upstairs.

As his running shoes hit the beach, Ryan cast one last glance over his shoulder. Leah was back in her spot under the umbrella, a book in her hand. The orange cat watched from the porch rail as Ryan paused only a second before turning in the opposite direction.

The beach was less crowded here, he justified. Fewer beachgoers meant a faster run, for Chief was one curious mutt around strangers. This afternoon was proof that moving to the beach hadn't changed that part of the bullmastiff's personality. Nor had he changed his mind about cats being more friend than foe. If he had, Leah's orange fuzz ball wouldn't have survived the battle over the toy.

He rounded a curve and found himself nearing the harbor. Beyond the cluster of boats was a stretch of highway that led to Houston. On the opposite side of the cove was the lighthouse and dock where he'd taken Leah for their thank-you picnic.

Glancing back, he could see them both. Just beyond the lighthouse was the Berry home. From his vantage point, he could just make out the black smudge of the ruins. The setting sun had painted the broken columns with a golden brush, giving the place a surreal look.

Chief's bark caught his attention. "What's up, buddy?" he said as he turned toward the harbor where a flash of light danced off the waves. Again the dog barked, this time at the bride and groom who posed at the end of the dock for a photographer intent on capturing them before the sunset.

"Hush, boy," he said as he clenched the leash tighter and slowed his jog to a walk. The bride wore white, the groom deepest black, and together as they posed and teased one another, Ryan couldn't help but thinking about his own wedding.

Before Ryan could stop them, thoughts of Jenna in a flowing white gown and veil tumbled forth, as did snatches of other recollections. Fittings. Meetings with caterers. So many details. What had happened to just them, the Lord and a way to profess their love?

Ultimately their wedding had gone from a sunset

service on the beach with family and a few friends to a ridiculously formal affair in the biggest church in Houston complete with a country club reception. Somewhere between the asking and the I-dos, the planning of the extravaganza had taken over their relationship and made Ryan feel like a hamster on a wheel. What had begun as *their* wedding became THE wedding—a production that would outdo any of the other Junior League affairs held before it.

Their first fight had been over some ridiculous detail of the wedding and it had been followed in quick succession by too many more to count. At some point he'd left Jenna and her mother in charge and relegated himself to nodding when asked and keeping his mouth shut the rest of the time.

Not for the first time, Ryan wondered what might have happened if they'd declined to accept the fancy honeymoon gift from Jenna's parents in favor of the trip to the rustic Hill Country bed-and-breakfast Ryan had originally planned as a wedding surprise.

She'd still be alive. That much he knew with complete certainty.

And he'd be back on that hamster wheel, this time as husband to a woman whose life was bent around the will of her prominent family and appearances. A life that was no life at all for a guy who preferred to ride horses and fight fires rather than escort the former Miss Texas Rodeo to her unending social obligations.

Jenna's death was a tragic accident that he'd have wished on no one. Had she lived, would their marriage have been a tragedy of a different kind?

The thought shocked Ryan. He yanked Chief's leash and headed back toward the cabin at top speed. It chased him through the rest of the evening, barging in while he grilled his steak and watched the evening news.

After several sleepless hours of tossing and turning, Ryan gave up on his bed, snatched up his Bible from the kitchen counter and headed toward the deck to meet the Lord along with the sunrise, looking for some insight into the revelation he'd held at bay since Jenna's death.

Three days into his job as fire chief and Ryan had almost completed his inspections of all the public buildings in Vine Beach, including the nursing home and the three public schools. Public buildings then private businesses, that was his mandate, though the mayor did make it plain once again at their meeting this morning that he wanted Pop's moved near the top of the list once he began checking private businesses.

Ryan leaned back in his chair and laced his hands behind his head. He knew things would likely not go well once he got around to taking a closer look at the restaurant.

A knock diverted his attention, then Riley Burkett peered around the door. "Catching you at a bad time?"

He rose and beckoned the Realtor to come in. "Have a seat," he said as he gestured to the chair across from him.

"Don't want to interrupt anything," Burkett said, "but I just wanted to check in." He settled onto the chair. "You said something last week that made me think you could use some help...with grief?"

"Yeah," came out on a long breath as Ryan rose to walk over and close the door. "Look, I'm no good at talking about my loss. I lost my wife," Ryan explained.

"I wouldn't expect it comes easy to anyone," Burkett

said. "Especially someone as young as you. I doubt a man stands at the altar on his wedding day and contemplates the fact he could lose the woman he's pledging to spend his life with."

"I know I didn't." Ryan returned to his chair and rested his palms on the desk. "Tell me about this Starting Over group."

Riley smiled. "I'd be glad to. We're a bunch of guys learning to live with the reality of our losses. Some have been at this awhile. Others have gone on to remarry but don't want to give up the fellowship. Then there are the ones who are new at it. All are welcome. Oh, and did I mention we play a little basketball, too?"

Ryan chuckled. "No, I don't believe you did."

Burkett gave him an appraising look. "You're decent height and seem to be in good shape. Ever play?"

"Actually I went to A&M on a full ride. Coach blames the fire department for keeping me out of the NBA. Personally, I know better." He shook his head. "Haven't played in way too long, though."

"Well now." The older man's grin broadened. "I'll certainly take that into consideration next time we divide into teams. That is, if you're planning to show up at a meeting."

"I might," he said slowly.

"Eight o'clock Saturday mornings. We offer strong coffee, a nice selection of doughnuts and breakfast burritos and a good dose of the gospel." His expression sobered. "We get into some serious stuff, so don't think it's all playing around."

Ryan nodded. "The administrator at the nursing home mentioned that a bunch of your guys were there putting up Thanksgiving decorations earlier in the week."

"Yep, and we did the same thing over at the hospital. Word gets out that we're free labor and we never know where we'll be called next. But I have to admit that's part of the fun of it."

"Must feel good to help."

"It does," Burkett said. "In my experience, a man's a whole lot more content when his attention is off himself and focused on others. Having said that, I don't want a single man to leave feeling like he's got to manage his grief alone so we keep that in perspective. We're brothers in Christ and we stand together."

"Understood."

He nodded. "All right. Now that you've heard my sales pitch for Starting Over, let's talk about that counseling appointment. Still interested?"

"The truth?" When Burkett nodded, Ryan continued, "Talking about what happened is the last thing I want to do. Ever."

"And yet?" he urged.

"And yet I know if I don't I'll never be free to…"

"Love again?"

The question stunned him. Especially when Leah popped into his head.

Burkett must have sensed his reluctance to answer, for he pulled a small day planner from his pocket and thumbed through the pages. "I'm free tomorrow morning and Friday afternoon. Either of those times work for you or should we look at next week?"

He agreed to an appointment as much to get it out of the way as to give him the rest of the day to change his mind. But as Burkett left, Ryan knew he'd keep the appointment. He had to.

It was the only way to move forward and possibly put down the terrible burden of guilt that he'd been carrying with him for a year now.

It was time.

Chapter Seven

"Good morning, hon," the head nurse called as Leah stepped through the double doors that marked Pop's wing of the care facility.

Since her last visit on Sunday, the halls had been decorated in an autumn theme for the coming Thanksgiving holiday. Everywhere she looked paper leaves of multiple colors filled the walls around posters of Pilgrims and turkeys and the traditional fruit-filled cornucopia baskets.

"Good morning, Geneva," Leah responded. "The place looks great. Tell whoever did this that I heartily approve."

Geneva grinned. "Can't credit this to us," she said. "Thank the Starting Over fellows from the church. You probably just missed them on Sunday afternoon."

"Well how about that?" Leah ran her hand along the fat beanbag turkey decorating the nursing station before moving toward her father's room. "They did a good job," she cast over her shoulder.

"They did, didn't they?" Geneva paused. "Now you tell your daddy I'm watching him."

Leah stopped to turn around. "What's he done now?"

She shook her head. "Nothing terrible. Just thought he was going to take a walk last evening. Said he needed to talk to the mayor about something he'd made him promise. Anyway, the night shift supervisor found him halfway out the door in his pajama pants and suit jacket."

Leah frowned. Pop's doctors had warned that wandering was one of a laundry list of symptoms that could appear in the future, but thus far the issue had not occurred. For that reason, her father remained happily in a small studio apartment on a ward where there was little need for close supervision.

Perhaps it was time to have another chat with his doctor about the level of attention Pop received. Given this new turn of events, her plan to speak to Pop about the needed fire inspection might have to wait.

But then with Pop she never knew. His episodes, as he called them, were rare now that his doctor had found a medication that eased the symptoms. Some days he was the old Pop. Others he was close enough to fool most folks who didn't know him like Leah did.

"Don't worry, hon," Geneva said. "Your daddy was sweet as he could be when the orderlies told him they'd convey the message he was intent on delivering. Went back to his room and wrote down what he wanted to send to the mayor then went right to sleep without a single complaint. Least that's the report I got."

She backtracked to the nurse's station. "Would you know what happened to that note? I'd like to see it."

"Well now, that's a good question. Why don't you go on and visit with your daddy and I'll see if I can find out about it?"

With a nod, Leah headed toward Pop's room. She found him watching a game show in his recliner and shouting out prices along with the television audience.

As always, his room was neat as a pin, but then Pop had never quite managed to leave his military mindset behind when it came to housekeeping. The room boasted a bed in one corner and a small sitting area with a television in the other. Beneath the south-facing window in between was a tiny table just big enough for the two chairs drawn up to it. The stack of books she'd brought from the Vine Beach Library remained in the center of the table where she'd left them yesterday.

"Leah," Pop said when he spied her. "Now, isn't this a nice surprise? Let me turn off this noise." He pointed the remote and silenced the television then rose to greet her. "Either I'm further gone than I thought or you just came to see me yesterday after church."

"You're close. Sunday was three days ago, Dad," she said gently as she fell into his strong embrace. As ever, he smelled of Old Spice and Ivory soap, a combination that took her back to childhood every time.

"So it's Wednesday, is it?" Pop offered a broad grin. "Come and sit," he said. "I've still got some of the cookies you brought last week. Want some? I bet I could fetch us cold milk from the cafeteria to go with it."

"Sounds wonderful, Pop," she said as she followed him over to the little table and took a seat across from him, "but I'm not going to risk getting in trouble with Geneva for ruining your appetite so close to lunch."

"Is it close to lunch?" He lifted up his sleeve to reveal the watch he'd worn as long as Leah could remember. After staring at the dial a moment, he shrugged and removed the ancient Bulova then thrust it toward her. "Better have Sam Carson take a look at it."

Leah bit back her response. Sam Carson's jewelry shop had been closed for nearly ten years. Instead she slipped the watch onto her own wrist with a nod then glanced at the time. It was correct.

Mustering a smile, Leah rested her hands in her lap. "So, Pop," she said slowly, "what's this I hear about you wanting out last night?"

Pop blinked hard then his face went blank. "Last night?" He shrugged as his fingers worried with the cover of the book on the top of the stack. "I don't know what you mean. This is my home now that Berry Hill's a pile of ashes. Why would I want to leave?"

There could be any number of reasons why her father wouldn't want to own up to his actions last night, not the least of which was his pride. But when his gaze collided with hers, she knew he was sincere.

She reached for his hand and held it tight. "What did you want to tell Jack Murdoch?"

The familiar look of frustration she'd come to know all too well formed on his face. Any thoughts of discussing the restaurant's safety inspection history evaporated.

Finally he loosened his grip on her hand. "Goodness, girl," he said as he pushed back the chair and rose. "I haven't seen Jack in at least a week. Maybe two." Pop ran his hand through his still-thick salt-and-pepper hair then focused his attention on a spot somewhere outside the window. "Unless you know something I don't. Did I miss a City Council meeting?"

She mustered a smile. "How about we change the subject and talk about Christmas? With Thanksgiving two weeks away, we need to make a decision on holiday plans."

"What kind of decision?"

"Well," she said slowly, "I know how much you loved opening up the restaurant to the public on the night of the boat parade, and the folks in town have come to look at the buffet we serve as a yearly tradition."

"As well they should," he said. "The money we collect goes to a good cause. Think of all the things that have been done with our little donation."

"It's not such a little donation, Pop," Leah continued. "In fact, the money we earn from that evening alone could pay for..." She paused to once again search her father's face.

"Leah Berry," Pop said slowly, "you're not actually thinking of profiting from the Christmas buffet, are you?"

"Well, Pop, I'm expecting some big expenses at the restaurant."

"Answer me," her father said. "Are you considering keeping the money that the citizens of our town will expect to be donated?"

His eyes pierced her soul and punctured her big plans to settle her accounts quickly and simply. "When you put it like that, it sounds awful."

He squared his shoulders, his eyes narrowed. "It is awful, girl. I'll not hear of such a thing. Do you understand?"

Leah let out a long breath and closed her eyes, taking a moment to recover from doing battle with her formidable father. She opened her eyes at the sound of the game show filling the room again. Pop was happily assisting the current contestant choose the proper price for a can of creamed corn.

"Guess I'll see you again in a few days, okay, Pop?"

He nodded, though it was difficult for Leah to tell whether her father was responding to her question or the amount the contestant pledged for the corn. Her heart heavy, Leah kissed her father on the top of his head and left him before his mood changed again. At the nurses' station, she found Geneva scribbling notes in a file.

"That was a short visit," she said as she handed Leah the folded note she'd found.

"'The desk fixes everything?'"

"Didn't make sense to me but I hoped maybe it would to you," the nurse said.

"Not a bit." Leah dropped the note into her red purse. "He doesn't remember anything about last night's escape attempt. Is that cause for concern?"

"It could be," the nurse said. "I sure wouldn't have expected something like that out of him. I will say he hasn't been as social lately. Most days he keeps to himself at mealtime, which isn't like him."

"Definitely not," she said as she recalled the days when Pop spent as much time in the restaurant dining room as he did in the kitchen. He'd been as interested in finding out the latest goings-on in Vine Beach as cooking, which suited Orlando just fine.

Geneva reached over the counter to pat Leah's shoulder, jarring her from her thoughts. "I'll keep close tabs on him. Don't you worry, you hear?"

Don't worry. She almost laughed at the absurdity of the statement.

Geneva's eyes narrowed. "What's he doing back here?"

Leah followed the direction of the nurse's stare and

spied the new fire chief walking through the doors. Before their gazes met, however, Ryan disappeared into the administrator's office.

"That is one handsome man," Geneva said, "even if he does make me nervous."

Leah turned to face the nurse, shrugging off the thought of Ryan as handsome. "Why does he make you nervous?"

"He was here for almost two hours doing his fire inspection." She craned her neck as if to better see what was going on in the office.

"So he was tough? I guess that's a good thing, right? I mean, it's good that he wants the facility to be safe." Leah began to once again consider what it might be like when Ryan showed up to inspect Pop's Seafood. The thought was not a pleasant one.

Nor was the idea that Pop might somehow meet up with the man who'd taken his job.

Leah decided to take a seat on the bench outside the administrator's office to wait for Ryan. As she watched the staff go about their work, her mind tumbled back to a time when she, too, did something of value. Not that keeping Pop's open and its employees in their jobs wasn't valuable work, for it certainly was. But it wasn't a Paris symposium or a Smithsonian consultancy, the selfish part of her reminded.

Nor was it as mentally challenging and satisfying as the curating she'd done for multiple public and private entities. Leah sighed. And yet caring for Pop and the business he loved was exactly what the Lord would have her do.

So despite the fact she missed so many things about the career she'd left, she wouldn't have it any other way. Though she knew she could return to that work someday, there would be no recouping of missed time with Pop.

A few minutes later, Ryan emerged with the administrator. "Glad you stopped by," the older man said as he shook Ryan's hand. "Very, very glad indeed."

Leah sent up a prayer that she, too, would come out of the inevitable inspection unscathed. For though the Lord had never promised an easy path, He'd never failed to walk beside her and help navigate the rough spots.

"In all things give thanks," she said under her breath. Her mother's favorite saying, and one that Leah had learned at an early age. *I'm trying, Mom. I'm really trying.*

If only her mom were here to offer advice. She'd know what to do about Pop. And the restaurant. And the handsome fire chief who had the power to turn her life upside down—in more ways than one.

But mom's battle with heart disease had taken her far too soon, leaving Leah and Pop to fend for themselves the past three years. It was almost a blessing that her mother hadn't lived long enough to witness Pop's sad decline.

Leah sighed as she realized she agreed completely with Geneva. *That man makes me nervous, too.*

Chapter Eight

After saying their goodbyes, the administrator disappeared down the hall and Ryan headed toward the exit. Quickly Leah moved to follow him.

"Hey," she called as she fell in step beside him. "Got a minute?"

"Oh, hi." The fireman checked his watch. "Sure."

"I feel kind of silly seeing as you're obviously leaving…"

"I am," he said, "but why would you feel silly?"

She met his stare as her heart did a slight flip-flop. "It's just that…well… I saw you walk in and was a little concerned that you might…"

What was wrong with her? She could barely complete a thought.

Leah forced herself to continue. "I felt I needed to ask a favor of you, seeing as you've been here twice this week."

One dark brow lifted. "Tracking my movements now?"

She laughed then tried not to cringe. "Of course not. I only wanted to ask that you avoid any contact with my father while you're here."

He shook his head. "Not a problem, Leah. I was just leaving and don't expect to be back anytime soon."

"Good. Well...thank you. I just don't know how Pop would react if he found out he wasn't...you know."

"Still the chief? I don't expect he'll hear that from me." He nodded toward the door. "Are you leaving or arriving?"

"Leaving," she said.

"But what about my request?"

"Yes. I just need more time to introduce Pop to the idea that he's been replaced."

"I'll think about it." He nodded toward the door. "I'll walk you out."

"So," Leah said as the doors closed behind them, "are you settling in to your new job?"

"Going pretty well so far." He gave her a sideways glance. "Any luck finding that paperwork for Pop's Seafood?"

"No." She clutched tighter the strap of her purse. "There wasn't anything in the files at the restaurant that looked like a fire inspection. You know, they may have been out at the house. It's unlikely as Pop had a rule about not bringing work home, but in those last months before the fire I understand he wasn't completely himself."

A niggle of regret snaked into her thoughts. If only she'd known...

"It's very possible," Ryan said. "I'm still working on my end to see what I can turn up."

"Something about my fire?"

"I've got my doubts that it was accidental."

They arrived at her SUV, and she reached into her purse to grab the keys. A slip of paper fluttered out and landed at Ryan's feet. He grabbed it and handed it to Leah. "Don't figure you want to lose this," he said. "Looks like something written on nursing home stationary so I'm guessing it's important."

"No," she said as she opened the door and tossed her purse onto the passenger seat then returned her attention to the folded sheet of paper in her hand. "It's the note my father was intent on passing on to Mayor Murdoch last night. He actually tried to leave here and take this to him."

He shifted positions to cross his arms over his chest. "Is that allowed?"

"No, of course not, but Pop must have thought it was important at the time." She sighed. "Unfortunately, he doesn't remember a bit of it today. Swears he never tried to leave."

"I'm sorry," Ryan said. "Must be tough to deal with this kind of thing."

"It is, though it's the first time he's tried anything like this. Kind of makes me wonder what was so important and whether this is the beginning of his decline."

"I'll protect him as much as I can, Leah." He gestured to the letter. "As to the letter, I don't mind dropping it off with the mayor. I'm headed back to City Hall now."

"Thank you but I don't think that's necessary. I'm sure it's nothing," she said as she climbed into her car.

"Guess so."

As she watched Ryan walk away, she thought of the steaks she'd smelled last night and almost asked him what was for dinner. Almost. But not quite.

She had far too many reasons to keep her distance from the handsome fireman. Not the least of which was the man who now lived in the nursing home. Hurting Pop was the last thing she intended to do, and he'd never understand why someone else had taken the job he loved.

She closed the door and jabbed her keys into the ignition then reread Pop's note. "The desk fixes everything." What sort of nonsense was that?

Leah shook her head as she stuffed the page back into her purse. Just another nonsensical thought from a man whose memories were fading. If only Ryan could be more trustworthy. Saying he would try to protect Pop while insinuating the fire wasn't accidental concerned her. So did the idea that Ryan might press the issue of the fire inspection.

Saturday morning arrived far too early. After his counseling session on Thursday, Ryan had promised Riley to give the Starting Over group a try. Now that the day had come, he was already regretting the decision.

A few cars clustered on the far end of the parking lot near the church's basketball court as he stopped in the parking space next to Riley's car. A black truck pulled in beside him, and a man about his age jumped out.

"You must be the new guy," he said as Ryan stepped out of the Jeep. "Dad told me to look for you."

"Yeah, I guess I am." Ryan reached to shake his hand. "Ryan Owen."

"Nice to meet you, Ryan," he said. "I'm Eric Wilson. Town veterinarian. I'm newly remarried, but still attend sometimes. Riley's married to my mom. You probably met her at the real estate office."

"Susan? Yes, I remember her." He paused. "Small world."

"No, small town. Everyone's either related or about to be. At least that's how it seems."

"So, town vet, eh? You're on my list of folks to call," he said. "I've got a bullmastiff who's going to need an update on his shots before the end of the year."

The vet glanced down at his attire—basketball shorts, sneakers and a sweatshirt emblazoned with the logo of the Vine Beach Rams—then held up both hands. "Sorry, but I don't have a card on me. We're easy to find, though. Right across from—"

"The courthouse," Ryan supplied. "That's where my office is. I'm the new fire chief."

"Well how about that?" Eric grinned. "Glad the mayor finally made good on a campaign promise and filled that job. Guess you know about the former chief."

"Carl Berry," he said. "Yeah, I do."

After an awkward moment, Eric gestured toward the basketball court. "Come on. I'll make the introductions."

Two hours later Ryan left with a new perspective, a half-dozen new friends and sore muscles he'd be soaking in Epsom salts by bedtime. As Riley had predicted, he'd not only enjoyed himself but he'd also felt a shared acceptance among the men whose journeys had aligned loosely with his.

For once, he wasn't the odd man out. And that counted for something.

"Coming back next week?" Eric asked as they walked toward their vehicles.

"Yeah, I think I will."

"Glad to hear it. You've got some moves on the basketball court. I'm glad we were on the same team."

Ryan laughed. "It's been a long time since I played. Felt good getting out there."

"Hey, do you sail?"

"That's something else I haven't done in a long time, but yeah, I used to sail quite a lot when I was younger." He clicked the lock on the Jeep and reached for the door handle. "Why?"

"A couple friends and I were going to take my boat out tomorrow after church. Figured I'd see if you were interested in coming along."

"Sure," he said with a grin. "Sounds great."

"We generally end up making an afternoon of it, then head over to Sand Island to throw some steaks on the grill. I'll have you home by dark."

Ryan laughed. "Only if you'll let me bring the steaks this time. My dad owns a cattle ranch north of Austin, so he keeps me pretty well stocked. Unfortunately the freezer in my rental isn't nearly as big as the one I had in Houston."

Eric shook his head. "Say no more, my friend. I will be happy to help you with that problem. You bring the steaks and we'll supply the rest."

After exchanging phone numbers and agreeing on the time and place, Ryan climbed into the Jeep and headed back to the cabin. This time when he spied Leah sitting on the beach under the umbrella, he headed right for her.

"Shouldn't you be working or something?" he asked as he stood between Leah and the waves.

"Kate's covering the lunch shift so I don't have to be there for a couple of hours." Leah closed the cover on her e-reader and set it in her lap then regarded him carefully. "What have you been up to?"

"I just spent the morning being reminded of all the muscles I haven't used in a while."

"Oh?" she asked. He could tell she was keeping her distance.

"Yeah." He flopped down on the sand and stretched out his long legs. "Spent the morning playing basketball. I haven't done that since college."

"I see."

He shifted positions to look toward the horizon. "Over there. Is that Sand Island?"

"Yes, it is." She dug her toes into the sand, likely to warm them. Fall had finally come to Vine Beach, and with it a chill wind that kicked up at odd moments. "It's accessible only by boat."

"What's on it?"

"Not much. Shells, a few trees and a nice wide beach. It's perfect for picnics. I used to go there a lot but it's been ages since I've been." She paused. "Why?"

"Met a guy playing basketball this morning who offered to take me and some others over there for a barbecue. Just wondered what it was like." He rose and moved downwind to shake the sand from his legs. "You happen to know Eric Wilson?"

"The vet?"

Ryan nodded. "That's the guy. Seems nice enough."

"He is. Of course I'm biased. I went to school with Eric, and his wife, Amy, is one of my best friends." She paused. "You met his youngest daughter at the pier last week. Remember Brooke?"

"Sure, the little blonde who was fishing with Riley. I remember her."

"She's a big sister now. As of six weeks ago. Amy and Eric had a little boy. Cutest thing." Leah clamped her mouth shut. She was finding it really tough to keep her distance from Ryan, which, of course, was exactly what she should be doing.

"No wonder the guy needs a break. Four kids. Wow."

Leah stifled a frown. "You make it sound like a burden."

"I just can't imagine one, much less four. I mean, I have enough trouble keeping my dog in line. Can you imagine trying to raise all those kids?"

She could, actually. Would have welcomed it had the Lord offered up marriage and family as an option. Instead she'd been relegated to a whole other field than motherhood.

Ryan's phone rang, and he answered it. Leah picked up her e-reader and tried to concentrate on the page that had held her enthralled before her neighbor's unexpected arrival. Instead, she could only listen as he spoke to someone about a change in plans. About the need for a new departure time. The wind once again kicked up, this time causing Leah to reach for the beach towel she'd stowed in her bag. Wrapping the towel around her legs, she settled back onto her chair.

Abruptly he turned to face her. "I'll ask. Hey, Leah, want to go sailing with Eric and Amy and the girls tomorrow afternoon?"

"Uh, well…" She shrugged. "Sure, why not?"

Ryan repeated her answer then, a moment later, hung up. "Okay, we're set. Eric's girls talked him into taking them sailing instead of the guys. He arranged for Riley and Susan to keep the baby so Amy can come along. He figured you'd want to come and hang out, too."

Simple as that. And just as complicated.

"Well, all right. I guess."

He gave her a sideways look as he shielded his eyes from the sun. "You guess?"

Leah rose and tucked her e-reader into her bag then folded the chair and pulled up her umbrella. "Okay, it's a plan. Unless it gets any colder. I don't like sailing in a parka, and it *is* November."

"November in Texas," he said. "It'll be fine."

"You sound pretty sure of yourself."

Ryan snagged the handles of her bag then reached for the chair and umbrella. "I do, don't I?" he said as he set off toward their shared property line.

"That's because I am. Remember, I'm the guy charged with the public safety in this town. You'll be fine with me."

Chapter Nine

Amy Wilson greeted Leah with a hug and a grin. "I'm so glad you could come today. I haven't been sailing in months because a certain veterinarian thought it wasn't safe while I was pregnant."

"Did she mention that she gets horribly seasick, Leah?" Eric called from the other side of the deck where he was helping the girls into their life jackets. "And that her obstetrician suggested she avoid anything that might make her any more nauseous than she already was?"

"Yes, well, on that lovely note, welcome aboard." She looked past Leah then back at her. "Where's Ryan? I thought he'd be with you."

"Ryan?" She shook her head. "I don't know."

"Oh," Amy said as she pressed a curl behind her ear. "I just thought that maybe you two were... I don't know...together?"

Leah handed her bag to Eric and watched him stow it in the galley. "Why would you think that?"

"I guess I just heard...well...that is..."

She lifted a brow to give her friend a look. "Amy? What have you heard?"

Amy motioned to the cushions that surrounded the forward bow. "Come over here where we can talk." When Leah settled down beside her, Amy continued, "Okay, Susan told me she suspected there was something going on between you, what with the picnic at the pier and the fact that you were seen talking to him at the nursing home. And you live next door to one another."

"A thank-you lunch and two complete coincidences, I assure you."

"What happened to my friend who swore there were no coincidences?"

"All right, you've got me there, but trust me, there's nothing going on. Honestly, how could I introduce him to Pop? Ryan took his job."

Amy seemed to consider the statement a moment. "You know, I've given up trying to figure out what God's going to do next, but I have the strangest feeling that things are going to work out better than you could imagine."

Her gaze cut past Leah. "And there he is," she said a bit louder. "Honey, you want to go see that Ryan finds us? I think that's him coming up the dock."

Eric waved at Ryan as Brooke squealed, "I know him!"

"And I know you," Ryan called as he stepped into view. "And I know you, too," he said when his stare met Leah's.

She smiled even though she didn't much feel like it. She took a deep breath and tried to remember what Ryan had said about today's trip being about taking her mind off things. So what if he was the guy who might have to deliver bad news about a certain fire inspection? Today he was just that handsome guy who lived next door and had a nice smile.

"Where do you want these steaks?" he asked Eric.

"Here," Eric said as he shook hands with Ryan, "I'll show you."

When the men disappeared into the galley along with the three Wilson girls Ella, Brooke and Haily, Amy returned her attention to Leah. "Okay, I saw how he looked at you and I'm only going to say this one more time—there are no coincidences. Now let me see if I can get those guys out here so we can get this fun underway."

From the steaks Ryan grilled to perfection to the clear blue sky that dared not allow a single cloud, almost every detail of the late-fall afternoon on Sand Island was just right. The lone irritant in the day was the Wilson girls and their obvious matchmaking.

Thus, Leah was relieved when Eric suggested he and Amy take the girls on a shell-hunting expedition to the other side of the uninhabited island. Unfortunately, that left Leah alone with Ryan.

While the fireman carried on the business of putting out the campfire and packing away the items they'd carried over for the meal, Leah settled on the blanket to enjoy her view of Vine Beach. Though she'd made trips to Sand Island all her life, she never tired of the feeling she got when she saw the Berry property from this vantage point.

Only the black smudge where the house at Berry Hill used to stand marred the view. She turned her attentions to the lighthouse instead. From there, recollections of childhood rowboat trips and thoughts of other picnics sent Leah down a rabbit hole of memories. Only when

Ryan sat down on the blanket beside her did she realize time had passed.

He said nothing, which suited her fine. Instead, Ryan reached over to drop a perfectly formed sand dollar on the blanket beside her. "Peace offering," he said when their gazes met.

She smiled as she picked up the shell and held it in her palm. With her finger she traced the five points of the star imbedded in its center.

"Thank you," she said.

He shrugged as if his offering had been of no importance. "Just a small down payment on the amount of shells I owe you."

Leah shook her head. As Ryan leaned back on his elbows, a silence fell between them.

Finally, he sat up to study something across the bay. "Palominos, aren't they?"

She followed his gaze to the meadow behind the restaurant and the highway that split Berry land. "Yes," she said. "The last half dozen of what once was a decent-sized herd."

"What happened to the rest of them?"

She let out a long breath. "A combination of things, but mostly economics. When you've owned the land as long as the Berrys have, keeping it's the most important thing. So, as funds were needed, the horses were sold." Leah looked away, painfully aware that she'd said too much.

"I take it you're a native then," he said.

"Born and raised in Vine Beach." Leah set the sand dollar on the blanket between them. "Went off to college and never figured I'd be back except to visit."

"And yet here you are," he supplied.

"Yeah," she said slowly, "here I am."

"It must have been beautiful." He gestured toward the horizon. "The house, I mean."

"It was. Why?" she asked as she wondered what his purpose for asking might be.

"Just wondering," he said casually. "How old is it?"

"Built in the 1850s," she said. "There was a smaller home—more of a cabin, really—on the property that suited my great-great-grandfather just fine. Then he fell in love with my great-great-grandmother, a girl who grew up in a big mansion in Galveston with the best of everything. According to family legend, she came over from Galveston and took one look at the cabin he intended for their home then told him she'd be back to marry him when a suitable dwelling could be had."

"Apparently he took her seriously," Ryan said.

"He did, and spared no expense making Berry Hill the most beautiful home in the county. Before he built the home, he hired someone to have the hill built. The land's as flat as a pancake around here."

Ryan shook his head. "Why did he do that?"

"An inside joke. He told her that he'd built it up higher than anything around to reflect the fact that marrying her had made him come up in the world. I'm surprised she waited—the whole project took almost three years. Guess she really loved him after all."

They shared a laugh.

"I don't know what he would have done if they'd built the lighthouse before he finished the house. Rumor has it he paid off the powers that be to have that lighthouse delayed by a full year so that he and his bride could settle in first."

"Must have been terrible to watch the house burn."

Leah sighed. "God spared me that," she said. "I was in Paris with a delegation from the historical society when it happened." She paused. "Ironically, I was teaching a workshop on nineteenth-century coastal archaeological preservation when I got the call."

"So you're a teacher?"

She shook her head. "Not exactly. More of a researcher, I guess you'd say. My background is in history but archaeology has always fascinated me. I blame that on growing up with all the old family stories. Until I started delving into the history of this area, I thought they were just silly legends."

"Such as?"

Leah thought a moment. "Well, such as the fact that one of my less-reputable ancestors scammed a few of the area's more gullible female citizens, then, when he realized he was about to be caught, he hid the gold in a hollowed-out fence post on the property. His plan was to come back for the money and beat a hasty retreat as soon as the heat died down. Unfortunately, he didn't plan on the hurricane of 1875. When the wind and rain ceased, there wasn't a fence post standing on the entire property." She laughed. "They never did find that fence post or the gold."

"Seriously?"

"It's true." She shrugged. "Look it up. Last time I checked, there was actually mention of it in the Texas history textbooks the public schools use."

"Are you ever tempted to go out looking for that fence post?"

She sighed. "Every month when the bills arrive." An awkward silence fell as Leah wished she could take back the words.

"Leah, Leah!" Brooke called from somewhere behind them. "Leah, come look at the shell I found. Mama says you'll know what kind it is."

Once again she traced the points of the star before braving a glance at Ryan. "Guess I should…"

"Yeah, probably so." He shrugged. "In my experience, what Brooke wants, she gets, and patience is not her favorite virtue."

"True." Exchanging a smile with Ryan, she rose. "Thank you for the peace offering," she said. "It's lovely."

He met her steady gaze. "Lovely indeed."

Ryan nearly called himself a fool as he watched Leah walk away. Did she have any idea that the lovely comment was directed not at the silly shell but at her?

What was he thinking? He was the last person she'd want a compliment like that from, especially now, with the inspection of Pop's right around the corner.

He hadn't had the heart to tell her it was tomorrow.

He watched as the redhead bent down to inspect Brooke's new treasure, and couldn't help but think how beautiful she was. And interesting. With a brain behind those green-as-the-sea eyes.

He sighed. He'd put off the city's less-pressing fire inspections in favor of checking out the area schools and health facilities first. But as of tomorrow he would move on to the next level of need: local restaurants.

His thoughts immediately traveled to Leah and the growing closeness he felt to her. A closeness that was oddly comforting and uncomfortable at the same time. The comfort came from spending time with her, time that seemed to fly. The discomfort, however, arose from a deeper place: guilt. For the feelings of closeness he already had for Leah were different than anything he'd felt for Jenna.

The guys at Starting Over said every man's recovery from tragedy was different. Some fell right into the next relationship, while others might never find another with whom to spend their lives. Since Jenna's death, he'd been certain he was in the latter group. His worst fear was that he was joining the former.

No, he amended. Not fear, for that would mean he didn't want to go forward with whatever the Lord had for him. And if God led, he would lift Ryan through the process, also something he'd learned from the group.

If only he could stay out of Pop's and not mess things up for Leah. He almost considered it. Almost, but not quite.

For as much as he cared for her, his duty was to perform his job to the best of his abilities. This he would do no matter what it cost. All he could do was pray it didn't cost Leah her father's legacy and the family restaurant.

When Ryan walked through the door of Pop's on Monday afternoon, Leah's grin faded when she realized he was there on official city business. "I suppose you'll want a tour," she said lightly, though there was no missing the tremor in her voice.

Nor could he miss the splash of red across her cheeks. Sunburn from yesterday or something else?

"Want me to handle it, Leah?" The burly cook stepped up behind her and glared. "I'm sure there ain't nothing here to see, but I guess we've got to show it to him anyway."

Leah turned to rest her hand on his arm. "Orlando,

be nice. Ryan, this is Orlando. He's been with Pop's since before my father could rightly claim the name."

"Her pop and I served two tours of duty together." His glare intensified. "We got each other's back, if you know what I mean."

Ryan nodded. "I'll do a cursory examination and then I'll need access to some specific areas of the restaurant. I'll start with the FA system and suppression module, then we'll talk about a few other things." At Leah's confused look, Ryan continued, "Why don't I let you know when the inspection gets to that point?"

"Yes, that would be fine," she said as she nudged Orlando.

"Yeah, great, you do that, slick." Another nudge from Leah, this one a bit sharper, and Orlando's expression softened. "Whatever you need," he said.

Unfortunately, by the time Ryan was ready to see the internal workings of the restaurant, he already knew the place was going to fail miserably. He'd save that information for another day, he decided as he followed Orlando into the kitchen to complete the inspection.

"So," Leah said when Ryan returned to the dining room. "Red snapper's on the menu tonight. As I recall, you're fond of our snapper." She smiled. "And pie. You still haven't taken me up on that offer to try buttermilk pie."

"Sounds tempting," he said as he made a valiant attempt at a casual expression. "But I need to get going. Maybe I could get a rain check."

"Sure." Her smile wasn't quite as broad now. "So..." She fiddled with the stack of laminated menus on the counter in front of her. "I guess I'll be hearing from you."

"Yes," he said.

"And you'll let me know if…" Leah wrapped a flame-colored tendril of hair around her finger.

"I'll let you know," Ryan said.

With each step he took toward the door, Ryan wished he didn't have to make good on that statement.

But he had a job to do. And he would do it.

Leah watched Ryan go, her heart pounding. They'd failed. She knew it. If he'd found nothing wrong, the chief would have said so. And given the appetite he'd shown for Pop's redfish and pie, he surely would have accepted the offer of a meal.

But he had been in a hurry to leave.

Because they'd failed.

Fear, pure and simple, seized her and she knew it had no place in a believer's world. She took a deep breath and let it out slowly. *Lord, please don't let me panic. Remind me You're with me in this.*

Orlando came to stand beside her, resting his arm on her shoulder. "Either way, it'll be okay," he said.

She leaned into his comforting hug. "You think so?"

He nodded. "I know so."

"He sure seemed in a hurry to leave." She looked up at Orlando. "What do you think that means?"

"I think that means he's a busy man." He paused. "And beyond that I won't speculate."

The door jingled, and Leah jumped. Her heart in her throat, she hoped it was Ryan coming back to admit his somber demeanor had just been an act. That it was all some sort of awful joke.

Instead she watched the mailman deposit the day's mail on the counter in front of her.

"Got anything going out?" he asked.

Leah could barely make herself reply. "Not today."

"Well, all right then," the fellow said. "See the two of you tomorrow."

Unless we're forced to close before then.

Leah shooed away the thought. It would be all right. She had to believe it.

Orlando sorted through the mail then solemnly handed an envelope to her.

Her heart sank. "The tax bill," she said under her breath. "I'm afraid to open it."

She weighed the envelope in her palm and then quickly tore it open to see a number that made her breath catch. Orlando whistled soft and low.

"Worse than I thought." Leah let the paper flutter to the counter then watched it slide onto the floor before she looked up at Orlando. "So much worse."

Again he placed his hand on her shoulder. "You've got options, Lee-Lee."

She steeled her resolve and nodded, the moment of pity over. "Yes, there are options."

"You've already decided what you're going to do, haven't you?"

"I've been thinking about it." She paused only a moment before giving voice to the ideas that had been churning for days. "I've known since the mayor hired the new chief that we'd likely have some expenses in bringing the restaurant up to code. So my guess is this number will go up, though I hope not by much."

Orlando shrugged. "Depends on what he's found. I'm no expert but this place is older than you and me put together, so it's going to have some things that'll need to be brought up to standard. I'll do what I can and put out some feelers to see who can do the rest at the best price."

Leah patted Orlando's hand. "I know you will. Thank you. From me and Pop."

Again he nodded. "It's what we do, your pop and me."

She sighed. "Assuming we can get these things handled quickly without much interruption of business, I've also been considering a sort of fundraiser." Leah lifted her gaze. "What would you think if we used the profits from the Christmas buffet to pay for the repairs?"

One brow rose, but otherwise the old sailor remained silent for what seemed like an eternity. Finally he let out a long breath. "Have you talked to your pop about this?"

"I mentioned it," she said slowly. "Just as a possibility. But to be fair, I don't think he understands the gravity of the situation with our finances. He couldn't possibly or…"

"Or he would have agreed to your idea."

"Yeah," came out in a defeated sigh.

"Honestly," Orlando said. "Did you pray about that?"

She hadn't. "It seemed like a good idea," was the best response she could manage. "And Pop's won't be around to raise money for anything next year if we don't pay the bills this year." A poor defense for an idea that sounded more selfish every time she tried to defend it. "All right," she admitted. "It was a bad idea. But I've got to do something."

Orlando shook his head. "Maybe what you've got to do is wait. Right now you're just going on suppositions and fears."

She turned to face Pop's best friend. "Maybe I'm

being proactive," she said. "I made a promise to Pop to keep this place going, and I plan to keep that promise."

"Honey, you know you're not bound by something a man said when he wasn't in his right mind." His pleading look broke Leah's heart. "But I won't waste my breath trying to talk you out of it. You're every bit as stubborn as your daddy ever was."

"There's a difference in stubborn and sensible," she countered. "And while I'll admit I can be a single-minded on occasion—"

"Single-minded, is it?" Orlando asked with a chuckle.

"Yes, single-minded." She paused to suppress a smile despite the tears threatening. "But I'm also practical. And whether or not my promise to Pop should be kept, I plan to honor it as best I can. So, that leaves just one thing to do, and that's figure out a way."

"Wait, Lee-Lee," Orlando said. "Just wait. The Lord will lead."

"Nothing wrong with doing a little getting ready for when He leads," she said as the cook disappeared into the kitchen.

Leah reached for the stool and settled on it then grabbed a pen and paper from the drawer under the cash register. At the top of the page she wrote the amount of the tax bill. Then, she began to add the expenses that were looming beneath it. Care and feeding of the horses and the cost of Pop's living arrangements went at the top of the list followed by the lesser expenses such as food and utilities. Then came the big question mark that held the place of the amount she would have to pay to keep Pop's open.

Now for the positives. She drew a line down the middle of the page from top to bottom then paused to consider what to put there. Finally on the plus side of the column she wrote Berry Hill Farm and Stables, Pop's and the cabin where she lived.

All three sat squarely on Berry land, something she would keep until the bitter end. Thus, she drew a line through all of them.

What else?

The only furniture worth anything was the old desk, and she had no idea of its value. Perhaps one of her colleagues could come and give her an estimate of what she might get for it at auction. Thus, the desk went in the positives column.

Next went the horses, though Leah wrote that with misgivings. She loved those animals and couldn't imagine parting with any of them. And yet she knew the sale of even one would bring a tidy sum. Several might fix the budget issue altogether.

Much as she hoped she wouldn't have to make the decision, she left the item on the plus side of the page. *Maybe just one of them, Lord? Or maybe the antique desk is worth a fortune. Anything to make these problems go away.*

Leah sighed and yanked the page from the pad, then wadded it up and tossed it into the trash. Orlando was right. She was letting supposition and fear take hold.

However, based on how quickly her feelings seemed to be growing for a man whose job it was to possibly close down Pop's, that fear was justified. But it wasn't just fear. She also felt a nagging frustration that her heart and her head were saying two different things.

While her heart said to see where these emotions led, her head told her there were too many risks involved. She had already given up her life in Galveston to come here.

Leah sighed. Her traitorous heart missed that life, though she rarely allowed herself to consider what it had been like when she could immerse herself in her work on historic restoration or perhaps collaboration on some project destined for a museum and forget any other responsibility. Some might find it odd that she felt keeping Pop's running was much less daunting than delivering a paper before an international audience of historians in London or Barcelona.

But that was the easy work. Knitting back the life in Vine Beach that kept coming unraveled was the tough job.

Then she spied Ryan Owen walking back into the dining room. And fear turned to a certain knowledge that the news he bore was not good.

Chapter Ten

Ryan squared his shoulders and tried to forget that he'd taken the easy way out the last time he'd been confronted with those bottle-green eyes and the freckles decorating her still-pink-from-the-sun cheeks. As fire chief he had a job to do, and he couldn't let anything distract him from that job.

Not even a beautiful woman like Leah. Even if it meant destroying her livelihood.

Walking out of Pop's without warning the owner of the establishment that she was in violation of multiple fire codes had been inexcusable. Thus, he'd returned to try again.

"Got a minute?" he said as casually as he could manage. "There's something we need to talk about."

"Sure," Leah said she rose from the stool. "Did you change your mind about that pie?"

"Leah," he said as gently as he could, "I'm back on official business." He paused to judge her reaction. Unfortunately, she showed no emotion beyond a cursory nod. "The restaurant didn't pass inspection." He added, "I'm sorry."

Other than a slight tremble of her lip, her expression still showed no hint of her thoughts. In fact, her direct look and her wide eyes almost seemed to dare him to feel pity for her.

"Don't apologize, Ryan," she said firmly. "Remember I've got a little bit of experience in restoration of old buildings. Given the age of this structure, I'd be more surprised if it had passed."

He nodded. "There are some definite issues that have to do with the age of the building, but some of those are grandfathered in. Others will need fixing but shouldn't be too difficult to repair. It's actually not the structure so much as the..." Ryan shook his head. "Look, I'll write all this up and get it to you quick as I can. There's nothing here that can't be brought up to code with some work."

"I suspected as much."

Ryan stuffed his hands in his pockets as he felt the weight of the silence between them. He glanced behind her at the photograph of a young man—the sign beneath declared him to be her father. Jack Murdoch had told him just enough about Leah's father to let him know that Chief Berry would be no help in solving the issues facing Pop's Seafood. Looking into the eyes of that guy with a military haircut and a smile made him feel even worse.

"Do you have any questions about the inspection?" he asked.

She rested her palms on the counter and looked beyond him. "No," she said. "I can't think of anything."

He took a deep breath and let it out slowly before proceeding. Along with it, he sent up a prayer that he might handle this properly. And that she wouldn't cry. He hated it when women cried.

"All right, then. I want to be sure you understand what's happened. The restaurant has failed the fire safety inspection. You've got some time to get things fixed. Once the repairs are done I'll come out and inspect again anytime you're ready."

"Yes, I understand." She returned her attention to him.

He paused. "Look, Leah, I'm sorry. I wish I had better news for you. But I can't let violations go. It wouldn't be right."

"Nor would I ask that of you, Ryan," she snapped. "Please don't think I am."

"No, I didn't think…"

He stopped speaking just short of making the situation any worse. Or at least he hoped he had. When she seemed reluctant to speak any further, he decided to place the sign on the door and make a quick exit.

"Just one more order of business and I'll be done." He nodded toward the door. "I left the notices out in the Jeep, so I'll have to get them. Then I'll head back to my office and get the papers written up for you so you'll know what to tell the contractors when you start taking bids for repairs." He hesitated. "I can drop them by your place this afternoon if you'd like."

"You can leave them under the doormat."

"You sure?"

Leah frowned. "I won't be home until late. Pop's is open until nine, but depending on the crowd, we may be here cleaning up and getting ready for the next day's lunch until eleven or twelve."

"Leah," Ryan said gently when he realized what she intended. "You won't be serving here. Not tonight."

"What do you mean? Of course we will. Tonight I've got the back room reserved for the Beach Reads Book Club ladies at six and Eric asked for three tables over in the corner to push together and hold an introductory meeting for participants of the Boat Parade. That's at seven-thirty. Then I've got two reservations for eight and another..." Her voice wavered as it became apparent that his words had finally sunk in. "You're closing Pop's."

His heart hurt as he nodded. "I have to."

"No, you don't," she said fiercely. "You do not have to. Next week's Thanksgiving, Ryan! We do our biggest fall business during the week before and after. Instead of closing us, you could..." Again her voice wavered. This time tears shimmered beneath her thick lashes.

"No, I can't," he said with as little emotion as he could manage. "The rules are the rules, and I'm sorry but a restaurant with serious fire violations cannot remain open. It's a danger to the public."

"Great, Ryan. Why don't you explain to the public why Pop's won't be the site of the annual Christmas buffet fundraiser this year? And while you're at it, maybe you could tell the kids at Vine Beach Elementary that they won't be getting new playground equipment because there's no money for it?"

He paused only a minute before deciding a nod would suffice as a sufficient goodbye. He would not apologize for doing his job, much as he wanted to. And he'd never allow a lapse in safety to harm anyone again. Not after what happened to Jenna.

"Hey, Ryan," Leah called, stopping him in his tracks.

He turned, hoping she'd had sufficient time to understand his predicament and appreciate his attention to safety. One look at her face and he tossed that hope away.

"Want to buy a horse? Maybe two or three?"

Ryan headed for his car, the sound of her angry voice ringing in his ears.

The remainder of the week was spent watching for an accidental meeting with Leah, dreading the possibility. Somehow she managed to avoid him, leaving well before he went to work and coming home who-knew-when. Where she spent her days, he could only guess.

It certainly wasn't anywhere in the vicinity of the courthouse or, for that matter, downtown Vine Beach. And each night as he sat on the deck with his Bible as the light from the cabin spilled down onto the pages, he wondered how she was, if there was anything he could do to make things better.

By Friday evening he was ready to walk over and ask. Instead, he decided to put off the question until after the Saturday morning Starting Over meeting. If Eric was in attendance, maybe he could shed some light on the mystery that was Leah Berry. Failing that, he'd go to Riley. Surely either of them would know her better than him.

The following day was gray, dull with clouds that hugged the horizon and threatened rain. The warm weather than had followed almost to Thanksgiving was gone and in its place were temperatures that put frost on the windshield of his Jeep.

He arrived early and found Riley and a few of the others setting up for the game. As he pitched in to help,

Ryan tried to figure out how to broach the topic that was troubling him.

"All right," Riley finally said. "Enough of this. Let's take a walk and have a chat about whatever it is that's on your mind."

Ryan tossed the basketball to one of the other guys, then nodded. Falling in step beside the older man, he waited until they were out of sight of the basketball court before taking a deep breath and letting it out slowly.

"Can I save you a little trouble?" the older man asked.

"Sure, I'd appreciate that."

He stopped in a sunny spot behind a hedge of oleanders and regarded Ryan with a thoughtful look. "This is about our Leah, isn't it?"

Our Leah?

"Yes, actually, it is." Ryan paused to shrug deeper into his hooded sweatshirt. "I had to do my job, Riley, and I won't apologize for that."

"Of course not. But?"

"But I feel for her. With the restaurant closed, I'm worried she won't have the money to make the repairs that will allow it to pass inspection."

Riley crossed his arms over his chest. "What makes you think this?"

"She's thinking of selling her horses." He shrugged. "And maybe that's not a big deal, but I got the impression it was."

"I see." He gave Ryan a sideways look. "Have you talked to her about any of this?"

"Not since I left the restaurant after closing it down." He paused. "I tried to catch her at home, but haven't had any success."

"That's probably by design," Riley said. "I wonder if you've come up with a solution to this problem?"

"I have. Sort of."

The older man inclined his head toward Ryan. "Go on."

"All right. I can't help her with these repairs. It would be a huge conflict of ethics, since I'm the guy who has to inspect them once they're complete." He shifted positions. "But the Starting Over guys could."

Riley's brows gathered. "What are you suggesting?"

"I wonder if Leah might be able to come up with enough to pay for supplies if the Starting Over group were to provide the labor. Most of what needs to be done is simple. I'd say only a few things would require an electrician or plumber. The rest are hammer-and-nails type work."

He seemed to consider the idea a moment before nodding. "I think you're on to something, son. Carl Berry has served this church and our city well for longer than most of those men have been alive. I for one would love to pay a little of that back, but we'll have to see what the others say."

"Fair enough."

"And what of the horses?" Riley met his stare. "I don't know how you're fixed for money, but have you thought of buying one?"

"No," Ryan said slowly. And yet the idea held some appeal. The palominos were beautiful, this he'd admit. And though his plan wasn't to stay in Vine Beach forever, there would likely be no trouble boarding one more horse up at his dad's ranch.

"You're thinking about it."

Ryan nodded. "I am."

"Good." They turned to walk back toward the basketball courts. A moment later, Riley stopped short. "There's just one thing. If the men agree to help, I want you to be the one who gets Leah's permission."

Ryan laughed. "Are you serious? She won't even speak to me."

"I'm sure you'll think of something, but I'm going to insist. Think if it as your contribution to the project." Riley clasped a hand on Ryan's shoulder and nodded toward the group who milled around waiting for them. "Let's go put it to a vote, then, shall we?"

"Hey, I wondered where you two were," Eric called as they turned the corner. "I was afraid my team was going to have to lose without you." He jogged up to join Ryan and Riley. "Everything okay?"

"Yes, it's fine," Riley said. "Actually we were talking about the Berry horses. What's your professional opinion of them?"

"Best palominos I've had the privilege of treating," he said without missing a beat. "Why?"

Riley turned his attention to Ryan. "I believe your friend here is in the market for one."

"What? Are you serious?"

"Yeah," Ryan said slowly. "Before I left Pop's the other day, Leah mentioned she was going to sell one to raise the money to pay for repairs."

"I see." Eric ran a hand through his hair. "Well, this is the first I've heard of it. Seeing as how you're renting that cabin, I'm guessing you'll need to board the horse. At least until you can make other arrangements."

"Yeah, that would be great if she'd allow it." He shrugged. "There's just one problem. She's not happy with me. I'm thinking she might not sell to me."

Eric seemed to be considering the idea a moment. "You may be right."

"But she's going to need some cash to get that project done."

"Then what if I broker the deal?" Eric asked. "Let her know I heard she was looking to sell and that I might have someone in mind to buy."

Ryan grinned. "That would be great. Thanks."

"Hey, I'm not just doing a buddy a favor. I'm also saving a hardheaded woman from herself." He chuckled. "And if any of you tell Leah or my wife I said that, I'll deny it."

Riley laughed. "Why don't you gather up the guys before you start the game? I've got a proposition they need to vote on." When Eric had complied, the older man turned his attention back on Ryan. "All right, now what else is on your mind?"

"Nothing," he said.

"I don't believe you." Riley shook his head. "If I didn't know better I'd think you're beginning to care for that girl."

"Leah?" He shrugged off the nagging thought that Riley might be right. "I feel responsible for her predicament, at least in part. It's not her fault her father didn't keep that place up."

"And it's not your fault you had to make a hard choice while you were on the job." He gave Ryan a hard look. "But the hardest choice you're going to have to make is whether you choose to either pursue a relationship with Leah or step back and miss out on the opportunity."

Ryan didn't bother to respond. He knew Riley Burkett was right.

After a quick rundown of the idea of helping over at

Pop's, Riley called for a vote. The decision was unanimous. Once the Thanksgiving projects were behind them, the men from Starting Over would tackle the repairs at Pop's Seafood Shack. And while Ryan would have given anything to join them in that endeavor, he had to settle for agreeing to draw up a checklist of items that needed attention, then discreetly following up on the work as it was completed. At least that much could be done without violating any oaths of office.

That and buying himself a palomino.

He groaned. For a guy who was determined not to sink any roots into this tiny town, he sure was putting a whole bunch of seeds into the ground.

Chapter Eleven

On Thanksgiving Day, Leah sat with Pop until the orderly came to fetch him. Unfortunately, her father was in a mood and refused to budge from his chair.

She was in a mood as well, but his discomfort was brought on by her decision to tell her father about the situation at Pop's.

"You'll miss the Thanksgiving celebration, Mr. Berry," the sweet young man told Pop. "They've got all kinds of good things to eat there." He gave her father a conspiratorial look. "And not a one of them was made here in the kitchen, if you know what I mean."

The beginnings of a grin touched Pop's face. "Well, that almost tempts me." He looked up at Leah. "You know, I appreciate that you've put me in such a nice place, but honestly a man can only survive so long on all this healthy food. Would you believe they don't even own a fryer? I know because I went in the kitchen and saw for myself."

"And got in plenty of trouble for it," Leah reminded him. "You're here as a guest, not as a cook, Pop. Leave that to the ladies and gentlemen who get paid for it, all right?"

He waved away her statement and punctuated it with a resounding *harrumph*. "All that good fresh seafood they get, and what do they do with it? They broil it. Fresh Gulf shrimp and red snapper that just left the boat! Or, worse, they bake it until it tastes about as good as the bottom of my shoe."

"Pop, that's enough. You know what your doctor said about fried foods. Only on special occasions and in moderation."

Another *harrumph* and a shake of his hand was apparently his final word on the subject.

"Come on, Mr. Berry," the orderly said. "I know you're not going to miss the turkey and dressing. And the sweet potatoes with real marshmallows." He paused. "Nah, you're right. It's nothing you'd like anyway. I don't figure you for a man who'd be interested in the pies, either. At last count, there were five or six different kinds. 'Course, the church folks were still unloading them when I left to come get you."

Leah waited for Pop to indicate any sort of reaction. When he ignored them to reach for the remote, she took the offending item from his hand. "Thanks so much for trying," she said to the orderly. "Why don't you leave the wheelchair here and I'll bring him down there in a few minutes?"

"Yes, ma'am," he said. "Just call down to the nurses' station if you need help."

"I will." Leah waited until the door slid shut before turning to face her father again. She found him still in his chair staring at the blank screen on the television. "All right, Pop. What's the matter? Thanksgiving was always one of your favorite holidays, and now you're turning down turkey and all the trimmings?"

He crossed his arms over his chest. "Is there something wrong with wanting to watch TV?"

Leah moved to kneel beside him. "Pop," she said gently, "you're all the family I've got left, and I want to celebrate today with you. Is there something wrong with wanting to do that?"

His expression softened. Still he didn't budge.

Placing her hand atop his, Leah rested her head on his shoulder. "I miss you, Pop," she said into the warm flannel of his plaid shirt.

He shrugged into her embrace and slowly stroked her hair. For a moment the antiseptic smell of the long-term-care room faded away and she was back at Berry Hill with a father who was as familiar as he was predictable.

She allowed a memory of riding horses while they waited for a Thanksgiving turkey to cook. Of Pop's persistent joking that he'd cut one of the coastal scrub plants to haul back and turn into a Christmas tree. And finally of the three of them all dressed up and seated at one end of the massive table in the formal dining room, Mama's best china and glasses sparkling beneath the glow of the silver candelabras.

After Mama died, she and Pop had tried to continue the tradition, but it just wasn't the same. Eventually they'd abandoned the idea altogether in favor of serving at the nursing home then enjoying a platter of fried shrimp afterward.

"Hey, Pop," she said as inspiration struck. "How about you and I get out of this place for a while?" She lifted her head to look up at him. "We could go for a drive. Maybe go back to my place and fry up some shrimp?"

For the first time since she had arrived, Leah watched her father actually smile. "I'd say that sounds like a winner of an idea, kiddo."

She matched his grin. "All right. I'll just go let the nurses know what we're doing. Why don't you put on your sweater? It's a little chilly out."

By the time she returned, Pop had complied and was sitting at the little table ready to go. "Can we stop at the library and get more books?" he asked.

"We can return these, but it's Thanksgiving so the library is closed."

"All right," he said as he scooped the books into his arms. "I'll just bring some back from home." He walked past her and the wheelchair and out the door before she could respond. Leah caught up with her father and gently turned him in the direction of the side door nearest where her car was parked. "Are you sure you don't want me to wheel you out, Pop?"

"Long as I can go standing, I plan to," he said.

"All right, then." She waved to the nurse at the station, then headed toward the parking lot a step behind her father.

"Say, isn't that Eric Wilson?" Pop gestured to a blue Suburban. Another step and she spied Eric opening the back door of his vehicle.

"It is," she said. "Would you like to go say hello?"

He handed Leah the stack of books then set out across the parking lot with the speed of a man half his age. Leah quickly dumped the books in the backseat, then hurried to catch up.

Of course, the first thing Pop asked after the greetings were done was about the horses. "Is my Leah taking care of them?" he added.

"They're beautiful, healthy animals," Eric said. "And your daughter's been taking great care of them. In fact, Leah's going to be giving the girls riding lessons starting this Saturday."

"Is that so?" He grinned. "Well, be sure you pick just the right ones for those babies to ride. That Maisie, she loves to be ridden, but she wants to be at a trot most of the time. Peep, she's a good one for the littlest of your bunch. Now Boo, she's a feisty one but with just the right rider she'll be your favorite. I know she's mine."

Leah rested her hand on her father's shoulder. "That's because you're the only one who can ride that ornery horse."

"That reminds me." Eric hit the button and the Suburban's lock chirped. "I heard through the grapevine that you were looking to sell one of the horses. I know a guy who is anxious to take a look at them, but I wasn't sure which one you were willing to part with."

"What's this?" Pop's eyes flashed fury. "We're not parting with any of that herd. It's the last of what my grandpa started with, and not a one's been sold off since before I was born."

Not exactly the truth, but Pop believed it at this moment.

"Who told you we had horses for sale?" he demanded.

"I, well, uh…" Eric looked to Leah, a combination of surprise and regret etched across his face.

"Pop," she said gently, "we'll talk about this in the car, okay?"

"I don't want to talk about it in the car. I want to know why my horses are for sale." Hands on his scrawny hips, her father made an attempt at a formidable presence. "And I want to know now, young lady."

"Look, maybe I misspoke," Eric offered. "I just thought that—"

"No, it's all right. Give me a second, okay?" She linked arms with her father, then escorted him to her vehicle a few spaces away.

"Well, look at that," he said as he leaned into the backseat and grabbed one of the library books. "You brought me something new to read."

He fastened his seat belt, then opened the book and began to read.

Satisfied Pop was settled, she walked back over to Eric.

"Hey, I'm really sorry," he said. "I had no idea he didn't know. Ryan told me you'd mentioned it last time you two spoke so I figured... Anyway, I feel awful."

So Ryan had been talking with Eric about her. Interesting. Her curiosity rose.

What else had they said?

"I planned to talk to Pop about it today." She glanced over her shoulder to see that her father was still reading. "So, tell your buyer he's welcome to arrange a trip out to the stables. Just let me know ahead of time so I can be there, too."

"About that," Eric said slowly. "The buyer, he, well, he's not keen on letting anyone know who he is just yet."

She shook her head. "Why?"

He shrugged. "You'll have to ask him when the time comes."

"I suppose that's all right." She studied him. "Will you vouch for him? Much as I need to raise cash fast to get started on those repairs, I won't do it at the expense of sending one of my horses to someone who doesn't appreciate what he's getting."

"About those repairs…"

"Hey, Eric, did you find the—" Ryan Owen came around the side of the Suburban then stopped short when he spied them. "Leah. I didn't expect…that is, I figured since your dad is here…" He shook his head. "Anyway, Eric, did you find the extra spoons?"

Leah took a moment to allow her gaze to slide over her neighbor. Despite the grief his presence in Vine Beach had caused, she couldn't completely blame her current situation on Ryan.

Partially, yes, but not completely. Still, she didn't have to like the fact he was still here.

Still next door.

And still causing her to remember their afternoon at Sand Island when she spied the sand dollar he'd given her as a peace offering.

Eric looked back and forth between Leah and Ryan before setting his attention on the fire chief. "My guess is the spoons were either left at the church or they're in someone else's trunk. I don't have them."

"Yeah, okay." He stuffed his hands into his pockets and rocked back on his heels. "So, Leah, how have you been?" he said.

She crossed her arms over her chest. "Good."

"Good," he said. "Glad to hear it."

Ryan leaned toward her, his expression somber. "If you have a minute, I'd like to talk to you about something."

She spied Pop getting out of the car and suppressed a groan. "If this is about the restaurant, I really don't want to discuss it. Not here. And not today."

"I understand, but you're not making it easy to find you, Leah."

Pop was closing the gap between them to grasp her arm. "Honey, why don't you introduce me to your gentleman friend?"

"He's not my gentleman friend, Pop," she said as she felt the cold fingers of dread about what Pop could learn snake around her heart.

"He's with me, actually," Eric supplied. "Ryan Owen, meet Carl Berry."

Ryan took her father's hand and shook it. "Pleased to meet you, sir. I've heard very good things about you from Leah."

"Is that so?" Pop met Leah's horrified stare. "And what sort of things are those?"

"Well, sir," Ryan continued. "Your daughter tells me the buttermilk pie recipe at Pop's comes from your mother. I'm going to have to admit I haven't tried it yet, but I've been promised it's better than the coconut cream. I'd appreciate your opinion on that because I find it hard to believe."

"Oh, I've got an opinion, young man. Tell me who you are again."

Leah's heart nearly stopped in her chest.

"Owen," Ryan said, "Ryan Owen."

"And how do I know you?"

"He's my neighbor, Pop," Leah supplied.

"Oh, I see." Her father nodded, his expression curious. "And what is it you do here?"

"Okay, well, I hate to interrupt." Eric clasped his hand on Ryan's shoulder. "We ought to get back inside."

"Yes, please don't let us keep you," she said before

linking arms with Pop and turning to head back toward her car.

In the quiet of her vehicle, Leah allowed herself a moment to collect her thoughts. Turning the key in the ignition, she swiveled to face her father. "Pop, we need to talk about something important."

He put aside the book and gave her his attention. "Sure, honey. What's up?"

"The horses," she said. "I'm sorry you had to find out that way. I really had planned to tell you today. After lunch. We're going to have to make some hard decisions if we plan to keep the restaurant open."

Pop seemed to be considering her words, for after a moment he nodded. Then he picked up the book again.

"Pop," she said softly. "Do you understand what's happening? Our taxes have gone up, but worst of all, we need to make some major repairs to the restaurant so we can reopen. I need to sell one of the horses."

He waved away her statement. "You don't have to do that."

"Yes, Pop, I do." She paused. "There's no other way."

He met her stare, his eyes clear and his expression intense. "Yes, there is. The desk is worth a whole lot more. Just don't sell it without telling me first. It holds a little secret."

It took all she could manage not to roll her eyes. Pop had spoken frequently about the desk and its secrets in recent years, but when questioned he always played coy. Thus, she left the tale alone this time in favor of gently guiding him back to the topic.

"So, the horses. Would you like to go see them?"

Pop shook his head. "Why would I want to go see the horses when we've got a perfectly good Thanksgiving meal waiting for us in the cafeteria?" He nudged her with his elbow. "Rumor has it there are pies. Four or five different ones at last count."

"I thought it was five or six," she said as she shut off the engine and pulled the keys out of the ignition.

"Where in the world did you hear that?" He shook his head. "Truly, Leah, you need to pay more attention to the details. There's no telling how much you miss."

"Never mind." Leah spied Eric and Ryan emerging from the building to climb into the Suburban and leave. *Thank You, Lord.* Any chance of further awkward moments with Ryan Owen had been delayed or, she hoped, eliminated completely for today.

Had Eric not spilled the beans about the horse, she might have opted to tell Pop about Ryan's new job instead. In either case, her father could only digest one surprise at a time.

"All right, Pop," she said as she opened the car door. "How about we go have a Thanksgiving meal together?"

He grinned. "Good idea."

"Want me to bring the library books back in?" she asked as she paused to reach into the backseat.

"Those?" Pop said. "Leah, you're getting awfully forgetful. Remember you were going to drop those off on your way home."

She closed the door then linked arms with her father. "Right, Pop. Sorry about that."

They walked together as far as the door before Pop stopped to face her. "Have I told you about the desk?"

Leah nodded. "Yeah, you did."

His smile was swift and broad. "Good. Then all your problems are solved."

"Yeah, Pop," she said as she followed him inside. "All solved. Thanks, Pop."

Again he stopped. This time he reached to hold her in a strong embrace. "Anytime, sweetheart. Anytime. What say we go take a ride after we eat? Maybe go fetch us a scrub tree to decorate for Christmas."

For the first time in what felt like an eternity, Leah laughed.

Chapter Twelve

The day after Thanksgiving, the reality of her situation had more than set in. Leah hung up the phone and pushed it away. One more contractor, one more far-too-expensive quote. And yet she had to do something. Orlando had already begun work on the things he could manage, but technical repairs were beyond his level of expertise.

Tracing the edge of the antique desk, Leah closed her eyes. If only Pop were right. If she could just find enough money in the value of this one piece of furniture to fix all her troubles.

But that was silliness. Pop's version of reality. Still... if only...

Her phone rang, causing Leah to jump. Eric. She pressed the button and greeted him.

"Got good news," he said. "You've got a buyer. He wants Boo."

"Boo? Boo is Pop's horse."

"I know, Leah," he said gently, "but realistically, will Pop ride again?"

She paused to reach for her pen. "So, what's the buyer offering for her?"

"He said he'd pay full price in cash no later than Tuesday."

Hope welled up despite the fact she'd have to explain to Pop that his favorite horse was gone. Cash on Tuesday meant she could pay a contractor on Wednesday. With a month to go until Christmas, it just might be possible that the yearly celebration could be held on schedule after all.

"There's a catch, though," Eric said. "He's asked if Boo can be boarded at your stables, at least for a while."

"That's it? He just wants to board her? How much is he willing to pay?"

"I think you could probably name the price, within reason. What do you think?"

A flash of red caught her attention down on the beach, and she turned toward it. There she spied Ryan Owen in dark sweatpants and a red T-shirt jogging past, his monster of a dog happily ambling at his side. Thankfully, the beast was on a leash, a fact that Baby missed as she puffed up and hissed in defense of home, hearth and the dog toy that had already gotten her in trouble the last time she stole it.

"Leah?"

"Tell your guy I'm happy to do that as long as he needs me to." She watched Ryan disappear just past the oleanders.

"When am I going to find out who this mystery buyer is?"

"Good question," Eric said. "When I spoke to him this morning, he told me that he'd be coming around to introduce himself soon."

"Oh?" She spied the same flash of red again, this time walking past without the dog in tow. Baby jumped to race down the stairs, presumably to greet him. Sure enough, the fat cat ambled near to allow the next-door neighbor to rub her ears. *The traitor.*

When Ryan looked up at her, Leah ducked away from the window.

"So if you're agreeable, I'll let the guy know the deal is a go. And you can let your contractors know, as well."

Leah sucked in a deep breath. "How did you know I needed the money for that?"

"I'm sorry," he said. "Is that…a secret?"

"No," Leah said quickly, "of course not. I'm sorry. And yes, I'll get the workmen started on Pop's. We need the place open before the Christmas celebration."

"Leah," Eric said. "Do you think it's wise to plan on having the charity buffet at Pop's when we don't know if it's going to be available?"

"It will," she said with a bravado she only half felt. "It has to be."

"Right. Well, if you're sure then I'll have the billboard go up. Same as last year, right?"

"Sure," she said. "Same as last year. Christmas Eve parade viewing party at Pop's. I've got faith it will happen."

But as she hung up the phone, Leah felt her faith shake. Even if the repairs were completed in time, the restaurant still had to pass inspection. And then there was the matter of the tax bill. A bill that would come due one week after Christmas.

She let out a long breath and rested her forehead on the desk. What happened to the days when her worst conundrum was whether to jet off to Milan for a conference or accept an invitation to tour the restoration of an antebellum mansion stateside?

And how had she gone from an expert who talked about restoration to one who could only wish she was able to fry shrimp and wait tables again?

Lord, this is so hard. Orlando would say she was getting ahead of herself by worrying. Pop would tell her things were already handled.

Both were right.

Leah swallowed the remainder of her self-pity and lifted her head to open her eyes. The Lord had gone beyond what she'd prayed for—not only a buyer for one of the horses, but also a monthly payment for boarding.

Why couldn't she trust Him to do the rest?

Before she could take another breath the tears fell. And then came the sound of breaking glass from somewhere under the cabin.

He'd come over to get her permission for the repairs and own up to the horse purchase, but considering the mess he'd walked into, Ryan decided he'd probably put off that news for another day. He returned to the scene of the crime with a broom and dustpan. This time Chief had been innocent, but the end result of the thievery that led Leah's cat to haul the dog's leash through the oleander hedge was scattered on the concrete around his feet. Until the leash caught a branch, Ryan expected there would be little trouble in returning it to its peg next to the stairs.

But now that the cat had hauled the branch across the shelf that held Leah's canning jars and a pair of empty clay pots, there was little left to tell what had been there. When the orange menace dropped Chief's leash at Ryan's feet, he reached down to extract the stick then throw it over his shoulder.

"What in the world?" Leah stood at the bottom of the stairs, hands on her hips and an expression of disbelief on her face. Her gaze dropped to the concrete floor and the leash tangled up in the broken glass. Then, slowly she returned her attention to Ryan.

"Don't worry," he said casually. "I've got this." He swept up the glass while Leah watched. "Where's your trash can?"

She gestured to the same closet where he'd retrieved the ladders the last time he cleaned up a mess at the Berry place. "So," she said when he had dumped the glass, "your dog strikes again?"

"My dog?" He shook his head. "Actually, this all happened because—"

"Because that monster was off his leash," she supplied as she walked over and retrieved the leash then dropped it again. "So where is he?"

Chief was home, behaving himself nicely. Unlike the felonious feline who stared back at him from the rafters above.

Leah shook her head. "You don't know? Really, Ryan. You should be more careful."

"Actually the real problem is…" He bit back the remainder of the comment he wanted to make.

"Is what?" she asked, her tone as frosty as the cold front that had blown through last night.

"Never mind." Ryan picked up the leash and took it over to the trash can to shake off the remainder of the glass shards. That accomplished, he said, "I'll just be going."

"Be sure you find your dog and take him with you,"

she said with ice in her voice. "And please try to keep him where he belongs."

Again he thought about responding, but good sense won out. He'd caused her enough grief without letting Leah know her cat was the real menace.

Like clockwork, Chief started barking as soon as Ryan's foot landed on the first step. "That's enough," Ryan called, halting the bullmastiff's noise instantly.

He reached the deck and paused, as he usually did, to appreciate the view. Out of the corner of his eye, he spied Leah standing on her deck. He looked over, risked proving himself right to an already irate woman, meeting her stare before reaching to open his door. "Come on out, Chief."

The big dog pressed past him to stop and sit at his feet. Ryan patted Chief's head, still watching his neighbor's surprised stare over the fact that his dog had not been running free as she had claimed. Had his phone not rung just then, he might have gloried in the moment of triumph a bit longer.

"Hey, Uncle Mike," he said after checking to see who was calling.

"Missed you at Thanksgiving," he said. "Figured you'd come celebrate with us."

"Yeah, about that." Ryan glanced over to see that Leah had busied herself with plumping the cushions on the deck chairs before turning his back on the redhead. "I meant to, but…"

He couldn't face another family gathering where no one knew what to say.

Last time he was there, his parents still had his wedding photos on the mantel.

Plus so many other ways to complete the statement.

"Hey," Uncle Mike said, interrupting his thoughts, "no worries, kid. How's Jack Murdoch treating you? Things going all right for you in Vinc Beach?"

"Things are going pretty well," he said as he slid another glance to the east to see the redhead still hard at work on her deck. "And the mayor treats me just fine. I don't ask for favoritism and he doesn't show any."

The old fireman chuckled. "Yeah, didn't figure he would. Jack's tough but fair. He gave you the chance but I knew you'd have to earn the job." He drew in a long breath. "Actually that's not why I called. I wanted to talk to you about something in person yesterday. So, you got a minute?"

"Sure." Ryan stepped inside and waited for Chief to follow before closing the door on the sound of the wind and waves. "What's up?"

"Just wanted to give you a heads-up about what's going on." He paused and Ryan could hear the television blaring in the background. "I spent a little time with your former captain last week. You know they still want you back at HFD, right?"

He did, though it had been a while since he'd heard from any of the guys. "Yeah," he said. "Or at least that was the plan. Six months and I go back. Far as I know that hasn't changed."

Uncle Mike didn't respond. Okay, so this wasn't the social call Ryan had expected. Something was up. And unless he missed his guess, it wasn't good.

Ryan moved over to the sofa and got comfortable then propped up his feet on the coffee table. Chief jumped beside him and made three circles until he landed in a heap. Still Uncle Mike hadn't said a word.

Instead, the television blaring into the silence told the story.

"Something you're not telling me?" he finally asked his uncle.

"They want you back, kid. And sooner rather than later." He hesitated before continuing. "Your captain said if he had his way, he'd head to Vine Beach with a moving van and haul you and your mangy dog back to Houston tomorrow."

"What happened to my six months here?" Ryan said, ignoring the dig at Chief.

"Look," he said, "here's the deal. I don't know how much you've been following things here in Houston, but we've got a new mayor and there's no love lost between the mayor's office and our guys. What that means for the rank and file is that there will be a whole bunch of scrutiny put on budgets going into the new year."

"Yeah, well it happens like that, doesn't it?" Ryan shifted positions. "A few months of belt-tightening until the bad blood's forgiven and everything will go back to normal. What does that have to do with me?"

"Cap needs your spot filled or he'll lose it."

"My spot is filled," he said. "I didn't give it up. Six months leave of absence was the deal, and I'll keep my end of it." He scratched Chief's head. "Cap knows I mean what I say, and besides, I've only been here a month."

"That may be, but are you willing to risk losing your spot should the department make you choose between coming back sooner than you planned or staying where you are?"

His "yes" wasn't as easy to voice as Ryan expected.

"I keep my word," he added. "Cap knows that, and so do you."

"Glad to hear it." He let out a long breath.

"So he'll understand when I ask him to keep *his* word. Maybe I ought to set the record straight on that Monday morning."

"No, don't do that," Uncle Mike said. "He doesn't know I've called you. I just wanted to give you time to think about what you'll say if and when you're forced to make a choice."

"Well, I appreciate that," Ryan said with a chuckle. "But there's no choice. Three generations of Houston firemen came before me. How can I end that legacy?"

"Exactly," his uncle said. "Which is why I want to be sure you're ready when you're called back. And honestly, Ryan, you may not have to make that decision. Political folks change their focus all the time. Unfortunately, his is on the cost of running the fire department right now."

"Understood."

Chief lifted his head and sniffed at the air then let out a low rumbling growl. A moment later, someone knocked and the dog's growl became a full-fledged bark.

"I appreciate the warning," Ryan said. "But I better go see who's here before Chief goes through the door."

"Yeah, all right. But promise me one more thing."

"What's that?" he asked as he moved toward the door.

"Call your mother sometime, okay, kid? She misses you."

Ryan laughed. "I promise. I'll call her today, deal?"

"Deal," Uncle Mike said before offering a quick goodbye.

Ryan quieted the dog then opened the door to see Leah standing there looking a little sheepish. "Well, hello," he said. "Did I miss a spot cleaning up the glass?"

Chapter Thirteen

Leah cringed as the jab found its mark. "About that," she said. "I'm pretty sure I owe you an apology."

"Pretty sure?"

Ryan leaned against the door frame, his arms crossed and his expression giving no clue as to whether he was serious. Nor did he appear to feel the icy wind that blew across the deck now that the sun was setting. Leah shrugged closer into her hooded sweatshirt and tried to ignore the goose bumps rising on her arms.

"Well," he continued, "how about you let me know when you make up your mind?" The twinkle in his eyes let her know he'd been teasing. She responded with the beginnings of a smile that quickly died as she realized she still must make her situation right.

"Okay, look. I'm sorry." She peered at the dog that sat silently awaiting his master's command, her teeth chattering and her fingers going numb. "I made an assumption that was wrong."

And not just today. For she also assumed an unfair dislike of Ryan's duty to hold the restaurant to city standards. But one apology at a time.

"Really?"

She leaned down to allow Chief to sniff her hand then straightened to return her attention to Ryan. Time to get on with the apology so she could go home and warm up.

"Really," Leah said. "Apparently my cat was the source of the trouble today."

He lifted a dark brow. "Apparently?"

"You're not making this easy, Ryan," she said.

"Well," he said slowly, "I'm wounded here. You've made assumptions about my dog…" The fireman paused and offered a purposely pained look.

"I see." Leah stifled her own smile as she realized he was not through teasing her. "Well, I apologize to you both, then."

She turned to go only to hear him say, "Wait. You can't leave me in despair."

"Despair?" She stopped to look over her shoulder. "I had no idea it was as bad as all that."

"Well, there is a fix for our pain." He shrugged then knelt down to scratch the dog behind the ear. "If you were truly interested in making things right with us, that is."

Leah shook her head in disbelief. "Us?"

"Yes, us." He gave her a pitiful look as the dog rolled over on his back and urged Ryan to rub his belly. "Chief and me," he said as he complied.

Laughing, she rested her hand on the stair rail. With the sun warm against her back, the wind felt less bone-chilling here. Or perhaps amusement had trumped hypothermia.

"I don't know a whole lot about dogs," she said, "especially monsters like that one. But Chief looks pretty content."

Ryan straightened to leave the dog sprawled at his feet. "Looks are deceiving."

"Aah." She folded her arms over her chest. "So, just to be sure I understand, you and your dog—who appears to have fallen asleep—are still grieving over the wrong done to you."

He looked down at the beast then back at Leah. "Exactly."

"All right," she said with a chuckle. "What will it take to make things right again?"

Ryan once again lifted a dark brow. "Take a ride with me."

A ride? Not what she expected. "I…" She searched for something to say. "That is…wait. How will that help Chief?"

"He's my best friend, Leah. And he wants me to be happy. Don't you, Chief?"

The dog opened his eyes and looked up at his owner. A moment later he closed them again.

"See," Ryan said. "He's already on the mend. So, what do you say?" After a moment, he added gently, "I really do need to talk to you about some things."

"Sure," she said, though she half expected to regret it. Instead, she felt a surprising tinge of excitement along with a case of nerves. "But I need to change my shoes and grab a jacket."

Ryan changed his jeans once and his shirt twice before finally opting for wearing the same thing he'd had on all day. *Wouldn't want her to think I'm dressing up for this.*

The question of whether to get her or wait was answered when Leah appeared on the stairs. She'd changed from the sweatshirt and yoga pants she'd worn earlier and now wore a green sweater a shade darker than her eyes and a pair of slim-fitting jeans. A pair of dark brown boots completed the outfit.

"You look…"

Ryan paused to tamp down on his enthusiasm. It wouldn't do for Leah to know how much he'd anticipated this moment. After all, he was a man on a mission. Besides, he was pretty sure he was the last person on earth she'd want to receive a compliment from.

"Ready for a drive?" he finally said as they climbed inside the Jeep.

"Where are we going?"

"Not far," he said as he backed out of the driveway and headed east. The afternoon sun slanted across the waves and warmed the interior of the Jeep despite the November chill.

Up ahead he spied a billboard newly emblazoned with the red and green colors of Christmas. Marching above a photograph of sailboats decorated with Christmas lights was an invitation to join this year's Vine Beach Boat Parade festivities on Christmas Eve.

In smaller letters at the bottom of the sign was a reminder that Pop's Seafood Shack would be hosting a viewing party along with their customary buffet to benefit local charities.

Leah noticed him reading the board and shrugged. "It's faith. The event does so much good in the community. I just feel like God will find a way to make it happen at Pop's."

"I think He's already done that." Ryan slowed to

allow a car to turn ahead of him before braving a quick glance at his companion. "I've been trying to tell you this since Saturday. The Starting Over guys are willing to help however they can to make the necessary repairs."

"Oh, Ryan." Her voice was soft as if he'd overwhelmed her with the news. "I couldn't ask them to do that."

"It's already been voted on. All you have to do is say yes." He signaled to turn left at Berry Hill Road. "And don't worry about having to run into me there. I can't help. It's a conflict of interest since I'm the guy who has to do the inspection after it's done."

"Okay."

Did she sound relieved or was that just his imagination?

"So you'll let them help?"

"Well, yes, I suppose so." She paused. "I mean, yes. I would be honored to have them help get Pop's back open in time for the Christmas Eve event. Thank you." She reached to touch his arm. "I'm sure you had something to do with this."

"I'll let Riley know," he said. "And the thanks goes to the Starting Over guys, not me."

"I'm grateful all the same." She returned her hands to her lap.

"Ryan, where are we going?"

This time the tone of her voice was unmistakable. Apprehension colored her words and, when he glanced across the front seat, he could see it also colored her features.

He pulled the Jeep to a stop in front of the gate leading to Berry Hill Farms then let out a long breath. "Part of why I wanted to take you on a drive was so I could tell you about the offer the Starting Over guys had for you."

"And the rest of it?"

"The rest of it has to do with the fire."

"I see."

Ryan shifted the car into Park then swiveled to give her his fill attention. Her fiery hair curled around her shoulders and begged him to touch it while those beautiful bottle-green eyes regarded him with an odd mixture of what appeared to be suspicion and something else. Was it fear?

"I fail to see why you need to concern yourself with a fire that happened eight months ago. It's over and done. It was an accident, an awful one, but there's nothing further to be gained from worrying about it."

Ryan watched her with an investigator's eye. While he'd worked arson cases only a few times in his career at HFD, he'd been at enough fire scenes to point out a guilty party with reasonable success. What he saw wasn't guilt.

Leah Berry didn't burn that house, not that he'd expected she might be a suspect. But she knew who did.

"The case was never closed," he said slowly. "Did you realize that?"

She worried with the edge of her sleeve. "No. I guess I just assumed that since no one said anything and Pop's injuries were minor..."

Much as he would like to conduct an interview with her regarding the subject, Ryan knew from experience he could gain much more by bringing her to the actual scene of the fire.

He signaled to turn into Berry Hills Farm. "There's

a code on that gate, Leah. I'd like to take you up to the site and see if maybe you can help me close this case permanently."

"Ryan," she said softly, "I appreciate what you're trying to do but I don't see any benefit to dragging up a topic of conversation among the locals that has only just died down."

"I understand," he said, "but let me ask you this. Did your father file an insurance claim on the home?"

"No," Leah said. "Pop was adamant that since he didn't intend to rebuild, there was no need for it." She shrugged. "I called his insurance agent once I got the power of attorney over Pop's affairs."

"And?" he asked though he had a good idea of the answer.

"And she said that unless there was a finding from an inspector as to why the home was a complete loss, there could be no payment issued." She leaned back against the seat. "I just let it go at that point. Pop was the only witness and unless the agent caught him on a good day, there's no telling what he might claim."

A thought occurred. "Are you afraid he started the fire?"

She seemed to consider the question a moment. "If you're asking if I believe my father purposely burned down our family home, then no. I don't think he did."

He sensed she wished to say more. "But?"

Taking a deep breath, Leah let it out slowly as the waves crashed against the beach in the distance. "But if you want to know whether he was the cause of it, then I'd have to say I think he probably was."

"I see."

"Pop left a pan on the stove and the house caught

fire. The building was old, and the timbers were dry. That much I can verify. So given the facts, what other explanation is there?"

He could think of several.

She slid him a hesitant look. "So part of my reluctance is the fear that my father will be charged with a crime, that he somehow started the fire."

So there it was. The need to protect her father was the reason Leah was reluctant to cooperate. "Leah," he said gently, "if you get an insurance settlement, you may be able to use the money to make the repairs at Pop's. Not that I am encouraging you to cooperate so you'll get money," he hastened to add. "I can't be party to anything regarding the payments made for repairs to Pop's, not when I'm the inspector. Just consider this as advice but not a recommendation, all right?"

"No, of course. I understand." She considered his suggestion. "Yes, all right. Let's get this over with."

She released her seat belt and stepped out of the Jeep, allowing a cold north wind to blow in. Gathering her jacket around her, Leah punched in the code then stepped back to allow the gate to swing open. The moment she shut the car door behind her, Ryan shifted into Drive and headed up the gravel road toward the biggest mystery he'd found in Vine Beach.

Second biggest, he amended as he spied Leah watching him. As much as he wanted to put this case in the solved file, he wanted to figure out his feelings for Leah even more.

He hated to admit it, but the neighbor with the ornery cat and penchant for buttermilk pie had begun to wiggle her way into his heart. The fear that thought invoked must have shown on his face, for Leah reached across the distance between them to touch his arm.

"Something wrong?"

"What?" Ryan eased the Jeep around a dip in the road then headed toward the ruins, placing his palm over hers. "No, but your fingers are like ice."

"It's November in Texas," she said with a shrug.

"Same thing we said out on Sand Island when you were getting sunburned." He pulled to a stop at what must surely have been the main entrance to the grand home.

"It was so beautiful," Leah said softly. "I remember riding my pony at a full gallop up the drive and right to the front steps. My grandfather used to tell me that one day I'd just ride right into the kitchen to see what was for supper if I wasn't careful."

Ryan chuckled. "I actually did once."

"What?" She grinned. "No, you didn't."

"Yes, actually I did." He shrugged as he pointed the Jeep closer to the burned home. "I was seven and thought myself quite the cowboy. But in my defense, I did it on a dare. My dad was so mad at my brothers for putting me up to it that he fed the horse on the back porch and made Robby and Steve eat supper in the barn."

With the ruins only several steps away, Ryan pulled over and turned off the engine. "Since the case is still technically under investigation, we're going to have to treat this as a crime scene," Ryan said as he reached for the door handle. "Stick close to me and try not to touch anything, all right?"

She nodded and followed him out of the car the few yards that separated them from the spot where the front porch had once been. Here the jagged columns jutted up into the sky, blacked reminders of what once had been.

He could see through to the back of the house, though such was the intensity of the fire that very little was left of the interior. Leah came up behind him and unexpectedly reached for his elbow.

When he turned to face her, he spied the shimmer of tears swimming at the corners of her eyes. "Hey," he said lightly, "we don't have to do this now. Why don't we—"

"No, I *need* to do this," she said in a shaky voice. "Today. I'm fine. It's just that I'm surprised at the way I'm feeling, that's all."

"All right." Ryan waited a moment then urged her forward. "Let's walk the perimeter and you can tell me what you know about that night."

A strand of hair blew across her forehead and she reached to tuck it behind her ear. "But I wasn't here. I don't know what I can do to help."

He shrugged. "You never know. Let's try it."

A nod and she fell into step beside him. As they walked, he paused occasionally to take photos of pertinent evidence with his phone. By the time they reached what he assumed was the back of the home, Ryan realized Leah hadn't said a word.

"Hey," he said as he stepped into her line of sight, "are you all right?"

She walked around him to move toward a bench that appeared to have been built from a hollowed tree. As he moved closer, Ryan could see that what he'd thought was wood was actually concrete.

"Not really," she said as she settled onto the bench. "It's suddenly just so real."

Ryan eased down beside her and leaned forward, resting his elbows on his knees. From this spot—the highest elevation in the city—he could see all the way to Sand Island. His gaze tumbled down the grassy hill to the ribbon of highway, the shuttered restaurant and then finally the Gulf beyond. A glance to the right brought the lighthouse into view and if he squinted he could just make out the pier where he and Leah had had their picnic.

"It's beautiful, isn't it?"

He nodded as he straightened to turn his attention toward Leah. "Yes."

And she was, too. Even with the tears freely sliding down her cheeks.

Ryan cleared his throat then reached to once again cover her hand with his. "Hungry?"

The diversionary question was enough to capture her attention. "What? Actually…"

"Good. I think we're finished here."

They weren't but he'd not tell her that. He rose and stood in front of her then reached down to pull her to her feet. To his surprise, she fell into his arms.

Leah buried her face in the fireman's shoulder and, for a moment, tried not to think of what a fool she was making of herself. Something about sitting here on the bench where Pop used to read her stories had been the final straw that caused an entire avalanche of memories.

The rambling message Pop sent via email, the unsuccessful attempts to reach him by phone. And finally the call from Jack Murdoch.

She'd known something like this could happen. Had

tried her best to convince her stubborn father to either accept an aide from the nursing service or…

Or what?

A sob worked its way up Leah's throat. She had replayed the either-or part of that equation since March. When Pop refused the Home Health nurses, she should have walked away from the Paris trip and seen to him herself.

That was the *or* that plagued her.

By degrees she became aware of Ryan's hand on her back. Of the complete stillness with which he held her. The idea that this felt so right.

Too right.

Slowly the feeling of foolishness overtook her grief and she stepped from his grasp. "I'm sorry," she whispered though she'd hoped her voice might carry louder.

"Come on," he said gently. "Let's get you out of here."

While the idea was tempting, she needed something to stall him until she could find some measure of calm. The last thing she needed was to get into close proximity to Ryan in the Jeep then fall apart again.

"Wait." She let out a long breath. "Long as we're here, do you mind if I feed the horses? I was planning on doing that later but if it's all right with you…"

"Absolutely." They climbed into the Jeep and bounced across the prairie to the field where the palominos were grazing.

Leah went into the barn to fetch the food, leaving Ryan behind. When she returned, she found him lavishing attention on Boo. If he saw her walking toward them, Ryan gave no notice of it.

"I'm going to miss her," Leah said as a chill wind blew around her.

"About that."

Ryan seemed to fidget, causing the horse to spook. The fireman watched the horse bolt across the pasture before turning his attention to Leah. She could tell he wanted to say something.

"It's okay," she supplied as she gathered her jacket closer. "I'll miss her. So would Pop if he were the old Pop. But there are things that take precedence." She paused to look across the field. "Like family."

"Yeah," he said softly.

She gathered her wits and squared her shoulders. It was time to go now. "And a promise is a promise."

Chapter Fourteen

As they left Berry Farm, Ryan was furious with himself. Leah had all but served up his chance to admit the truth on a silver platter. And what had he done?

Nothing. Holding her in his arms had clearly addled his brain.

"You said you were hungry?" she asked.

"Starved."

She lifted a brow. "I hope you're not considering another picnic at the pier. It's a little cold for that."

"Oh, no. I've got another place in mind. How does pizza sound?"

Her smile warmed his heart, especially since he could still see evidence of her tears. Could feel the dampness where she had cried on his shoulder.

"All right. Pizza it is."

They rode the remainder of the brief distance to the Pizza Palace in silence. The restaurant had already added their Christmas decorations outside, complete with several dozen strands of lights and a gigantic snowman that played Christmas carols at high volume.

"You sure about this?" he asked as he joined Leah at the door.

"Absolutely," was her swift response.

"All right then. After you."

Once inside, the combined sound of children and carnival games stopped Ryan in his tracks. He looked around at the combination of lights and noises with the eyes of a man caught in a trap of his own making. By the time a waitress dressed in royal regalia arrived at the hostess booth, his flee-or-fight meter was drifting dangerously toward flee.

"No kids with you tonight?" She reached for two menus. "I'll take you to the grown-ups section of the palace then."

The tiara-and-evening-gown-clad teenager whose name tag proclaimed her to be Princess Bailey led them to a booth in the corner farthest from the zoo that was the children's playroom. While silence didn't exactly reign, at least chaos didn't, either.

Here the Christmas music was audible, something that was a mixed blessing. Leah slid into the crow-shaped booth and Ryan followed. In his haste to get seated, he scooted a little too far and collided with Leah. The reminder of holding her in his arms hit him, again.

"Sorry about that," he said as he inched over. *It's just dinner,* he reminded himself. *Just dinner.*

"I didn't know it would be this crazy," he said once their drinks had been ordered. "The last time I was here the place was closed for my inspection." He shrugged. "Not nearly as loud when the game machines are off."

"And the kids aren't here," she added as a pair of elementary-aged boys raced past. "But you know what? It's kind of fun."

"You think so?" He frowned. "Really?"

His neighbor looked up from the menu, grinning. "Really. Why? Does this bother you? Remember we're here to make you feel better. That's how I got conned into that drive."

He laughed at the reminder of a conversation that felt like it had happened days ago rather than less than an hour. "Serves me right for picking this place, then."

"Actually, I think it's kind of funny." She set aside the menu. "And maybe just a little bit of payback."

"Payback?" A kid squealed with what he hoped was happiness over in the playland area and Ryan flinched. "How do you figure that?"

She fixed him with an I'll-tell-you-why look. "Why didn't you stop me when I blamed Chief for breaking the jars?"

"Hey, I'm a nice guy," Ryan protested. "And I figured considering all that's happened since I got to Vine Beach, I owed you the right to get mad at me for something."

Her smile faded and she looked away. "You did your job. Now I'm doing mine."

Ryan took a sip of water. "What do you mean?"

"It's pretty simple really." She leaned back and rested her hands in her lap. "Pop left me in charge of all the Berry holdings, and I'm doing my best to be a good steward of that legacy. Some days I have no idea how he did it all. Others I have no idea why he bothered." She shook her head. "That sounded awful. Honestly, I am grateful to have a long line of history behind me. I just can't see where it's all going."

"I understand family history," he said. "It can weigh heavy on a person, can't it?"

"It can."

Was that relief or surprise he saw as her expression changed?

"Yeah," he said softly. "So your dad. How's he doing?"

"Some days he does great. You saw him on a pretty good day. Others, not so well. I never know which Pop I'll see when I visit. Or, for that matter, what he'll say or do while I'm there."

"Is that how he ended up at the nursing home?"

Her brows furrowed and she seemed to be considering how to answer. "Technically he's there because of the fire. When Berry Hill burned, there was really no place for him to go. The cabin's just too small and I'd worry about him going up and down the stairs all day." Leah worried with the edge of her napkin. "It was the best choice."

"You don't seem certain of that," he offered.

"Oh, I am, but that doesn't make it any easier." She paused. "And when I say technically, I should qualify that. I had concerns about Pop living alone before the fire."

"Oh?" he asked as he thought of the burn pattern he'd photographed in the ruins of Berry Hill.

"Yeah."

She didn't indicate a willingness to elaborate, and given his experience at Berry Hill, Ryan could figure no other way to ask. "That must be tough," was the best he could offer.

"It's not fun, but at least he's still around. I haven't lost him completely. I don't know what I'll do when that day comes. But then I know you understand."

"Actually my dad's still alive."

"No," she said as she unrolled the napkin. "I meant your wife. You understand loss."

He froze. When no better response came, Ryan finally said, "Can we change the subject?"

"I'm sorry," Leah hurried to say. "I didn't realize this was a topic you…" She lowered her head. "Forget I said anything."

He shook his head. "Sorry."

But was he? Yes, that was part of it. But part of it was the growing need he had lately to share with Leah his feelings of guilt over Jenna's death. The fact he even considered talking about the topic told Ryan that this relationship with the girl next door was becoming something more than a friendship. Was developing a trust that terrified him.

When it came down to it, he also had to admit he'd never had that kind of trust in Jenna. Which brought him back to his feelings of sorrow. And guilt.

They fell into a mildly uncomfortable silence. For his part, Ryan didn't mind not having to speak, and Leah seemed to feel the same. At least that's the impression she offered as they sat side by side.

Thankfully Princess Bailey arrived with their salads, making the lack of conversation less obvious. Still, Ryan took two bites then pushed away his plate.

"Look, Leah," he said. "We keep trading apologies. And it's my turn." He paused to rest his palms on the table while he gathered his thoughts. "When I say I don't talk about, well…my past, I don't mean to be rude about it. It's just that people tend to act weird around me when they find out what happened. And you've been nice—mostly." He punctuated the jest with a gentle nudge.

"I try." Her smile was fleeting as she stabbed at her salad. "Though you do have a way of making things difficult." Her grin returned full force.

At least she'd made a joke. That gave Ryan hope that the evening wasn't going to be a total loss. "So, anyway, how's the work coming at Pop's?"

She looked up sharply. "It's coming along okay, though I'll be glad to see the Starting Over guys. Why?"

"No reason. I just wondered." Ryan shook his head. "We're quite a pair, aren't we?"

Leah played with her meal. "What do you mean?"

He shrugged. "Seems like our safest topic of conversation is silence."

"I don't mind if you don't."

"Me? No. I like a woman who doesn't expect me to entertain her with my witty banter."

"You have witty banter?" she asked. "Really?"

"You wound me," he replied in mock disappointment. "And for your information, I am extremely witty."

"I don't know, Ryan." Leah dabbed at the corner of her mouth with her napkin. "In my experience if you have to tell someone you're witty, you're probably not."

"Ouch. Though you do prove my point about silence being our best topic of conversation." Ryan gestured to the kid-filled chaos corner. "If only they felt the same way."

It took a moment for her to get the joke, but when she did Leah began to giggle. Her laughter was contagious, and soon Ryan joined her.

"Okay, let's try some witty banter," she said after a moment. "Tell me something interesting about you I don't know."

He thought a moment. "Okay, I put myself through

junior college riding broncs and bulls on the rodeo circuit. Had to quit when the Aggies offered me a basketball scholarship, but I still miss it sometimes."

"Now that is interesting." She paused. "Which did you prefer, the bulls or the broncs?"

"Broncs aren't as bent on ruining your day by stomping you as bulls, but it happens so fast that either can be dangerous. One minute you're climbing into the stall and the next you're sitting in the dirt. If you're good and you're lucky more than eight seconds have passed between the two."

He chuckled as he motioned for the waitress to bring their check.

"That must be why you're so good with horses."

He paid the check then returned his attention to Leah. "What's that?"

"I saw how Boo reacted to you." She slid to the edge of the booth then stood. "She's not the easiest to charm."

Ryan followed her out of the Pizza Palace, his conscience stinging. After helping her into the Jeep, he went around to climb into the driver's seat. "Leah," he said slowly. "About that horse of yours. I'm the one who bought her."

Her expression went blank then slowly the corners of her mouth lifted. "Oh, that's good, Ryan. That's really funny." Her grin became a chuckle. "Or should I say witty?"

"No, really. I did."

She shook her head. "Okay, enough teasing."

Ryan turned onto the highway then let out a long breath. "Ask Eric. Boo is mine. Or she will be on Tuesday. I'm boarding her with you until I decide what to do with her."

The rest of the trip home was wordless. Ryan climbed out of the Jeep and trotted around to meet Leah.

Maybe this was the way the Lord wanted things to go. Whatever the reason, he'd managed to tell Leah the truth.

"You don't have to walk me upstairs," she said angrily.

"Sorry, but I do," Ryan responded. "I was raised to see a woman safely home. Nothing personal, but my dad wouldn't be happy if he found out I was ignoring his rules."

Leah reached into her purse to find her keys then stabbed one into the door's lock. When the door slid open, she turned to face him. "I think maybe we should stay away from each other, Ryan."

"Why?" he managed.

Chapter Fifteen

Saturday morning dawned sunny and much less cold than previous days. Ryan dressed quickly and took his Bible out on the deck to enjoy the warmth of the combination of sunshine and hot coffee.

Ryan leaned back against the deck chair and looked up into the cloudless sky. A few stars and the faint outline of the moon were still visible against the brilliant blue, but they were fading fast.

He opened his Bible to the place where he'd left off yesterday morning. *As charcoal to embers and as wood to fire, so is a quarrelsome man for kindling strife.*

Ryan stuck the bookmark back in and closed the Bible on Proverbs 26:21. Charcoal to embers. Wood to fire.

Images already in his mind from his argument with Leah last night. He'd said too much, and he felt awful. Frustration was no excuse. He set the Bible on the table beside him then picked up his coffee. By the time he'd drained the cup, Ryan was more than ready to see his pals at Starting Over and hear how yesterday's construction work had gone. He still wondered when they'd get around to asking him to talk about Jenna's death, but at least he felt like he'd regained some of his skills on the basketball court.

Last week he'd only had to soak his sore muscles for two nights. Maybe this time around he wouldn't have to soak them at all.

When he arrived at the church, he found Eric waiting for him in the parking lot. "How did it go?" he asked Eric.

"From what I understand they made a lot of progress on the deck. Not sure what else they worked on, but Mom told me Riley and the guys had a great time."

"Good."

"Hey," Eric said as he fell into step beside Ryan, "I wanted to catch you before the meeting started to ask if you'd do something."

His brow rose. "What's that?"

"I'm putting together a team to decorate my boat for the Christmas boat parade and I wondered if you'd join us."

He chuckled. "And what does this entail exactly?"

"A whole bunch of grunt work that may or may not include scrubbing decks, hanging lights and deciding what in the world we're going to put on the banner this year." He shrugged. "Honestly I don't know how you can say no. It's a sweet deal, especially when you consider there's no pay and the other team members are my daughters and, if our son allows, my wife."

"Count me in," Ryan said. "It sounds like fun."

"Um, right." Eric grinned. "Actually it really is. Except for that sign. We never decide what to put on it until the night before and even then…well, anyway, we can talk about that later."

By the time Riley arrived to call the meeting to order with a devotional and letters of thanks from the nursing home residents, Ryan had heard all about the previous day's work. Orlando and a few members of the church choir had joined them, making the work move fast and giving them the occasional song to hammer by.

As the tales progressed, so did Ryan's feelings of envy, though his concerns at joining a bunch of guys who talked about how bad their lives were had disappeared. An hour later, so had any thoughts that his basketball skills had improved since the last two times he'd played.

When the game ended and the guys split into smaller groups, Eric invited Ryan to join the men standing with him. As they all sat, Ryan's resistance to talking about Jenna's death rose.

"This morning I was reading the Word. How many of you use the Bible-in-a-Year version?"

Ryan nodded, as did several others.

"I don't know about you, but when I got to the verse in Proverbs about kindling and fire and the quarrelsome man, it stopped me cold." He looked at Ryan. "And not just because I made the new fire chief hang out in our group this morning."

When the smattering of chuckles died down, Eric continued. "Ryan's fairly new, so he probably doesn't know this, but we're not in the habit of forcing members of this group to bare our souls to one another. There'll always be a listening ear here for any man who needs to talk, but our purpose is less about spending time in the past and more about walking together toward whatever future the Lord has for us."

Eric paused a minute before continuing. "Bottom

line—our story got us here. It doesn't keep us here. So what does that have to do with the quarrelsome man?" He shrugged. "Every time I've read this passage I've thought of that guy we all know who's always up for a fight. He's the first one to challenge your favorite football team or your choice of food or car. In short, he's an opinionated pain who, for the most part, is uninformed and can't keep his mouth shut enough to listen to good counsel. Can anybody relate?"

Ryan could, and his nod said so. Others agreed.

"All right, here's where it gets good." Eric grinned. "What if that quarrelsome man was me? Or you?" He waved away the murmur of protest. "Hear me out on this. How many of us can say we've argued with God and taken a path He didn't send us down? How'd that turn out? Could you say you kindled some strife? Could you also say things might have gone better had you been less quarrelsome and not thrown charcoal into the embers?"

Ryan was still thinking about that question as he climbed the stairs to return home. He'd left his Bible on the table, a fact he realized when he found Leah's cat batting at the pages. Shooing the orange menace away, he let Chief out to prowl the deck before choosing a spot at Ryan's feet. Then Ryan picked up the Bible and read the passage from Proverbs again. *As charcoal to embers and as wood to fire, so is a quarrelsome man for kindling strife.*

What paths had he taken that kindled strife? Instantly his move-forward-at-all-cost marriage to Jenna came to mind, as did a few other recent missteps.

He closed his eyes and let free a long breath while he

poured out his heart to the Lord, then sat very still and listened. Even when Leah's cat returned to plop in his lap, Ryan remained still. So, oddly, did Chief.

Ryan opened his eyes and glanced down at the bull-mastiff who lay sprawled at his feet. "Guess you two have decided to make friends," he said as he scratched the cat behind its ears. After looking up at Ryan through half-closed eyes, the feline stretched, followed by nimbly jumping off his lap onto the table beside him. She took another leap and landed between Chief's front paws.

The big dog lifted his head to stare at the cat. Then, to Ryan's surprise, Chief laid his head back down and resumed his peaceful slumber while the cat moved a few feet away to a sliver of afternoon sunshine and began preening.

Mindful of the promise he had made to Uncle Mike, Ryan picked up the phone to call his parents. Of course his mother answered the phone. She always did, even when Dad wasn't at the firehouse.

After dispensing with the pleasantries, he paused to wait for the question he knew she would ask. "So, your dad's at the station," she said slowly, "but I'm asking this for both of us. How are you really, son?"

He sighed but sat taller. "Really, I'm good. Getting that way, anyway."

"Are you?"

"Mom," he said with as much patience as he could manage, "I am. I promise. And getting better every day." That much was true.

"All right, then. I'm glad. So tell me about your job. Is it everything you thought?"

Ryan propped his feet up on the rail and considered

his response. "It's nothing like I expected, mostly in a good way."

"Mostly?"

Again he paused. "Well, you know, it's difficult to tell someone her business has to close until it's brought up to code."

"Her?" his mother said. "Is this *her* someone you'd like to tell me about?"

"Mother."

"Oh, all right, but you can't blame me for asking. Now," she said, "is it too early to talk about your holiday plans?"

"Well, actually, it is. I'm not sure what the schedule is for city employees. I may have to be on call." He shifted positions. "But I'll ask the mayor as soon as I can, all right?"

"Ryan." Her tone held more than a little warning. "You're not trying to get out of seeing your family at Christmas, are you?"

"No, of course not." Or was he? Ryan cringed at the thought. And yet he also cringed at the idea of his family trying not to say the wrong thing. "Look, I promise I'll let you know my work schedule just as soon as I find out."

He changed the subject to ask about his mom's book club, which sent her off on a ten-minute and much-welcomed discussion of what she had been reading. Once the topic died, Ryan knew it was time for her favorite evening television show.

Thus he was able to hang up a few minutes later knowing he had fulfilled his promise to Uncle Mike without making any promises to his mom.

There were no plans beyond the idea that he would

help Eric prepare his boat to be in the boat parade on Christmas Eve. And so far that suited Ryan just fine.

He set the phone aside and rested his head against the back of the chair. As much as he loved his mother, he hated being evasive with her. Worse, he hated that he'd mentioned Leah, even in passing. His mom would want to know more next time, and all he could tell her was that he'd made a mess of what might have been a good relationship.

Or had he?

Ryan rose and snagged his phone. Maybe he could salvage their friendship with an overdue apology. He tried her home and saw her vehicle wasn't there, so he headed for the stables. There he found her grooming one of the palominos. She looked up when he drove through the gate.

"You just missed Eric," she called as she set down the brush. "He and the girls left right after the riding lesson. Something about hurrying home for dinner, I believe."

He closed the distance between them, then paused to offer the horse an apple from his pocket. "Actually I came to see you." Ryan met her gaze. "I need to talk to you about Boo. Or rather, about not telling the truth about Boo."

She rested her hands on her hips. "Oh?"

He gave her a sideways look and searched for something to say to lighten the mood. "So, yeah, I'm apologizing again. Making a habit of it, it appears."

Just when he thought his joke had fallen flat, Leah's expression softened. "It does appear so," she said.

"I have no excuse." He shrugged. "I wanted that horse and didn't think you'd sell her to me, but I should have taken my chances with the truth." Ryan paused.

"So if you want her back, much as I would hate to, I'll do that."

Leah looked away, then turned to lead the palomino into a stall. Once the stall was secured, she leaned against the door and regarded Ryan with an even look. "I appreciate that," she said, "but it won't be necessary."

"No?" A grin slid into place. "Thank you. I would have hated to return her even if it was the right thing to do."

She walked past him to grab the brush on her way to the tack room. "Do you always do the right thing?" Leah tossed the words over her shoulder as she deposited the brush, then returned to wait in the door.

"I wish I could say I do." He watched her move to the bench nearby before joining her. "I try."

She released a long breath as she stretched out her legs. "I believe you."

Spying a piece of straw in her braid, Ryan reached over to pluck it free. "Look," he said slowly, "I would never do anything to hurt you, Leah. So, this thing with Pop's…" He paused to consider his words carefully. "This thing with Pop's is hard. I'm not asking for sympathy, and I won't apologize for doing my job. However, I need you to understand that I will do anything I can to help you. Long as it's legal, of course."

Leah sat up straight to swivel toward him. "Ryan, I—"

"Hey," he interrupted, "not arguing. Just let me help however I can, all right?"

She shook her head. "I don't know what to do about you, Ryan Owen. One minute I'm so frustrated and the next…"

"The next?" he urged as his hopes soared.

Leah climbed to her feet abruptly, then started for the stalls. "Well, never mind about the next. Thank you for the apology and the offer to help in any way you can."

"I meant it," he said as he rose to follow her.

"Good." She reached over the rail and pulled a shovel. "Your horse's stall needs mucking."

"Great," he said as he began his first project in the mission to help Leah Berry.

Chapter Sixteen

"**M**ight want to go easy on the brushing," Ryan added. "I've seen horses kick for less than that."

Leah looked startled then nodded her head. "You're right." She tossed the brush aside and placed the blanket over the horse.

Ryan watched Leah close the stall door and then wander over to look out at the downpour. Even in silhouette, he could see her shiver, but with the rain came the darkness, and with the darkness a chill that permeated the drafty building.

"Hey, look," he said. "I wanted Boo, but more important, I wanted you to have the money from her sale to pay for the things the Starting Over guys can't handle."

Leah's expression went blank. Slowly she began to shake her head. "Why would you do that?"

"I care about you, Leah."

Something cold and wet hit him on the shoulder. He looked up at the rafters in the center of the structure to spy rain pouring in. Fetching an empty feed bucket from beside the tack room door, he positioned it beneath the leak.

The place was old and in need of repair, but Ryan would stake odds that this project was low on the list of things Leah could afford. With winters mild and storms generally fleeting outside of hurricane season, the old structure was serviceable. Still, he hated to think of these horses braving a cold winter in a wet stable.

A check of the stalls showed that at least there were no leaks where the horses were kept. However, he spied several other places where the rain was getting in. Tomorrow he'd come back with hammer and nails and see what he could do.

If Leah allowed it.

Ryan smiled. Or maybe if she didn't. As much as she had on her mind, it might be fun to take this item off the list and present it to her as completed.

He sighed. He was meddling again, even though she'd already told him once to stay out of her affairs.

"Where are the rest of the feed buckets?" he called.

Leah turned. "What?"

"Buckets," he repeated as he gestured toward the ceiling. "Anything to catch these drips."

She looked up at the ceiling then down at him. Though he couldn't see her face, her posture told him she'd not taken well to seeing the leak.

"There should be more up in the loft above the tack room. Probably an extra trash can or two, as well." She gestured to a spot behind him. "The ladder's on the side. Need some help?"

"No, I've got this."

When he ran out of empty buckets and trash cans, Ryan gave up. At least the horses would stay dry and the floor wouldn't flood.

He found Leah standing in the doorway, her damp

hair curling in long fiery ropes across her shoulders and down her back. She seemed unaware of his presence, so Ryan was content to stay some distance away and watch.

In profile she was every bit as beautiful, though she seemed restless and unable to remain still as she clenched her fists and worried with the hem of her shirt. Finally, Ryan went to fetch a blanket. Then, as he moved closer, softly called her name.

"You're soaked. Here, put this on." He draped the horse blanket over her shoulders then stood beside her and gazed out into the storm. "Looks like this isn't letting up anytime soon. Too bad you're parked so far away. We could make a run for it if you want."

When she did not reply, Ryan moved into her line of sight. "Okay then. What say we move out of the wind? You're not going to get dry standing here."

She turned around and looked down to spy the feed bucket in the center of the walkway. "I won't get dry in here either," she said as she stepped past it. "But I can't make a run for it. Not when it's lightning and thundering. I just…well, I can't."

He caught up to her and gestured to the bales of hay at the far end of the stables. Her reluctance puzzled him. "Go and sit down."

Though she appeared not to hear, Leah complied. He waited until she had settled atop a hay bale then went to fetch his own blanket. Though he was not soaked through to the skin like Leah was, the rain had still caught him unaware and done a decent job of dampening his clothes.

When he joined her, Leah mustered a smile. A brisk wind blew past, and Leah wrapped the blanket tighter.

The storm whipped up and something slammed against the wood on the other side of the barn. Leah jumped then huddled deeper into her blanket as a few of the horses whinnied in protest.

"I'll go check on that." Ryan rose to search out the origin of the sound only to find one of the window shutters had torn loose and was banging against the outside wall. Rain was pouring through the opening and soaking a mare that looked ready to bolt.

He edged around her, climbed into the gap and hauled the window shutter back into place. Then he calmed the mare until she no longer pawed at the ground.

By the time he headed back toward the hay bales, he was every bit as drenched as Leah. The cold seeped into his bones far quicker than he expected, causing him to detour to the tack room for the last of the blankets.

"Aren't we a sight?" Leah asked when he joined her. "What was making the noise?" When he told her, she shrugged. "The place is falling apart," she said softly. "But then it's old. That's what happens."

"Except when the owner is an expert in nineteenth century coastal archeological preservation."

Her gaze collided with his. "You remembered."

Ryan gripped the blanket as he shrugged. "I find it fascinating."

Actually he found *her* fascinating.

"It's a little like the fairy tale of the cobbler's shoeless wife, don't you think? I do fine at helping others preserve historical sites and buildings but I can't keep any property with a Berry name on the deed from falling into shambles. Thanks to the Starting Over guys..." She paused. "And to the money from Boo's sale, however, the restaurant should be ready for inspection soon.

I'm determined to reopen in time to host the Christmas banquet and viewing party."

Ryan nodded. "Just let me know and I'll make that inspection a priority. I owe you that much."

They sat in silence for a moment, and then Leah turned to Ryan. "You know a lot about me, but I don't know much about you. About why you're in Vine Beach."

Ryan gave her a sad smile. "I'm here because I said I'd be." He added, "And I keep my promises."

He could tell she wanted to know more. And for some reason, he wanted to tell her.

"To my wife," slipped out before he realized it.

"Oh, Ryan, I'm sorry," she said as she moved closer beside him.

"About Jenna." He swallowed. "I'd like to talk about how she died."

"Only if you want to," she said softly.

"No, I don't want to," was his response. "But I need to. I think the worst has been not talking about it at all." He took a deep breath and let it out slowly. "Classic cowboy-and-the-rodeo-queen relationship. I fell in love with her and she fell in love with love. And weddings. Oh, how Jenna loved planning our wedding. Seemed like that took over everything. Somewhere between arguing over the china pattern and choosing what color the tablecloths were going to be at the reception, we forgot we'd fallen in love."

She reached out to hug him.

He wrapped his arms tighter around Leah and she snuggled closer. Though the night air had grown colder, she felt warm in Ryan's arms.

"I should have called it off. I didn't. If I had, she'd be alive today."

She pushed away to shake her head. "Ryan, you don't know that to be true."

"I do, actually." He leaned against the rail and crossed his arms over his chest. "She died on our honeymoon."

"Oh, no," she murmured.

His expression softened. "We'd gone diving. Lost sight of her for just a moment. She was out cold. I tried... I tried..."

Leah rested her hand on his arm. "You don't have to tell me anything else."

He fixed his gaze on her. "She... I couldn't save her." Ryan paused. "The night we got engaged, she asked me to promise her a couple of things. The first was that I'd find a nice seafood place on the beach to celebrate our one-year anniversary." He looked directly at her. "That's the day I met you."

She slid her hand behind his back to lean against the rail beside him. Her smile encouraged him to continue.

"The second promise she asked of me was that we plan to move to the beach." He paused and seemed to be considering his words carefully. "To Jenna this was what she looked forward to, us someday living up here and acting like we were on vacation every day. She made me promise to follow through even if she died before we made it here."

"That doesn't sound much like you," Leah said.

"No, which is why I didn't get what she was asking, I suppose." He shrugged. "I figured a beach was a beach, and with Uncle Mike's connections, I could keep my promise to Jenna and still have my firefighting career." Again Ryan paused. "See, what Jenna never understood is that I'm a fireman. I come from firemen. I live, eat and breathe that life. She wanted to turn me into something different. And I probably wanted to do the same with her."

"Ryan, her death was not your fault." She bumped shoulders with him, and he began to smile. "Forgive me?" she asked.

Ryan shook his head. "I don't think it's your turn. I think it's mine." He pretended to consider the question. "No, wait, you're right. It is your turn. I apologized for buying your horse in secret. So yes, you were due to apologize to me."

"Well I'm glad someone's able to keep up," she said.

Silence fell between them punctuated by the soft sound of rain and the plopping of water into the various cans and buckets Ryan had spread around the place. "I always liked rainstorms," he said.

"Not me." She clutched the blanket tighter. "My grandmother died racing a storm back to this barn. She couldn't find me. Because I was playing hide and seek. I saw her go looking for me and I thought it would be fun to play a trick and hide in the loft. So I climbed up to wait for her to come back. I guess I fell asleep."

"Oh, Leah. I'm so sorry." He reached around to gather her into his arms. "And for the record it *is* my turn."

Her soft chuckle was buried in his shoulder, as were her tears. Ryan lifted his hand to cradle the back of her head. Her hair felt soft and the curls wrapped around his fingers as he let his head rest on hers.

How long they sat like that, Ryan couldn't say. At

some point he became so comfortable that he closed his eyes.

What seemed only a minute or two later was incorrect as Ryan opened his eyes. It was dark now, pitch black with only the slightest pale glow where the moon shone through one of the cracks in the wall. The rain had stopped, though the sound of dripping continued at irregular intervals around him.

Gradually he became aware that Leah was still fitted comfortably against his shoulder. Her slow, soft breathing told him that she was asleep.

He could have sat there all night just watching the slow rise and fall of her breath, counting the freckles that danced across her cheeks or feeling the comfort of her snuggled against him. With care, he leaned over and kissed the top of her head.

She smelled of rain and floral shampoo. With a little bit of the earthy scent of horse blanket thrown in for good measure. Or maybe that was him.

Unfortunately, his phone rang. Before he could silence it, Leah jolted awake.

She rose to stretch her arms over her head, and the blanket fell on the floor at her feet. "Don't you need to answer that?" she asked, her voice thick with sleep.

"No." He watched her move across the small expanse to peer out the window.

"It's stopped raining," she said. "What time is it?"

Ryan pulled his phone from his pocket, noting the call he'd missed was from Eric before checking the clock feature. "A little past nine."

Leah stifled a yawn. "Oh, wow."

"Yeah," he said. "I guess we both fell asleep."

She reached down to grab the blanket and began

folding it. Ryan rose and did the same, accepting hers when she handed it to him. Returning from the tack room, he found her attempting to remove hay straw from her hair.

"Here," he said as he closed the distance between them. "Let me do it."

Her thick hair rested in his palm as he pulled long pieces of hay from the fiery strands. She stood a full head shorter, giving him the advantage of height as he worked to remove as much evidence of her nap as he could. When he finished with the back, he turned her around to face him.

Their eyes met and he couldn't help but smile. "Stand very still," he said as he brushed his palm against her cheek. "You've got something—" he retrieved a strand of hay from just behind her ear then traced her jawline with it "—right here."

"Thanks," she said abruptly as the straw fluttered to the ground between them, "but I should go."

Ryan reached out to stop her, and his hand lingered on her arm. Again their gazes collided. Before good sense could prevail, he leaned down to touch his lips to hers. Her lips were soft, her touch light. His heart soared as he wrapped her in his arms. At once, Ryan Owen felt alive.

"We, um…" Leah said a moment later.

"Should we go?" Ryan supplied.

Eyes wide, Leah barely blinked. "Yes."

"Are you okay to drive?" he asked as he watched her unsteady march toward the door.

"I'm fine," she said. "Just a little tired. It's been a long day." She paused to turn and face him. "And it rained. But I survived."

"Yes, you did." He waited for her to say more. To acknowledge the kiss that was seared into his brain.

Instead he watched her palm her keys and disappear into the night to click the alarm on her SUV. He followed her in his Jeep the short distance home until Leah pulled into the driveway and turned off the engine.

Ryan climbed out of his car and escorted Leah up the stairs to her door. The cat met them halfway and trotted after Leah as she stuck her key in the lock.

"Ryan," she said without looking his way. "About that kiss."

He studied her profile in the moonlight looking for any hint of what she might be about to say. "Yes?"

She rested her palm on the door frame. "Is it your turn to apologize or mine?"

"This time," he said with a grin. "It's neither."

Leah turned to face him, and her smile matched his. "Good night," she said as she disappeared inside and closed the door.

Chapter Seventeen

On Tuesday afternoon, Leah left the bank with mixed feelings. She'd just put a nice deposit into an account that had dipped dangerously low, making it possible to pay the contractor for the restaurant repairs. She would still have to figure out how to pay the property taxes, but today Leah counted one hurdle off the list, and that was enough.

All that remained was to do a final walk-through at the restaurant followed by a call to Ryan to have him reinspect. Then she could aim for handling hurdle number two.

Her finger rose to her lips as Leah recalled last Saturday's kiss. Her next-door neighbor had been scarce since the weekend, and she hadn't seen him at church on Sunday, either. And while she'd considered the thought that the kiss might have chased him off, Leah consoled herself with the knowledge that it was Ryan who initiated it. At the same time she had to admit her heart lingered on the promise of a future together that his kiss seemed to offer.

Turning into the parking lot of the nursing home, she

steeled herself for the conversation she knew she must have with Pop. She tucked her purse under her arm and ducked between the raindrops to enter the nursing home. With no one at the nurses' station to greet her, Leah hurried down the hall to Pop's room.

When she heard the familiar voice coming from the other side of her father's door, she stopped short.

What in the world was Ryan Owen doing here?

The temptation to barge in and demand an answer was bested by the desire to listen in on their conversation. So she leaned against the door frame and waited.

"Are you sure that's your complete recollection?" Ryan asked. "That you don't remember how you ended up outside the burning home?"

"I smelled smoke, and I think maybe I was cooking something. I've been told I left something on the stove that caught fire," she heard Pop say.

"You've been told?" He paused. "So you don't remember cooking anything?"

"Son, I don't remember what I had for breakfast," Pop said. "How am I going to recall whether I was cooking something way back in March?"

"Because I think you do know, sir."

"Of all the nerve." Leah shoved open the door, following her outrage into Pop's room.

She found the men sitting across from each other at the little dining table under the window. Two cups of coffee had been poured though it appeared only Pop was interested in drinking any.

"What do you think you're doing?" she demanded of Ryan.

"Leah, honey." Her father rose to come over and embrace her. "Come and meet the fire chief."

"The fire chief and I are acquainted," she said, looking past her father to the man whose kiss was still on her mind.

"Well, how about that?" He ushered Leah over to the table. "Here, sit," Pop demanded as he gestured toward the chair he'd just vacated. Leah resisted the urge to sit in favor of standing and claiming the superior height over the fireman—for once.

She gestured toward the door. "Could I speak to you out in the hall, Ryan?"

He turned to Pop. "Since your daughter's here visiting, why don't I come back another time, Chief Berry?" Ryan pulled a card out of his wallet and handed it to her father. "If you think of anything that might help the investigation, I'd appreciate it if you'd give me a call."

Ryan shook hands with Pop then pressed past her to head for the door. Leah followed a step behind, her fists clenched and a few choice words on the tip of her tongue.

"I'll be right back, Pop," she said as she closed the door firmly then turned to face Ryan. "I repeat. What do you think you're doing? You know I did not want him to know about you."

"Apparently he's known about me for a while, Leah."

"How do you know this?" Concern etched on Leah's face as she wondered how Pop would feel. And yet if her father had known about Ryan and not said anything, he must be upset.

"The mayor told me." He grabbed Leah by the wrist and led her away from the door and down the hall, stopping only when they reached the front entrance. "All right, now let me get this straight," Ryan said. "You've lost your family home and you're not interested in finding out the real reason why?"

Leah looked around and, satisfied no one was in earshot, returned her attention to Ryan. "Yeah, honestly that's true. What good would it serve to open this again? It's not like I can rebuild. Apparently the policy Pop bought didn't come close to covering the damages."

He seemed to be trying to decide what to say next. Leah took his silence as an opportunity to walk away. Of course, the persistent fireman followed.

"Leah, wait." He stepped in front of her. "I'm trying to get at the truth. And the truth appears to be at odds with the report that was filed by the police officer." He looked away. "I'm not trying to cause any pain for you or your father, but I've looked at the scene of the fire twice now, and your dad's story doesn't add up."

"Which story?" She waited for him to return his gaze to her. "I've lost count of how many versions of that night I've heard. And in case you've missed it, he's here for a reason. Pop can't be relied upon to remember anything with any sort of reliability unless it happened at least three decades ago."

"You'd be surprised at what a few important details can reveal," Ryan said. "And I think he knows that fire didn't start in the kitchen."

"Again, what does it matter? The end result is the same whether Pop started the fire in the kitchen or some other part of the house."

Ryan leaned closer. "I'm considering the possibility your father didn't start the fire at all."

Leah's eyes narrowed. "If not him, then who?"

"You tell me," he said. "I understand offers have been

made for purchasing the entire tract of Berry land, including Pop's. Is that true?"

"How did you know?"

"I had a tip." He shrugged. "Took it to Jack Murdoch, and he admitted it was true."

"I see." She frowned. "Yes, it's true that the mayor and some group of investors he put together would like to have that property to develop some sort of beachfront condo and golf course resort. But it's not happening. Not now, and not ever."

"All right," he said. "And what if someone's trying to convince you to sell by setting fire to the home and breaking a few things in the restaurant so that it would fail?"

"Breaking a few things?" She shook her head. "Are you saying you've seen evidence of tampering with things in the restaurant?"

"I can't say for sure. It's possible that some of the damage was done over time. We've had a couple hurricanes come through in the last decade, and that could be the cause of some of the structural issues I found. I'm just offering the possibility. So what do you think?"

"I think Jack Murdoch would never be responsible for sabotaging Pop's or setting fire to Berry Hill."

"You're sure?"

Was she? Leah considered the question a moment. "Yeah, I'm sure. Now, he's never said who the members of this group of investors are, so I can't vouch for them. But I can say that the mayor has been nothing but protective of me and my dad, at least from what I have observed."

"All right," he said. "That gives me something to go on. I'll have Jack fill me in on these investors of his."

"What if he doesn't want to?" she asked.

"He has no choice." Ryan smiled. "I'm the fire chief and this just became an official investigation again." His expression sobered. "Look, Leah. I don't want to upset you or your father. I'm here to get to the bottom of what I've thought from the beginning was a suspicious fire." He paused. "I'm worried for your safety should someone be responsible for burning that home, they might come after the cabin next."

She nodded.

He gestured to the front doors behind her. "Then I'll go get started on this."

"Okay."

"Good. Now that things have changed between us, I can't help but want to protect you."

After a moment of silence, he ducked his head and pressed past her. "Oh, Leah?" he called as he reached the doors.

Leah turned to find him grinning in her direction. "Yes?"

"I'm still not sorry." And with that he turned and left her smiling in the lobby.

"Neither am I, Ryan," she whispered as she made her way back to Pop's room.

"All right," he said when she stepped inside and closed the door. "I want the scoop on this fellow and you'd better give me the truth."

"Sure, Pop," she said as she settled across from him at the table. Ryan's mug was still on the table, so she rose to empty it in the sink. "What do you want to know?"

"Is he courting you?"

Stifling a smile, Leah left the mug in the sink and

returned to her father. "No, Pop," she said. "It's nothing like that."

Her father looked skeptical.

"He's the fire chief," she explained, "and he's trying to decide what actually caused Berry Hill to burn. Apparently he's not convinced that the police report told the whole story."

"It didn't." Pop crossed his arms over his chest and stared out the window. "I'm the only one who knows that and I haven't told a soul."

"Pop," Leah said carefully, "what is it you haven't told anyone?"

He swiveled to look at her. For a moment she thought he might respond. Then he picked up his empty cup and handed it to her.

"Would you like more coffee?" she asked.

"No, but that's what caused the fire, you know."

"Coffee?" Leah rose to deposit his empty mug in the sink beside Ryan's. "Pop, coffee doesn't cause fires."

"No, but coffeemakers can."

"I suppose." She returned to the seat across from him, watching his face carefully as she chose her next words. "Ryan says the fire began in more than one place."

His expression remained blank. Then, slowly, he rose and walked to his recliner to reach for his remote. A moment later, the television was blaring. She went around in front of him to turn it off.

"Pop?" she said. "If you don't want to talk about it, that's fine. But Ryan's a smart man. He'll figure it out eventually. If you've done something you shouldn't, I'd rather hear it from you than him."

Pop shrugged. "What I've done is end up an old man

whose daughter should be out living her life. Instead you're here in Vine Beach trying to keep an old seafood joint running."

"About that, Pop." She shrugged. "We had to close to make some repairs. And I had to sell Boo to pay for the repairs."

"The desk," he began.

"I know, Pop. The desk." She patted his shoulder. "I'm having it appraised, but I don't think you realize how much the horses are worth."

"I do, but…"

"But what, Pop? What is it about that desk that makes you insistent on telling me it's so valuable?"

He reached down to lift the footrest on his recliner, a sure sign he preferred a nap to any further conversation. Setting the remote on the table beside him, Pop rested his hands in his lap.

"Pop," she said again as she came to kneel in front of him, "what is it about that desk?"

He shook his head. "I don't know," he said softly. "I can't remember. But Leah, I do know there's something…" Pop shook his head. "There's something…"

"It's all right, Pop," she said as she reached to hold both his hands. "Don't you worry about it. I'll figure out what's so special about the desk, I promise."

She rose and kissed his forehead. Reaching past him to the table, Leah snagged Ryan's card and stuck it in her pocket. As much as she wanted to know the truth of the Berry Hill fire, she didn't want Ryan to figure it out first.

"Leah," Pop called just as she was about to step out into the hall. "Berry Hill was mine, and I had the right to do with it what I wanted." He turned to face her.

"And what I wanted was for that house not to hold you here like it held me."

She froze. "What do you mean? You loved Berry Hill."

"No, sweetheart," he said. "I loved your mama, and she loved Berry Hill."

"But..." She shook her head. "I don't understand."

"No, you probably don't, but you will."

He reached for the remote. The sound of the afternoon game shows chased her down the hall. By the time she reached her car, Leah was more confused than ever.

She picked up the phone to call Ryan, then changed her mind. Better to discuss this in person.

Ryan clutched the phone as irritation rose. "But that doesn't make sense, Uncle Mike. I just talked to you last week and you told me there wasn't anything concrete happening that would make me have to return early."

"I said I was giving you a heads-up that something could happen," he corrected, "and now it has."

"But two weeks? That's an impossible deadline. I can't give my captain an answer by then."

"You'll have to, kid," his uncle said. "He knows I'm calling, so expect to hear from him personally in the next twenty-four hours. I just didn't want you blindsided. Bottom line is you've got two weeks to say yes or no. After that, your spot goes to someone else."

"All right," Ryan said. "Thanks for letting me know."

"So what'll you tell the captain when he calls?" Uncle Mike asked.

"I'll tell him I'm going to need every minute of those two weeks to figure out what I'm supposed to do."

"Well, good luck with that." He paused. "I know you

promised that girl the moon and stars, but sometimes promises made in the emotion of the moment aren't ones the Lord holds us to."

Ryan hung up thinking about his uncle's statement. Did the Lord intend him to leave Vine Beach so soon? If so, He would have to make that plain.

And so far, all Ryan felt was a strong tug to stay. A tug that was strengthened every time he laid eyes on Leah Berry.

Ryan set the phone on his desk. He hadn't promised Jenna the moon and stars, but rather just that he would spend their anniversary at the beach as they had planned and that he could make a life there in her absence.

At the time of their engagement, he would have promised her anything. Only after the funeral, after the last casserole had been tossed into the trash and the final potted plant given away to the neighbors did he allow himself time to really think about what he'd agreed to do.

What had seemed like a simple way to fulfill his promises had become something so complicated that Ryan was still trying to untangle all the emotions attached to it. Loss of his job in Houston no longer mattered, nor did the fact he'd be giving up a comfortable home in the Heights for a cramped one-room beach cabin.

What did matter was his growing feelings for Leah Berry. It had mattered so much that he'd gone to her father to admit it, even knowing Chief Berry might toss him out on his ear or, worse, not remember who Leah was at all.

Neither had happened, and while Pop Berry seemed genuinely clueless about details of the fire, he'd certainly had a sharp attention span when Ryan admitted he was interested in seeing Leah. Gaining the old fireman's blessing hadn't exactly been achieved, but Ryan had left the encounter encouraged that there would be no opposition from Leah's father should he decide to pursue a relationship.

He let out a long breath and shifted positions. Now, if he could just keep her safe. Ryan was willing to admit that a good portion of his protective instinct came from the knowledge that arsonists rarely strike only once. Thus, Leah's home was a target, as was the restaurant and possibly the nursing home should Carl Berry be the source of the arsonist's wrath. Or the next victim could be anyone in Vine Beach.

He rose to push away the thought. No, Ryan decided, his goal was to keep Leah from harm and to find out exactly what had happened to that old home. With that as his focus, he could keep Leah safe.

And nearby.

Chapter Eighteen

Leah followed the contractor through the restaurant as he showed her the electrical and plumbing work his men had completed. Orlando tagged along asking questions and making sure things were done to his tough and exacting standards. At the end of the walk-through, she wrote a painfully large check then watched the man fold it and put it in his pocket.

"That sound you hear is my bank account draining," Leah muttered as the door closed behind the contractor. She tried not to think of how she got the funds—how Boo had been sold to pay for the repairs.

"He did a good job," Orlando said as he came to stand beside her. "You going to call the fire chief or should I?"

"Why don't you?" she asked. "I think I'll go home. It's been a long day."

"You sure?" Orlando asked with a lift of one gray brow.

"Yes, I'm sure. Why?" she asked.

He shrugged. "I know you'll be surprised to hear this, but I respect the fellow."

"Ryan? You do?" She rested her elbow on the counter. "Really?"

"Really," he said. "I think it would have been easy for him to give us a pass on this place since it's obvious he's interested in you. But he didn't do that. He held Pop's to the same standard as the other restaurants in Vine Beach, and I have to give him points for that."

She shook her head, even as she recalled that kiss Ryan had given her. "What do you mean it's obvious he's interested in me?"

"Your pop told me the fire chief came to visit him this morning."

"Yeah, I knew that," she said. "I caught him cross-examining Pop, and I didn't appreciate it. Did you know he's been asking questions about the fire?"

Orlando reached to place his hand over hers. "Leah, honey, don't you see what he's doing?"

She sighed. "He's digging in something that's better left alone."

"He's concerned that there might be someone behind the fire other than your father. And that someone might be considering further action to cause you to sell."

She jerked her hand away and took a step backward to give Orlando a startled look. "You told him."

"I did," he said. "And while I was at it, I asked him a few questions." Orlando paused. "I saw the two of you coming home from the stables the other night. And before you think I was spying on you, girlie, I had come over to the restaurant to check up on the progress."

"So if you'll call Ryan, I'll go on home." She gave Orlando a look. "I guess I don't have to ask if you've got his phone number."

Orlando chuckled. "Nor do you have to ask if I approve of him."

"We're back to that?" Leah fished her keys from her purse. "Please tell me you didn't discuss me during this phone call."

Orlando sighed. "Leah, of course not. Other than for me to tell him I'd be standing in for your father in any matters where I was needed."

"What does that mean?"

He grinned. "I left that for him to figure out. Now go on and get out of here. When we pass inspection, we'll have plenty to keep you busy so enjoy your afternoon off today."

She pulled her purse strap onto her shoulder and headed toward the door. Before she reached the knob, Leah turned back in the direction of her father's best friend.

"Thank you, Orlando," she said as she wrapped her arms around him in an embrace. "I hope Pop realizes how well you look after me."

"I do like the Owen fellow, Leah. And I meant what I said. A man with feelings for a woman, he takes care of her. And that man's looking after you."

The next morning, Leah arrived at the restaurant for the inspection. Orlando and Ryan were already there. "Did I get the time wrong?" she asked when she walked in and found them enjoying coffee and eggs. "And since when does Pop's serve omelets?"

"Since Ryan showed up hungry and in need of breakfast. And no, you got here exactly when I told you. Want some eggs?"

"Thanks, no." She turned her attention to Ryan. "Good morning."

Orlando nodded toward the clipboard on the counter. "You'll need to sign that. After the two of you go over it. Together." Orlando fixed Ryan with a look then returned his attention to Leah. "If we're going to open back up tomorrow, I'll need to put together a grocery list and start the prep work. So, if you'll excuse me, I'll get started."

Leah placed her purse under the counter and regarded Ryan with what she hoped was an impassive stare. He was dressed in his official fire chief garb again, and it suited him. Actually, it suited him very well.

"Good morning to you," he said as he finished off the last of his eggs. "Your contractors did a good job."

"I hope Orlando didn't lure you here early to take advantage of the fact he makes the best omelets in Vine Beach." She paused. "Or to try to…"

"Pay me off so I would pass the restaurant?" He chuckled. "Leah, you know me better than that."

She did, but she also knew Orlando. He wasn't above securing their certificate of operation through any means.

"I suppose." She reached for the coffee pot and poured a cup. "So we can open tomorrow?"

He nodded. "Actually you could open today if you want. Soon as the certificate is signed, you're back in business."

She smiled. "No, tomorrow's fine. I'll have to make some calls and get my waitress back. And we'll need to put some kind of notice in the paper letting the folks know we're open again. In fact, I should make a note to call the *Vine Beach Gazette* before I do anything else." Leah paused. "And I'll need to let Eric know the Christmas celebration will go on as planned."

"I know he'll be happy about that." Ryan set down his mug. "So, tell me about this celebration. What's it like."

Leah settled onto the stool opposite him. "It's fun," she said. "While most towns have a Christmas parade, in Vine Beach, Santa arrives via boat. I understand you've been helping Eric decorate, so you already know about the parade."

"I know it's a pretty big deal. Eric's been getting emails from boaters who want to come all the way from Galveston and Corpus Christi for this event."

She nodded. "That doesn't surprise me."

"So while the boats are on parade, Pop's is serving a buffet to the people watching?"

"Yes, but we open up early and stay open after so that the boaters can get fed, as well." She took another sip of coffee. "The main point of the buffet is that the money goes to charity. Pop's doesn't take a dime of it."

Leah winced as she recalled how she'd considered taking all the proceeds to solve a problem that the Lord had ended up handling. Just another example of trying to get ahead of God. A poor idea indeed.

"Yes," Ryan said, "this year it's the elementary school playground equipment, right?"

"Right." She reached for the clipboard and began to read the documents. When she was done, she pulled the pen from its place beneath the clip and signed in all the appropriate spots. "Here," Leah said as she pushed the paperwork back in Ryan's direction.

"Thank you." His hands brushed hers as their gazes met. "Leah," he said slowly, "now that this issue of the restaurant's been handled, I need to ask you a question."

"What's that?" she asked as she looked into his eyes.

"Have dinner with me."

"That doesn't sound like a question."

"Guess it doesn't." He rose and tucked the clipboard under his arm. "Okay, wait, I've got a question. Are you free to have dinner with me on Saturday?"

Leah nodded without thinking about it.

"Great," Ryan said, a smile lighting up his face. "I'll pick you up at five."

"Five? Why so early?"

He winked. "Just be ready."

Leah followed him out onto the patio. "Oh, I get it. You want to get to the Pizza Palace before the Saturday evening dinner rush."

Ryan waved away her comment as he climbed into the Jeep and drove off. When she walked back into Pop's, she found Orlando waiting for her.

"Would it be inappropriate to say I told you so, Leah?"

Suppressing a smile, she brushed past the cook to freshen her coffee. Orlando's chuckle trailed in his wake as he returned to the kitchen. By contrast, Leah's smile lasted the rest of the day.

As he gathered his tools and the supplies he'd purchased during the week, Ryan called Riley to let him know he'd be missing this morning's meeting.

"You sure it wasn't something I said?" Riley asked with a chuckle.

"Actually it *was* something Eric said." He closed the back door of the Jeep then went around to climb into the driver's seat. "I'm trying not to be a quarrelsome man."

"Is that so?"

"Yes." Ryan started the Jeep then cradled the phone

between his shoulder and ear to buckle his seat belt. "The barn at Berry Hill Stables has a roof that leaks like a sieve and that's just one of the things on the long list of repairs I'm going to try to tackle this morning."

"By yourself?" Riley asked.

"Sure. I don't mind. Actually, I enjoy it."

"Need any help?"

Ryan thought a minute. "Well, Leah doesn't exactly know I'm doing the work. But she'll likely figure that out today. Unless I'm wrong, she should be teaching riding lessons today to the Wilson girls."

"So? What do you think? Could you use a hand with the work?"

Ryan grinned. "Why not?"

"All right," the Starting Over leader said. "I'll make some calls and see who can show up ready to work sometime later this morning."

"Hey, that's great," Ryan said. "But one thing. I don't plan on working much past two-thirty or three."

"Oh?" Riley said. "Why not? Got a hot date?"

"Actually," he said with a chuckle. "I do."

"Really. Anyone I know?"

"Yeah," Ryan replied as casually as he could manage. "Leah Berry."

"Is that so?" he said slowly. "Don't guess you plan to say anything more about that, do you?"

"Don't guess I do." Before Riley could press further, Ryan offered a word of thanks for his help, then hurried to hang up. As he slid the phone into his pocket and rested both hands on the steering wheel, he let out a long breath.

He'd gone and done it now. Admitting to himself that

he was considering starting a life that included Leah
was a big step. But telling Riley? Even bigger.

And yet it felt good. Right.

He shifted the Jeep into Drive and headed toward
the Berry place. As he drove past the restaurant, he
was glad Pop's would be open now and later when the
Christmas festivities rolled around. Not only was it best
for Vine Beach, but it would also do Leah a world of
good to be able to help the people here, whom she loved.

And she did love the people here.

Ryan signaled to turn, then eased the Jeep around
the bumps in the narrow road leading to the stables. If
the truth were known, he loved it here, too. And though
he'd considered staying and giving up all he'd earned at
the Houston Fire Department, he had to wonder if loving a place was enough to derail a career.

Though Leah gave a good show of it, Ryan knew in
his heart that she couldn't have just walked away from
the career she'd loved to live here happily forever. She
had to miss some of what she'd done.

As the Jeep edged to a stop at the gate, so his mind
edged to an idea that at first seemed impossible. But
as he punched in the code and watched the gate slowly
swing open, Ryan began to allow a possibility to take
hold.

What if she could do the work she loved? And
he could go back to the HFD without losing the one
thing—or rather person—he loved? His heart soared.
If they were together as husband and wife, it was possible. All of it.

Ryan stopped the Jeep in front of the stables, allowing his gaze to sweep the horizon. They would come
back here. Often. With the drive being only an hour,

Leah could see to her father's care from Houston almost as easily as she could from here. And the running of Pop's could be left to Orlando. With the cabin here serving as a second home base, he could dispense with the other properties and still have a place on the beach.

He smiled. Yes, of course. This just might work.

Houston during the week and Vine Beach on the weekends. At least the weekends when he wasn't at the firehouse or Leah wasn't traipsing the globe.

Opening the back of the Jeep, he snagged his toolbox, then headed toward the stables with a spring in his step. *Yes, this will work,* he amended.

All he had to do now was figure out the right way to ask. And the right time.

Chapter Nineteen

Leah arrived at the stables to find Ryan there. She climbed out of her SUV and went in search of the fire chief, only to find him perched atop the barn with a hammer in his hand.

Her heart did a flip-flop as he spied her and waved. "What do you think you're doing?" she asked as she shielded her eyes and squinted against the glare of the freshly risen morning sun.

Ryan rose to move toward the edge of the roof then peered down, hands on his hips. "Trying to see that next time it rains you don't have to buy more trash cans and feed buckets."

"Very funny. Now come down from there before you fall."

"Can't do that," he said. "Besides, I'm certified on ladders, remember?"

"And on roofs?"

"Here's how I see it, Leah," Ryan said in his sweet-as-sugar Texas drawl. "I've lost count of the burning roofs I've crawled all over. So, I figure one with a few holes is easy." He took a step back and appeared to stumble. A moment later, he recovered to grin. "Just teasing."

"Seriously, Ryan," she said as her heart lurched. "You scared me to death. Now please come down and tell me what you're doing. And why. And no more jokes."

He paused and appeared to consider her statement then nodded. "All right. Coming down."

Disappearing from her view, Ryan rounded the corner a minute later. His long-legged stride made her smile, as did the grin he wore. Since the last time she'd seen him, he'd changed from his official uniform to a pair of faded jeans and sweatshirt bearing the logo of Texas A&M University.

At that moment, Leah couldn't say which she preferred. Actually, she decided as Ryan moved closer, she liked them both just fine.

"What I'm doing," he said when he reached her, "is repairing a barn that's falling down around some beautiful palominos." He settled his hands on her shoulders. "I understand you're a woman who likes to be in charge of these things. And I can't say I'm a specialist in nineteenth-century architectural restoration, but I am decently handy with a hammer and nail, and right now there's a whole stack of shingles up there calling my name. So," he said as he leaned slightly closer, "if you don't have any further objections, I'd like to go back to what I was doing."

Looking up into his eyes, Leah promptly forgot the clever retort she'd been planning. Something about stubborn men and leaky roofs. Or was it about getting around to hiring someone as soon as she could afford it?

"Leah?"

She blinked.

"Does this silence mean you're in agreement?"

Slowly she managed a nod. He'd already turned and walked halfway to the barn before she managed a witty parting shot. "After all, we are the couple who thrive in silence."

He stopped short and turned to look in her direction. "I like the sound of that," he said.

"The sound of silence?" she asked with a chuckle.

"No, the sound of you calling us a couple."

Ryan disappeared around the side of the barn. When she heard hammering, Leah knew he'd gone back to his work.

A man with feelings for a woman, he takes care of her. And that man's looking after you. Orlando's words returned, and Leah allowed them to chase her into the barn where she prepared the horses for the Wilson girls' lesson.

Before long, Amy arrived with the trio who piled out of the Suburban with giggles and squeals. "Leah," Brooke called. "Look, I've got riding boots."

The youngest Wilson led the pack as they tromped through the muddy barn in leather boots that surely cost Eric a fortune. All but Brooke also wore riding pants fit for dressage and dark brown boots to match. Brooke, however, had chosen to outfit herself in pink from head to toe to match her boots.

She looked up from saddling the last of the horses. "They're beautiful," she said. "And so are you."

Brooke offered her a hug then leaned close. "We've got a secret," she said in what was probably supposed to be a whisper. "And I can't tell you."

"Really?" She looked over Brooke's head to find Amy regarding her with amusement.

The sound of hammering drew Brooke's attention. "Someone's up there."

"Yes, that's Ryan. He's fixing some holes in the roof so the horses don't get wet."

"Come on," Brooke said to her sisters. "Let's go show him our boots."

"Stay off the ladder, girls," Amy called. "And do not bother him if he's working," Amy added. "You'd better watch these three," she told Leah when Brooke and her sisters had raced from the barn.

Leah grasped Maisie's reins and led her out of the stall. "Why?"

"Let's just say I hear things around my house." She smiled. "And we both know what matchmakers those three are."

"Are you saying—"

The sound of Ryan complimenting the girls echoed in the barn, as did his laughter. Amy looked up then back at Leah. "But then maybe their help isn't needed. Are you and Ryan a couple?"

"No," Leah said emphatically.

"Leah Berry," Amy said. "You're not telling me something. What is it?" She reached over to touch her arm, halting Leah's progress.

She glanced up toward the rafters. "Orlando and Pop have stated their opinion about Ryan. I'm guessing you've got one, too."

"I hope they agreed with me. I think he's great. And I would like it very much if you'd find a nice guy and settle down."

"Hold on, it's just dinner, Amy."

"Dinner? What do you mean?"

"I mean I'm going out to dinner with Ryan tonight."

When Amy squealed, Leah shushed her. "Don't get too excited. He's picking me up at five, which I figure means we're going back to the Pizza Palace, only this time he intends to miss the crowds."

"Oh, Leah," Amy said. "Do you want me to have Eric talk to him? Maybe drop a few hints on alternative dinner plans?"

"Don't you dare," Leah said. "It's just dinner."

"Oh, Leah," Amy said. "It's never just dinner."

"You're wrong. Why else would he be picking me up so early unless he's thinking of it as just..." The sound of an approaching vehicle caused Leah to forget the rest of the claim. "Are you expecting Eric?" she asked Amy.

"No, he's at the marina meeting with the Boat Parade committee." She released her grip on Leah's arm and walked toward the door. "It's Riley Burkett. And he's not alone."

Leah led the horse toward the exit then stopped short when she saw a half-dozen vehicles and twice that number of men. "What's going on?" she asked Riley when he climbed out of his truck.

"We heard Ryan might be able to use a few extra hands to whip this barn into shape." He looked up. "Hey, buddy," he said to Ryan. "Put us to work."

Ryan came down and made the introductions before leading the dozen or so men over to a pile of supplies to give them assignments. Leah was astounded by Ryan organizing all these people to help her once again.

She was astounded by him in general.

The girls kept her so busy during their lesson that it felt like she barely got started and then it was time for them to go. When they returned to the barn, Leah noticed that Eric had joined the men working on the barn.

"They're doing great," she told Amy as the girls raced toward the Suburban and climbed in. "Especially Brooke. She's a natural on a horse."

"She loves it, that's for sure. Almost everything on her Christmas list is horse related."

"I remember going through that phase."

"Well I don't. I'll be calling on you for some help in that department. And speaking of help." Amy nodded toward the barn. "So, are you sure I don't need to take Eric aside and have him give Ryan some pointers on how to romance a woman?"

"No!" Leah lowered her voice. "No," she said again. "Don't you dare."

Amy laughed. "I won't. Tempting as it is to help the poor guy, I'll let Ryan fail miserably without help."

"Or succeed," she said under her breath as she watched Amy and the girls drive away.

When she turned around, the man himself was standing in her path. "Do you mind taking a look at some things? I want to be sure we've done them the way you want," Ryan said.

"Sure," she said as she followed Ryan around the corner of the barn.

He grinned as he gestured to the roof. "Most of what we've done is up there. Do you want to view it from above or should I take you inside the barn and show you from there?"

She judged the height of the roof and the amount of ladder rungs she'd have to climb with knees that had inexplicably begun to shake in the fire chief's presence. "No, I think I'd prefer to see it from ground level."

"Right this way then," he said as he led her into the cool recesses of the barn. He gestured at the wide center walkway between the stalls. "No more puddles for the horses to muck through," he said. "We stopped short of putting a new beam in there, but that'll probably have to be done in the next few years. We were able to match the shingles so you'll have a watertight roof to keep the horses from getting wet."

He continued to tout the improvements he and the others had managed in so short a time. "Now we'll need to come back next weekend and do the rest. This time around we hit the more important items on the list, but there are a whole bunch of things that need doing."

"Ryan," she said as she touched his sleeve. "You don't have to do all this. Really."

He looked down at her, his smile touching his eyes. "Just trying to take care of you." He punctuated the statement with a wink. "Now come over here and take a look at the tack room. I've got an idea I think is a good one."

A man with feelings for a woman, he takes care of her. And that man's looking after you.

Leah shook her head to clear her thoughts and followed Ryan.

The shadows fell long in the tack room, and the earthy smell of leather permeated the space. Pop's favorite saddle was stowed in its place beneath the shelf where his riding trophies used to sit.

Where were those trophies? Probably stowed away along with hers in a box somewhere up in the loft. She ran her hand over the tooled leather, resting her palm on the soft horn. How many times had she climbed up and ridden with Pop as a child?

"Leah," he said softly, capturing her attention. Then

his fingers captured hers, turning her around to face him. "I brought you in here for a reason."

Her heart jolted against her chest.

He lifted her fingers to touch his lips. "What I wanted to show you is that one kiss just wasn't enough."

"Oh." The single syllable was all she could speak.

His grin broadened. "But I'll need your approval." Ryan released her hand to wrap his arm around her back and gather her to him. He smelled of wood chips and sunshine, a combination that she knew would forever be seared into her memory.

And so was the kiss.

An idea she heartily approved.

Chapter Twenty

Leah left Berry Hill Stables with the Starting Over team still busily making repairs. The temptation to call Pop and tell him about the blessing bestowed on the family by these men was strong, but she didn't want anything to ruin this glorious day. And catching Pop in the wrong mood would do just that.

She checked the time and saw it was almost five. Ryan had told her to wear something nice but warm. With those cryptic instructions, she dug through her closet and came up with an ensemble that might fit the bill.

Owing to the season, Leah chose a sweater dress in a Christmas red with matching tights and her favorite red cowboy boots. While the warmth was questionable, the outfit would certainly go well beyond the dress code of the Pizza Palace.

Though she'd begun to suspect that might not be where they were going.

At precisely five, Ryan knocked on the door. Leah opened it and stepped back for Ryan to walk inside. Instead, he remained on the deck, motionless.

"What?" she said as she looked down at her outfit. "Don't like it? It's the boots, isn't it?" She turned to walk toward her closet, but Ryan snagged her wrist.

"Don't you dare. You look...." He shook his head. "You're gorgeous."

Leah felt the heat rise into her cheeks. "Thank you." She reached for her purse then recalled she'd planned to use the red one. "Just a second and I'll be ready."

Stepping into the closet, she fished out the purse she'd last used several weeks ago. As she opened it, a piece of folded paper fluttered to the floor. Leah retrieved it.

Leah returned to find Ryan studying the shells in the jar on the table. An image rose of him crushing the shells underfoot, and she stifled a grin. "I'm ready," she said.

Ryan looked up and smiled, then offered her a small brown bag from his coat pocket. "I've got something for you."

She accepted the bag then opened it slowly. Inside were three perfectly formed sand dollars. "Ryan, they're beautiful," she said as she leaned down to place them in the jar.

"No, Leah," he said softly. "You're beautiful." He nudged her toward the open door. "But we've got to get moving. No time to waste."

Giving him a skeptical look, Leah grabbed her coat and followed Ryan outside. "Ryan," she said after they'd settled into the Jeep. "It's a little early for dinner."

"Yep," was all Ryan would say as he headed down the highway out of Vine Beach. Finally he took pity on her and said, "All right, if you must know, I'm taking you to Galveston."

"Galveston? That's almost an hour away."

"Exactly." Ryan offered a smile before returning his attention to the road. "Which is why I picked you up at five."

She smiled and settled back for the ride. Until she saw the lights of the city glittering across the bay, Leah hadn't realized how much she had missed her adopted hometown. Driving past the Seawall was like coming home, and seeing that Murdoch's Bath House had been rebuilt in her absence made her laugh out loud.

"What is it?" Ryan said after her outburst.

"Murdoch's," she explained. "I love that place."

Ryan made a U-turn in the middle of Seawall Boulevard and brought the Jeep to a stop in front of Murdoch's. "Come show me what you love about this place."

She escorted him up the many steps to the tourist shop that held a place of honor on stilts over the beach. Though she'd feared the new version of the old favorite might be missing the flavor of the original, Leah was not disappointed.

"So what is it you love about this?" Ryan asked as he gravitated toward a shelf of eclectic items. "Is it the coconut monkey saltshakers or the selection of shells made into kitchen utensils? Or maybe it's these?"

He turned around and held out both arms, his hands covered in pot holders that made his fingers look like neon-green fish. Striking a pose, he offered a serious expression. Leah could only laugh.

"Put those away," she said as she shook her head then turned her back on him.

Ryan quickly caught up and fell into step beside her, minus the mitts. "All right, then," he said as he reached to grasp her elbow and stop her progress. "Tell me what it is you love most about this place."

"Other than the coconut monkey?"

"You don't really like that?" he said as he glanced behind him.

"I do, actually." She shrugged. "But what I like about this place, really, is the history of it." Leah paused to offer a wistful smile. "My history."

"Oh?"

"I've been coming here since I was a little girl. It was always my favorite part of any trip to Galveston." Leah paused. "I think the first time I stepped inside Murdoch's I was probably three or four. My grandparents brought me. The picture of that moment was in a frame on Granny's dresser the rest of her life."

Ryan smiled. "And what did you get that day? Do you remember?"

She lifted one brow and gestured behind him.

"You're kidding."

Leah shook her head. "Would I kid about a monkey made from the shell of a coconut?"

They left with broad smiles and the odd-looking souvenir. "That is the ugliest thing I have ever paid money for, Leah," Ryan said as he eyed the treasure in Leah's hands.

"It is not," she said. "So what's next on the agenda?"

He checked the time on his phone, then started the Jeep and headed back down Seawall Boulevard. A few minutes later, he made the turn to head inland. As they crossed Broadway, she glanced to her right and looked at the beautiful homes that lined the street.

She'd had the good fortune to rent an apartment over the garage of one of the more lovely estates on the street.

Letting that go had been difficult, though definitely the right choice. Pop needed her.

And she might never have met Ryan if she'd stayed here.

That thought took Leah by surprise.

Ryan continued on until he reached the Strand. Bordered on both sides by turn-of-the-century brick buildings, the oldest part of Galveston was also the busiest on this Saturday evening. Owing to the combination of the Christmas season and extremely nice weather, shoppers and diners were out in droves.

Wherever they were going, Leah hoped Ryan had thought to secure a reservation. Otherwise, they'd be spending quite a bit of time waiting.

He turned onto Mechanic Street then pulled into a parking lot that was zoned for residents only. She was about to point this out when Ryan pulled a key tag from his pocket and held it out to scan it.

They parked and he came around to open her door and help her out, then gestured up to the penthouse of the building. Someone had strung lights around the railing and across the roofline. Even the palm trees were strewn with tiny white lights.

Leah gave him a sideways look. "Ryan, what are you up to?"

"It's just dinner," he said as he offered her his arm. "And for the record, I promise we're not going to be alone." He gave her a trust-me grin.

"All right," she said as she allowed him to escort her into the Art Deco building and across a lobby that could have hosted a gathering of a hundred people or more. Above her were glittering chandeliers of the same period, their tips shining beneath a ceiling of pressed tin.

The effect was heightened when she turned to see the Christmas tree. At least twenty feet high, its mirrored star still did not reach the roof. On its branches were silver reflective ornaments of every size and shape and lights that twinkled bright white. Someone had strung a lush ribbon of thick silver rhinestone-studded velvet through the branches and tied it in a giant bow midway up.

An ancient elevator car arrived, and Ryan opened the door to help her in. Closing the gilded cage, Ryan pushed the penthouse button then gave her an admiring look. "Have I told you how pretty you look?" he asked.

"Thank you," she said though she was rarely fond of such compliments on her appearance. Coming from Ryan, however, she liked it very much.

His fingers encircled her wrist. "Get used to hearing it," he told her. "I plan to say it a lot."

The doors opened onto a marble lobby that spilled out into a room completely devoid of furniture. The ebony hardwood floors gleamed beneath the light of the candles that had been placed across the brick mantle.

Leah blinked to allow her eyes to adjust to the dim room before following Ryan through the entry and into the penthouse apartment. There the view unfolded into a breathtaking three-hundred-and-sixty-degree vista that included all of Galveston.

A table had been set up in the center of a lush outdoor garden. The lights she'd seen from the parking garage circled the garden and provided just enough illumination to see that there were potted palms and hothouse flowers of all sorts blooming around them. Overhead, the stars made for a glittering canopy.

"Ryan, this place is breathtaking." She pushed a

strand of hair from her face. "Please tell whoever owns it that I absolutely love it."

"I'm glad." He shrugged. "Because it's mine."

"Yours?" She turned to face him. "Really?"

"For the evening anyway. Excuse me while I tell the chef we've arrived," Ryan said as he disappeared back inside.

Not what she expected, but then so far this had been a most interesting evening.

Leah walked past the table, decorated with candles, gleaming white tablecloth and fine china, to the edge of the balcony to look over at the bustling activity below. Thankfully the patio design included heaters, for the air was brisk and the temperature quite chilly now that the sun had disappeared beneath the waters of the Gulf.

"All right," Ryan said as he returned to the deck. "Dinner is served."

He pulled out her chair and settled Leah into her place at the table before joining her. With her back to the doors, she had an amazing view of Galveston's Strand District.

And of Ryan.

"I hope you don't mind, but I've chosen the menu. I had some help, though."

She met his amused stare across the table. "Oh?"

Ryan nodded at a spot behind her, and Leah turned around to see Orlando dressed in his Sunday best and carrying a tray of food. He sat the overflowing platter on the table with a flourish then took a bow.

"Orlando?" Leah shook her head. "What are you doing here? Who's running Pop's?"

"I volunteered for this duty," he said. "And a couple of guys from Starting Over are manning the grill and working as sous chefs. Eric's mom, Susan, is supervising and running the register. Turns out Riley Burkett is a decent fry cook, so he's in charge of the kitchen. When I left he was trying to teach Eric how to stuff the shrimp."

Leah returned her attention to Ryan, tears threatening. "You planned all of this?"

Ryan nodded toward Orlando. "I had a little help."

She rose to hug Pop's best friend. "Thank you," she whispered against his ear as she leaned up to kiss his cheek.

"You deserve a special evening. Now enjoy your dinner," Orlando said. "I'm going to go check on dessert. But don't think I'm taking my chaperone duties lightly."

Leah chuckled as she returned to her chair and let out a sigh. "Ryan, this is amazing." She gestured to the table then took in her surroundings with a sweeping glance. "All of it. Just amazing."

He grinned. "I'm glad you like it."

"Like it?" She settled her napkin in her lap then met his stare. "No one's ever gone to this much trouble for me. Ever."

"I wanted to be sure you enjoyed yourself." He paused to lift his water glass in a toast. "Here's to just dinner."

She lifted her glass to touch his. Something in his expression put her on guard. He seemed just a little nervous. Or perhaps he had something on his mind. Before long they were dining on fresh Gulf seafood and laughing about today's adventures in carpentry and horseback riding. By the time Orlando came out to clear away the dishes, Leah couldn't believe where the time had gone.

"So much for us being the couple that is better in silence—or whatever that silly thing was I said."

"I'd say that myth is busted," Ryan agreed.

When Orlando returned with two slices of buttermilk pie and a pot of coffee, Leah clapped. "I won't even ask how you remembered this was my favorite, Ryan."

"I may have mentioned it," Orlando said with a wink as he disappeared back inside and left them alone.

Leah sat back and watched as Ryan poured coffee. He even knew how she liked it: half of one pink packet and a dash of milk. When he brought out the cinnamon to dust the top, she smiled.

"Did Orlando tell you that, too?"

"Drink up," he said as he stabbed at the pie. "The night is young."

"What are you talking about?"

His gaze fell to her empty plate. "I'd rather show you than tell you about it."

"All right." She sipped at the steaming coffee. "Perfection."

"Indeed," was Ryan's whispered response.

After Leah finished her coffee, Ryan rose and beckoned her to join him at the rail. Below the Strand had been festooned for the holidays in swags of red and green with lights everywhere she looked. Off in the distance, someone's laughter floated up to them.

Reaching across the distance between them, Ryan grasped Leah's hand. For a moment he merely held her fingers entwined in his. Then he turned to face her.

"Leah, I need to tell you something. I'm not the kind of guy who makes pretty speeches or falls in love with someone he barely knows, so bear with me, okay?" When she nodded, he continued, "There's just something about you—about us—that makes me happier than I ever knew I could be." He squeezed her hands. "You're that special one I almost missed."

She felt tears threaten and blinked them back. "Ryan, I don't know what to say."

"Don't say anything," he replied. "You don't have to. Just be you." He paused. "I hope I'm not coming on too strong here. It's just that when I see something I want, I go after it. And I really want to figure out why I can't get you out of my mind." He leaned in close. "And out of my heart."

"Oh, Ryan."

She fell into his warm embrace and rested her head on his shoulder. How long they stood like that, Leah couldn't say. When he moved to hold her at arm's length, she felt his absence keenly.

"Leah, I've fallen in love with you," he said. "And I didn't mean to do that."

Her heart thudded against her chest as she gave up fighting the tears. "Is it your turn to apologize or mine?" she asked as she swiped at her cheeks.

"This time," he said with a grin, "it's neither."

Leah tilted her face up to stare into his eyes, and her smile matched his. "That's what I thought, too."

He gathered her to him once more. "I need to ask you a question."

"Hey, you two about done here?" Orlando called before stepping out onto the balcony. "I just talked to Burkett and we've got a packed house at Pop's tonight, so if you're ready to call it a night here, I'll clean up and head back to Vine Beach."

"Thank you, Orlando," Ryan said. "And I mean that."

The men shook hands and then Orlando embraced

Ryan. "You're a good man, Fire Chief. Don't let this woman get away, you hear?"

He nodded. "I don't intend to."

"I'm right here," Leah said. "I can hear you."

Chapter Twenty-One

Ryan rolled off the sofa bed that had been so comfortable the past few weeks having slept only a few fitful hours at most. Standing to stretch, he tossed the blankets back into place, then converted the bed back into a sofa and walked toward the kitchen.

Though the coffeepot had been fixed last night, it was far too early for the timer to activate the device. With the sun not yet slanting over the horizon, Ryan dressed warmly, then donned his running shoes and set out for a jog down the beach with Chief.

Though the morning was cold for this part of Texas, Ryan soon worked up a sweat trying to outrun the thoughts that had kept him awake most of the night. And while the memory of time spent with Leah was sweet, the decision on how to best move forward with the relationship was giving him trouble.

Soul-searching had always been best done while running, and this morning was no exception. Ryan reached the pier, then circled around and headed back toward his temporary home, with Chief in stride beside him.

From there he could see the first orange tint of the

coming sunrise threading across the horizon. The waves lapped against the beach and a few vocal gulls flew overhead. But in the homes that edged the waterline, few lights were burning.

Even the running was better in Vine Beach, he decided. Nowhere in Houston did he have a view like this.

But it wasn't the view that held him here in Vine Beach. It was Leah Berry. She was the one. The woman God had sent him to spend the rest of his life with.

The clarity of that statement hit him hard, as did his understanding of exactly what that meant. He would do whatever it took to be with the woman he loved.

Even if that meant giving up his job at HFD to stay here with her.

Pouring his best effort into the remainder of his run, he lurched forward to arrive at the cabin in record time. Poor Chief kept up, though the effort caused his tongue to drag and his eyes to plead for a quick trip upstairs to his water bowl.

Ryan complied and then, as he showered, he thought over his next move. By the time the coffee was ready, so was Ryan.

He took the phone and a fresh cup of brew and went outside to sit on the deck. Leah was obviously still sleeping, for her curtains were shut tight and the porch light was still on from last night.

Settling in his favorite chair, he pulled out his phone, then set it on the rail. *Thank You for this new start,* he prayed. *Show me how to be the best husband I can for Leah. But first, give me the words to break this to my parents.*

He called Uncle Mike first, giving him the bad news and the good. "So I'm losing a fireman but gaining a family member?" his uncle asked. "Guess that's not a bad deal."

"Trust me," Ryan said as relief flowed. "She's much easier on the eye than I am."

They shared a laugh, then Uncle Mike paused. "Hey, kiddo," he said, "you sure about this?"

The porch light went off at Leah's place, then the curtain beside her desk moved just enough to let him know she was sitting there. "Never been more sure about anything in my life."

Ryan hung up promising to bring Leah for a visit, then took a sip of coffee before making the next call. To his surprise, his dad answered then quickly put his mom on the other line.

"Two for one, son," his father said with a chuckle. "Now, what's going on that you would call us so early? Everything all right with you?" His mother echoed the statement.

"I'm great," he said. "And that two-for-one thing, Dad? Well, I'm hoping to offer that right back to you."

"What are you talking about?" his mother said.

"All right." He prayed one last time for the right words to come. "I'm not coming back to Houston or the fire department. My life is here in Vine Beach now." He paused just a moment. "With Leah."

Both parents started talking at once, and it took a full minute before silence was restored. While he waited, Ryan spied Leah watching him from the window next door and waved. She returned the gesture and added a smile.

"All right," he finally said as his parent's rush of words slowed. "Let me get this all out at once, then you can ask me anything you want. I'm staying in Vine

Beach because I've fallen in love. You'll love her, too," he said. "She's just…amazing."

"And this girl doesn't want to live in Houston?" his mom asked.

"Oh, I don't know. I think she might be willing if I asked." He let out a long breath. "But I don't intend to ask. Our life together is here. And before either of you blame her for my decision to leave HFD and the city, you need to understand that all of this is my choice."

"Is it?" Dad asked.

"It is," Ryan said firmly. "She doesn't even know I'm about to ask her to marry me, so it's not like she could influence me on the subject."

Leah opened the curtains completely, her grin widening as she lifted her coffee cup to salute him. All Ryan could think was that he hoped she didn't read lips. He preferred to keep the surprise proposal he was considering just that, a surprise.

How much of a surprise would depend on Leah's feelings on the topic. Since their evening in Galveston, Ryan had known Leah was meant to be his wife. Whether she knew was a different matter altogether.

"So you're leaving the fire department, but I'm getting a daughter-in-law?" Dad asked.

"That's about the size of it," Ryan said. "Hey, I need to go. But I promise I'll keep you posted."

"Bring her to visit," Mom said as the line went dead.

"That went well," he said to Chief, who had come to rest his massive head in Ryan's lap.

One last glance at Leah's place and a wave to its owner, and Ryan went back inside to grab his computer and secure Chief for the day. After arriving at work, he checked his messages, then walked down the hall to find the mayor's door open, his secretary not at her desk.

"Got a minute, boss?" he asked the mayor.

"Sure, come in and sit down." When Ryan complied, he continued, "What's on your mind?"

He leaned back against the chair cushion and looked Jack Murdoch in the eyes. This conversation had to happen so Ryan could best figure out how to keep the woman he loved safe. If an arsonist walked free, he was the man who would track down the criminal. Going into a marriage with this hanging over both of them was not what Ryan wanted to happen.

"I need to get to the bottom of something, sir," he said. "Someone burned down Berry Hill, and I believe you know who it was." He studied the mayor's impassive expression before continuing. "It was either you or Pop."

"Nobody's proven anything but that it was an accident." He sat back and crossed his arms over his chest. "What've you got that tells you otherwise?"

"Instinct," Ryan said. "I should tell you I know about the deal you and the investors put together to convince Leah to sell."

The mayor looked away. When he swung his gaze back to meet Ryan's, all the bluster had gone out of him. "All right," he said. "Here are the facts. There isn't any group of investors. That was a story Berry and me concocted to convince Leah to sell."

"Wait. Why would you do that?" He shook his head. "And what would be the point?"

"The point was to get that girl back to the career she left. I promised my buddy I'd do right by him. Once he got to where he couldn't take care of himself, he had me to do for him. He never wanted Leah to give up her life to take care of him. Much as he loves her, he thought that was too big a price for her to pay."

"Fair enough," Ryan said, "but Leah's made no secret of the fact they're not wealthy. If her father was going to secretly buy her out, where was the money going to come from?"

The mayor scratched his head, then leaned forward to press his palms on his desk. "I wondered the same thing. Berry said he had the gold and he'd arrange to get it to Leah when the time came. Said it was hidden in the family vault. I figured that meant down at the bank. Then he showed me where he put it. Clever, I'll tell you."

"But where would the money have come from?" Ryan asked.

"You heard the legend of the fence post full of gold that some Berry relative hid then lost in one of those hurricanes? My guess is Berry found that fence post and set the gold aside for Leah."

Ryan considered the statement a minute. "I guess that could be true. But the fact remains that the house was burned to the ground."

"The better to send Leah packing, don't you think? No family home means no more family ties to Vine Beach." The mayor paused. "And I'll swear under oath I didn't set fire to that house."

So it was Leah's father all along. The woman he loved had a father who was an arsonist. And he was the town fire chief.

He shook his head.

"I see you're figuring on what to do. Care for some advice?"

"No," Ryan said.

"I'm going to give it to you anyway. Let it go. And before you get all bothered about what I'm saying, pause to consider that there's a man sitting in a nursing home tonight who loved his girl enough to set her free from the bondage of seeing him die." He shook his head. "Now, I know all the arguments against that being a good idea, but you just try and get one of them past Carl Berry."

Ryan sat very still as Jack Murdoch admitted what Ryan already suspected. And likely what Leah suspected, as well.

"Nobody was hurt and no crime was committed. That house belonged to Carl. What he did with it wasn't nobody's business. This is Texas, after all, and a man's got the right to do as he pleases with his own property long as it doesn't hurt anybody else."

The mayor had a point. He'd have to do some checking to be sure no laws were broken, but unless there was something else he'd missed, Carl Berry hadn't committed any crimes other than the crime of bad judgment. And even that was subjective.

The last time Leah had been inside the City Hall building she'd been headed for a showdown. Now she was here to say goodbye. She much preferred the showdown.

She found him exiting the mayor's office.

"Where are we going?" Leah asked as Ryan escorted her to his Jeep.

"Your place. I need to show you something." He raced around to climb into the driver's seat. A few minutes later they were climbing the stairs to enter Leah's cabin.

"All right, what is it?"

Ryan pointed to the desk by the window. "Is that the one that used to belong to your grandfather?" When she nodded he hurried over and pushed away the chair. A moment later he'd cleared the desktop of her computer and had the piece leaning on its side. A bang to the bottom panel and a large piece of wood fell into his hands.

"Ryan! What are you doing?"

He laughed, then gestured for her to join him. There on the floor was a scattering of gold coins. More were visible inside what must have been a secret panel in the desk.

"I'd say expenses won't be an issue anymore."

"But…" She shook her head. "Ryan, the gold in the fence post. It was here all along just like Pop's note said."

"Just like you," he said softly as he embraced her. "A treasure just waiting to be found."

Christmas Eve dawned gray and cloudy but by noon the clouds had parted and the sun shone. Preparations for the buffet were complete and all that remained was for Riley and the guys from Starting Over to appear to help with the serving and cleanup. Leah was bustling around making sure the decorations were done just as they had been in years past, for tonight Pop would return to the restaurant that bore his name so everything had to be perfect.

"Where's Ryan?" Orlando asked when he arrived in full Santa gear.

"I'm not sure," she said. "He left early this morning.

Something about helping Eric with the banner for the parade. I thought he'd be here by now."

Orlando patted her back. "I'm going to fetch your pop," he said.

When Orlando had gone, she sat back on one of the stools and looked out over the water. So much had happened in such a short time. With the taxes paid and plenty of money in the bank, Leah was free to go wherever she wished.

But the only place she wished to be was at Ryan's side.

"Leah," Kate, the waitress, called. "We need you in the kitchen."

She went to handle things, and before she realized it, the citizens of Vine Beach had begun to arrive for the annual Christmas Eve buffet dinner. Still Ryan was nowhere in sight. Pop, however, was moving from table to table greeting guests and generally acting as if he'd never left.

It was a good night, and not just for her father.

"It's time for the boat parade," Orlando announced as he helped Pop to his traditional place of honor on the deck.

Leah stood beside Pop just as she always did while the mayor made the speech that started the annual Christmas Eve Boat Parade. A few minutes later, Ryan appeared at her side.

"Where have you been?" She pointed to what looked like a smudge of green paint on his cheek. "And what is this?"

"Top secret," he said.

"Look," Leah said, "there's Eric and Amy's boat."

As the craft drew closer, she could see a banner unfurled from the mast.

"Oh, I heard about the big argument regarding what would go on that banner. I wonder who won."

Ryan stepped in between Leah and her view of the water. "I did," he said as he moved out of the way and allowed her to see what had been written there.

"Leah, will you marry me?" she read.

"Hey, that's my line."

Leah's heart thudded against her chest as Ryan dropped to one knee in front of her.

"Will you?" he asked. "Marry me, that is?"

And the bride-to-be said yes.

* * * * *

Dear Reader,

Thanksgiving and Christmas are my favorite times of the year. While many of you associate these holidays with snow and ice, those of us who grew up along the Texas Gulf coast experienced a different type of holiday. Indeed our turkeys were just as often fried or stuffed as baked in the oven, and some of us—including my family—substituted traditional Christmas fare for steaming hot tamales and a delicious bowl of homemade *chili con queso* and chips. In a sense, what is usual for some is unusual for others. But isn't it awesome that while God made us all unique, He also gave us the ability to appreciate those differences?

Of all the things Leah and Ryan deal with in *Her Holiday Fireman,* it is their differences that cause them the most grief. While considering what sort of holiday story I wanted to offer, the Lord led me to the verse in Proverbs, about kindling and fire. The correlation to my fireman hero was unmistakable. However, it wasn't until I began writing this book that God showed me what the rest of that verse meant, the part about the quarrelsome man, that is. Don't think you could be that sort? Think again. Have you ever discovered a difference in your plans and the path the Lord appears to be sending you down?

I have. The quote at the beginning of the book—"It's just dinner"—is proof that God not only has a divine plan that is so much better than ours, but He also has a sense of humor. You see, my husband, Robert, and I began our relationship vowing there would be no relationship. It was just dinner—nothing more—and to be sure of that, we invited his daughter, Bailey, and my daughter, Hannah, to come along as chaperones. I had other plans. So did Robert. But so did God, and we recently celebrated our first wedding anniversary.

Leah and Ryan must learn that what makes them different—be it holiday traditions or life plans—is what the Lord uses to bring them together. As with Robert and me, it wasn't just dinner.

Merry Christmas from my family to yours!

Kathleen Y'Barbo

Questions for Discussion

1. Both Leah and Ryan make promises they struggle to keep. Have you sacrificed something to keep a promise? What was it and why?

2. Ryan admits he got caught up in the wedding his fiancée was planning and forgot all about planning for the marriage. By the time his misgivings were beginning to surface, he was afraid to speak up. Have you ever been caught up in something only to realize later that you shouldn't have gone through with it? How did things turn out? What have you done to remedy the situation?

3. Leah's father has Alzheimer's disease, and as such is unable to live independently. Thus Leah has made the difficult decision to place her father in specialized care. Have you faced this decision? Do you know anyone who has? What sort of support do caregivers need?

4. Leah makes the point that although she is an expert in restoration of older properties, she cannot seem to maintain the historic buildings entrusted to her. Have you ever felt like Leah: unequipped to keep up with the responsibilities you've taken on? How did you get into this situation? What steps can you take to make the changes that will remedy this?

5. Ryan comes from a family of firefighters. Training in the fire academy then taking a job as a fireman

is a tradition that the Owen family honors. What sorts of traditions does your family honor? What new traditions can you begin in your family?

6. Leah is plagued with a nightmare that has its beginnings in the guilt she feels regarding her grandmother's death. Is guilt something you deal with? If so, how has it manifested itself in your life? What can you do to break its hold?

7. Animals play a big part in this story. While the horses are as much pets as they are property, the bullmastiff and orange tabby definitely seem to be in charge of their owners at times. Ironically, these polar opposites—cat and dog—learn to live harmoniously next door to one another well before their owners do. Do you have a pet? What, if anything, has your pet taught you?

8. Leah's father insists there is more value in an old desk than in a beautiful palomino pony. While the statement defies logic, in the end it is proven true. Often the things the Lord asks of us also defy logic. Do you have a story about how you went against logic to follow God's leading? How did that turn out?

9. Leah approaches her father with a plan to pay off the taxes only to find Pop refuses to allow it. Instead he, and his friend Orlando, tell Leah to wait on God and turn the problem over to Him. Have you ever had to wait on God? Were you tempted to "help" Him respond sooner? How did it turn out? Was His way best?

10. Leah and Ryan are an unlikely pair—one might say they are opposites! Have you ever fallen in love with someone who was your opposite? Was God behind it? What did you learn from being with a person so different from yourself?

11. Orlando is a good friend to Leah's father. He's even stood in as a substitute parent to Leah. In a sense, God provided Leah with someone to be the father her own dad couldn't be. Have you experienced this sort of divine substitution in your life? Who did God provide and why?

12. The holidays are full of traditions, and each family is unique in the ones they celebrate. What are your family traditions? Where do they come from and how have you blended them with your spouse or partner, if you have one?

WE HOPE YOU
ENJOYED THESE TWO

LOVE INSPIRED®
BOOKS.

If you were **inspired** by these

uplifting, **heartwarming**

romances, be sure to look for

all six Love Inspired® books

every month.

Love Inspired®

Get 2 Free Books,
Plus 2 Free Gifts—
just for trying the Reader Service!

Save $1.00

on the purchase of any
Love Inspired® book.

Available wherever books are sold, including
most bookstores, supermarkets, drugstores
and discount stores.

Save $1.00

on the purchase of any Love Inspired® book.

Coupon valid until July 31, 2018.
Redeemable at participating retail outlets in the U.S. and Canada only.
Limit one coupon per customer.

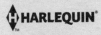

HARLEQUIN®

Save $1.00

on the purchase of any

Harlequin® series book.

Available wherever books are sold, including most bookstores, supermarkets, drugstores and discount stores.

- ✂

Save $1.00

on the purchase of any Harlequin® series book.

Coupon valid until July 31, 2018.
Redeemable at participating retail outlets in the U.S. and Canada only.
Limit one coupon per customer.

52615203

Canadian Retailers: Harlequin Enterprises Limited will pay the face value of this coupon plus 10.25¢ if submitted by customer for this product only. Any other use constitutes fraud. Coupon is nonassignable. Void if taxed, prohibited or restricted by law. Consumer must pay any government taxes. Void if copied. Inmar Promotional Services ("IPS") customers submit coupons and proof of sales to Harlequin Enterprises Limited, PO Box 31000, Scarborough, ON M1R 0E7, Canada. Non-IPS retailer—for reimbursement submit coupons and proof of sales directly to Harlequin Enterprises Limited, Retail Marketing Department, 225 Duncan Mill Rd., Don Mills, ON M3B 3K9, Canada.

U.S. Retailers: Harlequin Enterprises Limited will pay the face value of this coupon plus 8¢ if submitted by customer for this product only. Any other use constitutes fraud. Coupon is nonassignable. Void if taxed, prohibited or restricted by law. Consumer must pay any government taxes. Void if copied. For reimbursement submit coupons and proof of sales directly to Harlequin Enterprises, Ltd 482, NCH Marketing Services, P.O. Box 880001, El Paso, TX 88588-0001, U.S.A. Cash value 1/100 cents.

5 65373 00076 2   (8100)0 12314

® and ™ are trademarks owned and used by the trademark owner and/or its licensee.

© 2018 Harlequin Enterprises Limited

HSCOUP0318

Love Inspired®

Inspirational Romance to
Warm Your Heart and Soul

Join our social communities to connect
with other readers who share your love!

Sign up for the Love Inspired newsletter
at **www.LoveInspired.com** to be the
first to find out about upcoming titles,
special promotions and exclusive content.

CONNECT WITH US AT:

Harlequin.com/Community

 Facebook.com/LoveInspiredBooks

Twitter.com/LoveInspiredBks

LISOCIAL2017